Come and Take It

Eden Chronicles - Book Two

S.M. Anderson

The Eden Chronicles: Book Two

Come and Take It

First Edition
Cover Art by Alecia Burke

Author's Note –

This is volume **two** of The Eden Chronicles. If you have purchased this book as an introduction to the story, I heartily recommend reading "A Bright Shore" - Volume One, first. While this book can be read as a standalone, there is a good deal of back story that you will find yourself in want of. I purposefully did not include a great deal of expository musing on the past where our characters think back and remember what happened. There is some, as a writer, you can't escape it entirely.

What I have tried to avoid is the first three chapters being a rehash. I personally feel that adds a level of artificiality to stories that are written in a series. In my mind, it accomplishes little besides driving up word count and taking the reader out of the story. I usually skip that 'stuff' as I strive to read multiple volumes in the order they were intended. I wanted to keep this story in the present; well, not our present, but theirs.

To my readers that are rejoining this adventure, Thank You. I don't wish to do anything with my writing besides entertain. Your reviews are very much appreciated. To the one reader that offered sky writing his review, thank you! I have enjoyed getting to know many of you through my website www.smanderson-author.com. I promise to respond to all the e-mail I receive.

I'd also like to thank my beta readers and editors, particularly Matt, Craig, and Ray. They know who they are, and their help was much appreciated.

A special thanks to my family who manage to tolerate me while remaining supportive. The latter is expected in family, the former is much harder.

Thanks, Scott

Chapter 1

Earth 1.0

The flight had been mercifully short after the helicopter he'd been bundled into had fired on and destroyed the ISA agent's jeep. The minute the missile was released, Sir Geoffrey Carlisle had assumed he was on his way to a black site. Somewhere deep and dark, where he could be interrogated by General Gannon's people without the public wondering where he was. Kyle and Jake had been right, and he'd been wrong. The government it seemed, wasn't willing to give him a public forum. He had no doubt that he had already been reported dead along with the incredibly naive ISA agent in the jeep.

They'd been flying for maybe twenty minutes when the Colorado mountain that had been so central to their plans for a decade, collapsed in on itself in a fiery bowl. The glow from the explosion and fire was visible on the distant horizon as a back light framing the outlines of the Rockies. His friends and colleagues were gone. Safe, he had to assume, on Eden. It had been a long time coming to fruition, but he had managed to keep the operation secure and safe from the prying eyes of Washington. He'd done his job. It would now be up to a younger generation to protect what had been built on Eden. He'd volunteered to accompany the ISA agent, Mr. Reed, off the mountain.

Or so he had intended. When the helicopter, transporting a single special forces soldier had stopped their jeep, taken him on board, and then proceeded to destroy the jeep along with the luckless Mr. Reed - he knew his intentions were less than wind. He began to wonder how deep a hole he was going to be put in. His solitary guard on the helicopter had been very matter of fact. "The President wanted you dead, you're dead."

The soldier didn't seem one for conversation, not after his single question of whether he'd been telling the truth during his final webcast from inside the mountain. The same mountain, whose insides were by now a tortured hell of melting steel and burning concrete. Everyone else associated with the Program would have made it to Eden by now, he was the sole living witness on earth. This earth. He'd never imagined he would be granted a public trial, he had imagined a secret prison surrounded by government shrinks and interrogation teams. This though? This was something different. According to his captor, General Gannon, the Chairman of the JCS wanted to talk to him in what was a direct contradiction to the orders of the President.

His guard looked like one of Kyle's companions, mid-thirties, fit, bearded and very wary as the helicopter touched down at a small airport in the dark. He recognized the type, a career soldier, special forces. It should be familiar to him, he'd been an SAS man all those years ago. When the man drew his sidearm and held it tight against his own body and looked out the side of the door at an approaching figure, Sir Geoff was even more certain that whatever was happening was off the books. His own guard was worried, and not so much about him.

"Took you long enough," a woman in civilian clothes, baseball cap with a blonde ponytail hanging out the back emerged from the shadows and yelled over the rapidly diminishing noise of the helicopter's turbines. He noted that his guard relaxed instantly.

"We good?"

"Waiting on you," she smiled and turned to glance at him as she stuck her head into the helicopter's open side, "and you."

"If you would, Sir."

Geoffrey realized his guard was talking to him and shooing him out the door, "I promise you, our next flight will be more comfortable."

The young lady helped him step down from the helicopter. At his age he was well past caring about the propriety of such things and took her hand with appreciation.

She kept a hand on his elbow as she escorted him to a G-5 Lear jet with no markings other than a tail number parked at the end of a runway at what he could tell was a very rural

6

airport. There was a tell-tale glow on the horizon that had to have been the Denver/Boulder area.

"That story you were spinning during your broadcast, it true?"

Her companion had asked the same question on the helicopter.

"All of it," he nodded as they reached the fold out stairs and he was hustled up into a wood paneled cabin, smelling of cigar smoke and whiskey. He almost felt like he was home.

"Sit anywhere you like." The woman motioned to the couches and half dozen plush swivel chairs and stuck her head in to the cockpit. He could see the backs of two heads in the pilot's seats, a man and a woman. When he turned back to the cabin, his companion from the helicopter had joined him, and was already shedding his combat gear. The rest of the plane was empty.

"Grab a seat," the man said as he retracted the stairs with a whirring grind of an electric motor that he could barely hear over the growing whine of the Lear's jet turbines. The pavement below the door was starting to creep past before it had fully closed.

He fell into a seat just moments before the jet turned sharply and hurtled itself straight down a runway and leaped into the air as if it couldn't wait to leave the great state of Colorado. The soldier grunting with effort against the acceleration, plopped down in the chair opposite his and ran a hand through his sweat soaked hair regarding him closely.

Sir Geoff just stared back expectantly and watched as the woman came aft slowly, leaning backwards into the incline of the jet's climb. She settled in on a couch across the aisle from him. From the looks that passed between the two, he gathered there was something there more than collegial friendship.

"I'm Brittany," the woman waved at him across the aisle, "you've already met my gentler half, Tom."

He nodded at the soldier. "Briefly."

"Here's the deal." She leaned forward, elbows on her knees facing him. "We don't have the slightest idea what's going on, other than to get you to a safe house and keep you there, safe that is. The government wants you dead, and as far as they know, you are."

"You're not the government? Whose prisoner, am I?"

The woman tilted her head to the side. "We don't take prisoners. Let's call it protective custody, shall we? You going to behave until we can figure out what we're supposed to do with you?"

"My days of being an escape risk are well behind me. Where would I go?"

"Kinda the way we see it as well. General Gannon said he'd be in touch when he could. He's very interested in speaking with you."

"I see."

The woman looked over at her husband or was it boyfriend for a moment before turning to back to him. "So, this Eden place? The planet? It's real? You guys really have been going there for some time?"

"It is, and yes," he replied. "We tried to get as many there as we could before the powers that be shut us down. You saw the broadcast?"

"We did," she nodded, and then turned back to her companion. "You never take me anywhere like that, nowhere nice."

"Tbilisi, three months ago," the man said defensively. "Before that, we had that all-expense paid trip to Kamchatka. Bear sausage!"

The woman turned up her nose. "My husband thinks exotic food that he gets to kill, makes the trip. Personally, I like the night life and room service. Can you imagine what goes for nightlife in Kamchatka?"

He was so confused he found it easy to keep his mouth shut.

"Precious little," she answered for him.

"You're married? Both military?"

"Married, and yes, both Army. We represent exactly one third of Task Force Chrome," she answered with one sharp nod of her head. "Brittany, Captain Brittany Souza, you can call me Britt, Brittany or Mrs. Souza if he's around," she motioned her head to the side. "I gave in and took his name, kind of came with the assignment."

"Your marriage is part of your cover?" Usually in a situation like this, he would have professed confusion to buy time to think. He didn't have to pretend.

"Oh, we're married," Tom smiled. "I have scars to prove it, we all are." He pointed to the cockpit, "the Bowdens are our pilots, husband and wife. The Mills, another couple you'll meet later, make up TF Chrome."

"Made up," Captain Souza piped in shaking her head. "The DoD didn't renew our budget this last year. We've been sort of free-lancing until Gannon reached out earlier today."

"This isn't official then?"

"There wasn't anything official about us, when we were active," the prettier half answered. "When they cut our budget, it wasn't because the bean counters saw a line item that read 'special forces unit masquerading as suburban professional couples.' No, whatever six-hundred-dollar toilet seat that had been paying for us got its budget cancelled. Outside of Gannon and a few other top brass, we don't exist, never have."

"I see, and the aircraft?" he pointed around him. "Not a government plane I take it?"

"Nope," Tom Souza shook his head. "Belongs to a corporate client that owes us. Big time."

"Relax Mr. Carlisle," Brittany leaned across and patted his knee, "no dark site for you, you'll get our guest bedroom."

"It's man cave," Tom protested.

She ignored her husband and shook her head at him. "Guest bed room. You'll be with us until Gannon gets a chance to talk to you."

"It certainly beats the alternative, or what I was dreading."

"It's not that nice," she smiled. "He's got a bunch of hunting trophies mounted on the wall in there. A little freaky and hard to sleep, if you ask me."

"It's a man cave, and I'm right here."

Sir Geoff felt his eyebrows go up. He'd been out of his element before, but this was a new one. This wasn't just Gannon going against orders, the General was going rogue calling in this... this Task Force, former Task Force he corrected himself.

"If this place you were talking about is real, how do you get back there?" Captain Souza asked suddenly all business.

"Is this my interrogation?"

"Nah, I leave that kind of stuff to him," she jerked a thumb towards her husband.

He didn't doubt for a second the female half of this pair was the one calling the shots and quite possibly the more dangerous of the pair. She might be able to order her husband to beat a confession out of him, but something told him she'd be much more efficient in the doing. He glanced at Mr. Souza, he still didn't know his rank. '*Tom*' shook his head as if to say ignore her.

"I'm afraid I don't get back," he answered her initial question. "We destroyed the gate facility inside the mountain."

"So not another facility hidden away somewhere?"

"It was hard enough to build one, not to mention keeping it secret."

She smiled at him warmly, a picture of a pleasant suburban professional. Sir Geoff thought she'd look more at home dropping children off at a school, than sitting in a black ops G5.

"Not exactly an answer to the question I asked."

He smiled in return. *Aahhh, so it is an interrogation.* "I'm afraid I'm stuck here, same as the two of you."

"Damn," the male half of team Souza said, "ever since I heard your speech, I can't stop imagining what the hunting and fishing must be like on a virgin earth."

"Never understood those hobbies myself," he answered. "Many of my colleagues seemed to live for it."

"Seriously?" The team's leader sputtered as she came to her feet. "An empty, earth like world, dedicated to liberty, and you can only think of the hunting?" Mrs. Souza marched off towards the cockpit, muttering to herself.

"Don't mind her," Tom shrugged. "Been too long since she's gotten to shoot someone."

*

Chapter 2

Eden

"You sure, you're up for this?" Elisabeth was looking at him like she didn't believe he was. She was probably right. Kyle's week-long headache was down to a dull throbbing that seemed to be synched with his heart beat. It was a marked improvement over what had felt like an ice pick in his ear for his first couple of days after regaining consciousness back on Eden.

And they *were* back, barely in the case of Colonel Pretty and himself. Jake and Carlos had gotten both their unconscious bodies to the gate room with less than 90 seconds to spare before the HAT's fuel air scuttling charge had turned the inside of their mountain complex into a man-made incendiary hell. He remembered nothing after the SF Osprey had exploded. Eight additional members of Pretty's combat team had made it as well, including his executive officer Captain Nagy who was still in the hospital recovering from his injuries.

"I'm sure," he lied. What he was certain of, was that if he spent another day lying in bed he was going to have to hurt someone. It would have to be someone small, slow, and incapable of putting up much of a fight. The truth was, he still felt like shit.

Elisabeth led him out of the elevator and down the gray carpeted floor of the New Seattle operations center's top floor. The conference room's door was glass, so he could see the large number of people gathered around the table, some he knew at a glance. There were many new faces around the edges of the room that he didn't recognize. He assumed they were program personnel who had made it across in those final days. He paused on the hallway side of the door.

"He's in there, isn't he?"

"Who?" Elisabeth asked, a little too innocently for his taste.

"Your step brother." Elisabeth had a half-brother in Paul Stephens, the Program's founder. Kyle had figured that out quickly, but somewhere in that crowd was a step brother that Elisabeth insisted he'd already met, and even teased him with a "he likes you." So far, he'd been unable to figure out who it was. No one in the Program seemed inclined to help him either. In fact, the longer it went on, he was sure they were all actively keeping it from him.

"It's not Colonel Pretty?"

"Is that an official guess?" Elisabeth asked. "How many of those do you get by the way?"

He must have pleaded with his eyes,

"It's not Colonel Pretty, come on," Elisabeth said pushing the door open, and leaning in close to him. "Promise me, you'll leave if this is too much."

He nodded at her in agreement, he wasn't going to fool anyone that he was back to a hundred percent. He ignored the looks of surprise at his presence and walked around the table to slide into a seat next to Col. Pretty. Elisabeth had gone the other way around the table and sat across from him.

Paul Stephens looked relieved, Kyle thought. The last time he'd seen the Program's leader, Stephens had been worried about the government arresting Phil Westin, learning of what they were doing and moving to shut them down before they could make it to Eden. The government had nearly succeeded, but in the end, as usual had moved too slow and they'd made it to Eden. Barely, in his case.

Stephens had a right to be relieved. At the moment he was looking at Kyle with that look of concern that he was already tired of seeing on other people's faces.

"I've already questioned Colonel Pretty," Stephens shook his head at him. "Are you certain you're ready to jump back into this?"

Kyle glanced over at the Colonel. He had one arm in a sling, had lost a slash of hair on the back of his head and was still wrapped up in what looked like a sterile turban. The man shared the same waxy complexion he'd seen in the mirror this morning. They were both lucky to be alive. Two of the Colonel's men weren't. They'd been running for the relative safety of the HAT's garage and been caught in the fireball of the exploding Osprey. They'd all known the government would try to shut them down. Pretty's SF unit had been the tool they'd sent.

No one had planned on having to deal with the Airforce. They were supposed to have been locked up tight in that mountain before anything could be scrambled. They hadn't counted on additional members of Pretty's assault team deciding to come over at the last moment, and they'd re-opened the blast doors.

"I'm alright, Sir."

Stephens paced back and forth at the head of the table. "I won't repeat what I've already said in thanks to Col. Pretty for Kyle's and Elisabeth's sake; it's enough for all of you to know that Mr. Lassiter's team was no less central to what we've been able to do and we all owe him our thanks."

"I'll second that," Phil Westin put in from across the table and several chairs closer to the front, "Emily and I owe Mr. Lassiter and his team our lives, something I'm not likely to ever forget."

Kyle nodded at Westin's upraised coffee mug in acknowledgement. Westin's company and personal wealth had funded a good deal of the Program. He and his wife had been captured by the government's new Gestapo arm, the ISA, before Kyle and his team had been able to rescue them.

Paul saved him from any more embarrassment as he stopped his pacing as if he'd just remembered something. Stephens wasn't just a genius, he was a master at getting people to forget that he was a genius. Kyle didn't doubt for a second that the second skill was as critical as the man's intellect for his success. It didn't fool him, Stephens was probably incapable of forgetting.

"Which," Stephens looked over at him again and shared a conspiratorial glance with Col. Pretty, "brings us to Kyle's position here within the program. Something I've overlooked while we dealt with our logistical issues and he convalesced."

Kyle felt his stomach lurch, in a manner that had nothing to do with the post-concussion nausea he'd been dealing with. At a glance, he could see Pretty smiling at him. That was never a good thing. It was a senior officer's non-verbal for 'bend-over here it comes.'

"As most of you know, Sir Geoff invested Kyle with the responsibility of leading our efforts to secure the settlement sites, a process that continues and will continue until the defenses are needed or the threat is no longer there. Sir Geoff also left me additional notes regarding Kyle."

Stephens smiled to himself for a moment. They were all going to miss Sir Geoff, but Stephens had relied on the old man.

"I won't repeat what he actually said, but suffice it to say he believed I'd be some sort of drooling idiot if I didn't take Mr. Lassiter's council to heart. So, in conjunction with Col. Pretty's elevation in status to the head of our military defense, Kyle will join him and remain in charge of our tactical security measures at the settlement level under Hanks's authority."

"The need for such doesn't require an explanation. We are now worried about our new arrivals, their health and welfare and their readiness to meet any threat which may present itself. The job may lack some of the flair of Sir Geoff's former security portfolio," Stephens smiled, "his *spook* work, I guess he called it, but I hope we're done with that now. We've made it, we're here, but the work of securing the settlements in the face of what we may face is no less critical."

Stephens bowed his head towards Hank Pretty. "Which is why Col. Pretty wants Kyle to act as his second in command."

A heads up would have been nice, he thought, staring across the table at Elisabeth. She was acting as if she was focused on her half-brother at the head of the table and ignoring what he felt had to have been a look of panic on his face. Sir Geoff had already warned him this was coming, both in person during that last night inside the mountain as well via the notes on the compad that Sir Geoff had gifted to him. The old man had said he'd threatened Stephens to make certain Kyle would have the authority he needed to do his job.

The other written information, some of it rambling treatises on politics, some hard data, were less instructions and more operating principles. Musings on what Sir Geoff thought would be needed before they were done here. Much of which, Kyle knew wasn't going to be popular. He didn't feel bringing up any of that here would constitute wisdom or good timing. Certainly not when Sir Geoff's primary concerns for the future revolved around the role of the Program itself.

"You and your fellow hooligans will need to be the Praetorian Guard before it's over," Sir Geoff had written him. The old man had seemed very certain on that point.

"That's if he's up to the task," Stephens was looking at him in question, with a half-smile playing across a face that couldn't imagine anybody not wanting a position with the Program, "and wants the job?"

He didn't want Sir Geoff's old job, or the new one. Not even close. He wanted to disappear into the hills of this empty planet, toss his compad into the nearest stream and go mountain man. At least for a while. He'd already told Pretty the same, and the Colonel, the same man that had recommended him for the Program in the first place, had just shook his head back and forth slowly from the chair in his hospital room a week ago. Pretty wanted out too. There was far too much to be done though, and they both knew it. At some point, he promised himself, he was going to take some serious down time. Screw the Appalachian Trail, he was going to start on the East Coast and follow in Lewis & Clark's footsteps. But not yet.

"I'd be honored," he said. Elisabeth was smiling at him. Pretty just glanced at him with a firm nod that seemed to say, 'Yeah, me too.' He had seen Jake here when he walked in. His friend and fellow 'knuckle dragger,' was seated behind him against the wall, no doubt sadly shaking his head right now. Jake would be certain to remind him, 'how you never, ever, volunteered for anything'.

"No one is happier about that," Stephens gave him a warm smile, "than I am. If anybody is capable of getting here from Earth and chewing me out, it would be Sir Geoff."

Everyone had a good laugh at that, but Kyle knew Sir Geoff's distrust of the bureaucratic side of the Program was well enough known, that not everyone around this table was a member of the Sir Geoff fan club – nor of his, by extension.

"OK," Stephens called them to order again. "To the situation at hand – our final count."

Someone activated the power point on the wall above and behind Stephens, it just showed a number. 1,298,578.

"I'm told several very pregnant women are in competition to deliver the first child born on Eden from the New Arrivals Group," Stephens crowed. "The number will grow, but that right now is our total population."

Dr. Jensen sat next to Elisabeth across from him and was shaking his head. "We need to be careful with that, Paul. Sitting up two distinct groups, early arrivals and the Noobs."

"N.A.Gs," Paul countered, "New Arrivals Group.".

"You can label them anything you want Paul, everyone is calling them Noobs out there." Jensen jerked a thumb over his shoulder towards the window. "*They* call themselves Noobs, and the first time they or we start crowing about a baby being born, some early arrival is going to point out the fact that all her kids were born here." Kyle liked Dr. Jensen. For a PhD in molecular engineering the guy could still speak English. The former 101st Airborne medic, didn't sugarcoat anything.

"I hadn't thought the divide between the two groups was so pronounced," Stephens seemed genuinely shocked.

"It's pronounced, and it will get worse before it gets better." Elisabeth continued with a nod to Jensen. "It's only been ten days, but our new arrivals are quickly starting to figure out that they've got some real adjustments to make. This isn't coming as a surprise to any of them, but I think the scope of change is throwing a few of them. It's an adjustment the pioneers have lived with for years, and that later group is in a decidedly superior position at the moment.

"For the most part, everyone is helping out as much as they can," Elisabeth continued. "But people don't like being in a position of needing assistance, over time it just reinforces the divide we currently have.

"It runs the gamut; housing, employment, you name it, but its focus is location," Elisabeth glanced at her notes. "We have nearly two hundred thousand people here in New Seattle, that were or are slated to move out to secondary settlements and in some cases to outposts. Long story short, they aren't leaving."

Kyle listened to the competing voices in the room as his mind wandered to Sir Geoff, wondering where he was, if he was even alive, and what he'd do if he were here. He'd cut through this shit definitively and piss off everyone in the process, but they'd leave the room knowing he was right. Now they were looking to him, even Paul Stephens seemed to be waiting for him to speak.

"The fact is," Dr. Jensen saved him. "A great many of our new arrivals signed up for the brochure – which admittedly is pretty damn good. But seen in the light of day, with their families here and possibly at risk from a... I can't believe I'm going to say this – an alien invasion, the marketing doesn't sing quite as loud. They want security, assurances. Most of these hangers-on see New Seattle as our hub, which, let's face it, it is. But the fact is, we weren't designed to even have a hub after the arrivals phase was complete. The current situation goes against our planning. You can't really blame them. Back on 1.0 the four wealthiest counties in America were the four in Virginia and Maryland that surrounded Washington, DC. That wasn't a coincidence. They think, if something is offered, employment, housing what have you, it will be offered here first."

"A nanny state?" Paul Stephens stood back up. "No." He glared around the table at everyone. "We are not going to go down that route, we couldn't if we wanted to and we most assuredly don't."

"No one is suggesting that, Paul," Elisabeth spoke up. "The nut of the problem is just this body of people that won't leave New Seattle for the outposts or other towns. They see the supplies and infrastructure here, and well...here they stay."

Kyle shook his head. "You're all looking at this as members of the Program. You see the grand plan, most of you have worked the program for more than a decade, the mission, the program itself is your life. You are committed to it, you derive your own self-worth from what we are trying to build here and the reasons you are here, the reasons we left colors everything. These people out there came for the same reasons, some will just be wanting to contribute. We see it all the time working in the settlements. You take a former executive, university department head, whatever, someone who is used to a position of responsibility, maybe even authority and tell them that the best way they can contribute is to build a new life elsewhere, away from what they see as the center of it all? Factor in that they've dragged their families with them."

No one in this room had spent as much time in the settlements as he had, he had no doubts about what he was saying. "Nearly all of them are white collar professionals, and while they may believe at a basic level what we are trying to do, many have a rough time seeing a role for themselves. What do you tell a stock broker, insurance executive, a publisher what their role is in building a new world for their children? Most are fine with it, once they get to a settlement, they're usually too busy to complain." He shook his head, remembering his own run-ins with the type he was talking about. It was ego driven for a lot of people. "Some don't see a role for themselves, and they are questioning their value and probably their decision to come here."

"Idle hands...." Colonel Pretty nodded.

"I can almost wish we didn't have the nano-production, they aren't wrong you know, not really." Paul's lips were pursed and he had his hands steepled in front of his chin. "We can produce anything they need."

"Scarcity, we need scarcity...We can't build an economy on the backs of warehoused goods and nano-production." Kyle sat forward and looked down the table at the young man who had spoken. He knew this had to be Jason Morales, Sir Geoff's masterpiece of misdirection and intelligence gathering, aka *"the kid."* Kyle knew from Elisabeth that the economics wunderkind had worked his way into the administration of the most devoutly socialist politician in American history and was in large part responsible for running them in circles, chasing their own tails for the last year while the Program carried out its final preparations and ultimate escape.

"There is going to be a severe dislocation in the local economy, there simply has to be. It will involve two steps, per our long running plan. The first is we recognize, what we have now is complete nationalization of most major industries, at least most of those involving either capital equipment or complex processes. I don't mean at the local levels of most settlements, they are far ahead of us in this for the simple reason they are farther away from those major lines of production and they are, quite literally supplying themselves as they hack a new home out of the wilderness. Almost everything produced anywhere, is consumed locally. We don't have the transport, excepting the river communities and coastal town for inland logistics. No Fedex, no highways and no rail, at least yet."

"Two," Morales leaned a little further forward, "we view that nationalized capital plant and the precious metal reserves that were collected by the Program over the last decade as the national reserve, well global reserve in this case, but it's all going to be denationalized. We are in the process of monetizing that reserve and have already staked everyone with a portion of the M1."

"M1?" So, Jake was awake. His head hurt too much to turn and look.

"Um, sorry," Morales said, "yeah, M1 is the money supply. The value of the reserves and our production will equal the value of the currency. The economy from that point forward is based on the circulation of that currency at it chases goods and services, which will be provided by the same people that received their initial shares of currency. There's going to be fortunes made and lost, it's going to be ugly and it's going to be beautiful. We have designed some safety nets, but nothing approaching a nanny state. Like I said, the economic dislocation, which is needed, is being delayed and will be made worse the longer we delay."

"We didn't expect to be fighting off a potential invasion from a planet where clan warfare seems to be a way of life

20

when we drew up the economic time-table." Colonel Pretty explained throwing his hands up in apology. "We may be needing state-run production plants in the short term."

"Granted," Morales answered. "I fully understand and agree with waiting until we at least know what we are dealing with before implementing the economic plan. But at every opportunity, where we are able, we must work to make certain that the industry and businesses that supply our security needs are farmed out to settlements, and privatized where possible. The longer the wait, the harder it is going to get people to adapt to their new realities and make those changes that Mr. Lassiter described as being needed at the level of the individual."

"Makes sense," Dr. Jensen nodded.

Morales smiled, "It pleases me that there's finally a conversation around this table that I understand, usually its quantum theory or politics." When the laughter died down, Jason continued.

"Mr. Lassiter hit the nail on the head, we actually need people to revert a hundred and fifty or two hundred years in the labor market, as has been done by early arrivals and to be fair, a good many of the Noobs," Jason turned to the head of the table, towards Stephens, "Sorry, New Arrivals. They've learned new skills, emphasizing production and extraction, services are coming albeit slower. But the services aren't for investment advisors, life coaches or HR professionals. In general, right now services in the outposts means putting food, tools or some creature comfort in the hands of people doing some hard work. It's the Levi pants model."

"The what?" Jake again.

"Back in the California gold rush, the real fortunes weren't made by miners, but by those enterprising enough to fulfill the needs of the miners. Levi pants, the farms and ranches that fed the influx of people, the iron works that produced the tools, the wagon routes and shipping lines, the banks that boomed in San Francisco and so on.

"But to the problem at hand, the longer we wait," Morales continued, "the problem grows. With added time, the greater

21

disadvantage there will be for those who have been slow to adapt, or continue to resist the move out to the settlements, or" he pointed out the window, "are already out there stirring up trouble as they are in the process of convincing themselves they've been duped. The demonstration we had last night is just a beginning. As long as we have those people here, who have no real impetus to start over, we are all at risk."

"I'm not about to shut down the nano-plant," Dr. Jensen barked. "We are in full production for arms, ammo and equipment we may desperately need very soon, as well as spare parts for the military and transport gear we already have - it has to be a priority. *The* priority, or all else could be made moot." Dr. Jensen looked at Colonel Pretty and then at Kyle, almost pleading.

"No one's going to disagree with that." Stephens nodded. "But as to these slow adopters, we can't force them out of Seattle. Well we could, but I'm not about to take that route." Paul looked at everyone seated around the table, and those against the wall. Most hadn't spoken up at all. "Somehow, I think Sir Geoffrey would have already presented a viable solution that none of us would have liked."

The laughter died down quickly. "Elisabeth, keep working your advertising campaign for the settlements, we'll get them out of here slowly, but we have to move them."

The meeting broke up quickly.

"You coming?" Elisabeth looked at him like she couldn't wait to get him back to resting.

"No," Kyle looked over at Colonel Pretty, and winked, "I need to bend the Colonel's ear. I promise I'll be done in a few."

Pretty looked at him for a moment and nodded to Elisabeth. "This won't take long."

Elisabeth rolled her eyes at both of them and walked out.

"You are so out classed by that lady." Hank said quietly.

"Can you introduce me to Morales?"

"Sure," Pretty caught Jason's attention and waived him over, before turning back to look at him in question. "You look like a man with an idea. The light bulb just come on?"

"Trust me, the only flashes going on up there hurt, but I do have an idea about this scarcity thing."

"Scarcity," Jason broke in as he walked up, "sounds bad, but every economic system is built on it."

Pretty introduced them, and they shook hands. Kyle explained that he'd heard a great deal about Jason's exploits from Elisabeth.

"It wasn't that hard," Jason said with a shrug. Kyle didn't get the feeling Jason was being falsely modest. "Truth is, I had lived a lie for so long, nobody questioned me. You guys, you ran the real risks. I'd be willing to bet my old boss in the Administration still thinks I was taken out or kidnapped by the Program. No way his ego would allow him to think I had played him." Jason shrugged again. "I was above suspicion, it was easy."

"Being somebody else for that long, couldn't have been easy," Kyle added.

"What's this about?" Jason changed the subject quickly. "Scarcity? I'm enough of a realist to know economics isn't that exciting to most people."

Kyle looked at Pretty for a moment, and then back at Morales, before making sure no one was standing within ear shot.

"I might have an idea..."

*

Every time he did something that seemed natural or commonplace for the first time on Eden, Kyle was struck by how much societal habit they had all brought with them, as well, by how different some things were here. He stood at the bar of the New Planet Pub, a large plasteel Quonset hut that some entrepreneurial early colonist had taken over with his hobby brewed beer.

Kyle waited for his pitcher of beer, while Audy and Jason Morales sat at a table towards the back, away from the evening crowd that was a loud mix of Program personnel, early colonists and recent arrivals. The latter were a mixed bag of emotions. Many still carried the excitement of their arrival,

23

even after two and for some three weeks. Some were bitter at the short-term, no-vacancy status of some of the more popular settlements, or just on general principle that things were different than they'd imagined. Everyone, founder and noob alike, were anxious for what the future held. Some though, were less than happy to find that the future wasn't scripted and ready to be handed to them.

Mixed into the 'noob' community were a select few, who were genuinely angry at, or worse in Kyle's opinion, jealous of the 'founders.' It made no sense to him, but this group seemed to be centered here in New Seattle and they wanted a larger say in running the Program, as if the Program had some role to play as a future government. It didn't and wouldn't, if he had anything to say about it. But, he knew there were already Program members who held different opinions on that subject, and they were all bending Paul's ears on a daily basis. To Kyle, they were more dangerous than the upset Noobs. They were the example the Noobs would point at and say they wanted authority too.

When they did point, the word, 'founder' wasn't used with a respectful tone. It was usually preceded by an 'F bomb' and followed by some imagined slight or unfair advantage that the founders had over the noobs. The fact was, the founders did have an advantage, especially the young adults that had grown up here. They possessed a sense of independence and "can-do" attitude that probably hadn't been seen in America since the 1800s.

Everything was possible to them, they just had to make it work. No one was going to drown them in red tape, no one was going tax them, and no one was going regulate them out of business. That said, no one was going to bail them out either. Their safety net, if they had one, was their family and the fact most founders could live fairly well off the land.

The noobs, particularly the trouble makers who were refusing to leave New Seattle were a different set altogether. Unlike the vast majority of recent arrivals, they weren't out learning new skills and working on building a new life in the settlements. These made up about a third of the crowd inside

24

the Pub. They were hanging on to their old jobs, their old-earth status, power, what have you. They simply didn't have or were unwilling to learn the skills that founders took for granted. The skill disparity had a secondary effect that would have been comical if it didn't carry such a destabilizing risk. Kyle was thinking of the meat market, which was in full swing at the Pub, as always. Every teenager, single man, and a surprising hell of a lot of women from the founder community were trolling for dates and mates among a suddenly insecure noob community.

As a noob, hitching your future to a Program technocrat or founder in New Seattle was just about the only way you could currently guarantee you wouldn't eventually have to go live in one of the far away and scary settlements. That thought made Kyle grimace. Elisabeth had received an anonymous resume from a potential suitor the other day. "Someone dependable to share your life with," it had read at one point. They had both had a good private laugh over it, but Elisabeth, who was a student of human behavior, was worried. A lot of founders, especially the teenagers and young adults, were taking advantage of a situation where they were suddenly "great catches." It was just one more dynamic between the two groups that was causing friction.

Kyle thanked the teenager behind the bar that slid the pitcher of Hefeweizen towards him and he almost reached for a wallet on his back hip that he no longer had. He smiled to himself because he wasn't even sure where the damn thing was. He put his thumb on the biometric reader the bar tender pushed towards him on the bar top. The cost would be subtracted from whatever the Program was paying him. He moved through the breakwater of the crowd, holding the pitcher out in front and over his head and was half way back to the table before he realized that Jason and Audy's table was surrounded by half a dozen men and three women.

He could feel the tension at the table as he approached, centered around one stranger leaning forward, two fists planted on the table and his face about a foot away from Jason's.

25

To his credit, Kyle thought the young economist was doing fine. He was smiling and evidently not giving the asshole the argument, he was looking for. Glancing at Audy, he was relieved to see an amused look on the outlander's face. If Audy had felt threatened, Kyle didn't doubt for a second the half dozen Noobs would come out of it with a very short and painful portion of the stick.

And they were Noobs, he could tell at a glance. Program members all wore a badge on a lanyard, and these days, dark circles under their eyes from the long hours. Founders in general just looked healthier, and tired as well from working hard. These people just looked upset.

He put on his most cheerful face and squeezed through the ring of flesh to the table. "Sorry about that. If I'd known you had friends here, I would have brought some more glasses."

"Not friends," Audy piped in, with a tone that could have been used to discuss the fact that it was raining outside.

Kyle groaned inwardly. Audy's English was progressing remarkably well, but there was a cultural divide that the language couldn't quite span, maybe never would. Audy was as stubborn as he was intelligent. His alien friend's ability to recognize hyperbole, irony, or cynicism in English was almost non-existent. He'd tried to talk to him about it and explain that earthborn humans didn't always say what they really thought, nor believe what was said. It was a steep learning curve. Kyle knew Audy had grown up in a social world of stark divides between dark and light, good and bad.

"No," Kyle said clearly to Audy. "They are friends, just a little upset it would seem." He turned to face the lead trouble maker, who was shorter than him by a head but very clearly had a hard intelligence behind some very cold, dead eyes. Attorney, Kyle guessed immediately.

"You're the Lassiter fellow, Sir Geoffrey put in charge of our defenses."

It hadn't been a question, so Kyle just tried another smile that he could feel dying on his face and held out his hand after sitting the pitcher down. "I am, Kyle Lassiter."

26

Another hand was offered, and Kyle couldn't help but put a little extra pressure on it.

"Richard Kiley, Director of American Rebirth. We were a conservative think tank based in Washington." Kiley paused for a moment as if that detail should mean something to him. When it was clear that it hadn't, the man changed tactics.

"I knew Sir Geoffrey well, we worked closely for years and I'd think he'd be demanding an election by now. When is the Program going to stop being run by fiat?"

Kyle glanced at the man for a moment as if to confirm what he'd just said. If this Kiley had been a confidant of Sir Geoff, he'd chew off his own arm. Sir Geoff had as about as much use for career politicians on the corporatist right as he did for those on the socialist left.

"Elections are being held every day. Constitutions, by-laws, articles of federation and commercial laws are being written and enacted as we speak in every settlement on the planet. If you knew Sir Geoffrey as well as you claim, you'd know he wanted Seattle burnt to the ground the minute everyone was safely resettled."

Kyle waved a hand around the room, "New Seattle is the Program's corporate headquarters. It is not meant to be and will never be a settlement or part of a government – it's Ellis Island. Someplace you land before moving on."

"Convenient for the people living here, wouldn't you say?"

Kyle checked his rising anger. "They hacked a home out of this wilderness. At one point during the first year, they went six months without a supply shipment from Earth. A few died of starvation. Another settlement was attacked, nearly wiped out in the early days before they had defenses. They built this and the other settlements for you, and they don't expect a thing for it. They don't expect to play a role in how you will live in the settlements, but they've definitely earned a right to make their own laws in their own home."

Kiley wasn't listening, just preparing his next sound bite. "But this is where the power is, decisions being made here affect us all, hardly representational is it?"

27

His mother's words to him, *"don't argue with an idiot, bystanders won't be able to tell you apart,"* were echoing in the back of his head. He just couldn't let it go.

"No, it isn't." It was difficult to ignore the mental image of him driving his fist into the former lobbyist's throat. "It's not meant to be, any more than the man in the street is allowed around a corporate board room to vote. There are technical decisions being made here regarding the overall program and not surprisingly, right now those decisions are focused on keeping your asses safe. You suggest those decisions be put to a vote?"

"I do, we all do. I still believe in civilian control of the military," Kiley sounded indignant. "Furthermore, you talk about citizens voting around a board room, I used to remember people could buy shares in a company and get a vote."

Kyle took a step toward Kiley, around the table slowly. "So, go buy a share, make a commitment to of the settlements, sacrifice, work, earn your share, earn your place around the table." He looked up and met every eye in the circle.

"The table, as Mr. Kiley referred to is open to everyone. We desperately want and need everyone. But the seat at the table is earned. You all came here because you believed in liberty. It's being offered in nearly 300 settlements that have every creature comfort New Seattle has, and they are all made up of free citizens that are committed to civilian control of the military."

Kyle paused and leaned into Kiley, "Because those same people *are* the military. Volunteers, all of them willing to fight for what they believe in, willing to fight for your right to hang out on the streets of New Seattle and get your temporary housing and three meals a day."

"Are you threatening us." Kiley took half a step back.

"He ain't threatening you, Dick," another man spoke up from the circle, "he's just talking."

Kyle did his best to soften his tone and looked at others in the group. There were a few hard cases there half sneering at his words. Some though, he gauged, were at least listening.

"There's every type of representational democracy imaginable to choose from and a few that are still in the process of deciding. You want to vote, vote with your feet. You want to go as a group somewhere new, petition the Program and they'll get you the gear and infrastructure start you need to do it. But what you want, will not, I repeat, will *not* be found here."

"Come on, Dick," a woman pulled at Kiley's sleeve, "leave them be."

"I'll leave," Kiley sputtered, "but this isn't over, not by a long shot."

Kyle sat down in his own seat and nodded at the backs of the group as they moved back towards the crowd nearer the bar. He looked over at Jason who was staring at him.

"Nice speech."

Kyle shook his head and drained half his beer that Jason had poured for him. Sitting the glass down and wiping the delicious foam off his lips. "How often does that happen to you?"

"First time," Jason said. "Usually it's just mumbles and glares as I walk past. By the way, you should run for office, I mean if we had offices here. I think you just convinced a few of that group to get out of town."

Kyle shook his head and looked over at Audy. "Audy, if I ever run for office you have permission to shoot me."

Audy's face lost some color. "I would not shoot you."

"I'm just kidding, Audy – a joke."

"Not a funny one." Audy shook his head.

"I wasn't being serious," Kyle explained, "just a funny way to explain I do not want to be a politician."

Audy smiled suddenly, and pointed towards the front of the bar. "That man Kiley, him I would shoot for you."

Kyle sat his beer down. His understanding of the politics on Audy's world was incomplete but he knew enough to know it revolved around honor, clan loyalties, and blood ties.

"Are you joking Audy? Or serious?"

Audy looked at him for a moment before his face cracked open in a smile. "I joke. I have listened to you explain this."

"Had me worried too," Jason added, regarding Audy with a smile.

Audy put his beer down and held both hands up. "Truth... I do not understand. You," he pointed at Kyle. "You are Seraph, a leader in your tongue, you can't allow a man to challenge you without giving answer."

Kyle shrugged. "I did answer, I answered with my own ideas, my own words. If my words are stronger, my ideas win." Kyle pointed at Jason, "the two of us just met a week ago, we may argue tonight, but we can argue and still be friends." Kyle pointed at Audy. "You and I don't have to agree with each other. We are friends, we'll be friends after we argue."

"You wish to be friends with that Tardan?" Audy pointed at the bar again, "with that man?"

Kyle looked towards the entrance, the group around Kiley wasn't as big as it had been, but he had no idea if that had anything to do with him knocking the asshole down a peg or the New World's Pub's meat market ambience.

"No. But, I can argue with people I don't like as well." Kyle said and took another drink.

"Although, sometimes," Jason added with a wink, "shooting them would be easier."

Audy picked up his glass and regarded Jason a moment before turning to Kyle. "I like him."

Jason tapped his glass against Audy's. "Ok, so Audy has established that the Chandrian contingent of Eden likes me," he turned to face Kyle. "I'm guessing you don't have some long-hidden interest in macroeconomic policy, what gives?"

Kyle regarded Jason in silence for a moment. He was about to take a huge risk with Jason and all he had to go on was hearing the man speak at one planning session. The couple of times that Sir Geoffrey had mentioned Jason to him, it had always been as "our Ace in the Hole."

"Can we speak in confidence?" Kyle asked.

Jason nodded. "I understand you were pretty much brought under Sir Geoffrey's wing, if the two of us can't keep a secret, who could...."

"Good point, and here's to Sir Geoff," they clicked glasses together. "What I wanted to talk to you about was something you mentioned during the meeting in terms of these folks not wanting to leave the mothership. I found myself wondering what Sir Geoff would do if he were here."

"You'd mentioned at the meeting having an idea, before Paul walked over to join us. You suddenly clammed up. You thinking of rounding folks up at gunpoint?" Jason asked, smiling with his eyebrows cocked in question.

"Sir Geoff would only joke about that. Secretly, I think he loved civil disobedience."

Jason nodded in agreement. "So, what's your idea?"

Kyle leaned across the table. "The old man always said Paul kept him around to make those hard decisions that he couldn't. I'm confident I've got an idea that might work, but I need your opinion and your blessing. If we get caught, it's on me, and Paul can fire me anytime. But I'd really like an opinion on whether you think it would have an effect. I really just want to go build a cabin in the woods anyway."

Jason just stared at him for a moment. "As I mentioned in the meeting, we need the nano-production. In particular, the military builds that are roughly sixty percent of the total right now. If Audy's relatives show up, we are going to need those arms, ammo, and spare parts, and by we," Jason pointed back at him and then at Audy, "I mean you. I'm just a geek, a number cruncher."

Kyle nodded. "If I can't get Doc Jensen to agree with me, it's a no go. But if I get his buy in, would I have your OK? if ....."

Kyle went on for less than a minute. It was simple in his mind, it all came down to the question, what would Sir Geoff do?

He finished and watched as Jason refilled his own mug and drained it. "You're serious?" The young economist's eyebrows had crawled halfway up his forehead.

"Yeah, I am."

"It's insane, you're insane."

"Is good plan," Audy tapped his mug on the table for emphasis.

Jason turned to face Audy, a confused look on his face, "you understand this economic stuff?"

"No," Audy shrugged, "I meant the other part. It will be fun."

"Forgetting the fun part," Kyle smiled and shook his head at Audy. He looked back across the now empty pitcher at Jason. "Would it work?"

"It might, but you can't ... I mean, could you?"

Kyle just smiled back at Jason. "I've got some friends who will show up for the fun part."

*

Chapter 3

New Seattle

"Is it wrong I'm enjoying this?" Jake shifted a wad of tobacco to his other cheek and spit on the polished concrete floor.

Dr. Jensen, the Director of the nano-production facility just glared at him over the top of his glasses.

"What?" Jake shrugged innocently. "Nothing going to be left of this place in an hour, you want the floors cleaned before we blow it to shit?"

"I do not understand this either." Audy stood next to Kyle where the last load of invaluable nano production template servers and production beds were being crated up and moved to an adjacent assembly warehouse via the tracked assembly line in the subbasement. From there, everything necessary for restarting production was being air trucked to a facility the Program had on Whidbey Island, a forty-minute round trip to the North. With nearly two dozen air trucks pulled in from settlements on the Columbia and Willamette as well as two from Chief Joe, and every personal friend that Kyle and Jake had on Eden, they were making quick work of it. The air truck traffic wasn't anything unusual, as a couple of times a week manufactured goods were flown out to various settlements or directly to the harbor warehouses in the area of what used to be Fishermen's Pier in 'old' Seattle.

The beauty of nano-production was that the templates were nothing more than computer files, albeit very complex and massive files, but they were all backed up by the Program in several places. All that really needed to be moved were the actual production beds that kept the hundreds of billions of molecule-sized nanobots happy, fed, and ready to work. Everything else, all that was about to be destroyed, the new assembly lines for raw materials and output-assembly stations were nearly completed at the Whidbey facility.

Kyle had worried that Dr. Jensen, who managed the nano-pro facility for the program would be difficult to convince, but he'd actually served up the best idea yet to cover their tracks

33

and perhaps win a few public relations points in the process. This whole operation was being done in the name of an imaginary Program employee who had written a simple, yet quite convincing manifesto, detailing how he'd come to Eden with the hopes of getting back to nature but had found the level of technology stifling. He could no longer sit by and watch as humans become welfare recipients from an infernal technology that answered basic needs at a whim while destroying everyone's work ethic in the process.

Kyle thought the note was a bit over the top, and there would no doubt be people calling bullshit on both sides of the Noob/Founder divide. That couldn't be helped, and since their imaginary luddite terrorist didn't actually exist and was going to be unfortunately killed in the blast, they were all hoping the act of sabotage might actually bring some people together. If the Program played along.

"Can't say this is my proudest moment."

Kyle turned to see his father pulling off his work gloves with an impossible to read half smile playing on his lips.

Kyle shrugged at his Dad. "You know, there are fathers around the world, on Earth at any rate, that would praise their God of choice if their sons would just stop talking and blow some shit up."

His Dad just grunted. "You sure about this? These people trust you."

"I know." Kyle was thinking of Elisabeth whom he had lied to, several times in the last few days making the preparations for this evening.

"They brought me in to make some hard decisions, I'm doing the only thing the situation here has left us. We need a watershed event, and we have got to fix this before..."

"Before we go to war with another planet?" His dad finished for him.

"I doubt if they'll send everyone."

"Oh, I feel better already." His Dad looked off as the last of the crates was lowered into the well in the floor where a conveyer belt whisked it away to the loading yard two warehouses away.

His Dad clapped him on the shoulder. "I wouldn't have agreed to this if I didn't think you were right." Roger Lassiter's big smile looked ready to break out in a laugh. "But, damn!"

Kyle spun in a circle taking in the empty space except for one production bed that had been taken off line for repairs anyway. Next to it was a waist high pile of battle ship grey dust, so fine a light cloud was visible near the floor kicked up by the passage of pallets and people walking past. It was the broken production bed's nanobots, and somewhere underneath that pile was a piece of C-4 the size of his thumb which would kick off the fireworks and infuse the chamber with a cloud of metallic, microscopic, non-union workers, just two seconds before the main charges of plastique brought the building and the adjoining warehouse down.

Kyle imagined the mess it would make and grimaced. Truth was, Paul Stephens' nano-technology and production had already vastly altered man's relationship with labor and they were in effect consumers of a near endless supply. This facility itself, had been up and running for half a decade. They had plenty of produced stock that would be well outside the blast zone. Within the zone however, were two warehouses full of food. History was replete with examples of hunger driving mass migrations of people. In just a short while, the noobs would definitely have some impetus to move on out to the settlements as he half expected food was going to be launched over the industrial quarter of New Seattle.

What they were doing wasn't nearly as drastic as what he knew Sir Geoff had intended for New Seattle. The old man had foreseen what could happen if Seattle was allowed to continue as a defacto capital city, directing and controlling what was happening on Eden. Sir Geoff had wanted the entire Program itself shut down as soon as practicable. The threat from Audy's home world had nixed that option. No one doubted they needed some semblance of centralized authority or command structure. What they were doing would undoubtedly land him in hot water, maybe get him fired. A big part of him considered that a win-win proposition.

He put his fingers to his lips and the shrill whistle brought everybody up short.

"OK, as soon as Dr. Jensen confirms the last truck is loaded and, on its way, get to your assigned positions. We'll starburst out of here, on every road, alley, and horse track. Make sure your area is clear as you go. You guys moving west, use your night vision. I don't want to blow up any teenagers making out under a tree in the park. Jake, you and Carlos get airborne, give me a green light when everyone has reported all-clear. Luis," Kyle looked over at Carlos' uncle the retired Marine. He was a legitimate demolitions expert and had assured them he could bring the building down with limited risk. "You bring the Christmas tree, you are with me."

"Any questions?"

"Can we share a cell?" Jake called out

"No! Hell no!" he answered. "Remember, when you leave, get to wherever you left your compads as quickly as you can. I imagine a lot of us will be on call as soon as this thing goes up. You out of towners," he looked over at the Chief Joe contingent and could still not believe the changes that Eden seemed to have worked on Lupe Vasquez, "thanks for your help. Remember... you're in town for some supplies, and a night on the big town. I recommend the New World Pub, too many entrances and balconies for anyone to notice when you got there. I imagine most of you have been drinking already."

That got some laughs.

"Anybody gets questioned, you know nothing, forever." Kyle caught as many eyes as he could. He was asking a lot and he didn't like putting friends in harm's way.

"Forever. This story, at least publicly, has to stay whole, or things could get nasty. We all have bigger problems to worry about. I'll take the hit with the program in the near term, but publicly, you know nothing but the story you've been told and whatever hits the news feeds. Forever."

Twenty minutes later, from an intersection separating the industrial zone from the rest of the city, Kyle and Luis, watched the running lights of the air car above the facility

36

about 700 hundred meters distant and circling at an altitude of about 500 feet. Inside, Jake and Carlos were collecting the 'all clears' from the rest of their motley crew. Kyle saw the air car's nose dip and move off to the south towards them, screaming almost directly overhead of their own position.

"We're all green." Luis intoned, looking at the jury-rigged circuit board.

Kyle reached over and thumbed off the safety lever and flicked the button before he could change his mind.

The explosion was designed to implode the building but a good portion of the roof was launched about fifty feet in the air on the back of a massive gout of flame. A split second later the shock wave and sound washed over them.

Kyle looked over at Luis who was grinning like a kid. "Anybody related to you that isn't crazy?"

Luis' grin grew a little, "Not a one."

The second explosion of the warehouse was muffled in comparison.

"Is that right?" Kyle asked

"I rigged the warehouse with mostly incendiaries, you didn't want anyone killed by flying barrels or number 10 cans, did you?"

Kyle shook his head. "Good point."

*

Whether it was his imagination, ego, or guilty conscious, Kyle felt like everyone else in the emergency meeting of the Program's management staff was throwing a knowing glance his way. Elisabeth was doing it now. He could feel her eyes boring into him from across the table. He knew there were going to be people disappointed in him today. He could not have cared less. Elisabeth's opinion was the only one that mattered. As far as he held it, a lot of people associated with the Program needed an attitude adjustment. He hoped she could come to see they hadn't had a choice. He'd intended to come clean from the beginning, but given the community's reaction to the bombing he wanted to see where this discussion went.

37

It had been nearly a week since the explosion and Dr. Jensen had the new nano-pro facility up and running on Whidbey Island. He'd been noticeably absent the last few days, at least by Kyle's guilty approximation, but the scientist now sat next to Elisabeth with a calm demeanor listening to a Noob, a former FBI Field Office Chief, deliver her investigative report in short staccato bursts.

Everyone had thought it wise to turn over the investigation to someone from the Noob community, an independent party as it were. Although, much of the remaining Noob community in New Seattle felt Mrs. Lawry was too pro-Program to be truly independent. From what Kyle had seen so far, they needn't have worried on that score. He could only imagine the efficiency that the former FBI SAC had brought to her job in the past.

Watching her deliver her report, no one in the room doubted that she took her job seriously. To look at her standing just over five feet tall, her gray streaked hair in a tight bun, she could have been the church lady in any community, until she opened her mouth, that is. Speaking loudly enough to cater to the large conference room and the audience that filled it, she held the entire senior staff in suspense.

Kyle feared she was about to point at him like his second-grade teacher had and call him out for bringing the electronic fart machine to class. He'd been as guilty then as he was now.

"In summation," she paused and looked around the room, "the heat from the fire destroyed any hard-forensic evidence. The CCTV cameras were cut into and fed some generic night footage, circumstantially proving that our perps had at least some rudimentary knowledge of the minimal security protocols that were in place."

"Excuse me," Paul Stephens raised one hand while the other rubbed at a headache between his eyes. "You said, 'perps' – plural?"

Agent Lawry, nodded once curtly and pivoted. "That's right, there is no way in my opinion that this act, which included spoofing the CCTV, getting through the outside door alarms, through the double keyed locks of the production floor, which we know they did, because whoever brought the building down, wired it from the inside. Every internal support stanchion was explosively cut. They did all this, as well as gaining access to the adjoining stock and outflow warehouses which were wired with fewer explosives and some well-placed incendiaries clearly designed to burn down rather than explode."

"If they had used explosives there, we'd have food stuff, supplies whatever was in the warehouse all over the industrial quarter, and we'd also undoubtedly have a great deal of injuries as well. I can only surmise that the intention was to deprive the community of the goods in the warehouse, and more specifically the production facility and not just haphazardly blow the building up to deliver a message. Given the flyers left around town, I personally believe the intent was as stated; basically, back away from the temptation of nano-production and make do with your own work.

There is no evidence, and I mean none, that suggests this was done by a lone ideological driven individual, Founder or Noob. Everything points to a group with at least a solid understanding of the Program's security. There were no personal compads registered in the area, whoever did this knew how to cover their tracks, which again, points to Program personnel.

"You sound certain." Stephens asked.

"It's circumstantial, but it all points that way. Not enough to prosecute, even if we had laws against such a thing or anything else for that matter," the former FBI agent smirked, leaving no doubt as to her personal opinion regarding the dearth of laws. "But I'm certain," Mrs. Lawry looked around the room again, "in my 30 years of investigative experience, I've rarely seen a case that stands so firmly against the public narrative out on the street."

Paul Stephens stood slowly. The last couple of days had clearly taken a lot out of him and Kyle felt like shit for doing that to the guy. But Sir Geoff had warned him in no uncertain terms that Paul would be the first to get seduced into supporting the central role of the Program.

"That is my problem to fix," he declared. "I'll make a statement this evening highlighting your findings. Thank you, Mrs. Lawry. I hope we won't need your services again in this capacity, but it's nice to have your skills and experience to call on."

Mrs. Lawry nodded. "Never thought I'd have to do this again, but if I may make a suggestion, Sir?"

"Certainly."

"Don't change the narrative. The event has been transformative, at least within the Noob community, those that are still here. I'm speaking as a Noob, and as somebody who was part of this program for the last seven years. There is still some heartburn over *having* to go to a settlement, but they are starting to go, and people in the settlements are that much more motivated to make their own go of it. They realize it will probably be a while before the safety net of Seattle's production is back on line."

Stephens looked a little surprised by the statement. "If you had to guess Ms. Lawry, how widely shared is your sentiment?"

"It's difficult to measure sentiment," she replied evenly. "Certainly not everyone, and in most cases the probable shortages are what people are concerned with, regardless of what they may think what happened or who was behind it."

"Jason?" Stephens called on his Chief Economic planner. "What do you think?"

Jason Morales shook his head wistfully. "I stated in our last meeting that I wished we could shut down the production. I won't now act as if my job and that of my team just didn't get a whole lot easier. We actually have a shot at monetizing the economy now that we may have some scarcity, or a perception of scarcity. Not to mention what it'll do to the labor pool. If I didn't know better, I'd ask if anyone has seen Sir Geoff around, because from my perspective somebody just cut the Gordian knot."

"Kyle, what of the military situation?"

Kyle hoped he hadn't jumped out of his seat at his name being called. Somehow, he knew this wouldn't be laughed off like the fart machine had been.

"We still have no idea from where an attack from Chandra could come, so we've been moving gear and ammo out to the settlements all along, as they are produced. Same for the caches we have sprinkled across the map where we don't have settlements. For basic supplies, guns and ammo, we're solid. What we lost were some critical spares for our four jump jets, as well as the helo, and Osprey fleet. They all eat spare parts through normal use. Needless to say, we won't have any more than those four jets or any more Ospreys until we get production back up." He was hedging, production was pretty much already back up.

"Dr. Jensen, how long to get production back to where we need to be?" Stephens sat back down and steepled his fingers under his chin. Kyle wondered for a moment if Jensen was going to come clean.

"As you know, we have a small nano-production unit at the gate station. It always made sense to have a unit there, and most of the hub settlements have an independent production capability. I've already began constructing new production beds and control units, but the runs need to be completed in series. As a result, we'll have all the parts to build twenty new production beds in the same time it would take to construct all the parts for one bed. Shutting the damn things down, reprogramming them and restarting as you know, is the real bottle neck time wise. But we can do that in say seven, maybe eight weeks..."

Hedging again, Kyle nodded internally. Jensen hadn't lied. He'd just described the production schedule for an increased nano-production capacity that had already been approved.

"That's not so bad," Elisabeth's mother piped in from somewhere behind Kyle. He didn't dare turn around and look.

"It's not as easy as that," Dr. Jensen continued. "The real kicker is that a new production bed, once constructed and assembled, has to go into what we call a breed phase. Basically, they each produce their army of nanobots that will

41

carry out the programmable construction, just shy of a month to do that, call it three months all told."

"So," Stephens looked slowly around the room, "what I'm hearing is the destruction could have been much worse, and it actually solved an intractable problem. Problem is, I'm not in the habit of and don't want to start lying to our people. I already feel, as if we've got a bait and switch situation with the threat of a Chandrian invasion hanging out there."

"That's just horseshit, Paul," Hank Pretty announced in his command voice. Stephens was laid back and didn't ask for any deferential treatment, and Kyle knew Hank and Stephens went way back. That said, he doubted if anyone else in the room could or would have taken the same tone with the head of the Program.

"Have to concur with Hank on this." Phil Westin was nodding his head and he looked over at his fellow Program board member and former Earth 1.0 competitor, Matteus Tagliasano before continuing. Kyle figured the two industrialists would have ended up owning Eden had they wanted to put their collective experience to work for themselves but they were both very firmly retired and occupied advisory roles.

"Paul," Westin continued. "Many of us argued for shuttering the food line to force these last holdouts to the places their children will all grow up. I was among that contingent as you know. I find myself in agreement with our young economist here," he nodded respectfully towards Jason. "The whole thing smacks of Sir Geoffrey. He had a knack for knowing what needed doing even when it was ugly, unpopular and downright nasty. Yeah, somebody broke a few eggs, and we'll undoubtedly break more if we have to fight a war. Our ideals are fine, but we can't be slaves to them, creating a situation where those principles work against us. Besides, whoever did this... gave you, I can't believe I'm about to say this, but you've got plausible deniability. I say you roll with the story line that's out there. Use it"

"We still would seem to have a problem of a rogue Program employee or employees." Stephanie Kurtz tapped the table. "Is it something we need to worry about?"

"I would imagine it was a one-off," Hank Pretty offered. "It solved a problem."

Kyle glanced up and looked at Elisabeth. She was staring back at him with an evil smile barely playing on her lips.

"I arranged the destruction of the factory." Kyle leaned forward, put his elbows on the table and looked at Paul Stephens directly even as he could feel every eye in the room turn towards him. "We all sat around asking ourselves what Sir Geoffrey would have done. I believe he would have said you know what has to be done. I did it. The actual production units were not destroyed, they are on Whidbey Island, awaiting re-installation."

There was a good four or five seconds of stunned silence. Until Dr. Jensen leaned forward, "I appreciate what Kyle just said, but I was in on it as well, and the new production site went operational two days ago. All essential spare parts were moved prior to the explosion as well. We'll deal with a one week or so delay in getting nano-bot levels back to where they were, they don't like being inactive, but that's it."

"I gave my blessing," Jason raised a hand. "We have to get away from playing nanny quickly, or our grand-kids will all be eating at some future government trough."

"As did I," Hank looked at Paul as he said it. The look of surprise on Paul's face was unmistakable.

"I don't want Kyle to get all the credit," Jake smiled, leaning back in his chair to the point he looked about to spill out of it. "We took precautions, we were as safe as could be and it needed doing."

"If this were to get out," Paul Stephens threw the pen he was holding across the table. "It would set back the Program for years to come. People would never trust us again."

"Sir," Kyle said as evenly as he could. "I'll resign now and go feeling good about what we did. You only have to ask. But, this concern *for* the Program, its standing among the colonists, how it's viewed... we have to get past it. Eden and our communities have to get used to living without constantly looking for guidance from the Program. The Program's mission was to get people here, that's done."

"We are all in agreement there, Mr. Lassiter," Paul looked from him to Colonel Pretty. Kyle figured if what he had done had surprised Stephens, the fact that one his oldest friends had signed on must have come as a real shock. "I'm just not used to this devolution, I think we can call it, of authority."

"I'm not looking for any authority, Sir, or power or a title. Sir Geoffrey got a promise out of me that I would always act for the long-term survival of our principles, and not specifically for the Program. He believed there were more than enough people looking out for the Program. He warned me that there was far too much power and authority already vested in New Seattle. I know that's something we all agree on, but when push came to shove, a week ago in this very room, the Program firmly backed itself, its role. It's a slippery slope."

"So is vigilantism." Elisabeth surprised him by speaking up across from him.

Kyle nodded at her in complete agreement and turned back to Stephens. "Sir, I'll happily resign any position here at the Program.

"I'll continue my role with coordinating our defenses if Colonel Pretty agrees to it. But I have to say Sir, as long as I am here, I'll keep doing what I think Sir Geoffrey would have done. I think he understood the lure of central authority and power better than anyone I've ever met and I made him a promise I will not break."

The room was oddly quiet when he finished, and Stephens was just staring at him. Slowly the man nodded at him. "I think we made a mistake with you Mr. Lassiter, your time under Sir Geoffrey's wing may have given you the idea that you can pull a stunt like this and walk away with no consequences."

Kyle glanced across the table at Elisabeth, who had studiously turned in her chair looking directly at her half-brother speak.

"I'm going to remedy one shortcoming you pointed out a moment ago." Stephens said. "If there are no objections, I would formally like to name Mr. Lassiter as our new Director of Security." Stephens paced in a tight circle for a moment thinking, "I think we can all agree that he'll do whatever it takes as he sees it to keep us honest. Sir Geoffrey told me that I should trust you. We should have listened to you a week ago. Any objections?"

Stephens looked around the table and settled his eyes on his old friend Colonel Pretty. "Hank, can you still get what you need out of Kyle if he has other duties not specifically related to our Defense?"

"I think we can work something out." Hank said.

"Can the record state that I'm taking this role under duress?" Kyle said, feeling the room needed a break in the tension. It couldn't have been easy for Stephens to learn so many of his team had gone behind his back and Kyle was acutely aware that some of the bureaucrats around the table and standing against the wall were less than amused.

"For what it's worth, sure." Dr. Jensen said, "but I don't think it's going to help."

He bowed his head to Paul Stephens and at his friends around the table. "I'll do this, but I'd like to make a request, actually it's an idea that Sir Geoffrey had, so I can't take credit for it no matter how good it sounds to me right now."

"What is it?" Stephens asked.

"I be allowed to step down as soon as our current threat has passed. I'd further suggest and this is Sir Geoffrey speaking here; the entire Program, minus our economic team, be dissolved as soon as possible. A guiding hand, no matter how benevolent or light can't help but strive to protect itself, its institutions, its power, its bureaucracy and its authority over time. Sir Geoff's words, not mine. If we become, in any manner, Eden's government...How many generations would it take until we are right back where we started?"

"I don't think we have much to worry about there," Elisabeth turned and smiled at him.

45

"I've been keeping tabs on the constitutions that have been written in the settlements," Elisabeth continued turning back to the room. "They have pretty much written the Program off in terms of a political role, and that's all to the good. Our residents have the combined history of mankind to look back on and make value judgments. They are writing laws, and Bills of Rights that are so strongly in line with the individual, I'll be surprised if we have any centralized authority anytime soon. But with a security threat looming, that presents additional challenges as well."

"Some of these settlements though, are almost antagonistic regarding the Program."

Kyle didn't recognize the woman that spoke up, but what worried him were several perceptible nods of agreement in the room. As far as he was concerned, the settlements should be looking to get out from under the Program.

Stephens rapped his knuckles on the table top putting an end to the voices that started bubbling up.

"Kyle and the rest of his criminals have given the economy the chance it needs. I think that as much as our military situation allows, the Program should initiate its planned draw-downs. We still have thousands, tens of thousands of people to get to their eventual destinations, and Jason's economic team has their work cut out for them. We should keep up the advisor programs in the settlements for as long as they want us, but other than that, I don't see a reason that we can't immediately lower our profile and impact as it goes. Comments?"

"I see one big problem," Colonel Pretty answered immediately. "No central authority is great, but I remind everyone that in all likelihood we are going to face a military invasion at some point in the future. We are pretty sure from Audy that they are focused on North America, but that's a lot of ground to cover, and military recruitment not to mention fighting a war with that kind of scope is hard enough under a central authority. I don't think it's ever been done without it. We, and I mean humanity here, hasn't had this kind of fight for hundreds of years. The nearest recent analog I can think of is Afghanistan, and this time we are the Afghans. No centralized power, disparate centers of populations, religion and ethnicity, they get attacked locally, they fight back. But, and it's a big but, getting them to take the *'local,"* Hank held up his one good hand and made a quote sign, "out of their considerations of when to join, when to fight, and when to run.... is going to be a challenge."

"Sir," Mrs. Lawry spoke up. "It's just my opinion, I'm pretty tight with the Noob community. I've never pretended to be anything other than a recent arrival with a lot to learn as to what it's going to take to survive here. We all feel Eden is our lifeboat and we know we don't have a shore to swim to. I can't guess as to how they'll fight, but they'll fight."

*

Charlotte, N.C.   Earth 1.0
Gone was Captain Souza. The young woman standing in front of him was simply a mother. Her husband stood just inside the door of their home in the suburbs Raleigh, looking anxious to be on his way.

"You sure you can do this?" She had that typical blue-eyed, blonde hair look of a healthy, attractive soccer mom who'd grown up in Nebraska. But Sir Geoff had spent enough time over the last two months as a *'guest'* in their home to know that Captain Souza, aka Brittany Souza, wouldn't hesitate to bury him in their back yard.

"I'll be fine." He lied, he had never been less sure of anything in his life.

"Ok, they've eaten," she continued, "but tell them to go bed by ten, but not without brushing their teeth."

'Them' referred to the seven-year-old twin children of the best 'covered' special forces tandem he'd ever met.

"Ten pm, affirmative."

"You've got our number, don't hesitate to use it, we'll be less than twenty minutes away."

"Britt...."

"What?"

Tom Souza looked at him in apology. "Given Sir Geoff's resume, I'm pretty certain he can handle the twins for a few hours."

He wished he shared that confidence. He'd rather be leading a contentious debate in Parliament, or back in the African bush than be left alone with the Souza twins. *Needs must.*

"Right," Mrs. Souza shook her head as if remembering who he was. "You'll be fine."

"Assuredly," he managed.

The door shut with a click and for a moment the Souza's house was quiet. For just a very short, blessed moment. There was a squeak of tennis shoes upstairs in the hall way, followed by what sounded like a stampede of horses coming down the stairs. He turned in time to see two young faces peering around the corner at him.

"Are they gone?"

"They are," he assured his charges.

"You going to let us have ice-cream?" One of the lads asked, he didn't even try to tell them apart.

He nodded in resignation. "Only if you scoop me some too, and clean up afterwards, bowls, spoons washed and put away."

"We can just stick them in the dishwasher," the other one said.

"Tradecraft, idiot," the other brother admonished, "leave no evidence, right?"

"Quite right." He mumbled to himself as he moved into the kitchen wondering what story he was going to be forced to tell them tonight. The Napoleonic wars he'd already covered with them, maybe something classical.

"What story you going to tell us tonight?"

"The wars of Sparta and Athens?" he suggested, grateful for something to keep his mind occupied. There'd been no word from Gannon, no summons from a dark SUV in the driveway. He wasn't too surprised. America was coming apart at the seams. The General was no doubt a very busy man. Of late, the reports on television were redacted to the point of silliness.

48

One only had to look out the window to see cities burning. The suburbs of Raleigh-Durham that the Souzas called home were so far safe, but there'd been several demonstrations and riots downtown.

The boy's parents were meeting this evening with the other two couples of their so-called task force. He felt for them, not just the Souzas, but the Bowdens and Mills as well. They seemed to have been forgotten by the DoD. He knew they were meeting to discuss contingency plans should the local situation, in the words of Tom Souza, 'hit the fan.' A potentiality that by his reasoning seemed more likely with each passing day. These boys certainly didn't deserve what was coming, any more than their parents did.

The bowl of ice cream was slid in front of him.

"This is the story of the three hundred, right? Thermapie?" One of the twins seemed proud of his knowledge.

"Actually, that was a different war." He tried to let the lad down gently, the brothers were incredibly hard on each other.

"Who's the idiot now?" The other one grinned. "Thermapie was the Greeks against the Turks, dummy."

"First off," he spoke up, stopping them with an up raised palm. "You are both very much mistaken, the battle's name that you both have butchered past embarrassment is called Thermopylae, and it was Spartans against the Persians. A different war entirely."

"Tell that one!"

"Yeah, it's cool."

He just looked calmly at both of them in silence.

"Sorry, could you tell us that story, please."

"Fine," he relented. "This was a long time ago, 480 years BC, and it wasn't the first time these two peoples had warred."

"And a long way away," one of the twins added laughing, "like Star Wars!"

He could feel the vein in his forehead pulsing. "Just so," he admitted reluctantly. He glanced at the clock on the wall. Three hours to go until their parents returned. He'd been in tougher scrapes before.

*

Chapter 4

Peter Curran still hadn't gotten used to the fact that he was living on a planet other than the Earth of his birth. Earth 2.0. The local kids in his settlement, referred to them all as "twofers." It was still Earth, even with the differences. The nights were darker than any he could remember seeing at home. The stars were that much brighter, and you could walk five minutes outside of most settlements and not see another soul. That was certainly the case in Great Woods, their small community nestled into the shallow meadows of the North Woods.

All that aside, it was a different world than the one the fates had granted him when his father had been killed in an accident at the fertilizer plant when he'd been 9 years old. Different than when six months later his oldest sister had disappeared from the freeway truck stop she worked at and ridden out of town with a long-haul trucker. Different than when his oldest brother had been dragged from home by the police a year after that.

Growing up with a mother who vacillated back and forth between severe bouts of dementia and a focused lucidity intent on extracting every last cent of welfare possible for the family had ingrained in him the belief that welfare was evil. It was welfare that allowed his mom to stay drunk. It was welfare that would have rewarded his mother for having another child fathered by a stranger, had she lived through child birth at the age of 43. He knew it played a role, helped a lot of people, and he was big believer in charity, though in his mind there were too many people who taken advantage of a bureaucratic system that did nothing but reward weakness and indolence.

High school sports had been his only outlet from raising a younger sister. He'd been the only one on the team that had to go to work after practice, every day. Starting his sophomore year, all year long, he changed tires, picked up around the place, and helped with the books at the local tire shop. He worked hard and by the time he graduated from high school he was practically managing the place for the aging owner.

Two years later, the owner wanted to sell and get away from Wisconsin winters and move to Florida. The owner had made certain the local bank knew who had been running the shop the last few years and arranged that he could get the loan he needed to buy the business.

He hadn't grown up with the American Dream, but he embraced it, and had risen with nothing more than a solid work ethic and a reputation for honesty. He'd soon found himself involved in local politics. The Chamber of Commerce for starters, the City Council followed and then a term as County Commissioner, before serving two terms as a State Representative in the Wisconsin Legislature. Two terms in Madison were enough to convince him that he enjoyed business and hated politics. By then he'd been noticed, and eventually recruited into the Program.

His first trip to Eden, years ago, had seen him fishing in a pristine river that had been nothing more than a polluted strip of damned up back water on Earth 1.0. He'd sold his business, which by then was a chain of tire shops across three states, and moved away with his family four years ago and counted himself one of Eden's original colonists even though many had been here far longer than he had. As far as the Noobs went, he found that he generally liked his new neighbors, even those he could barely communicate with. The Finns in particular; he'd never met a group of people that liked to fish and hunt as much as he did.

He liked them well enough that he half considered trying to learn his first foreign language, though their English was pretty good in his opinion. Even with the influx of the 'new people' as his wife insisted on calling them, because she somehow thought the term 'noob' was demeaning, he found that he could still walk for five minutes outside of their settlement and escape into virgin wilderness.

He'd walked a lot longer than that today. He'd started out in the air car and flown close to forty miles north of their home and then hiked for hours into the same forests and hills, new planet or old, that he'd fished and hunted for most of his adult life. Which was why the echoing thunder clap explosion and rumbling echo rolling out of the hills to his North scared the shit out him.

He'd never heard anything like it in his life. It was a series of pops, unnaturally loud and regularly spaced beyond anything nature had thrown at him in these woods or anywhere else for that matter. Snow was expected for most of the day, and he'd heard thunder with snow clouds once or twice in his life which was why he knew this was something else entirely.

The rumbling echoes rolled and faded. The forest was completely still. More than the explosion of sound, the eerie absence of noise from the birds, or squirrels jumping from branch to branch, sat his nerves on his edge. Even the forest itself seemed to know something was wrong. The wind picked up for a moment in a soulful moan among the tree branches, wisps of powdery snow blew in front of his pop-up ground blind.

He'd never been a nervous type, hell with the life he had lived, he'd learned early on it didn't pay to worry about shit you couldn't control. This just didn't feel right. He played with the trigger on his bow release strapped to his wrist, flicking it back and forth, the bow grounded between his knees. Back and forth, the trigger's action was smooth, almost silent and it was the only thing above the occasional wind's whistle through the branches that he could hear.

He glanced at his 30.06 snug in its soft sided case and tied to his backpack. He almost laughed at himself, the rifle was for the grey wolves which were thick in these woods. Wolves hadn't made that noise, and they'd be as spooked by it as he was. Which was why he was reaching for his com-pad when the damn thing vibrated against his thigh. He was so keyed up he nearly levitated off his log seat in surprise. He brought up the screen and the first thing he saw was a giant red exclamation point.

His stomach churning, he opened and read the message.

Massive disturbance in magnetic field, indicative of a large-scale translation has been detected in your area. Please advise ASAP.

He hit the link-up button and waited until a face appeared on the screen.

"Mr. Peter Curran?" The young face was looking at something off screen.

"How do you know that? What's wrong?" His mind went a thousand directions at once, none of them offered any comfort.

"Sir, your Com-Pad is accessed by your biometric, we see your ID."

He knew that. "Dammit – I knew that. You calling about that big noise?"

"Yes, Sir." The kid sounded excited and he didn't take that as a good thing. "You were close enough to hear the event, Sir?"

"Don't know what I heard. Hell, I almost felt it, sounded like the sky was being torn apart a bit North of me. Woods have gone quiet, nothing is moving at all, I mean nothing."

"We have your location, what is your status, Sir?" The kid seemed to be reading the question off a list.

"Son, why don't you just tell me what's got ya so excited... Translation? These those ones we've been worried about? I'm just out here trying to do a little meat hunting, but I guess that isn't going to happen is it?"

Another face swam into view on his screen. Whoever he was, he pretty much lifted the kid out of his seat as he turned to the camera at his end. The man was far too close to the camera which gave his face a bit of a rounded fish bowl appearance but he thought he recognized the man as one of the soldiers that had been out to Great Woods to conduct some training not two months past.

"This is Captain Bullock, how's the hunting?"

"Hello .... Sir." He had no idea how to address the man, he wasn't in the military, and as far as he figured it, this Bullock wasn't either. There was no military.

"I just got set up, when whatever it was popped, as you can imagine I haven't seen shit since."

"If you had to guess, how far away was the source of the translation?"

"There's that word again, is it that other planet, the one we're worried about?"

"Looks that way, yes. Mr. Curran. The Chandrians. How far away would you estimate the source of the noise was?"

"Lotsa hills out this way, thunder echoes, and bounces all around. Just guessing, but I'd say 5 or ten miles north of me, it was that loud. Could be less I suppose. The wildlife here definitely thinks something is close. You hunt, Mr. Bullock?"

The face smiled back at him. "Only when I'm hungry."

"These North Woods are thick with squirrels, noisiest damn things in the woods, and I haven't heard so much as a leaf rustle since."

The face nodded knowingly back at him. "Understood. How are you armed and are you on the ground or in a climber?"

"Bow hunting from my ground blind, I know that's not smart, but I hiked in and this pup tent is a lot lighter than my climber. I have my 1911, as well as my 30.06 with me for the wolves. I'm no soldier, Captain."

"Don't worry about that Mr. Curran, right now I'm glad you are a hunter, one who obviously isn't afraid of the winter. You know the storm you are about to get right?"

"Ya, another reason I brought my ground blind. Makes a decent little tent."

"We need you to get moving south Mr. Curran. Your settlement has already received an evac order and they'll be moving out within the hour. You are too far North to get there for the air buses, but we'll send in an aircar once we are assured you are a safe distance from whatever translated in. Frankly we are flying blind here, and you are our closest thing to a witness."

He was sharp enough to pick up on the hint. "My family is being evac'd? They're safe?"

"Yes, sir. The settlement at Great Woods is entirely accounted for, except you and three Finnish Noobs, they

55

wouldn't be up there with you and forgot their Com-pads would they?"

"I know em, those boys went way south, flew down to the Wisconsin River to do some fishing."

"Ok, that helps, Mr. Curran. We'll make sure we find em and pack them out. For now, let's get you moving to somewhere safe."

"You want me to bird-dog these Chandrians for you?" He was here. Offering to help was the right thing to do.

"Mr. Curran, these Chandrians are a nasty bunch. We have a QRF, a Quick Reaction Force leaving for your general location in a few minutes, but they'll move slow once they are on the ground. They are hunters too."

"Why not let me see if I can get a look at these aliens, your guys can just fly in and get me."

The face shook his head back at him. "That would make it easier, but I'm afraid our air transport capability is something we need to keep secret for the moment, otherwise I'd tell you to stay put, keep quiet and we'd just fly in and get you."

"Ok, but if I head south right now, your team will be that much further from where these guys landed, or translated, popped, whatever – you know what I mean. Why don't you let me bird-dog the bad guys. I grew up in these woods back on Earth, I know the terrain like my daughter's face."

"Mr. Curran, I very much appreciate what you are offering, I really do. We could use a set of eyes on the ground, I won't bullshit you on that. I'm not sure you understand what you may run into out there."

He nodded firmly at his com-pad, "I do Captain. Sounds like it needs doing though. Besides, I always liked playing army when I was a kid."

"Any intelligence you can gather would be more than we know now and the nut of our problem is that we don't have a satellite pass there for almost a day. To the best of our knowledge they are likely to send numerous two or three-man teams, scouts, in all directions."

"OK, so I may have company here soon, what you need me to do?"

"I need you to stay alive, Mr. Curran. That's your priority."

"I like that."

*

Jake glanced away from the Com monitor at the large overhead map the command team had brought up as they listened to his conversation and then back to his camera and Mr. Curran.

"Can you move straight west from your location until you get up to Mossy Lake, then move Northwest along its western edge?"

Curran looked away from his compad for a moment, from the flare of light on the screen, he knew the man was looking outside his tent.

"It's starting to snow again. I'll have to move all night, but I should be able to make it, yeah."

"OK, break down your blind, let the snow cover your tracks and keep your com-pad in whatever light you have left. Keep that battery charged up as best you can, and..." Jake scratched his beard knowing he was asking a middle-aged civilian to make a movement that a soldier would bitch about. He wondered what he was forgetting.

"don't take any risks, Mr. Curran."

"Right ..." Mr. Curran smiled back at him. "OK, I'm moving."

Jake switched off the com session at his end and looked up at Col. Pretty.

"Could be worse, he might have been some back to nature bird watcher or some shit."

"Agreed," Pretty was looking at the large projected map of North America. Across its northern face were three large red circles representing circular error probability of the insertion sites. The gravimetric sensors they had managed to employ weren't very accurate, hell the science behind them was as new as the ability to translate. Within each of those three very large circles spread across the continent the Chandrians had just invaded. The middle Circle, over the Great Lakes shrunk

57

down while he watched to where it was a bare fifty-mile-wide circle. The accuracy was based on Mr. Curran's position and the fact that he had heard the "thunder" of a massive volume of air being instantaneously displaced. They were naturally referring to this group in the Great Woods of Northern Wisconsin as the 'Central Group.' The Eastern Group took up about a third of the area of what used to be South Carolina and included a big chunk of northern Georgia. About 15% of that circle was off shore in the Atlantic.

"Probably too much to hope they were dumped out to sea."

"No way, we get that lucky." Jake answered Pretty.

They both looked up to the Northwest. "About halfway between Calgary and Edmonton, or where those cities would have been," Pretty said to himself. "We have only a small farming settlement well south of that and nothing but plans for some remote well-heads in the gas fields. Evacuation has begun, but even with small numbers, it is going to take a full couple of days, air trucks are worthless in that storm."

"Where do the bad guys go from there?" Jake asked the room, "it's the middle of nowhere, in winter."

"I think I have an idea on that," Dr. Jensen was sitting at a key board and manipulated the image on the screen. "Bear with me, I'm picking hypothetical points of entry in the middle of our probability models to demonstrate something."

The three red circles were replaced with black dots connected via a nonsymmetrical parabolic arc stretching from Western Canada eastward. The line curved slowly south until it intersected with the Central Group in Wisconsin before diving sharply south and east to the South Carolina/Georgia border near the Atlantic.

"If what we've gotten from Audy is correct, and I believe it is." Dr. Jensen paused and looked at both of them.

Jake believed Audy as well, not that they had much of a choice and he knew Pretty didn't think they had an option either. The former Colonel had to keep his options for their defense open though and that included the chance that Audy was mistaken or worse, a plant to provide misinformation.

"I think the Chandrians maintained their target pattern, at least with the three groups relative to each other, but their whole line is off to the right," Jensen pointed at the map, "watch."

"I'm now anchoring the whole line in the east, in south central North Carolina, the one place we know they've been before." The line and formation of dots held and shifted to the west.

"I was just a corpsman in my war Colonel," Jensen pointed at the map, "but I can read a map. We can't forget they are from Earth as well, they know the geography. Anchoring all three pointes 160 miles to the west, would have put the Central group at the headwaters of the Mississippi, and the Western Group comes out on the west coast, on the warmer wet side of the coastal range just east of Vancouver Island."

"Damn," Colonel Pretty whistled. "You earned your pay today doc."

"It's just a theory," Jensen added.

"Makes sense," Jake added. "If they'd hit those marks, the Eastern group comes out right next to where they've been before. Where we've been expecting them."

Pretty was nodding in agreement, "If they'd hit that target in force and won, they could have gone north or south or both, and controlled the East Coast. And they naturally protect the flank of the central group which I imagine would try to force its way down the Mississippi, cut us in half at the river and eventually control the Gulf. That western group though," Pretty shook his head, "even if they'd hit their mark, that's brutal terrain to march down the west coast. As it is they came out on the wrong side of some very ugly mountains, in winter. They have to be hating life."

"If they know their targeting sucks, they'll have planned for contingencies," Jake added. "No way would they intentionally plan to cross the Canadian Rockies in winter, if that group comes south, they'll wind up in Montana and could pick a pass to come west on, but not until spring, no way now."

Pretty nodded in agreement. "Dangerous to assume they would do what we would, but that makes sense to me. No matter how you shake it, that western group is in for a hard time. Snowed a foot and a half last night and a bigger storm is already in the Rockies moving East."

Pretty walked the width of the room to the east coast side of the wall map and pointed back to the middle of the continent.

"The Center Group could move south west through forest terrain though, nothing too difficult to get to the Mississippi, or hell they could pull a Champlain in reverse, and move northeast through the Lakes and the St. Lawrence maybe meet up with the East Group moving north up the coast."

"They going to build their own boats?" Jensen asked. "They are in a massive forest."

Pretty looked at Jake. "Add that to the questions for Audy. For now, we need confirmation of which direction the Central Group is headed, that's the group that immediately threatens settlements, regardless of which direction they go.

Jake pointed at the East Group. "General Majeski has our best gear and best unit in North Carolina, he's chomping at the bit to launch his birds."

"Dr.?" Pretty turned back to Jensen. "How long before we get another satellite pass?"

"It's on a polar orbit, and their timing was perfect, for them. Twelve hours for the Western Group, call it sixteen or so for the Central group, and about 18 for the Eastern Group."

Pretty shook his head. "Tell Majeski to cool his jets, literally. We need intel. He can send in his recon team on the Eastern Group. We do not show our air capability, not even for transport, observe only. We have to give Kyle and Audy's plan a chance, and for that, we have to know which group is which."

"We're going to need to get close, real close," Jake answered.

"I know." Pretty said. "If we can't pull it off and these groups are as large as Audy says they could be... I don't want to have to fight on three fronts against a bunch of Audy clones."

Jake shook his head at that mental image. The man had a talent for understatement.

Dr. Jensen stood up, holding his compad. "I'll get the formal report disseminated soon, but initial requests for musters and where relevant, evacs have confirmed receipt."

Jake shook his head. "We'll get our volunteers until people start coming home in body bags – they're just civilians, Doc."

"I know you have doubts Captain," Pretty's voice had an edge to it as he turned to Jake, the command tone he rarely used these days. "You are free to express them with me, just be careful. They are all looking at us to be their backbone. We are their morale."

"Understood sir." It had been something he knew he needed to hear. "It's not their heart I doubt, it's how most of them grew up. We aren't exactly dealing with the greatest generation here, especially with the late arrivals."

Pretty smiled and nodded in agreement. "That's why we avoid pitched battles until we know what we are dealing with and we have a better idea of how our people will stand and fight."

"Who knows," Jensen added sounding like a New Jersey longshoreman. "A hundred years from now, those same settlers might be spoken of in the same terms as the Minutemen."

"Doc, if we don't win, there won't be anyone saying anything about us in a language we understand." Jake looked over at Pretty. "Sorry, Sir."

Pretty flashed a feral grin back at him. "I think that sentiment is pretty well understood Jake. That's why we are going to win. There's nowhere to retreat to. No government to hold us back and pretend we can wait the enemy out. We are going to make these people wish they'd never heard of this planet."

*

Three hours later they were monitoring reports and Jake was starting to think it was time to check in on Mr. Curran.

"Oh shit," Jensen's voice interrupted, speaking directly into his computer monitor behind them.

"What is it?"

"Multiple sightings reported from the settlement at Deep Lake. The Central Group, at least part of it is further north than we thought."

"How many settlers there?" Pretty voice carried enough worry for all of them.

"Twelve hundred," Doc Jensen almost whispered. "They were part of the general evac."

"Get them out of there," Pretty said.

Jensen's hands flew over his keyboard. Jake and Col. Pretty watched as the large ring indicating the probable area of landing for the Chandrian Central group shrink even more and twitch to the north and west. A few miles away from the small settlement.

A half hour later, Jensen turned in his chair. "They got the general evac order, but only have enough local transport for about half their population, much of the remainder is moving southeast on foot, one hundred forty-five of their militia are remaining behind to buy them some time."

"Patch me in to whoever's leading their defenses." Pretty glanced over at him with a knowing look.

Jake felt his own stomach do a flip. He shouldn't be here, safe in Seattle, listening to reports. There was a battle on and those settlers didn't stand a chance.

*

Chapter 5

"Well? What they say Norm?"

Norm Patenski, shook his head as he zipped his compad back into thigh pocket and put his heavy gloves back on.

"Bout what we figured, be two hours before they can get us any help. If we can buy them that much, they'll be able to pick up our people."

"What about us?" He couldn't tell who has asked the question.

Norm watched the faces of those around him. Some looked back at him with a grim determination, the realists, who had known what it meant as soon as the alien army could be seen gathering at the edge of the cleared fields north of town. Others looked back at him in shock. It wasn't supposed to be like this, they were supposed to have had some warning. Besides, Deep Lake was a long way from the Carolinas, what the hell was the enemy doing here?

Somebody clearly wasn't with the program. There were close to two thousand Chandrians standing out on the edge of town, their numbers had been growing for the last ten minutes. He secretly hoped they'd wait until they all got here, burn some more clock.

"Nothing we can do about it now," Sara Thompson, glared at the faces around her and turned to look at him directly. "Tell us where you want us."

Norm had served in the West Virginia National Guard, twenty years earlier. It was why they were all looking at him now. It was enough experience for the Program to have put him in charge of the local militia. He wasn't sure how being a motor pool clerk, versed in making sure M1 Abrams tanks and old Bradley APCs got their regular oil changes and maintenance was going to help him now. Sara should be in charge, he thought, at least she seemed ready for a fight.

"We've drilled," he said. "We do just like those soldiers told us. Find a position, shoot, move, communicate. Get those claymores set up, and let's move the two machine guns, get them up on the roofs, one on the commissary, the other on the school facing out over the field."

They stood staring back at him. "Anybody else have any other ideas?"

"Ok," he yelled, "let's get moving, they want this land, they're gonna have to fight for it."

They moved off, some quickly, others moving slowly, still in shock. There wasn't anything they could do to stop the force outside of town and they all knew it. The snow was picking up. It was going to be a real storm, they'd been preparing for it the last couple of days. It had already reduced visibility to the point he could barely see the outlines of his scouts atop the settlement's school. In this kind of weather, the enemy could walk to the edge of town before they'd even be seen.

He started moving to his own position atop the commissary building, and then stopped himself, glaring up in the leaden sky. The enemy wouldn't see them coming either.

He bit off his glove, pulled out his compad.

"Sam? You and Miller meet me at the commissary, bring your snow machines, NOW!"

He suddenly wished they had more of the machines available, but most had been sent south with those walking out. They'd kept two back as a plan to ferry men and ammo to where they needed it. He didn't think they'd last long enough to need much ammo resupply.

"What is that noise?" Bastelta Mar'tea asked.

"I don't know," Lard'selt paused trying to get a fix on the high-pitched machine noise that seemed to be coming from the woods beyond their left flank. "Like a Kaerin vehicle perhaps, but there are no roads between the main host and these Shareki, so we will not concern ourselves with where they are going. The enemy is within that settlement, prepare to signal the attack."

"Sir, the rest of the hand is still moving up. We are just over half strength."

"We've nearly three fingers here, those structures could not hold our number. We attack. The more honor for us."

64

"Sir, I'll form the hand."

Lard'selt nodded in recognition. He couldn't fault Mar'tea's caution, it was a Teark's position to offer his counsel.

The machine noise surged out of the blowing snow storm from the woods along their left flank in the form of two sleds, moving far too fast over the snow-covered field. The strange objects blew past his position before he realized they were there, on a track parallel with the front edge of his formation, standing in close ranks awaiting the order to attack.

The sound of gunfire erupted from the sleds, just before they passed beyond his vision in the swirling snow. Gunfire was a sound that he knew well, but it came forth far too fast, like a Kaerin hummingbird gun, of which his command had none. The rapid enemy fire raked his formation, and he then realized, there were men riding the sleds, one directing it and one, just one soldier firing that amazing hummingbird directly into his war band.

He watched passively as he saw portions of his front rank go down. Some got back to their feet, wounded, others did not. Amazing, he thought, a hummingbird gun wielded by a solitary soldier. Knowing the existence of such a weapon in the Shareki arsenal would be worth the lives of his entire force gathered here.

The machine sound faded, changed in pitch and suddenly grew again. More of his warriors went down, as the two vehicles screamed past firing those miraculously small weapons as they passed. This time his men were ready. A large number of the front rank had their rifles up and fired. Most fired at the second sled, the first was gone as fast as it had appeared at the edge of their vision. The targeted sled made a strange noise, a loud bang issued and black smoke poured from it. It burned in the snow where it had slid to a stop. Laying in the snow behind it were the two bullet riddled bodies of its riders. His men gave a cheer. They were veterans and didn't need to be told to reload. This was different than what he'd expected. The enemy had yet to show themselves in force, but this distraction of the strange machines was proving enjoyable and they would learn much today.

65

Lard'selt pointed at the fallen enemy. "Retrieve those weapons." There was still no sign of the other sled, they could not even hear it. Perhaps enough fire had struck the strange machine that it no longer functioned.

He almost ordered the attack to begin, but he wanted to see the nature of the weapons they would face. The strange firearm was handed over to him. It was clearly recognizable as such, even if it was less than half the length of one of their rifles. He turned the strange weapon over in his hand, far lighter than he had expected. But still a weapon of obvious power. His dead warriors laying around him were a testament to that fact. He made sure the barrel was pointed at the ground and pulled, then pushed the obvious trigger mechanism. Nothing happened. There were other buttons, some sort of mechanism that slid back and forth, and a strange small window atop the weapon that when he gazed through it, acted as a telescope.

He pushed a different button and a part of the weapon dropped away to fall in the snow. Had he broken the weapon? The Gemendi cadre would be furious with him, but they were miles away with the main host and they would have time to examine the device after the battle. He picked up the narrow device that dropped out of the bottom of the weapon and was amazed at the material it was made of. It was not metal, but not natural either. It had an opening at one end, within a strange piece that he could push down. It resisted him and came back into position when he released the pressure. It was beyond him, and he put it in his pocket and examined the breech that was visible on the side of the weapon.

"This must be where they put the ammunition," he wondered out loud, but that didn't track with how fast the weapon had fired.

He looked up at his Teark and gave the signal to blow the horn. He watched as his men shouldered their rifles and adjusted the belts holding their blades. An explosion ripped through his lines at the far end of the formation, unseen to his right, and he heard screams. As a group, his hand turned and surged towards the violence. He nodded in appreciation. The

66

Shareki had finally arrived, not from the front as they should, but at least they had come out to face them in battle.

An explosion from behind, shocked him, he turned to look as a double handful of the enemy surged out of the woods and swirling snow. They all fired the strange hummingbird weapon from their hips and his men in front of him fell as if knocked down by a wall of lead fired by an opposing army. It was an incredible display of firepower, but these Shareki were stupid. They should have faced him in a proper battle line, such weapons would be devastating in large numbers.

The men closest to him flowed around him shielding him from the new threat. The Shareki attacked at both ends of the lines instead of from the front. It made no sense. Many of his warriors went down but he gauged the attackers few in number and their wondrous weapons did nothing to protect them from the fire returned by his men.

One of the Shareki appeared blessed with battle magic as he remained upright firing and turning towards him. He dropped the Shareki rifle and drew his blade as the enemy ran towards him, screaming. The man's dark skin at odds with the faces of the other enemy he had noticed. The hummingbird weapon was on his shoulder.

The Shareki was close enough to him that he heard the empty click on the strange rifle. The man in a rage, threw his weapon down and charged him. Lard'sclt turned sideways, his short sword coming up and catching the Shareki in the arm pit, he spun and dragged the blade through the cut as the man surged past to collapse in the snow.

"Unschooled," he commented to himself as he approached the Shareki, noting how young he was. The enemy lay on his back, quickly going pale from blood loss. He reversed his blade in preparation, as the Shareki said something to him, and then laughed. He paused his strike in confusion, as the Shareki's hand, draped across his chest, opened on a small oblong object. The man's other hand stretched out towards him, his middle finger extended in what could only be a sign of submission. A weak gesture of submission, he thought, these Shareki had no honor. His hand tightened on his blade

67

but the look on the Shareki's face, in those hard, brown eyes were defiant. His vision shifted back to the fruit shaped object laying on the enemy's chest. It had no smoking fuse, but it was about the same size as a ...

The Shareki attack was repulsed quickly, there had been but a few hands of enemy warriors at either end of their lines. Teark Mar'tea looked down at the remains of their Bastelta Lard'selt and the Shareki that had shredded his superior's body, with what he surmised to have been some sort of hand bomb. He glanced up to take in the rows of dead Strema nearby. He knew there were more fallen Strema beyond, at the other end of the line where the attack had begun. Reports were shouted through the white out of the storm. The losses at the far end were heavier than here, yet he was looking at the body of the Hand's Bastelta.

So few of the enemy had done this, what awaited them at the village ahead? A Bastelta could be forgiven for seeking glory with the lives of his men, a lowly Teark would not be. He would hold the attack, wait for rest of the host to come up, as Lard'selt should have done.

*

Chapter 6

North Carolina, Eden

"Your father," Darius Singer shouldered his pack and glanced back up the hill to the concrete command bunker they'd just emerged from, "is a hard man."

"Him?" Domenik Majeski just smiled and looked back following Darius' eyes to the half-buried bunker, just a short 10 miles from where it was believed the Chandrians had emerged seven years earlier to ravage a small North Carolina mountain settlement.

"He just yells a lot. You should meet my mother."

They had just finished a pre-mission briefing, *scream fest,* courtesy of Dom's father, the former Polish Army General. They were both left with a crystal-clear understanding that if they started any shit with the enemy they couldn't finish, they'd better just plan on fighting to the death rather than requesting reinforcements that wouldn't be coming. Their mission was to observe and report on enemy scouting activity, hopefully discern which direction the Chandrians were interested in taking, and if possible, identify which clan had plopped itself down on the eastern foothills of the Appalachians.

The real reason General Majeski was upset had everything to do with the fact he wanted to go on the offensive right now, with everything he had, against an enemy force less than two hundred miles away. Col. Pretty, rank aside, was in charge, and had over ruled him based on nothing more than saying Kyle had something up his sleeve.

"You did some long-recon in the Caucasus didn't you?" Darius asked him.

Domenik thought back to the several two-week long stints shivering in a frozen cave, in the heart of the Caucasus Mountains, eating cold rations alongside some very good Romanian mountain troops that he couldn't understand. They had been there to observe Jihadi troops move through the valleys below them. The whole time, worried about their supposed Russian allies who would have attacked them for just being there.

"Yeah, it sucked." He answered. "I don't think I've ever been so cold."

Darius just laughed, "I used to do this in the Sinai and North Africa. Hot. Africa hot, but not in a funny way. The scorpions would circle your hidey hole waiting for the sun to kill you."

Domenik smiled back at his partner and then looked across the landing field where the Ospreys and half a dozen Blackhawk IIs were parked. Beyond them sat two F35 jump jets, half of their total fleet, framed by the backdrop of the west side of the Carolina Highlands where the two of them would spend the next several days trying to "out" scout the Chandrian scouts they hoped to locate.

"For winter, the weather isn't too bad." Domenik thought out loud.

Their pilot, a freckle faced kid walked past them on his way to their air car with a wave to follow. The kid was wearing a fur hat with some animal's tail hanging off the back of it and frowning at his compboard.

"Let's get you guys going. There's an ice storm due in tonight, and I'm sure you'll want to find a spot to hole up by then."

Darius looked up at the gray sky shaking his head. "Of course, there is."

Domenik took the passenger seat in the air car as Darius sprawled across the back seat atop their heavy packs. He watched as the pilot, rail thin as only a teenager could be, jumped in and fired up the turbines. The early colonists, especially their children, were easy to spot. As a group they possessed confidence and skills far above their peers among the Noob community. Right now, none of that mattered to Domenik.

"How old are you, kid?"

"Sixteen." Their pilot adjusted his fur hat and just smiled back at him. "If it makes you feel better, I've been flying these things since I was twelve."

70

"You know to stay below the hill tops, right?" Darius chimed in from the back seat.

The kid just gripped the wheel and slammed the throttle to its stop. The air car, screamed down the runway ten feet off the ground with a nose down attitude that had Dominik's hands against the dash board in front of him. The entire camp sat atop a flattened, cleared hill, resting between taller forested cousins. When the air car reached the end of the runway, it dove, building speed that the kid used to pull out of the dive and fly between trees as he climbed out of the valley taking a few branches with them.

Their 'pilot' leveled off, dodging tree tops at the bottom of the short draw, hills on either side of them close to enough to reach out and touch.

"Yeah," the kid drawled. "No worries, name's Jeremy, not kid."

A little over an hour later the air car settled into the dark shadowed woods on the eastern slope of the coastal range next to a half-frozen stream that eventually made its way down to the coastal lowlands and out to the Atlantic. The car crunched to a soft landing atop soggy pine needles and a thick carpet of sodden leaves, with a gentle touch completely at odds with how Jeremy had gotten them to this hidden valley.

"I'm going to be sick," Darius grumbled from the back as he crawled out. He stuck his head back in a moment and looked at their pilot, "and then I'm going to shoot you, kid."

Jeremy just laughed back at them. "I was told to get you guys here unseen. I've been dodging Seattle's radar since I was a kid."

Domenik smiled, not willing to admit that his jaw muscles felt like they wouldn't unclench. "That long huh?"

"Well..." Jeremy faltered, "since I've been flying."

Domenik watched Darius walk around to the front of the car, bend over and pull something from the grill over the primary air inlet. The former Israeli commando came up holding a pine branch which he threw at the windshield in front of Jeremy.

71

"He looks pissed." Jeremy's voice rose an octave.

"Don't worry, you are a very good pilot." Domenik smiled and popped his own door, thankful for being back on the ground.

They grabbed their gear and stood off to one side as Jeremy scrolled through a digital map on his compboard still seated behind the wheel.

"If we need a quick evac," Darius said. "You be sure to tell them, we want you."

Jeremy shook his head. "They won't let me fly combat missions."

"What are you thinking you just did?" Domenik asked.

"Nobody shooting at me." The kid sounded disappointed.

They stood at the edge of the clearing as Jeremy lifted straight up until the car was at the height of the surrounding trees before rotating and moving sedately off.

Darius casually handed his compboard to Domenik, turned away and blew his lunch out at the base of a tree. He came up and wiped his mouth with the back of his hand.

"Next time you ride in the back."

Dom laughed, without looking up from the map. Like so many of the things they took for granted on Eden, their maps were nothing more than the pinnacle product of what the United States had been able to produce before the Program had pulled up stakes and changed planets. The Program's map data base had every map the USGS, National Geographic, NGA and the DoD had ever produced, but at the moment he was using a US Forest Service topographical map from 2005.

There were always slight differences at the local level between the Earth 1.0 maps and the reality on the ground, on Eden. But, they were small differences and the USFS maps were perfect for what they had to do. What was less than ideal was the complete absence of roads or trails. They didn't even have abandoned logging roads, fire cuts, or dirt tracks from weekend mountain bikers to speed their way or use as reference points. The program had been able to orbit a dozen or so simple GPS micro satellites in the last few months. They had their way points programmed in. That aside, it was going to be cross country all the way.

"Which way we headed?" Darius asked, looking back at him over his shoulder.

"That way," Domenik pointed downhill to the east. "If their scouts are pushing it, they could be as close as maybe twenty-five kilometers by now. Audy said they'd move as fast as possible for the first day, and then go cautious."

Darius nodded, and pointed down at the map. "Makes sense, force out a safe perimeter, then scout. Let go as planned, they'll have to scout that pass, regardless of which way their main group goes. They'll have to send someone."

"Storm is coming, harder for us and them," Domenik handed back the compad.

"Ya, and I'm very warm blooded." Darius agreed. "Thank God we didn't pull the Central Group, it's in middle of a blizzard. This Jew is used to sand and dust."

"I know snow very well, we Poles have seven different words for snow." Domenik looked up at the heavy sky, the color of dark slate. "I prefer them all to ice."

Eighteen hours later, Domenik sat in his small ice box of a hole doing his best to ignore the cold cramped muscles in his legs. His body heat had long ago melted the half inch of crystal-clear ice that encased everything around him in a frigid exoskeleton. The promised ice storm had shit on them all night long. He hadn't moved from his hole since before sundown, neither had Darius, who sat in a similar hole a hundred meters north of his position. The two of them bracketed the narrow pass which looked to them to be the best route westward off the coastal plain up into the foothills of the Southern Appalachians.

The enemy apparently agreed. They'd watched as the three-man Chandrian scout team had slowly climbed the pass the day before. The ice storm had hit, and like sensible soldiers anywhere, the Chandrians had stopped and set up a camp with a nice roaring fire perhaps two kilometers below their position. The enemy campfire had looked painfully warm

73

during the long night in which the ice storm had sounded like a million snapping branches coming from all directions at once. Sleep had been impossible. Mission be damned, he'd half wanted to creep down in the night and collect what they'd come for so he could enjoy their fire.

Before they'd pulled in for the night, he'd watched the Chandrians through his rifle scope by their fire. They moved well, were clearly well trained and joked with each other in a manner that would have seemed familiar to any soldier anywhere. He could imagine them bitching about the ice storm, bitching about the men and officers they had left back at their camp and bitching about the lousy food from their packs. With his half-frozen joints and a growling stomach, he could commiserate and almost felt a bond with the Chandrians. A connection he actively ignored.

To do otherwise might cause him to hesitate for a moment in lighting the group up the second they entered his section of the kill box that he and Darius flanked. They would kill these men, Chandrians for certain, but men, probably within the hour, if not sooner. He'd done it before and lived with it.

A devout Catholic, he thought he'd be a priest as a child. Part of that he supposed had been his mother's great hope. Hormones and the religious wars had kicked into full gear by the time he'd finished prep school. His father the general, had almost seemed disappointed when he'd signed up for Poland's version of ROTC for college. But the old man had understood. He'd been soldiering all his life, and leading men in disparate fights around the globe under the aegis of NATO since Domenik had been six years old. He had long since learned to live with the memories that came with war just as his father had.

They were always there. He could laugh and joke with other soldiers who understood the black humor was coping not callousness. Men who knew the jokes and laughter weren't irreverence, but the only link to humanity that kept them sane.

He checked his compad for an update from the Carolina Base they'd boosted from and there was nothing. He knew it was getting increasingly difficult for their satellite comms to handle the increased bandwidth demanded from all the military traffic that suddenly involved everyone in every settlement. The all hands message two days before had referred to it as 'defense needs.' They would launch another satellite in a week or so, and it would be another week before the program's technical team had it integrated into the network. Until then, any emails or messages that were non-defense related, just piled up in an electronic queue.

Which to him, seemed to beg the question of how all these ridiculous admin messages from Seattle seemed to get through whatever filter had been designed to prioritize military comms. He didn't bother to read any of them beyond the first. It had been some bureaucrat's heartfelt proposal to institute, or would it have been reinstitute? the Geneva Convention here on Eden. To him and the rest of the troop it was laughable. The Chandrians were here to exterminate them. He was pretty sure they'd never heard of Geneva. Whatever battlefield laws or behavior the invaders brought with them, that's what they would all have to live with.

According to Audy, the Chandrian's general sentiment was reflected in the name they had for those they did battle with; 'Shareki,' which meant 'the soon to slain'. Before they'd left the base in the Carolinas, there'd been some messages from Seattle, about a fight at a settlement up north which had the misfortune of being within ten miles of that incursion site. He doubted if the defenders of that settlement were reading their email either.

Valid military messages or no, he had nothing from his mother, nothing from Katia though she was probably busy helping her family evac. His girlfriend's family was Lithuanian and they'd settled in New Boston, so had his mother. Safe for now, but definitely behind the enemy lines if this Southeast group that had sent out these scouts they were watching, decided to go north up the Atlantic seaboard.

His wireless earbud chirped softly. It was Darius. Their tactical radios felt like a luxury. It wasn't like the ETs were going to intercept their signals, or even note them. So different than the operations they were all used to back on Earth. They were trusting Audy on that score, but if the friendly exiled Chandrian was lying to them, they had much bigger problems than their radio signals being intercepted.

"Movement, up my side like we thought. I have the call." Darius's voice was calm. He wondered if his friend was as cold and stiff as he was. It didn't matter, the discomfort would soon be forgotten as the adrenalin kicked in.

Darius' position was in line with his own, on the north side of the narrow defile that constituted the pass they were in. It was a narrow track; its most significant feature was the ridge line of exposed rock running down the middle of it. The north edge had the best cover for the advancing Chandrians and just as Darius had expected, the enemy was using it to advance.

Dom checked the Chandrians through his scope one last time. The slight rise in the middle of the pass would hide them from his line of sight in a moment, just as Darius' hole was hidden from his view as well. Once Darius opened up, the Chandrians would have nowhere to go for hard cover except the ridge between their two positions and the hope was the action would force the enemy to where Domenik already flanked them from a well concealed position.

He sent a simple two pulse squelch back in acknowledgement and waited. He was dimly aware of the fact his hands didn't feel as stiff and cold as they had a moment before, he knees hurt less and the ground in front of him took on a cobweb scene of cover, sight lines and contingency plans. He flexed his fingers, rotated his neck to the popping of frozen gristle, and did the best deep knee bend he could manage in the too small fox hole. He settled into a firing position with the barrel of his assault rifle over the top of an ice encrusted fallen log.

A single gunshot blasted through the quiet of the frozen morning. It was a large caliber weapon, sounding more like a fifty-caliber sniper rig than an assault rifle. Dom fought down a momentary flare of panic. Had they got the drop on Darius?

The quick staccato burst from Darius' assault rifle washed over him in relief, as he said a quick prayer in thanks. A loud whump of an explosion and a white cloud directly on the other side of the ridge line was most definitely not Darius's doing. A grenade he guessed, was followed by more shots from Darius. A few seconds later, a single Chandrian appeared over the hill dragging another by a harness they seemed to carry their gear on. The enemy situated himself behind a rock as he took up a defensive position, his back to Dom, gun pointed back towards Darius' foxhole.

Dom watched through his scope for a moment, relieved that the Chandrian still thought Darius was a threat. The prone Chandrian, laid out on the ground behind the active shooter, held his chest but wasn't moving. The other began rotating from his squat, scanning the area behind him for another threat. Dom observed in slow motion, his own crosshairs centered on the Chandrian sixty meters away as the enemy swung his massive rifle in a slow arc that moved passed his position, paused and then swung back. With his rifle scope's magnification, he could see the shock of recognition on the enemy's face. There was no surprise there, no panic. Dom's tungsten tipped round was already on its way as the Chandrian began pulling his barrel up.

Domenik felt the heavy slug from the Chandrian impact the log a few feet to his left even as he saw the top half of the man's head turn to spray, painting the bare rock behind him. He remained still for a moment, waiting, wondering how the hell the guy had seen him so quickly. The heavy impact against the log in front of his hole had shocked him. These Chandrians were a definite step up from the normal spray and pray AK-47 carrying muj. The other Chandrian still hadn't moved. He waited another ten seconds and then sent a three pulse all clear to Darius and got a response a few seconds after that.

He kept to a tactical approach as he approached the fallen Chandrians. The one he'd taken out was not a worry, the other... he felt for a pulse on the man's neck and there was nothing. Darius came over the hill a few second later moving slowly. He had taken something on the shoulder, and one half of his face was covered in blood.

Darius waved away the look of concern. "Fucking grenade, I can't hear." Darius was almost yelling.

Domenik held three fingers up with a look of question.

Darius pointed back in the direction of the Chandrian's initial approach, and waved a flat hand under his throat.

"Ok, time to move," he said to himself, remembering that Darius couldn't hear him. He drew his knife and sliced open the harness, jacket and shirt of the Chandrian and ripped it open.

"Jackpot." He whispered and looked up at Darius who nodded.

"Just like Audy's" Darius yelled at him.

I hope they aren't related... Domenik shook his head at the thought. He did not need Audy pissed off at him, none of them did.

He snapped a few pictures of the tattooed eagle on the man's chest and sent it to the network. This com traffic would definitely be expressed. He signaled for pick up and then went to check on Darius, who pushed him away.

"Just a flesh wound." Darius smiled.

"Ok, then let's move." He gave Darius the sign for lead the way, hoping they'd get the same kid for the evac, Domenik wanted off this frozen mountain. The enemy's tech and gear were for shit, but these soldiers were most definitely the real deal.

*

"This is crazy, I can't see shit." Carlos cursed and dropped to a knee halfway under a natural overhang of rock that blocked some of the wind. They had a bearing on Mr. Curran's compad signal, but it was impossible to see more than ten feet in the heavy snow storm.

"Now you know why I joined the Navy and got the hell out of Detroit, winter's crazy up this way." Jeff Krouse dropped next to him, down on both knees. They all wore mic shrouds that attenuated the worst of the wind noise.

"I figured it was the race wars or the neighborhood jihad." Carlos fired back cradling his precious sniper rifle protecting it like a newborn.

"Might have had something to do with it." Jeff admitted with a shrug.

Hans Van Slyke and John Wainwright were huddled together in conversation a few feet away, a compad between them. Carlos watched Wainwright, and not for the first time since they'd departed from St. Louis Center earlier that same day, he sensed the man didn't want to be here. Wainwright had lost a lot of the edge the SAS man had typically shown. Kyle had put Wainwright in charge and Carlos knew there wasn't anything he could do about it now. John had gained twenty pounds in the six months since they all made it to Eden. A "solid stone," the Brit had laughed off the ribbing they'd given him, but Carlos knew there wasn't anything solid about it. The man was quickly going soft. Wainwright was out, *mentally* out, of the military and in the last six months since the Noobs had arrived he'd clearly lost a step or two. That was bad, but John's inability to flip the switch and get his head back on mission was worse.

John and Hans joined them. "For an old man he is moving damned fast," Wainwright claimed. "You think he's been nabbed?"

Jeff pulled off his winter white watch cap and rubbed his bald head. The man's black skin steamed in the cold of the storm. "Just send him a text and ask, not like the aliens are going to be able to read it."

"This is true," Hans spoke up.

Carlos watched Wainwright type out the message. He must have shown more on his face than he thought. He felt Jeff nudge his leg. He looked up and Jeff was watching Wainwright as well. Their eyes met and he saw the concern in Jeff's expression and he nodded in agreement. He didn't feel relieved in the slightest that his concern was shared.

Peter Curran was breathing heavy as there was no real point in stopping to listen or look around. The wind and the falling snow's white out made that impossible. He'd been focusing on nothing but putting one foot in front of the other for hours. He did feel his compad buzz against his leg. He stopped and hunched up against a tree trunk to try and block some wind.

He took the opportunity to open up his parka and let out some built up heat. He'd worked up a little sweat and there was nothing more dangerous in conditions like this than to have wet clothes against your skin when you did manage to stop. He read the message, with a smile spreading across his face. Pulling off a glove with his teeth he typed out a response.

- Snowshoes... you guys aren't out here in this mess without snowshoes are you?

Wainwright read the message out loud and looked around at them, smiling. "Cheeky bastard, this old man."

- following tracks, an hour behind them, I think – wind. I think they are skirting south edge of Mossy Lake, moving west. I'd guess three of them, maybe four. Been an hour since I had a real good track to look at. What you want me to do?

Wainwright spoke slowly as he typed. "Maintain contact with trail if you can, do not approach. Hole up somewhere for the night in the next hour. We will link up with you before dawn. We are four, white parkas."

Carlos zipped his own jacket back up. "I guess that means we walk all night."

"You have a problem with that, Carlos?" Wainwright asked.

"Just speakin truth amigo," Carlos answered. "We should have brought snowshoes."

Wainwright looked pissed off, but he hid it well. "Yes, we bloody well should have, but we didn't."

"If the Colonel is right, this group our old man is following is breaking trail west for the main party," Jeff spoke up

80

breaking some of the tension. "We could have an army on our tails come morning."

"Let us hope they stop to wait out the storm." Han's pulled off his pack, letting the heavy bag down slowly in an eighty-pound one-armed curl.

"Maybe they don't have snow shoes either." Carlos said to no one in particular. Truth was he was as pissed off at himself as much as he was Wainwright. It was a stupid mistake, they'd all seen the weather report. Bush league, something the consummate professional in him despised. They all, himself included had spent too much time in the last six months flitting around in air cars and not enough time humping hills. By his way of thinking, it was simply no way to start a war and Wainwright...

Wainwright had two girlfriends in St. Louis, one married, the other almost half his age and both of them Noobs. He'd discussed it with Kyle who at least, girlfriend or not, still had his shit wired tight. Kyle knew it was an issue, but he didn't have an answer other than putting Carlos in command and pissing off Wainwright in the process.

"Not enough of us to win this Carlos," Kyle had said over a beer. "Sure, you, me, and the guys will hit hard and often, but the whole thing rides on the militia. John's a good trainer which makes him damn near priceless."

Carlos put the conversation out of his mind watching Wainwright smiling at his compboard as he fingered a one-handed message.

"That better be command," he said as lightly as he could manage. "You texting your women out here I'll bust that board over your head."

"Relax mate." Wainwright's voice had an edge to it but he slipped the board back into its thigh pocket.

"What gives?" Jeff asked toeing Hans in the ass. Han's was on his knees pulling crap out of his bag. He came up with a spool of paracord and held it up triumphantly.

"Some green branches and twenty minutes to make snow shoes," Hans said coming to his feet with grunt. "We'll make up the time on the move."

Hans looked at Wainwright for an affirmative. Carlos had already pulled his knife, "sounds like a plan." He waded off in to the snow to find some green branches.

"Wish Kyle or Jake were here," Jeff smiled, "those two rednecks could probably do this in five minutes."

"Or go barefoot." Wainwright laughed at his own joke and looked over at Hans. "So how do we do this?"

Curran slogged through the storm until close to midnight, when the wind finally began to soften. Without the snow blow, it was easier to see just how hard it was snowing, but the flakes were getting bigger so he knew the worst of the snow was going to peter out sooner rather than later.

He crested a small rise near the west end of the three-mile-long Mossy Lake, which in the spare diffused moonlight was nothing but a flat, featureless expanse of windblown snow over probably an inch or two of ice. There was a dark shadow of open water at the edge of his vision far off shore.

The light from a small campfire, perhaps three hundred yards off was just barely visible through the snow. In his exhaustion, he stood there staring at it for a half second before he threw himself to the ground his heart hammering in his chest. He stayed down long enough to realize the stinging sensation on his face was from the snow he was laying in.

He raised his head and belly crawled to a point where he could again see the flickering pin prick of light of the campfire. His brain slowly kicked back in as the adrenalin rush subsided. He rolled on to his side to dig out his compboard and quickly checked the compass indicator in the upper left corner of the screen.

"Spotted bad guy's campfire," he whispered to himself as he slowly typed. "300 yards west by north-west of my position. Played out, digging in to sleep." Or die if no one came for him, he added in silent thought.

He sent the message, stowed the board and dug in his bag for a small tarp. With his feet and legs, he stomped out what looked like a small grave into the back side of the snowdrift. With any luck, it would end up being a shelter for the night, not a coffin. He'd spent enough time in the woods to know the single energy bar he had left wouldn't see him out of these woods. He'd left his bow with his ground blind, if he had to shoot some game, he imagined a horde of these invaders would be all over him.

Once in the hole, he positioned the tarp and as much snow as he could shift on to it to hold it down. The falling snow would do the rest. He stayed awake long enough to eat the protein bar and drink some water. He said a quick prayer that he didn't suffocate in the night. As an afterthought, he added a P.S. for it to please snow hard enough to cover his tracks. In the end, he was too exhausted to worry about it.

His eyes snapped open to a narrow shaft of bright, painful sunlight illuminating his cave. He had slept in a fetal position and the first thing he did was try to straighten out his legs.

"Oh shit," he managed as the pain and cramping started immediately.

"Quiet, Mr. Curran, if you please."

He froze in panic at the voice coming from somewhere outside the shelter and relaxed immediately as he realized the Chandrians wouldn't know his name. Even less likely, they probably didn't speak with a British accent.

"Come out if you can, real slow, downhill side." A white gloved hand snaked down the hole in his shelter and patted a side of his snow casket and then flashed him a thumb's up.

He did his best to position his feet and push against the snow, but the combination of the weight, the fact that it was partially frozen from his body heat, and the excruciating pain in every single one his joints demonstrated the futility of the attempt.

"Umm, a little help here?"

Curran looked at the tan colored foil container and read, 'Chicken ala' King.' It looked like baby shit with green peas, but it was warm and quite possibly the best thing he'd ever eaten.

"You're looking a lot better Mr. Curran." The black soldier smiled at him and shoved another water bottle at him. "Finish this too."

He smiled and drained half the bottle in a go. "I actually thought I was in pretty decent shape."

The soldier held out his hand, "I'm Jeff, and you tracked these guys fourteen miles through a storm. We couldn't have done any better."

"Pete," he said, shaking the man's hand. "They still there?"

The soldier nodded back at him. "For the moment, but they're breaking down their camp." Jeff jerked his chin above them where another soldier was lying flat near the top of the small hill, watching through his rifle's scope.

"That's John, we let him think he's in charge. We've got two more colleagues out there. Closer, keeping eyes on the bad guys."

"They really the folks we've been getting ready for?"

Jeff nodded again. "That they are. We just didn't think they'd invade in the middle of winter."

"Well they did," Curran said trying to stretch out his legs that were quivering in their recovery. "I think you boys should just leave me with some food, I'll just slow you down. I'm wrung out."

The soldier looked at him for a moment in concern. "I think we are done tracking them."

"Oh."

The soldier nodded to affirm what he was thinking. "This group beelined west, we know what they're doing. Our next job is to figure out if the main group will follow this track."

"How exactly do you do that?"

The soldier above them crawled backwards downhill to where he slid to a stop next them.

"We get a reconnaissance photo of the main group in a few hours or so, that's how we do it. But we need some intel from these scouts." The Brit had clearly been listening to them.

He turned to Jeff, "Carlos has positive ID on three ECs, let's get in position."

"ECs?" Curran asked.

Jeff smiled at him, "enemy combatants, tangos, targets, ETs ... the bad guys."

"Before the storm got really bad, I could have sworn I was following four sets of tracks, not three." Curran wondered at speaking out, but it did seem important.

The Brit shook his head in dismissal. "Carlos says there are three, there's three."

Jeff tapped his ear piece. "I heard him John, Carlos said he'd ID'd three, if there's another Tango we need to be sure."

"There's no tracks out from their camp, none." John responded tersely back at Jeff. Curran watched the by-play thinking maybe he shouldn't have said anything. "Unless they put some poor bastard outside of camp in the snow all night, there's only three tangos. We go, now."

The Brit broke off his glare down with Jeff, and turned to him, a smile suddenly on his face. "The sooner we get this unpleasantness over, the sooner we can return Mr. Curran to his family."

"Sounds good to me," he shrugged, thinking to himself he'd survived a night in the storm without a fire, why couldn't a fourth EC or tango, or whatever they called these guys, have done the same.

"Find Mr. Curran a hidey, let's get this done," John ordered Jeff.

"Will do."

It was clear Jeff wasn't at all happy with what, or how they were going to do whatever it was they were going to do. But the friendly talkative soldier had gone strangely silent as he helped him over to a small ravine behind the hill and sat him down on a log.

"Shouldn't be much to see, but if you can make it to that next log, up there," Jeff pointed at the fallen tree between them and lake. "You should be able to see what's happening - if you want. Wouldn't blame you if you don't."

The moment Jeff moved off, he stood, or tried to and did a hunchback's shuffle slowly up the side of the ravine where Jeff had deposited him. He dropped down and crawled the last few yards until his head came around the bole of a tree. In the clear light of the day, he could see the three 'tangos' squatting on their haunches around a fire passing a canteen or container of some sort back and forth. From probably 400 yards he guessed at the distance, he could just make out their faces. He was strangely disappointed. For aliens, they looked just like people.

But they did look different. The brown gray parkas were heavy and they wore what looked like fur boots but it was difficult to tell. Even at this distance, it was clear that the rifles they carried were huge. The long barrels at this range looked like Kentucky long rifles given how far they stood above the enemy's shoulders. The whole group kind of reminded him of those old pictures of the early arctic explorers.

He knew from the training courses the Program people had run them through that the level of technology the Chandrians had was well beneath their own. They'd also been told they were all full-time soldiers and not to be underestimated.

The bad guys seemed oblivious to him, as he watched John and Jeff work themselves closer between where he lay and the enemy camp, using the terrain to stay below the bad guy's line of sight. They might have been moving up on a herd of antelope as he watched them. They were steady and smooth in their movements and he wondered, knowing they'd hiked all night as well, how they could move, let alone skulk forward on their bellies so well.

Jeff had said there were two other team members out there somewhere, one whose name was Carlos, but he had yet to see any sign of either of them. He watched as both Jeff and John stopped moving and went still in the snow. Their white parkas were nearly invisible but he could clearly see the soles of their boots pointing back towards him.

One of the Chandrians around the campfire surged to his feet suddenly, and the area reverberated with the crack of several rifles. Two 'tangos' were spun around and blown back violently while the third had dove out of view. He tracked his eyes back to Jeff's boots and watched as another shot, this one much louder, sounding a lot like his own 7mm Magnum which was at home over his fireplace, kicked up a fountain of snow half a foot from where Jeff lay.

Another short burst of automatic fire came out of the woods behind the campsite and Curran saw puffs of snow blossom forth from where the third Chandrian must have dove.

They must have gotten word from the tree line that the third guy was toast, because both Jeff and John came up on a knee, rifles held up against their shoulders started moving towards the enemy camp.

Carlos cursed under his breath and keyed his mic once. Something had moved up the hill to his left when the shooting started, and he knew that Hans was well below him. The single click, meant danger, stop, oh shit and fall back – everything that should have stopped Wainwright and Jeff in their tracks. He watched as Jeff dropped into a prone position and started snaking backwards for the cover he had just left. He was dumbfounded as Wainwright just stood there looking into the trees in his general direction.

He watched Wainwright key his own mic, "Carlos, you have something, key again, otherwise sta.."

"CRaaaack!"

The massive rifle shot came from where he'd heard something, he rolled quickly to orient to the sound and went completely still.

The Chandrian sniper made a mistake as he shifted position to get a better angle on Jeff or Hans. Carlos saw the movement and shifted his gun. The Chandrian saw his movement and swung the massive barrel of his rifle downhill towards Carlos as he worked the action. They were less than 75 yards apart in the thick forest. Carlos gently squeezed his trigger just as the Chandrian laid his cheek against the side of his own weapon to take aim.

A half hour later, after they'd made sure the area was secure as the three of them and Mr. Curran were going to make it. Carlos watched, as Jeff zipped the body bag holding Wainwright closed.

"I'm sorry," Carlos heard the civilian hunter half whisper to himself.

"Not your fault," Carlos said

"S'all right" Jeff nodded at him. "He forgot what he was doing is all, stupid limey bastard."

"What the fuck was he thinking." Carlos asked no one in particular. "His head wasn't in this, he had no business being out here."

Curran watched as Jeff nodded in agreement as the third soldier, a massive blonde-haired giant walked back to them holding a small camera.

"Pictures of their chest ink, snakes. It is all Audy needs, yes?"

"Yeah," Carlos coughed up something and spit into the snow. "Grab up anything else of interest and one of their rifles."

"Ja," the blonde man said looking at his compad, "extraction is twenty minutes out." *

Chapter 7

"John wasn't even pretending." Carlos sat in a bare office, with one large window and what would have been a decent view of Mt. Rainier if the sky wasn't the color of lead and pissing rain. The office was Kyle's erstwhile home in New Seattle's Program Center. A heavy, nano-formed desk, made to look like some hardwood sat between them, and despite most things being electronic, it was piled high with paper and maps.

"It wasn't like the guys we've both seen who'd done one too many ops and just didn't care anymore." Kyle knew exactly what Carlos was saying. They'd both served long enough to have seen it countless times. Teammates that pretended to be frosty even though everyone on the team could tell they were ghosting.

"Wainwright just flat out didn't *want* to be there. Like he was pissed that his vacation had been called off."

Kyle had read Carlos' report, and the ones from Jeff and Hans as well. They all told a similar story. He nodded in agreement. Wainwright had dropped any semblance of the operational mindset once he'd gone civilian. He should have caught it, and hadn't. This was his fault.

Rare was the individual that could totally unplug and then re-insert their psyche back into something they'd had more than enough of. Special Forces worked hard and played hard, and always knew they needed to be ready. Too much down time, he knew. Wainwright had let himself unplug and the sad part was Kyle couldn't fault him. Wainwright had deserved some peace and quiet, they all did. "Not yet."

"What?" Carlos asked.

"Sorry, thinking out loud." Kyle answered. "We've called in every veteran we have, Program and civilian alike, not everyone is going to be wired tight. Most of them have been out of the field for a very long time, and a lot were hobbits when they *were* in."

"Hobbits..." Carlos snorted, with a cynical smile.

89

That's what they had called all the support people, back at base. That separate army of specialists that made certain the pointy end of the armed forces could do what they were actually tasked to do. The kind of skills that he would kill for at the moment. He and Pretty were trying to stand up an expanded training program, every Hobbit was worth two to three shooters. That would change, but for now, more trainers, personnel specialists or logisticians would be a godsend. He wasn't going to argue with Carlos, though. He knew where his friend was coming from.

To Carlos, Hobbits were the guys back at base, eating Pizza Hut every day for lunch and drinking coffee flown in from Starbuck's, without ever having to leave the safety of the heavily defended base or green-zone.

"Maybe show them Wainwrights' body as a wakeup call." Carlos was still angry, so was he in truth. He just had enough worry and concern on his shoulders at the moment that he knew he couldn't afford to dwell on it.

"We are going to have a lot of bodies before this is over, Carlos. You know that. I need you frosty without getting pissed off at anyone that can't operate at your level. Which don't get all big headed on me, is about everyone I have outside of us knuckle draggers. It's the militia that is going to win or lose this for us, and we'll lose a lot of them."

Carlos stared at him for a moment and nodded. "Sorry bro, I only have one speed. I told Zarena I'd be back, and there for her, when this over. I'm going to keep that promise. You know I liked John." Carlos crossed himself.

"But these new muj are hardcore. Their sniper that took him out? He sat through a snow storm all night, alone, when his buddies enjoyed a warm fire a hundred yards away. Basic overwatch role sure, but that's professional level discipline. Solid training as well. He saw us take out his buddies one-two-three. He could have stayed in the black, watched and reported and we'd never have seen him. He could have waited until we thought it was all over and we were out in the open and tried to service all of us. But no Hermano, he had to know once he fired, when he did, from where he did, that he was a dead man and he didn't hesitate.

"The guy basically went kamikaze when nine out of ten would have laid low. What's that tell you?"

Kyle rubbed his eyes, he'd slept maybe two hours in the last twenty-four. "Tells me what Audy has been saying is straight up. They are basically robots. Duty only, they win or die. They fail and live, they get stood up against a post back at camp. They'll all die trying."

"Well we got hobbits and civilians," Carlos flashed him a thumb's up. "What are we worried about?"

"I think our people may surprise you. No one's harder to beat than somebody protecting their homes and family."

"It'll surprise me all right." Carlos was still pissed. But Kyle was secretly relieved. A quiet Carlos was a bad Carlos, he'd seen that side too. The Carlos that had first showed up on the Program was cold and just a little bit bent. This was much preferred and he knew what was really eating his friend. The same thing that kept him up at night. Carlos had somebody, the first somebody in his life to truly worry about. Not a buddy, not a team member, but a loved one whose life was forfeit if they lost.

Carlos now had Zarena and the two girls that had quickly adopted him as their father figure, and Kyle had Elisabeth who pretty much refused to speak to him at the moment because of what he and Audy planned to do.

"I want to show you something." Kyle worked his mouse and pointed at the flat screen behind Carlos on the wall.

"We found a memory card for a personal camera that one of the militia defenders at the Deep Lake settlement was wearing when they attacked the Chandrians."

"They attacked?" Carlos asked turning his chair around.

"They did," Kyle nodded as he finished keying up the video. "A Noob, a former motor pool maintenance guy in the guard was in command. They had to buy some time for their people to get away to where we could safely extract them by air bus. Which they did. The helmet cam was on a Noob named Surya

91

Patilaranga who volunteered for the attack. A former IT guy, out of some unpronounceable town in India."

The TV flared to life, and they saw the edge of the tree that the wearer was hiding behind. His frantic heavy breathing was picked up as was the sound of a series of distant explosions partially drowned out by the howling wind and thick snowfall visible on the screen.

"Those were grenades thrown by a similar group of Noobs on the other flank of the massed Chandrians," Kyle said. "This group waits for the enemy to react, to flow to that fight, then they move in."

"Now," someone off scream yelled, and the clear video devolved into a jarring side to side movement as their cameraman surged forward through the swirling snow. Other figures were visible to the side and a few in front of him.

Gun fire erupted the moment the enemy's formation came into sight, most of the enemy was facing the other way. Their cameraman opened fire himself, on full auto, spraying his M-4 directly into the enemy formation until his magazine came up empty. Chandrian soldiers went down by the dozens, those that didn't reacted quickly and started firing back. The enemy fire, reliant on breech loading single shots, was a lot slower and a lot louder than the tiny 5.56 rounds killing them. The enemy fire was very accurate, though, and the much smaller Deep Lake's attacking force went down quick.

Somehow, their cameraman was one of the few that managed to survive long enough to reload. He started forward, firing again on full automatic. He wasn't trying to aim, he just waived his barrel back and forth into the still tight formation of Chandrians that went down in front of him, even as others worked the bolt actions on their long rifles. A few drew short swords in what both Kyle and Carlos recognized as practiced ease. One of these, wearing a red sash around his grey parka swam into Patilaranga's sight picture just as the M-4's bolt slammed to a stop on an empty magazine. The young militiaman didn't pause. He dropped his rifle with a curse and surged directly at the man, who stood there calmly, his blade held up defensively.

The image blurred as the Noob slammed into his quarry, and the desperate grunt of surprise as the Chandrian's blade slammed home.

The firing had almost ceased as the enemy leader's face appeared on the screen looking down at their now dying camera man.

"Fuck you!" The man said and then laughed between gasps of pain.

A look of confusion spread across the Chandrian's face, as an outstretched hand entered the frame of view. The kid was giving his enemy the bird, still laughing.

The Chandrian's eyes shifted and a look of surprise crossed his face. The image went to static with a suddenness that needed no explanation.

"Grenade?" Carlos asked quietly.

"Yep," Kyle said and shut off the TV with a remote. "That kid knew he was going to die before they ever started that attack. They all did, they all volunteered. It worked; the Chandrians waited an hour for more reinforcements before storming the settlement. The rest of the group got away while they waited."

Carlos shook his head. "Maybe they'll do."

"They'll have to," Kyle said. "Carlos, I need you to keep that in mind. Our survival, Elisabeth's, Zarena's, her kids, all of us depend on how we can bring these militia along. They're scared, but they'll fight. We can't run them down, we have to build'em up."

Carlos nodded once in acknowledgement if not enthusiasm. "Message received."

"Come on," Kyle stood up. "We've got the whole military brain trust to speak to and I need your input. Don't sit there like a wetback being pissed at the man, cause he's going to deport you."

"Mexico sounds pretty good bout 'now, hermano."

Kyle laughed. "It does. But, for how long?"

*

There were more people in the small auditorium surrounding the conference table than he had expected. Kyle took that as a decent sign. Anyone with former military "command" experience, from the Program or the civilian population was supposed to have been brought in. Then again it was a sobering thought that the whole cadre fit into the small auditorium. There were maybe a hundred and fifty people present, most standing. They had a bunch more people that had served, but almost everybody that had been an NCO or above was here. There were others linking in from their posts, like General Majeski and his team. Captain Nagy, Colonel Pretty's former XO, was just recently fully recovered and was with most of Pretty's old unit bird-dogging the West Group of Chandrians through a hellacious Canadian winter. Right now, this room was what he and Colonel Pretty had to work with.

Kyle had command at the tactical level, while Col. Pretty had overall command. Hank was already standing at the head of the table when Kyle took his seat. They had conferred and agreed that Pretty would lead the briefing. The Colonel had a much better overall footprint of authority, especially among some of the foreign military veterans. They were typically, as had always been the case, much more "class-and rank-conscious" than the Americans.

"Here's what we know."

Pretty had the map up on the wall and his laser designator was dancing. Kyle half listened and half focused on what Carlos had said about Wainwright. He could recognize that piece of himself which wanted nothing more than to just unplug. It was a big enough piece that it worried him.

"The main group here in the middle is roughly a hundred and thirty thousand strong. Do not make the mistake of thinking that equates to forty or fifty thousand shooters. It's a hundred and thirty thousand battle hardened veterans, members of the Snake clan. Basically, they're the Waffen SS of Audy's home world. You've all, I hope, read up on the intel packages we have sent out on Chandra and everything we know of our enemy. This Snake Clan, goes by the name of

'*Strema,*' in the Chandran tongue. When the Kaerin on Chandra need another clan to back them, the Strema usually get the call.

This Northwest group is roughly forty-five thousand strong, we are still working to identify which clan, but the weather has not permitted any action beyond recon yet. Thankfully, the weather hasn't allowed them to move but a few miles either. They are a back-burner issue for the time being. Their 'drop' location, if you will, has put them in a very cold world of shit, a long way off from anything we have to defend in the short term.

"The Eastern group," Pretty shifted his pointer to the east coast, "is thirty-five thousand strong, and we have identified them as the Jema, or Eagle Clan. More on them in a moment.

"What we know so far is that their infantry carries very large caliber, very accurate and ponderous rifles. Basically, akin to our .458 Weatherby in power, though perhaps a little hotter – so our body armor is useless at anything but extreme range. However," Pretty nodded at Jake who stepped away from the wall carrying one of the massive rifles and set it down on the table. "It's basically Boer War technology. Breech loading, single shot, ammo carried in bandolier or pouch, very slow rate of fire in comparison to our own. As you can see, that is a 39 inch octagonal barrel, the whole thing is just under twenty pounds.

"They have very basic, frequency hopping radios, limited range. Again, all of this, tracks with what Audy had already given us prior to recent events. We don't know if the larger groups have any communication with the others, but our best guess is that if they have even limited numbers of tactical radios, they'd probably have something akin to HAM radios. We believe it probable they have the capability but, short wave as you know is finicky. We have collection towers going up and we are trying to collect enough take to break the code. Unfortunately, Audy is the sole speaker of Chandrian we have access to," Pretty paused and rubbed the bridge of his nose looking at the sober faces around the room.

"I imagine we'll learn more as we go on, but I'll leave you with this as a possible source of optimism. The three groups out there are three different clans and they do not, I repeat, do not trust or like one another. Not distrust, as in the US and USSR in 1944, but are actively engaged in ongoing and pretty much regular warfare on Chandra itself. Audy's home-world is basically Yugoslavia, but instead of Tito keeping everything under his thumb, their priest class actively enforces a situation of highly regimented and rules-based warfare between different clans, and it's constant. This isn't a conscript army, war is what they do."

"There's a relative weakness inherent in a society you just described." Paul Stephens had been sitting unobtrusively at the back of the room along the wall.

"Absolutely," Col. Pretty agreed, "and the weaknesses are obvious." He looked to Kyle and pointed at him, "those weaknesses play a large part in our tactical planning."

A hand went up directly across the table from where Pretty stood. "We are putting a great deal of trust in this Audy fellow, yes?" The speaker had a heavy French accent and waved an unlit pipe when he spoke. Kyle thought it made him look more British than French.

"Captain Montrose?"

"Yes, it's good to see you again Colonel."

"I wish we had your regiment of heavy tanks for you to use." Pretty smiled.

"As do I," the French tanker replied.

"To answer your question, yes, we do. Implicitly trust Audy, that is. He's been absolutely spot on with everything we have been able to learn firsthand. He was a command rank officer. But remember, this is relatively low-tech culture, no internet, heavily censored news, everything of a technical nature is controlled by their Priest class, down to the control of the written word. They control the technology and the best troops. All religion has been outlawed for approximately the last ten generations. Audy has great recall but there is much he never had access to, and there is much we do not know regarding what they may have brought with them."

"What of air-power, transport?" Stephens piped up from the wall keeping the briefing on its track.

"According to Audy they utilize dirigibles and single wing aircraft, and occasionally two engine, bi-plane bombers on their home world. Audy has been through our historical Jane's database and made a note of everything that he thinks they have and our best analysis puts their flight technology at roughly late 1920's. But again, strictly controlled and not nearly wide spread as in our own history. Their priest class, the Kaerin clan, has all the air power such as it is.

"They don't share that out with the other clans. We have not seen any evidence of aircraft from the very limited satellite photos we've been able to shoot through these storm systems. We don't know what they managed to translate here or how they moved so many men and material in one go. Blimps would definitely be easier to manage without having to build landing strips though."

"Armor?" Montrose still looked a little pissed at the short answer he had received on Audy.

"We think we picked a shot of what may be artillery, but not a lot of it. We have seen zero evidence of any motorized transport or armor. But I caution, that is all we have seen. They may have something more, though I would imagine transporting fuel to keep them running would not be easy. At this early juncture, we haven't seen anything beyond an enemy whose TOE supports infantry tactics based on massed assault."

Montrose scratched the top of his head, "What is our AT capability if they do have armor?"

Kyle glanced at Jake, who was sitting against the wall behind Montrose. Jake smirked and rolled his eyes.

Typical tanker, Kyle knew. They thought they ruled the battlefield and put every tactical decision down to how many tanks, across how wide a front, moving how fast was the end all of tactical planning. Which was all well and good if you were fighting World War II on the steppes of Russia or sitting across the Fulda Gap during the Cold War. The war on terror had proven they were next to useless against an enemy that didn't play by West Point rules and who had learned to use mortars and IEDs like a scalpel. Though he had to admit, against the Chandrians he'd love to have a couple of Abrams or Bradleys on hand. But they didn't.

"We have limited US military production anti-tank weapons, javelin and AT-4s shoulder launched," Pretty answered. "Weapons production right now is focused on mortars, artillery and air delivered ordinance - this looks to be an infantry battle Captain."

Pretty walked around to the front of the table. "What we do have, is Four Joint Strike Fighters, F-35 Lightnings, helos and Ospreys, 4700-plus air cars, and a couple hundred heavy air buses. We are churning out the spare parts, but an F35 has over a hundred thousand distinct parts. We can concentrate on building more or we can work on keeping the ones we have in the air. We fabricate in batches, so you can see the problem.

"We'll have mortars and a lot of them, they're simple. We'll have simple artillery, probably 105s. And we'll have them in numbers beyond our capability to man the systems with trained personnel – that's our Achilles heel across the board. Numbers and training - training up our militia to take on a force of two hundred thousand battle hardened veterans, regardless of their technology."

The room was silent. A few of the heads were down looking at the table top.

"Jake? Kyle?" Pretty prompted them.

"It's not a problem with recruitment," Jake broke the silence after Kyle gave him the nod. "We are getting the numbers we need and they are all being mustered to Salt Lake and south of St. Louis except for a few select groups that are already into their training cycle at their settlements."

With a glance from Jake, Kyle sat forward at the table.

"It's training them up to the point they'll be effective rather than just cannon fodder or a 'meat shield' as one young recruit referred to himself. The first time we engage, we will win. We simply have to. We do not have the recruiting depth to fight through low morale, so we are going to use our strategic depth and buy time, hammering at their edges until we are confident we can prevail in a head to head engagement. At this moment, one for one, they are much more disciplined, and experienced than we are. They are highly motivated, but so are we, and on the tech front we have a significant advantage.

Colonel Pretty waved him off. "Kyle is our tactical commander on the ground, your communities have all benefitted from the training and preps that his people have been running for almost the last year. He is advocating, and I agree that our best initial moves are to utilize the full brunt of our air power from the beginning. Hit them hard, regularly, move, hit them again, move, give up ground as we grind them down."

"Thanks, Colonel" Kyle pointed at the map on the wall, "you just saved these good people from a twenty-minute Power Point presentation and I never learned how those things actually solve anything."

The laughter was real but subdued. Kyle stood and turned to face the larger audience.

"We are basically the Wehrmacht after the battle of Kursk. The Germans kicked Russian ass in just about every battle in local tactical terms on their retreat to Berlin. They ran out of gear, men, and depth and the Russians could afford to lose men at a seven to one ratio. As long as the Chandrians do not get reinforced, we trade ground for time and combat experience, and we don't expect to have the German's supply problems.

"Why don't we just let them march around?" Stephens piped in again. "I've no military experience but we know they are necessarily limited in what they brought with them. Guns need ammo, men need food."

Kyle shook his head. "What they have thrown at us is a reconnaissance in force. They have an almost non-existent picture of what is here, beyond the geography. If this force survives to report back, we can expect the main force to follow on. It's their SOP, and our intel says that was their overall plan as of a year ago."

"Our intel? You are referring to this Audy again?" Montrose was growing frustrated, and Kyle knew it didn't have anything to do with not getting any tanks to drive around in.

"I do." Kyle answered simply. He turned and pointed at Audy who had sat unobtrusively watching the proceedings with great interest. "I apologize for not introducing him earlier."

"Mon Dieu!" Montrose rubbed at his face, and waggled his pipe towards Audy. "I mean no offense Mr. Audy, but I'm sure I'm not the only one in this room concerned that you are here, in attendance at this gathering."

"I am not offended." Audy spoke calmly. Kyle grinned a little inside. He knew Audy well enough that he didn't doubt his friend's words. Montrose's 'concern' would seem wholly natural to him and Audy would no doubt take it in stride.

"As I was saying," Kyle broke back in, "Their translation capability is based on some sort of natural occurrence or flux in the... Doc? A little help?"

Dr. Jensen remained seated and coughed into hand. "We have no idea beyond its naturally occurring. The power needed to translate what they did in one instant is beyond anything we could hope to generate. Only some sort of planetary build up in their gravitational and magnetic fields could potentially power what they did to get here in such large numbers. That's why we are certain it's a natural phenomenon on Chandra, one they've managed to harness or more likely ... located and figured out how to time. Hell, one of our theories suggests all the planes and ships that got lost in the Bermuda triangle went there or to some other world, we just don't know. But we are certain the enemy is utilizing a natural phenomenon.

"We also believe," Doc Jensen continued, "they have to have the ability to get back to report. So clearly, they are aware of or believe in such a natural occurrence here. It's giving us a whole new way to look at the quantum... err," Jensen remembered his audience with a chagrinned smile. "We are actively working to identify and hopefully locate this planetary phenomenon here."

"And," Kyle raised his hand to forestall Montrose. "That theory is in keeping with what Audy told us six months ago. They are very limited as to when they can translate, usually once or twice a year. Their targeting sucks. If it didn't, we think the Eastern Group, the Jema, would have landed within a few miles of General Majeski in North Carolina. The Central Group at the Mississippi River and the Northwest Group just east of Vancouver on the mainland, which on Chandra is a site of a major city."

Kyle glanced away from the map on the wall back towards Montrose who was shaking his head very much unconvinced. Kyle couldn't do anything about that now.

"As it stands, the Chandrians up north are bogged down in the plains north of where Calgary used to be, in a total whiteout condition. They are in a world of hurt with no easy route to their target, that being the west coast. The Central Group has already started moving west, slogging across the great woods heading towards the Mississippi River somewhere below where Minneapolis was located on Earth. Everything points to an attempt at controlling our coasts and splitting the continent in half at the Big Muddy. So, we have some advantages, they're not supermen, just very good soldiers who missed their LZs by a long shot."

"What kind of people are they?" A man about his age wearing a very worn Angels baseball cap raised a hand as he started speaking.

"Sorry, Brent Phillips – formerly a short fuse 1st Lt, 101st airborne."

"What happened?" Kyle asked.

"Bad chute, messed my back up on deployment and broke it when I landed. Active duty three months and eleven days post OCS, and that was twelve years ago, so I'm not really sure why I'm even here."

"Because you have the experience and background to help us train our militia, and you are very welcome indeed. Colonel Pretty tells me you were being groomed to be the youngest company commander in the 101 since World War Two."

"That's nice of him to say, but he talked me into coming to Eden so I have some issues with the Colonel about now."

The crowd broke out into some much-needed laughter. Kyle laughed along with them and waited for it die down.

"It's a damned good question. What kind of people are they? I'm assuming you were thinking of maybe a goodwill gesture on our part. Try to buy some good will? Divide and conquer?"

"Something like that" Phillips admitted.

"I'm not the one to answer that question. Audy?"

He watched as Audy stood, taking a position slightly in front of Kyle, close to his end of the table.

"My name is Audrin'ochal. My friends here call me Audy, this I understand. Many of your names and words are hard for me. I have study your language very much and am still learning so I apologize of mistakes I make."

It was the rehearsed speech they had worked on, and Kyle knew Audy was more nervous about speaking in front of this group than he was of fighting his fellow Chandrians. It came across in his wooden delivery.

"I am from Chandra. I am a *Bastelta*, this means much the same as Captain, perhaps Major in your military. I am Jema, this is my clan. Jema in your language means of the Eagle. Jema is no longer a large clan. When I was a child, the Jema rebelled. We fought very hard against the Kaerin who now control all of Chandra. We paid a heavy price for losing against them and their allies. We are still the most heavily watched, controlled clan as we have this history of revolt against the Kaerin. Most clans have earned the right to live amongst their people, some clans lose this ...." Audy looked to Kyle for help.

"Privilege?"

"Yes," Audy nodded, "we lose this privilege. Though in recent years we have fought hard to regain that privilege of being allowed to have children and grow as a clan once again. All clans must fight for the Kaerin. They have the best weapons and are largest clan with the most technology. They use technology and access to food to control Chandra. Kaerin leaders live and rule like God-Kings and are greatly feared for good reason. The Kaerin will come here in large numbers if these clans that are here now are not killed."

"You mean stopped?" Jake broke in. "They must be stopped."

Kyle tried not to smile at the scripted set-up, but they needed to drive this message home.

"No," Audy shook his head. "I do not. They will not stop. They will follow the will and honor of their clan leaders. You must, you will have to kill them all. Their people's safety and lives on Chandra are in the hands of their Clan leaders to fulfill their duty to the Kaerin. You call these people hostages, they are all hostages. We have no concept of surrender. Kyle explains this to me, and I do not believe him until I read your histories. We do not have a word for this concept. You win in battle or you die. That is the way on Chandra. They are here now at Kaerin demand. There will be no cease fire, no retreat, no mercy.

"So, we kill eighty percent of them," Jake was right on cue. "The remaining twenty just keep on coming? How does anyone ever win a war?"

"The Kaerin always win." Audy said slowly. He failed to hide the smoldering anger that Kyle had learned to recognize in his friend whenever the Kaerin were mentioned.

"They end the fighting when their will is fulfilled, Chandra is always at war. Clan honor guarantees challenges will be answered, but it is all controlled by the Kaerin. Wars are started by the Kaerin to control a clan that is growing in power. Sometimes, very rare, a clan will revolt as mine did, the Jema, when I was a child."

"What of your Clan's honor?" Jake asked.

"Honor was kept. We paid a heavy price."

"And now," Jake asked, "your Clan is held hostage on Chandra?"

"No," Audy shook his head

"But I thought the clan's peoples are kept hostage to force you to fight," Colonel Pretty challenged Audy.

"Other clans yes. When our revolt failed, the Jema were all killed by the Kaerin twenty-two years ago, save a single generation of children to carry the Jema's shame and hope of gaining our honor once again. I was one of those children. You call this ethnic cleansing I think. There is nothing clean about it. At seven years old, I was among the oldest allowed to live and grow to fight for the Kaerin, in the hopes of restoring our Clan's honor. Millions of Jema were killed, executed. Men, women and children. Now in the Jema, among those that are left, we are only soldiers, we are allowed no children. Punishable by death, mother, father and child."

"Your women fight alongside you?" Paul Stephens asked.

"They fight very well. They want to regain honor very much. Almost as much as they want children. They are very fierce."

"Good God." Dr. Jensen sighed as the gathered sat in mostly stunned silence. A few people crossed themselves, as did Carlos.

"This is barbaric!" Montrose looked up at Colonel Pretty who nodded back at him.

"I am learning of your God," Audy started again with a nod toward Doc Jensen. "Understanding your people and how you … are, is hard for me without knowing what you believe. Your laws are good, but until I read your history and your religions I do not see how this came to be. We had God on Chandra many generations ago, the stories are legend now, but the Kaerin forbid it. The Gods are dead on my world. Perhaps what has happened there would not have happened had we chosen a different path or had we been victorious against the Kaerin."

"Audy," Kyle spoke into the shocked silence, "tell them what you are planning to do."

"The Jema are treated poorly, thrown away," the look of anger and disgust on Audy's face was clear. "You have a word …expendable? I think is correct. The Jema would be given the hardest fighting. The one target we know on this world is your North part of Carolina. That is where they were sent. To the one place the Kaerin had attacked before. The one place which the Kaerin would think, would expect, that you are ready for us. Perhaps hard fighting? Now we know, the Chandrians on your east coast are indeed the Jema, my people. They, I believe were to be sacrificed to your guns, as the Strema would be free to begin their march south."

"The Strema," Audy pointed at the map projection on the wall, "you call it the 'Snake Clan' is my clan's most hated enemy. They were the sword that carried out the culling of my people when I was a child. The Kaerin gave the command, Strema blades did the work.

"We will find the Jema," Audy pointed at himself and at Kyle. "I will go to them and ask them to follow a different path to honor, to fight against the Kaerin once again. To fight the Strema. I do not believe my people have anything to lose. The Jema need a home, and I would tell them of the freedom that you have. Freedom that I believe they will fight for, as will I."

Audy, paused and glanced around the room, "I do not believe your people can understand what I am saying. When I say – to fight against the Strema, we would give all that we are, even our future."

Kyle watched the room. These were men and women that had served in Earth's various militaries. He could see it in their faces. Most had just heard a plea for help that they could understand, others weren't convinced. Montrose was among the latter for certain. The Frenchman sat there chewing on the stem of an unlit pipe looking very concerned. Kyle couldn't blame him either. The French military had faced a series of difficult, no-win decisions over the last decade as many of its former colonies in the Levant and Africa had joined the global dumpster fire and large swaths of what used to be France had gone over to full Jihad. They'd made a lot of very hard, unpopular calls and Montrose certainly didn't look like was buying into Audy's plan.

"Col. Pretty?" Montrose pointed at Audy with pipe. "You intend to send this man back to the enemy with what he knows?"

Hank glanced at Kyle and then over to Audy. "I think if Audy meant us harm we'd know it by now."

"Indeed," Audy said with more than a hint of pride, "you would know it. I have given my word, on my honor, to Kyle." Audy glanced over at him and nodded once deeply.

"I'm sorry," Montrose continued, "and I certainly mean no disrespect here, but what else would an agent provocateur say? And if he is truly on our side, which I have no reason to doubt, who's to say that these Jema don't get their information out of him any way they can?"

Audy looked towards him, "I do not know this word, 'prova cure'."

"It means spy, Audy," Hank answered for him looking sternly at Montrose, "and I'll admit we all had similar concerns regarding Audy, in the past. Audy himself understands this. We have no concerns in that regard now."

"But Colonel?" Montrose started,

"Captain," Pretty cut him off with a tone that had served him well on the battlefield and even better around budget negotiating tables. "You've seen the briefing, the numbers we are up against which I remind you is a reconnaissance in force. We are up against an entire world here. A *truly* evil empire. We have to crush this invasion or a year from now Eden will be facing numbers far beyond what our technological edge can overcome. We need allies, and the Jema may be willing to fight for a future, that I say again - we won't have, unless we win."

Hank looked around the room. "If it were my call, I'd make it. It's well worth the risk in my opinion. But this isn't the US Department of Defense, and we aren't NATO. This is a gathering of citizen soldiers from around the world who came here for a reason. I've been placed in command by the Program, but the Program has little or no authority in these matters, they've simply turned over their significant production and organizational capability to the defense of Eden. It is for us employ that capability the best that we can."

"I think I speak for the Program," Paul Stephens spoke up from behind Col. Pretty. "I do not like having to do this," Stephens paused a moment, "or even say it, but if Mr. Audy fails, are we really any worse off?"

"They'll have our order of battle," Brent Phillips spoke up. "They'll know where our settlements are, how few we are. Yes, sir, we'll be worse off."

"That's true," Kyle cut in, "but it won't change the inevitable invasion of their main forces. When I said we were trading ground for time and experience, I was speaking tactically. Strategically speaking, we aren't playing for time; we don't have much. We have to beat them."

Kyle paused, "kill them," he corrected himself. "As Audy said, it's a binary solution set. If we don't win, it won't matter what they learn from Audy, because the rest of the Clans will be follow on forces in numbers we won't be able to cope with."

"It is a lot of trust to place in one man, who comes from the enemy." Montrose addressed Audy directly, "I mean no disrespect to your honor saying that."

"You are trusting me now." Audy replied.

"I'm sorry?" Montrose replied.

Audy stood at the foot of the table and pointed around the room. "You are all the war leaders of your people, of the highest rank and experience. You have men and women to follow you, to fight for you. You are the people that will train your people to fight and who will lead them."

Kyle's eyes flashed to Hank who was already looking at him. Audy was suddenly off script, ad-libbing. For someone with an alien mindset and a limited vocabulary, that was a bad place to be.

"Audy? What are you saying?" Pretty asked.

"I am not saying," Audy drew his side arm and laid it on the table in front of him. "I am showing. If I wanted to assist the Kaerin," he reached into his thigh pocket and pulled out a claymore mine and tossed it on to the table next to the .45 that Kyle's Dad had given him. He reached for his other leg pouch and deposited a grenade on the table.

"I could do much more, simply killing as many here as I am able, before Kyle, Jake or Carlos killed me. They are the only other people armed within this room. Without you, your people would be as sheep against the clans. Even with your tools and your aircraft, sooner or later you will have to fight."

Kyle had one hand on his own sidearm and let out a breath of relief as Audy walked up one side of the table towards Montrose away from the weapons he'd laid out.

Audy stopped in front of the Frenchman whose face had gone scarlet.

"Captain, I have no clan left. I lost that when I came here. I have only my own honor. I have given my word to Kyle that I will do all that I can, to help the Jema see the path they must take and all that I can to help your people. It is the same path."

Montrose nodded stiffly at Audy and then turned to Colonel Pretty. "I believe you have already made a decision. No? I do not like the decision and I do not agree that this option must be employed, but I sincerely hope I am wrong."

Audy nodded at Montrose solemnly. "You will locate the Jema camp and I will go to them." Audy gave the room his best smile, failing miserably. Audy was a handsome guy, but his forced smile, big eyes and jumping eyebrows made him look like a homicidal maniac. "I will give them offer they can't refuse. A day in which our blood debt to the Strema can be paid."

*

Chapter 8

"Hell of a way to spend Christmas." Kyle was standing next to his father watching the distant mortar team run through its exercise with binoculars. They hastily broke down their tubes, loaded the base plates, tube, and ammo into the jury-rigged gear carrier welded to the outside of an aircar that looked to have had its roof removed via a blow torch. Gear loaded, the four-man crew jumped into the 'convertible,' moments before the overloaded aircar clawed its way off the ground.

"They keep this up," Kyle answered, letting the binoculars hang from his neck, they might live to see another." He was impressed with the exercise he'd just seen. The mortars, and the teams running them had been great. That said, the aircars were not military vehicles, not even close. These early models they had converted into Eden style *'technicals'* – a distant cousin to the Toyota Hi-Lo truck found in every shithole war back on Earth, worried him.

"Your idea to coordinate the targeting with that UAV feed?" He asked his dad.

Roger Lassiter just smiled back at him and shook his head. "Nope, that nugget came from none other than Lupe Vasquez."

The look on his face must have said it all.

His dad shrugged. "You remember Randy's new Deputy? Theo Giabretti? He and Lupe have been using drones to track that herd of buffalo that took out way too much of our winter grain field just by walking through." The elder Lassiter pointed up at the UAV over their firing range. "Lupe's idea."

"Lupe Vasquez? Same Lupe that took a shit on Roger's police cruiser? The Lupe that..."

His dad stopped him with an upraised hand. "He's earning his keep, more than. Hasn't been drinking. Theo straightened his shit out. Course, I think this place had a lot to do with it, a new start and all."

Theo Giabretti, the former Cruise Ship bartender and Marine Corps veteran was now the Deputy Sheriff of Chief Joseph and had been adopted by the community. The same community most of the people from his hometown had settled in, including his parents. Chief Joe was also home to the volunteers that made up this new mortar squad his dad had just trained up. Chief Joe was no different than most settlements. They were enthusiastically behind the defense of their world and the numbers of volunteers proved that. It would be a different story the first time they lost some of the hometown militia. He knew he was worrying too much about it. He wasn't sleeping for shit.

Col. Pretty had pulled him aside over a beer and counseled him. Every one of these men and women joining the militia had a hometown, or a family. The ones he knew personally would hurt all the more if or when something happened. But Pretty had been very clear that nothing would destroy their morale quicker than the slightest whiff of nepotism. He knew he'd have to put these people, some of whom he had known all his life at risk along with everybody else.

Kyle pointed back at the UAV which was circling lower in preparation for landing. "I like it, Lord knows we don't have trained Forward Air Observers. Do you have an SOP I can share out?"

"For the newly christened AMMS, yes." His Dad pointed at an approaching team in their aircar. It looked like a barely air worthy beetle, with too much luggage tied to its shell.

"Air Mobile Mortar Squad?" Kyle asked.

"You're smarter than you look."

"I was well-schooled," Kyle defended himself.

"Genetics," his dad answered.

Kyle laughed and gave up. "The SOP?"

"You can share it out. It's training ready. Four, four-man teams or cars to a squad. One tube to a car. Four tubes per squad, sixteen militia. If I was designing from the ground up, and we had decent aircars with more lift, I'd add another man to each car and maybe another tube."

"That'd take a new production line, and that list is beyond full."

"Oh, I know," his dad waved the suggestion off. "I'm just talking. All in all, I think of our operational M.O. as high-tech Muj."

Kyle smiled and raised an eyebrow in question.

"Shoot and scoot, muj style. Cept' we'll hit a lot harder. Those new mortar rounds they are getting to us are the real deal, but supply seems to be the big issue."

Not turning out fast enough, Kyle thought to himself. He'd already apologized for the limited number of rounds they had for training. Nano-production was great, in that you could build almost anything or the components for almost anything as long as you had the feeder stock and a template. What they didn't have was enough production beds, or at the moment, enough assembly shops where people would put together the nano-constructed parts to make finished products. Whether it was a new air car or an air-to-ground missile, the nano-constructed parts still needed assembly.

They could build assembly robots, but that would necessitate detailing several production lines to those parts. It was a lot faster to nano-produce parts and assemble by hand. At the moment, twenty percent of their nano output was dedicated to producing additional capacity in the form of new production beds, rather than turning out war material. The first problem was being worked, it was just a matter of time before the production levels caught up with demand.

Assembly plants were springing up everywhere there was a hint of free capacity on the nano-production side. Most of that extra capacity was in and around New Seattle, and they were quickly re-creating the problem of Seattle becoming the center of all things. At the moment, it was the destination of choice for everyone with an entrepreneurial, patriotic, bureaucratic, or political leaning. It was already causing issues with the Program's die-hards. Their planned glide slope into a series of sustainable 'local' economies spread across the world was going down in flames in the face of the existential threat posed by the Chandrian invasion. Which brought him back to the question at hand.

"Supply is a problem just about everywhere, for anything we don't have warehoused. You'll have ammo waiting for you in your staging area, no need for you to travel with it." Kyle paused and looked back at his dad. Time for the hard part of this trip.

"How long before we can get them out to St. Louis Center?"

"They're rough Kyle," his Dad pointed at the approaching squad as they flared their nacelles to begin landing about a hundred yards off. "My best team leader was a plumber in La Paz six months ago. She's a natural leader, and a damned savant laying in the mortar. I'm still teaching her to drive... fly, you know what I mean."

Kyle barked a short laugh but waited for the response to his question.

"I need a month, and I can give you two full squads as long we get another four aircars and enough ammo to train."

Kyle just shook his head in sympathy. "The Central group has already reached the Mississippi, at least its advance elements. They're building a massive camp. Whatever you have now, this squad, I need them in a week."

"A week?"

"From the size of the encampment they're building, they're going to be grouped up. We assume to build boats or barges for the spring thaw. We need to hit them now."

"You'll lose some to dumbass mistakes a couple more weeks of training might prevent."

He knew that. His dad knew, he knew that.

"This squad, one week." The senior Lassiter wasn't happy.

Kyle nodded. "I have to start whittling them down, I'm worried we've already waited too long. These groups disperse? And we'll suddenly need to protect numerous settlement sites, and we aren't set up for that. Our civilians aren't either, too many of our volunteers are used to watching war on TV."

His Dad slapped a heavy hand on his shoulder. "Son, by the end this, there will be no civilians. I think more of them realize that, than you give them credit for. Just do your job and try to keep as many of yours alive and in the fight as long as you can."

Kyle nodded in appreciation. His Dad didn't quite understand. They were all his people.

*

Three inches of fresh dry powder atop the foot of old snow hid all but the tops of the stakes he had hammered out to claim his homestead site months ago. He wasn't that concerned; he'd chosen this location well outside the range of where most of the residents of Chief Joseph were in the process of homesteading. He was well into the tree line above what had been Wallowa Lake. Snow and spring fed streams flowed down the mountain on either side of him and he had or would have a view of the entire lake once he was finished. If, the log house he planned was ever built. The war was here and he wasn't sure he'd ever get back to actually build the damn thing, let alone surprise Elisabeth with it.

He'd found time during one of his training stints in Chief Joseph to fell the trees and clear the initial footprint for the cabin. Those he had debarked and stacked as best as he, Carlos, Jake and Audy could manage, to season. He brushed the snow off the end of a log and sat, trying to picture what it would look like. He was mentally marking trees that he'd have to take out, when the whine of an aircar broke through the sound of the creaking trees that had been gently swaying and dropping their loads of fresh powder. *And there goes my New Year's Day.*

The aircar circled down into the small clearing below and he was surprised to see Audy jump out. Dressed in a heavy barn jacket, wool watch cap and dark sun glasses the Chandrian looked like anybody else walking around the streets of Chief Joe. Kyle shook his head, smiling to himself. It was sometimes easy to forget Audy had grown up on an alien world amidst an even more alien culture. At other times, nothing could be more apparent.

Audy walked slowly, sinking up to just below his knees in the snow.

"Audy, what are doing up here?" he half yelled.

Audy waved and kept steadily climbing with his characteristic economy of motion.

"You believe you'll be able to live here? After?" Audy stopped at the edge of the building site, looking around.

"Figured this was my last chance to get up here, remind me of the future we're fighting for."

Audy nodded in agreement. "Homes that may not be built, lives that may not be lived."

"Something like that." Kyle agreed. "By the way, how did you find me? I got twelve hours down time, on orders from the Colonel, and pointedly left my compad in town."

"Your mother told me," Audy brushed a log free of snow and sat. "I must say, your mother's cooking is my favorite thing on this planet."

Kyle grinned back at him. "Means she likes you, she'll be trying to find you a wife soon."

Audy was quiet for a moment. "There is a woman with my clan, if she lives, that I would join with."

"Really," Kyle was surprised. "You've never mentioned that before, I just assumed you were unattached."

Audy shrugged. "Because I have, as Jake says, been conducting extra-terrestrial diplomacy?"

"I'm not judging you Audy." Kyle laughed.

"We don't have the worries about such things as your people," Audy explained. "Comfort is taken where it is offered. I am a good cultural ambassador for my people."

Kyle laughed and punched Audy in the arm. "You just made a joke, Audy!"

Audy smiled at him. "I'm told I am a very good ambassador."

"Great to hear." Kyle bit back on the 'TMI' he wanted to say as he didn't think Audy would understand.

"Audy, why are you here?"

"Col. Pretty says that we are good to go." His friend held up a single thumb that always accompanied the statement. This time he rolled his eyes and shook his head. "I do not understand when he says, it's been approved. By who does he mean? He is the leader, no?"

Kyle was fairly certain Audy had a better idea of the growing bureaucracy and the attendant checks and balances that he and Colonel Pretty had to deal with, than he let on.

Kyle wasn't in the mood to hear Audy's opinion on how stupid the 'sharing' of authority was in a time of war, again. He let the question slide.

"You sure this will work?" Kyle asked, feeling his mountain cabin slide further away into a future that may not be. "What are the chances they don't shoot you, on sight?"

Audy smiled to himself, looking out at the ice rimmed lake far below them. "I am Audrin'ochal, they *will* let me speak."

"And after you have spoken?"

"I will not be shot. The Jema, if they do not believe me, will treat me as a traitor. Some there, will already believe me to be a traitor. But I think they will let me speak. We do not shoot traitors. It is something... else. You ... I don't think have a word for it. But it is not quick."

"Well there's that." Kyle shook his head, not wanting to imagine what the 'something else' was. "I'd hate to see you get shot."

Audy turned back to him. "As Jake would say, the dog is worth hunting. Yes?"

Kyle laughed. "That's almost the right usage, close. How many times have I told you? Jake is just about worst language tutor you could pick."

Audy nodded knowingly, suddenly serious again. "Jake enjoys teaching me falsely, I know this. But it helps me learn."

"For example," Audy said changing the subject. "Do you realize, how much of your speech, among you soldiers is about your games of chance? I did not understand this saying 'Chances are.' It made no sense to me until I realized it was close to someone saying, 'there's a good chance'."

Kyle just looked at Audy and tilted his head in question.

Audy stopped him from speaking with a palm held out. "And then, there are *the odds,* the odds are good, the odds are, the odds are bad. So much is about the chances or the gambles you take. You don't even think twice about it. It is accepted in your culture, most among your soldiers. You say, time for a

Hail Mary when odds are bad, but you don't have a choice? Is this correct?"

Kyle actually had to think about it for a second. "I guess. Do you even know what a Hail Mary is?"

Audy ignored the question and was silent for a moment. "I think me going to the Jema is not a Hail Mary, the odds are better than that. There is an OK chance, not fourth down. And I think odds are good, the dog will hunt."

Kyle just shook his head trying not to laugh. Audy had clearly been thinking about this particular conversation for some time. "Ok, if we stick to the football metaphor, maybe you mean third and long, or maybe fourth and one. Hail Mary is literally, a last-ditch attempt, very low odds of success. Third and long is tough, but manageable, it just might work."

Audy nodded in understanding. "I like this football, but I still don't understand it well. Hunting dogs have no role in the game? Correct?"

"Jake tell you that?"

"I did not believe him." Audy answered, shaking his head. "This, me going to the Jema, it is an acceptable risk that I go, so third and long."

"I agree Audy," Kyle said. "But I don't like it."

Audy just looked at him with an inscrutable look of confusion. "What does that have to do with the price of tea in China?'

Kyle flashed him a thumb's up. "Correct usage, and you're right, not a damn thing."

"I don't understand that expression at all," Audy replied. "It seemed the correct usage though.

"It was." Kyle answered. "I'm amazed at how fast you have picked up our language, I guess all that diplomacy has helped huh?"

"Now you make a joke. But yes, I study hard."

"You know there are people that think you will get there, and tell the Jema how few we are, like Capt. Montrose."

"His concerns are well made," Audy said. "Do you think you are gambling with me?"

"Not in the sense of distrusting you. I trust you, you know that. But yes, it's a huge gamble to send you."

"You must continue gambling, Kyle. Doing your Hail Mary's – it's something people of my world do not do. Are not allowed to do. They will have a plan and they will ... follow... that plan, always. You are few, but your tools are far beyond ours and you understand the ... power of taking chances. You will fight them in a way they will not understand, not just your air forces," Audy waived at the sky. "Which will be as magic to them. Men like you, Jake, and Carlos have the right to do in battle as you see fit, no matter the plan. A Chandrian, even a Jema, who are the most free in our thinking, will take orders to battle and die with those orders in his hand. But you, you can..."

"Call an audible..." Kyle nodded in understanding.

"Football? Or hunting with dogs?" Audy asked.

Jake had been having way too much fun screwing with Audy's English lessons. "Football - a play or a tactic is decided before the play begins. But the quarterback or leader, once he sees the defense, can change the plan. He calls an audible on the field before they start."

"Yes, this is exactly what I mean." Audy was excited and nodded to himself. "A Chandrian leader would be scourged for doing so, even if he were successful – especially if he were successful. Others must not see something like that succeed. Control is everything."

"We know, Audy. We've been listening to you. We'll use that against them."

"You must." Audy waived at the sky again. "Your jets cannot be everywhere I think."

Kyle nodded in agreement. Truer words had never been spoken.

"There is another gamble of which I must speak, but I do not wish to. I do not want you to change your decision in letting me go."

"No promises, but what?"

Audy stood up and paced in a small circle kicking at snow. "Our technology is well behind yours, but we have some medicines that are very powerful. They are much used by the Kaerin and important in controlling the clans. The Kaerin and those among each clan, even the Jema who control most of our technology, the Gemendi, science - priests I think you would call them - they can make a man speak the truth. A translation would be heart speak."

"Truth serum?"

Serum?" Audy asked.

"A drug, a truth serum, that makes you tell the truth."

"You have this? Why did your people not use this on me when you found me?"

"We couldn't exactly understand each other, Audy. By the time you knew our language, you had gained our trust."

Audy glanced skyward and shook his head in what may have been disgust. "I'm surprised you did not use this method, it would have been wise to do so."

"Not our way, Audy."

"Foolish of you. But I understand we are different."

No doubts there, Kyle knew.

"If my clan leaders allow me to speak, they will use the heart speak ...the serum. I will tell them what my heart feels is true, the drug is very strong. It cannot be ... tricked. If I do not convince them to join with you, should they stay true to the Kaerin's writ, they will ask other questions."

"And you know a lot." Kyle kicked at some snow himself. "Not good."

"The heart speak will help my argument, improve our odds, but depends on...

"...the questions they ask, I get that." Kyle finished for him. "That puts a different spin on things."

Audy was silent and looked around him at the mountains. Kyle could sense Audy was getting ready to unload verbally. It was probably a speech he'd rehearsed. He couldn't fault his friend, compared to himself, Audy was the Einstein of learning a new tongue. Sadly, most people were compared to him.

"Sometimes the odds are balanced by truth, my people respect truth." Audy held up a single finger curling it into a fist as he spoke. "One truth is above all else. They hate the Strema and the Kaerin that control them. But seeing a new truth is hard. They are all here, all that is left of my people. I know... they have to know by now, they were brought here to die. Cannon fodder is your word for it. Hope can be a truth as well. I have hope, because of my trust in you and your people, they will hear that from me. Now - they have none."

"What?" Kyle rubbed at the headache that had suddenly sprouted between his eyes. "What exactly are you saying?"

"I think I have an audible." Audy grinned.

Kyle just looked at him for a moment. "I'll listen."

"They need to hear of the freedom that they could have here. From someone that can convince them that my words are more than just my... heart's hope. When they question me, they will hear the truth of what I believe. But I could believe a lie."

"You want me to go with you?"

Audy breathed a sigh of relief and nodded. "They would use the heart speak on you, and me as well, to translate. It makes the odds much better I think. Maybe as good as fourth and one."

"Audy, you're killing me here. How much football have you actually watched?"

"One contest at the local school, and one recording of the greatest team ever, the LSU Tigers with..."

"With Jake, I get it. So, you think fifty – fifty? The odds I mean."

"Better," Audy shook his head once. "Maybe six out of ten. Maybe."

"That's if they don't shoot us on sight." He could only laugh.

Audy smiled down at him and thumped his own chest. "They won't shoot *me*, I am Audrin'ochal."

*

Chapter 9

God was laughing at them, he was sure. The temperature had dropped fast during the last eighteen hours since the snow storm, and the mercury if anyone were still using the stuff would have hovered around ten degrees Fahrenheit. The Blue Mountain Brigade, having readied their mortar squad, would be among the first volunteer Militia, to go up against the Chandrians and they were deservedly proud of the fact. Kyle watched the men and women in groups outside the air buses joking and trading e-mail addresses with new friends. Little did they know there wasn't much in the way of free bandwidth to be sending shout out and status checks with friends and family.

The sooner these people realized this was for real, the better. For the moment they had more volunteers than they could train effectively. To the point, Colonel Pretty had decided to recreate a system the United States had employed just prior to its entrance into World War I. The Lilliputian US Army had suddenly realized that it needed numbers far beyond what its existing training capacity allowed. Instead of ingesting all the available recruits immediately, they took in only what they could realistically train and built up from that cadre.

Never far from his mind, was the sobering fact that if they got their asses handed to them, the negative impact on recruitment back in the settlements, would be hard to turn around. These first trainees barely had time to learn basic military discipline. There had been no time wasted in learning how to march in formation, how to turn out a clean foot locker, or how to properly salute. They'd had time for only three or four weeks of intensive skills-based training. They learned how to shoot, how to maintain their weapons, and how to follow orders.

The mortar unit trained by his father aside, the Blue Mountain Brigade had a single artillery battery of four 105 mm howitzers, the rest of the soldiers were infantry. How or even if, they would stand behind their guns in the face of the enemy was an unknown. *The* unknown, he corrected. They were training the trainers as fast as they could, and he had no doubt that some of these people waiting to board the airbuses would eventually find themselves veterans and be sent back to help train up the next batch of recruits. He was just as sure some wouldn't come back. He knew they accepted that in an academic sense. It would be different the first time they saw action. It always was.

The entire volunteer force from Eastern Oregon, Central and Eastern Washington and the Snake River Valley settlements in Idaho were marshaled here, just outside of what had been Baker City, Oregon back in the day, on another planet. The settlement here was just called "Blue Mountain" now, and the four howitzers he watched being loaded into air trucks were the heaviest ground firepower they possessed at the moment. Chief Joseph had what he thought of as their most effective militia force, he'd witnessed the wringer his father had put the group through. Exactly four mobile mortar teams, four tubes.

He had no doubt most of them were relieved to get out from under Roger Lassiter's thumb, but he knew they were a lot closer to ready than most of the raw infantry units that had mustered in from central Washington and Idaho. Those groups had a solid three weeks of boot camp and basic instruction to fall back on. It wasn't nearly enough, but it was all they'd had time for.

The whole group, numbering 1140 men and women, would board the transports and fly out to a base that Jake and his team had been frantically building southwest of where St. Louis had been. The infantry he would leave there for now, for additional seasoning as Col. Pretty called it. They would be joined by other groups arriving from other settlements, some from as far away as Chile and Argentina.

Jake, Carlos, Jeff, Hans, and Arne and some of Col. Pretty's Green Berets would work to scare the living shit out of them until they were ready. The mortar teams, due to their mobility, he planned to put to use immediately. That and of course the

F-35 Joint Strike Fighters, the four Marine VTOL FB versions that were based in North Carolina with General Majeski.

They'd decided on turning out the venerable but ancient in military terms, A-10 Warthog rather than more F-35s. They needed numbers and the A-10 was a great deal less sophisticated and easier to produce than more JSFs. That said, the first two A-10s were three months away from being finished. He and Pretty had won that argument over just about every flyboy they had, which admittedly wasn't a lot, but more than he would have imagined. There were two German Air Force pilots, cousins, both former JSF pilots back on Earth 1.0 who would take delivery of the Warthogs and Kyle was a lot more excited about that prospect than they probably were.

He checked his compad again for the weather report. North America was experiencing its coldest winter in a decade and so far, old man Winter was their MVP as far as he was concerned. They'd be moving out ahead of one storm front, and flying through another getting across the central plains. They'd get there, and a day later it would have continued its eastern track and would hit them again. Of course, it would lay into the Chandrians central group, the Strema, with equal abandon.

He watched as one of the airbus drivers shot a flare gun into the cold, heavy air, and the men and women of the brigade grabbed their personal gear and began piling into the massive aircraft. The transports looked like overgrown greyhound buses abandoned in the middle of a field. Their massive turbine nacelles three to a side looked like giant warts.

He'd grown up with some of these volunteers. Dean Freeburn and he had played baseball together from t-ball to American Legion ball and he commanded one of the mortar units. His son Jake, who Kyle had bounced on his knee when he was home after basic so many years ago, was now 17 and out there as well.

He was going to see some of them killed in the next few months or however long this took. He'd be calling for reinforcements before they were ready. He suddenly had an image of having to tell Dean that his orders had gotten Jake killed. Kyle felt the bile rising his gut and he wiped at some snow that might have melted on his cheeks.

"Permission to speak freely? Sir." Cynicism dripped off of every syllable.

Kyle turned in place to see Carlos standing there watching the procession alongside of him. He hadn't heard the man approach. Then again, most people who had experienced that with Carlos, were dead.

"Since when do you ask for permission?"

"Since I saw you standing there watching your troops, like a sad general in some shitty old war movie."

"That bad?"

Carlos smiled as him. "Stop worrying, mi hermano." His friend shrugged, "they know they are in for a world of hurt, hell if anything, these shit sticks are buying into the idea of sacrifice a little too much. They sure as shit, don't need to see 'The Man' worrying over them. Kick em in the ass, they expect that. The sackless wonders need it. Don't be sugar coating this in your own cabeza, Kyle." Carlos slapped his own head and took a step closer to him.

"We're gonna lose a bunch of them. Fuzz nuts and heroes alike. Your *only* job is to make it count." Carlos dipped his own head looked him in the eye hard, almost a physical challenge, as only Carlos could do. His friend was half bent. Kyle had been there himself and made it back. Carlos had been on the mend, and now a new war was throwing him back into it. Anyone dealing with Carlos over the last week would have said the guy had his 'game face' on. Kyle though, knew it wasn't a mask and it was far more than skin deep.

He could feel the same pull on his own psyche. His lizard brain getting ready, shutting down emotions that could cause hesitation when he could least afford it. Worse, he knew he was in the process of cutting off emotions and feelings that would only increase the pain when shit went sideways. Not if, when. Shit always went sideways.

"Your only job," Carlos leaned in a little closer until his face was inches away from his own. "Don't waste em, make it count."

Kyle nodded at his friend. He needed his ass kicked occasionally too. "You done with the pep talk?"

Carlos grinned and pulled his head back. "All done amigo, feel free to deport my ass for insubordination anytime."

Kyle spit a stream of tobacco juice onto the ground and looked back at Carlos. "I'm going to call on you too, Carlos. You're gonna get red, real red."

Carlos's eyes met his own. "Understood, just make it count this time."

Kyle nodded. He didn't have a choice. Not this time. Win or lose, it was going to count.

"Will do and thank you."

Carlos held both hands out to his side and shrugged in apology. "Motivation by Carlos, it's why I'm here."

He smiled at the sniper's back as Carlos walked away, actively looking for a slow-moving soldier to yell at.

Carlos, Jake, the other knuckle-draggers and hell even Audy, in some strange interplanetary bleeding over of experiences, they all understood. They were all brothers. The wolves were just outside the door, and they guarded those who could not guard themselves. It was the old way. This time they were fighting for hearth and home. If a war could be right, this was it. They'd either win or be dead. There would be no negotiations, no cease fires and no surrender. They were going to get red indeed.

"Sir?"

Kyle turned back around to see Lupe Vasquez standing there. He did a double take, confused. Lupe looked like a different person. He clearly had his shit together. Not a just 'took a shower and shaved' shit together, he looked tight.

"Lupe? What can I do for you?"

"Kyle, I mean Sir..."

Kyle stopped him with a wave. "Lupe, I went to kindergarten and graduated high school with your sister. It's just us here, you can call me Kyle."

Lupe looked a little embarrassed and maybe a little mad. Kyle didn't think it was directed at him.

"I'd rather say, 'Sir.' I'm going to ask you for a favor. I want to go with the mortar teams and I need to ask my Commander, not, ... the guy..." Lupe stammered, "well the guy from my home town."

"Lupe," Kyle started, "my dad told me how much you've helped out, the remote planes, the UAVs? Do you have any idea how many lives you probably saved with that idea? You need to stay and train up the next batch. You are very much needed there. Who knew spotting antelope out of season would be so valuable, huh?"

"This next group has a real army dude that ran his platoon's UAV in Africa. He'll be better at it than I'll ever be. This group," Lupe jerked a thumb at the air buses, which were beginning to fire their turbines, "all they have are the guys I trained, they need me. You know I can shoot and I don't back down from no fight. You know that too."

Kyle nodded in agreement with that. Lupe had the reputation as being more than willing to throw down, whether he was asked to or not. Of course, Lupe had usually been drinking when that happened. He looked at the man in front of him, and had to admit that he was a different human being from who he'd been back home.

"Lupe...

"I'm not the same guy, Kyle." Lupe rubbed his nose. "I ain't had a drink in five months, and yes, hell yes I want one. I ain't gonna bullshit you.

"Lupe...

"People look at me different now, people who didn't know me before, the other settlers. Even the folks from back home look at me different, most of all, when I see my face in the mirror, I see someone different. That old Lupe, I want to kill him and bury him so deep he ain't nuthin but a bad dream. I want to fight. I need to.

"Lupe!" Kyle interrupted him just as he started to say something else.

"Sir?"

"You brought your gear with you?"

"Yes, sir." Lupe stood at attention.

"Go get it and wait at bus four. If this new troop with UAV experience is real, and I'm gonna check, you can load up."

"I won't let you down, Kyle."

Kyle nodded, "I know you won't."

Lupe grinned back at him. "I'm gonna go get my stuff, Sir."

Kyle watched him jog to the marshalling area. *One more to feel guilty about.*

He shook his head in disbelief. Burned out Marine snipers, a Peruvian plumber and reformed alcoholic poachers. They just might have a chance. He checked his six to see who else was lurking, but he was alone. So very alone. It was time to go kick some ass.

*

January 6

Kyle's headache was just starting to recede. Moving east with just the one scrapped together militia brigade had been a logistical nightmare. The initial scene at St. Louis base, the mustering area for all of N. America had been an epic goat rodeo. Arne, whose original MOS in the Norwegian Navy had been logistics, had quickly remembered his early training. It didn't hurt that he'd grabbed one Program supply tech by the throat and lifted him off the ground with one arm, when he'd heard a lame excuse one time too many, for why gear wasn't being matched with an arriving unit. The local supply situation had shown a marked improvement soon after.

For the moment, the Chandrian Central group had stopped and set up shop near what had been Minneapolis/St. Paul back on earth. Kyle watched them through powerful imaging binoculars from a ridge line, three miles south on the west side of the river. The magnified scene in his scope reminded him of old pictures of a Civil War encampment. The Chandrians had constructed breast works across the entire perimeter and timber observation towers sprouted along it every hundred meters or so. There was a sea of canvas tents in orderly rows and every single one of the bastards looked to be hard at work laying waste to the heavy forests surrounding the area, building every kind of boat and raft imaginable. Already, dozens were complete and stacked on the frozen banks of the river. Larger, flat bottomed barges, some complete, others in differing stages of construction, sat on log rollers waiting to go south down the river with the spring melt.

The archaic looking camp was about to get a lesson in 21st century warfare. He was going to kill a great many people in the next few minutes. He reminded himself that this group would be reinforced if they felt they had a chance of winning. He was going to take them down as brutally as possible. Audy had told them, time and time again, that there was no quit in the Chandrian clan system and they would literally fight to the last man. Kyle took that on advisement, but he also knew Audy had never witnessed the kind of firepower they were about to unleash. If their count was accurate there were somewhere north of a hundred and thirty thousand men down there. The Strema, or Snake Clan, Chandra's version of the Waffen SS preparing to cut North America in two at the Mississippi.

"Lightning flight on station..." The radio bud in his ear almost surprised him. Somewhere, well behind him and above the clouds, four JSF F-35 Lightnings, the Marine VSTOL model, were loaded for bear and waiting to start the welcome to Eden party.

Kyle didn't take his eyes from his binoculars. "Light it up," he ordered Carlos.

Carlos had a laser target designator, a gift from Dr. Jensen, on a tripod mount in front of him. It was a little bigger than a high-power spotting scope but it split a laser beam into multiple adjustable fractals that Carlos could use to outline the camp below them, drawing invisible lines around the target area. Invisible to everyone with the exception of Carlos's view through the scope, the sensor suites on the attack jets above them and the terminal guidance modules of the weapons it carried. Precision strikes could come later, this was going to be a shotgun blast of high-power ordnance.

"Lightnings have the porch light."

"Come on in, Lightnings – not a party without you."

"Roger Ground, Inbound."

"They sound like real pilots." Kyle said to Carlos.

Carlos kept his focus on the laser designator. "They are, two of them have been flying puddle jumpers up in Alaska, the other two ... for some airline."

A minute later they observed the activity in the camp slowly come to a halt as the rumble of the jets slowly grew. The new F-35s, specifically the Lightning II's were more than capable of supersonic flight, but Kyle didn't want to use that trick yet. Let the enemy get used to the sound of death first, then he'd start delivering it with no warning.

"No more easy work days." Carlos intoned.

Kyle glanced over at his friend who was grinning ear to ear.

Most of the Chandrians were looking skyward when some of them started pointing. Many ran for where their weapons were stacked in neat, upright lean-to piles. Many of the enemy just stood in place, not understanding what they were hearing.

Kyle was watching carefully through his binoculars. He saw more than a few Chandrians glance towards the large structure in the center of the northern half of the massive camp as if they were looking for guidance or orders. Kyle smiled to himself, and noted that a great many of the Chandrians had been in the middle of burying the structure under ten to fifteen feet of dirt... *command bunker*.

The first jet came in about five hundred feet off the ground, following the river, its payload doors open. The cluster bombs it released wobbled in flight as they seemed to glide below the track of the fighter. Each successive bomb 'shattered' into multiple warheads that were retarded by small parachutes. Each of the hundreds of anti-personnel softball sized bomblets drifted down quickly until the leading edge of the dispersal was two to three feet off the ground at which point their proximity fuses fired.

The giant string of massive firecrackers ripped across and through the enemy encampment shredding anything caught within twenty meters of a bomblet. Originally designed to fire a secondary charge straight down into the surface of a runway, these were nothing more than massive grenades, distributed over an area the size of three football fields. There were a lot of bomblets, a lot of shrapnel.

The second jet flowed in over their heads just as the first climbed out of sight. The rumble from the explosions of the first attack run was still echoing as it blended with the sounds of the approaching second jet which released eight 500-pound, guided bombs. The control units at the back of each bomb homed in on Carlos's laser targeting.

They felt the shockwave from the closely grouped series of explosions as just the slightest waft of air. One of the last bombs to detonate, struck an ammo or fuel dump because the secondary explosion was massive. Kyle cringed inwardly as he could see dozens if not hundreds of the enemy silhouetted within the fireball or flung up and outwards with a force much greater than any human could survive. The fireball continued to burn, so he was thinking fuel rather ammo, but he'd yet to see a single vehicle. The crater at the base of the fireball was three times the size as those left by the bombs themselves.

He was still watching through his scope as some of the surprised Chandrians fired their elephant guns at the third jet which had just began its run. It was a futile effort. Kyle filed away the scene, these troops were utterly inexperienced at defending against attacks from the air. The aircraft was miles downriver from the camp, coming in much higher than the first two planes had. This would be the FAE or fuel-air-explosive and would be targeting the southern perimeter of the camp where the boat building activity was focused along the river's edge. The river itself was frozen except a dark channel of open water thirty yards off shore.

"FAE!" he called out to Carlos. They were three miles away but Kyle still blew out hard emptying his lungs when he saw the big 2,800 lb. cylinder deploy. It looked like an extra-long oil barrel swinging from a small drag chute. It was nothing compared to the big Daisy Cutters or MOABs that could be ejected out the back of transport aircraft, but it was the biggest single piece of ordnance the JSF could manage. He almost felt sorry for the Chandrians who ignored the departing jet and fired at the big barrel that plummeted to earth on top of them.

They saw the primary explosion when the barrel was about 500 feet above the ground. It created a massive aerosolized fuel-air cloud directly over the target area. A small bolt of lightning, looking like a spark igniter on a gas barbeque fired and ignited the cloud. The massive fireball, and its attendant shockwave wave slammed out of the sky like the fist of God, crushing and burning everything and everyone beneath it. A second later they heard the characteristic two stage CRACK ... WHUMFF, followed by the shock wave which was a waft of wind blowing out from the camp for a split second, followed by another blowing back in as the near vacuum created by the expanding shock wave was rapidly refilled.

"Holy shit," Carlos laughed. "Clean up on aisle four."

"Too bad we only have a couple of those." Kyle's binoculars swung from one end of the camp to the other.

"Ground, Lightning Flight Lead, do you have a target for me?"

"Carlos, paint that bunker in the north half of the camp."

"Half-buried roof?" Carlos asked, not pulling away from his eyepiece.

"That's the one."

"Lots of shit in the air, concentrating beam...." Carlos manipulated the control at the base of his 'scope'.

"Ground, Lightning Lead – I have a single target designated."

"Affirmative Lightning Lead, go for target. Suspect command bunker."

"Roger, Ground, AGMs inbound."

Kyle couldn't track the fast-moving missiles which came out of the clouds diving almost straight down on the target. He thought there were four but might have been as many as six impacts. It was all lost in a large secondary explosion like nothing he had ever seen before. An electric blue mushroom cloud emerged from the remains of the target bunker crackling and discharging lightning within.

"Ground, Lightning Lead, we just registered an EMP spike– status?"

"Lightning Lead, Ground - secondary explosion looked electric in nature, never seen anything like it." Kyle spoke into the radio.

"Confirm no nuke, Ground."

Kyle looked down again and the spastic discharge was already gone, though it had started several fires among the piles of debris and scrap wood. One entire side of the log palisade was on fire. Through his binoculars the whole area looked like a massive set of Lincoln logs that had just had gallon of gasoline thrown at it and lit while ants slowly started moving again over the wreckage.

"Flight Lead, this is Ground, we confirm no nuke, say again, no nuke. Don't know what it was, negative on nuke."

Kyle hoped it was their jump gate or whatever they were planning on using to bring reinforcements.

"Ground, Flight Lead – we've got strafing ammo and fuel for a couple of passes, target?"

"Negative, Flight Lead, save your ordnance." Lord knows we are going to need it."

"Affirmative, Lightning flight, RTB"

"Commencing BDA. Well done, we'll see you again tomorrow."

Three minutes later, Kyle and Carlos were recording all they could for bomb damage assessment or BDA. The fires were still burning in places but neither of them could believe what they were seeing through their camera lenses.

"They're like fucking ants," Carlos shouted almost sounding hysterical. Kyle could well understand Carlos' emotion, he was sick to his stomach at what was occurring in the distant camp.

The manner in which the uninjured picked up their tools and returned to work was nearly as horrific as the others dragging dead bodies by one limb or another and tossing them into various bomb craters with all the thought and concern one would have for an old pair of boots.

Hard, didn't begin to describe what they were seeing. Corpsman, or whatever the Chandrian equivalent was, were running about patching people up or quickly killing those who were badly injured. As he watched a "healer" through his powerful binoculars, he felt as if he was witnessing something

131

truly alien in a non-human sense. A machete looking blade fell and an injured arm was tossed away like a bone for a dog. The screaming victim couldn't be heard, but Kyle could see the only thing on the ground were the man's heels and the back of his head as he arched his back in pain. The bleeding stump was cauterized with the flat of short handled spade, glowing red when the Chandrian 'corpsman' pulled it out from a small hibachi looking pot carried by a second. The man administering 'first aid' watched the now thankfully unconscious man for a second and shook his head. Reaching to his belt he withdrew a small knife and drove it into the man's temple and moved on to the next 'patient.'

They weren't human, ants indeed. Already, the camp was back at work, repairing damaged walls and building more boats as if nothing had happened. There would be no breaking these people. They would not stop. Audy had warned them, but hearing a description of an alien culture was one thing, seeing it in action was another entirely. They would have to kill every last one of them.

"Let's get out of here." Kyle muttered, his mouth was dry and it was suddenly far too easy to imagine what would happen to a settlement full of people if the Chandrians got to one before they could evacuate the settlers.

Carlos didn't look much better. But he had already taken down his laser designator and packed away the tripod and as he slid backwards down and out of his perch atop a bare rock, he stopped and looked at him.

"Command ain't gonna believe this shit."

Kyle tapped his binoculars. "I recorded it, they won't have a choice."

*

Chapter 10

Bres' Auch Tun had known nothing but war on behalf of the Kaerin for his entire life. To be honored with the command of the Strema war host was the stuff of dreams for any warrior. If all proceeded on this strange, empty world as decreed, he would soon be endowed with Kaerin status. For the moment, that mattered less than the fact the Strema were his clan and of his blood. Taking a world while leading the Strema host would ensure his uptake to the Kaerin, but what mattered to him most, was that the Strema clan and his name would echo for all time.

He had heard the strange rumbling growl of the Shareki airboats as they had approached the host's main encampment. He'd left camp that morning, for the purpose of seeing to the destruction of a small Shareki settlement, discovered by his outlying scouts and recently abandoned by whomever had lived there. There were many things about the settlement, or about these strange people in general, that they did not understand.

The Kaerin, though he would never voice his thoughts, had been less than helpful. They knew precious little of this world other than to say they had found the Shareki living here to be strangers to the way of war. Concerns and questions were dangerous, for the host and especially for war leaders like himself. Where were this world's Shareki? Where was the enemy? No doubt marching to him even now, he thought. When reports of the strange Shareki village reached him, he had felt the need to see it for himself. He would know this enemy before he destroyed them.

He had thought these Shareki strange, in that they did not challenge him in battle, the village confirmed his thinking. They built roads in their empty villages that ended abruptly, going nowhere. Their dwellings had dark windows on inner walls, that when activated showed images that were beyond the imagination. The whole settlement had a power source, buried, whose nature was beyond his Gemendi cadre to understand and those same technicians were given access to most, not all, but most of the Kaerin's technical knowledge.

Gaining an understanding of one's enemies was a difficult proposition when it seemed there were so few of them. Did they run from his host? Surely, they were preparing to meet him in battle? It mattered not, if they delayed. The mirror gate would be complete within a couple of days. Once its assembly was complete, he would be able to send a message to the Kaerin; that this world, while full of strange wonders, had offered little resistance. He was in no hurry to send such a message. There would be much honor to be gained in taking a world, and presenting it to the Kaerin. The harder the struggle, the more honor.

He had set out that morning with most of his senior officers and Gemendi cadre to explore the abandoned Shareki village. He had received the scout's reports and wished to see these strange things for himself before they destroyed the village. He had taken no pleasure in its destruction, as it was empty. It was the occupants of this world his writ implored him to destroy, not their edifices. On their return, they were almost within sight of their own encampment when the Shareki's flying boats appeared.

He had hurried his party to a hill top two ridges away from the Muddy River by the time the second flying boat had just finished its attack. The Shareki apparently took great offense at the destruction of their empty village to warrant such retribution. He had wanted to force an engagement, but nothing in his lifetime of experience could have prepared him for the power and speed of the Shareki airboats. He had flown in a Kaerin airboat one time. It had been a great honor for one not so ennobled, but that craft which he had thought powerful, could not have touched these incredible Shareki machines.

A third Shareki airboat appeared over the river moving faster than he could have imagined anything could move. It released a large object that seemed to drag a small parachute behind it. Such a strange weapon. Why would they attach a child's toy to a weapon?

The Fuel Air Explosive. The concept of such a thing was unknown to him. The massive fireball and the shockwave that bent the trees around them, snapping more than a few as it drove them all to hug the ground was easy to understand. The Kaerin had underestimated these Shareki, and perhaps this world was not as empty as he had believed.

He stood in shock and watched the rising fireball. His commanders and the Gemendi cadre stood behind him in silence. No one dared speak. The final attack was from an unseen airboat that was only heard in the far distance and its small weapons, leaving a thin trail of distorted air, moved far faster than even the airboats had.

They couldn't see the camp directly from their vantage point but they all recognized the impacted target when a large fireball of electric blue light erupted from the camp's location and boiled above the intervening hills.

"The mirror gate?" He asked the three Gemendi who accompanied him without turning away from the smoke, from the fires. The mirror was their sole means of communicating with the Kaerin on Chandra.

"Sir. That was definitely the battery pile's destruction. The mirror itself may be undamaged, but without impetus it will not function."

"Can another pile be constructed here?" his second in command, Bsrat'Auld asked.

"Not here, Sir. We don't have the material."

Or the knowledge, he knew. The Kaerin would not have shared that. Not even with their trusted Gemendi cadre.

"Could the source that powered the Shareki village be used?" Bsrat asked.

Bres'Auch Tun turned to look at his second. It was a very good question, Bsrat was no Gemendi, but it appeared he was doing their thinking for them.

"Possibly, Sir. But we destroyed the village and we would need time to come to understand their system of impetus."

"See that your people are prepared to do what they must," Bsrat replied stonily. "There will be other villages, Gemendi. Many more, I suspect."

Bres'Auch Tun nodded in agreement. *Would the destruction of each bring such retribution?*

"Come, let us join the host and prepare for battle. We have finally found the Shareki." The Strema had not faced defeat in over two hundred years, they would not let these strange birds of prey change that. He sat off on a loping run through the snow-covered ground, knowing his men would follow.

An hour later he stood alone atop an undamaged tower on the western perimeter of the camp looking at the craters of destruction filled with their dead. Sounds of Bsrat climbing the ladder behind reached him. No one else would have dared join him unbidden.

"Report." He asked without looking away from a rock outcropping that had taken a direct hit, the rock had been shattered and there was a carpet of dead in the surrounding area.

"The mirror is destroyed as well."

"Unfortunate," he answered without surprise. The central hall the Gemendi had under construction had been reduced to a smoking hole. He hadn't been expecting that anything within could have survived.

"There was no attack from the ground?" he turned and asked his second. Bsrat's face reflected his own sentiment of relief at a change of subject.

"Nothing, our scouts report nothing. Do you find that as strange as I do?"

He looked at his second in command and nodded. "It makes sense only in certain conditions."

"Sir?"

"Perhaps they are as few as we were beginning to suspect, or perhaps their host is still distant." *Or perhaps this is how they fight and airboats would be his only enemy.* He dared not speak that. He had his writ, and his writ was to destroy the Shareki. If they were all in airboats he did not see how this was possible and failing to carry out the writ was unthinkable.

"If either is the case, they would be wise to attack from the air again and often." Bsrat looked out at the destruction.

136

"What are our losses?"

"Still counting, Sir. My guess is close to four or five thousand."

An entire hand of warriors destroyed. Bres'Auch Tun knew he had one to blame but himself.

"They caught us penned up here, like wasps in a nest and applied a torch. That won't happen again. Disperse the host, before nightfall. Divide into eight kamarks, seven to march up and down the river, a half day walk from here and commence building fortifications, one kamark will remain here. One hand of each kamark will be posted on defense at all times, build a forest of towers. If airboats are all they have, we'll have some warning. If they find us difficult to see from the air in the forest, they'll have to come in and find us. We'll quickly learn how many they are."

"Sir." Bsrat bowed his head. "A wise strategy and if they attack a kamark on the ground, the others can assist and counter."

"Just so Bsrat. I made an error, I won't do so again."

"The Kaerin, Sir. We should have been told."

He just looked at Bsrat who should have known better than to question the Kaerin, even if they were a world away.

"Perhaps they did not know." It was as far as he was willing go in criticizing his masters.

"Of course, as you say, Sir."

Bsrat's response expressed the required amount of enthusiasm, just.

"The host remains Bsrat, and we will prevail, as we always do."

"Sir!" Bsrat saluted and turned to go.

"Bsrat, see to it that the Gemendi are sent to me. I must try to long message the other clans."

He despised the idea of warning the other clans, the Koryna and Jema that had been ordered to support the Strema. The Koryna, as the Kaerin dictated, had been yoked to the Strema for over a century. Whatever honor the Koryna gained here on this world would flow to the Strema and to him. The Jema were a different animal all together. That miserable excuse of

137

a clan, remnants of a once proud people, had no honor. They served no one beyond their attempts to regain what they had lost. It had been nearly thirty years since the Jema had rebelled, and all that remained of them were the grown children that had been allowed live as witness to their clan's undoing.

This world, would see the Jema's end; either at the hands of the Shareki or by his own. The Jema were to have been sent to the Shareki strongpoint far to the southeast in the hopes they would focus the Shareki there, even as they were destroyed. In the end, whether the Koryna and Jema clans lived mattered not at all. Only the Kaerin's writ and Strema honor mattered. He would use the others until they were destroyed. In the case of the Jema, if the Shareki did not destroy them, his host would. It was part of his writ.

When the history of this world was spoken, it would be his name and that of the Strema host alone that would echo. The Jema would be lost to history.

*

Hank was quiet as Paul watched the video of their first attack and the immediate aftermath that Kyle had recorded. For his part, he gazed out the window of Paul's office window in the middle of New Seattle. He'd watched the recording twice, more than enough to form an opinion.

The city, which they'd finally been able to 'de-populate' of the Noobs that had been too enamored of the Program's material largess, was quickly filling back up. Much of the industry behind the war production was centered here. A fact that was recreating the initial problem, driving the Program technocrats and especially the young Mr. Morales and his team crazy. This time, if there was a silver lining to be had, it was that the people flowing back into Seattle were working. It was still going to be a problem, especially for his friend behind the desk. He though, had different concerns keeping him awake at night.

Paul turned off his monitor and tossed the remote across his desk. Hank looked up and Paul was rubbing his eyes with both hands.

"I don't think I would have believed any of that, if I hadn't just seen it." Paul said.

"Did you catch Delgado's comment?"

Paul nodded. "Ants..." His friend looked up from his desk. "That's exactly what it was. We kicked an ant hill."

"Audy warned us," Hank had a foot crossed over his knee and he rubbed the knee that hadn't been quite right since being nearly blown up in Colorado, during his last few minutes on earth. "I thought, maybe I hoped, some of what he was saying was exaggerated."

"Or cultural pride," Paul nodded. "I've always believed him, but he described his culture at least parts of it, with some pride. I assumed some of what he said was hubris." Paul looked back at the blank flat screen, pointed at it. "But, that... there's no chance of integrating that."

Hank nodded in agreement. Kyle was headed into 'that.' A different clan to be sure; but how different could the Jema be to have survived in the same cultural ecosystem with the Strema? He knew battlefield psychology as well as anyone. Not just the troops under his command but that of the enemy. It was an essential part of the Special Forces' mission, which was to get behind the lines and gain the trust and eventually train allies among the indigenous population. Across his career, he'd had experience with every flavor of military culture Earth had to offer. The manner in which the Strema had reacted after the attack hadn't been human.

"Kyle and Audy leave St. Louis Base tomorrow for Fort Carolina," Hank spoke woodenly. "I know it's a different clan, but I like the idea of it less now than I ever did, but ..."

"But...it may be even more necessary," Paul finished the thought for him.

"Something like that, yeah."

"Elisabeth asked me to forbid him from going. She knew I didn't like the plan on principal."

"You couldn't have stopped him," Hank said. "Neither could I, he's convinced, as am I, especially now. We need a force, or an ally that can stand toe to toe with the Strema, while we can employ our firepower from a distance and from the air. We don't have the capability of pinning down a force like that, and won't for some time. They'd roll over our militia dying by the tens of thousands, taking us down by the thousands. In the end it's a numbers game, one we'd lose. I don't need to remind you we are against the clock as well."

"You didn't used to be such a pessimist," Paul smiled at him.

"I had a friend that convinced me to bring my family to a new world, I had a lot to look forward to then." Hank grinned back.

Paul shook his head as if waking from a bad dream, "God, what have I sentenced these people to?"

"Don't take me so seriously Paul. I'm a soldier at heart, we see the downside in everything. We still hurt them, ants or not. I've already put in an order with Dr. Jensen for a napalm deliverable. Unless their commander is a complete idiot, they are going to disperse and we may have to burn the forest down around them."

"Hopefully with them in it." Paul pulled a sick grimace, "I can't believe I just said that, or thought it. What is this war going to do to us?"

Hank remained silent. Paul was a close friend, but like most civilians he could never really appreciate the real toll of a war. At least not in the way that someone who had seen it up close and personal could. He'd had a commander tell him once that the military and those playing in the shadows of espionage were the 'sin eaters' of civilization. Doing things that the everyman wouldn't or couldn't imagine. Paul didn't have the stomach for this and Hank was glad for it. For himself, Kyle, the others who knew the score, they were soldiers. They would act so others could sleep safely. It had always been this way. Perhaps it always would.

"You saw that electrical explosion that coincided with the EMP spike the pilot reported?"

Paul nodded.

"What the hell was that? Their gate? Could they be sending people back? Getting reinforced?"

"I'll put my team on it," Paul answered, "but given their general low level of technology, no way it was a gate. A translation requires a level of power that we struggled with making mobile. You weren't involved, but the first mobile gate we translated here, for that first manned, round trip, had a small nuclear reactor powering it. It took several days to build up a stored potential that was sufficient to power the translation back home, and that was four people in the physical space of say a minivan."

Paul rubbed his hands together, shaking his head. "No, I think it was a massive battery storage, probably chemical in nature, for what I can only guess."

"So, guess..."

"They might have developed a way to communicate, send a signal back or receive one. It would still be power intensive, but orders of magnitude less than an actual translation. Just a theory, but it fits the evidence."

"Why didn't we do it then?" Hank asked.

"It utilizes extremely low frequencies, massive wavelengths, you basically turn the planet into an antenna. The signal, had we used that technique, would have been discoverable by any government or college science department on Earth. We never had a strategic need to communicate with Earth beyond the ability afforded by just translating an encrypted e-mail file. They perhaps, have developed a way to communicate with their home world."

Hank just raised his eyebrows, "I could really use an answer to that question, it could very well determine how we have to prosecute this fight."

"You have your field of expertise, I have mine." Paul nodded to himself, Hank knew his friend was a scientist at heart and was already working the problem. "Let me and my eggheads take a look at the data."

"They wouldn't have a need to send people back," Hank shook his head. "But a message? My God, we waited for them to stop and bunch up to hit them. What if they messaged back earlier? What would they have said? Other than no resistance encountered?"

"If I'm right," Paul was shaking his head, "and I usually am, it wouldn't be something that could be put up and taken down like an antenna. You'd literally have to dig the antenna in, turn the planet into a transmitter. Dig it in deep. And that half-buried housing that was the epicenter of the explosion? It wasn't complete, maybe we got lucky."

"In military parlance that is what is known as a fatal assumption."

"Unless you're correct." Paul wagged a finger at him. "Then you'd call it a calculated risk, a flash of brilliance."

Hank couldn't argue that point. "Speaking of calculated risks, if Audy and Kyle aren't successful, Kyle thinks a tactical nuke is our best bet, maybe our only play."

"No," Paul shook his head.

"I understand your principles Paul, but we might be talking about our survival here. We may not be able to afford those kinds of principles."

"And where would it lead?" Paul asked. "Say we survive and fifty years from now, some settlement becomes a political entity that wants some more real estate, or just hates their neighbors. It's just the same bullshit we all walked away from."

"If we don't survive this, Paul, fifty years from now is a pipe dream."

*

"Audy, my friend," Jake drawled. "For all your bullshit about these ass-munches being too stubborn to change tactics, somebody down there knows what he is doing."

Kyle had the aircar on autopilot circling high above the much expanded and dispersed enemy deployment. All three of them had binoculars out and watching. Occasionally a Strema would fire one of their massive rifles at them. For the most part, the enemy had clearly begun to recognize the high flying aircars as invulnerable spotters for the twice daily attacks from the F-35s. Kyle knew the first few air-to-ground missile, AGM equipped aircars were getting ready to go into production. He was looking forward to the surprise they would deliver. Each car could only carry one belly mounted missile but it would significantly increase the frequency and pace of their air attacks.

They'd need to, because the Chandrians were clearly learning how to avoid the worst of the air strikes. Their boat building was still suffering. Eventually the larger boats had to be brought out from under the forest to the water's edge, and there they could be destroyed. The best they could figure it, the Strema only took about a day or day and half to build a smaller boat. As soon as one was completed it was dragged under cover and all but impossible to spot from the air. It was time to start hitting them on the ground and the mortar teams were as ready as they were going to get without stepping out to gain some real experience.

Audy dropped his binoculars against his chest. "I was speaking of strategy, they will not be swayed in that. I did not say they were fools."

Kyle observed the smoke from the fires from that morning's airstrike. It was hard to discern what was a burning. A valid target? Or just surrounding forest? The Chandrian's monolithic camp was gone. In its place, spread out over a rough rectangle almost ten square miles in size, was a forest of observation towers and smaller camps which seemed to have sprouted like mushrooms after a Spring rain.

The ground spotters hadn't gotten close enough to laser anything in the central camp since the first day's strike. To do so, would have entailed threading a rat's nest of smaller camps and interlocking Strema patrols. It was clear a sizable portion of the Strema Clan was on guard duty, warding off an expected ground attack.

"Jake, I don't want the birds pounding solely on the boat building they manage to spot."

"Isn't that the goal?" Jake asked dropping his own field glasses and spitting into a Styrofoam cup while looking at him.

"If we force them to abandon the boats, they'll walk south. If I was them, I'd already be doing it. Divide my forces and march south along both sides of the river. I can't believe they are still preparing to float out, because they have to know we'll catch them on the river at some point. We'll hurt them bad, sitting ducks. On ground?"

Jake nodded in agreement. "We don't have the mass to stand against them."

"Not until we get the APC's here in the spring and I doubt we can get enough to stop them." Heavy lift capability was just something they didn't have a lot of and there weren't roads to transport supplies on. Infantry was far easier to move, but they didn't have enough of them either.

"I hear ya, boss man." Jake turned back toward the window, "I'll start taking the mortar teams in closer to the satellite camps, but the reception's liable to be ugly."

"They must not remain in one place for long," Audy commented. "The Strema will rush any local attack with speed. No matter the cost, to hold the enemy in place until the host arrives in force."

Kyle thought about the aggressiveness of the enemy. "You need to pull a rope-a-dope."

Jake looked at him for a moment, and then nodded with a grin. "Yeah... that might just work, I can see that. That's a lot of coordination to ask of green troops...

"What is a rope dope?"

Kyle smiled at Jake who turned around in the front seat to face Audy who was alone in the back. "Rope-a-dope... It's a term people who raise hunting dogs use."

Kyle couldn't hold in his laughter.

"So, I understand this is not about dogs?" Audy shook his head in disgust. "Yet again."

"Audy, it means to use their aggressiveness against them," Kyle explained. "Lead them to an area where we have constructed a fire zone with an overwhelming advantage. If they chase us, we can lead them to where we want."

Audy tilted his head. "This may work, but they will not be easily fooled."

"I'll be careful, dad," Jake drawled.

"You must be, Jake." Audy was suddenly all business. "You have seen how losing warriors does not affect them. The Strema who are used to having superior numbers always look for an opportunity to counter attack. The numbers they lose in your trap, any trap, will mean nothing to them if they hold you in place long enough for numbers to arrive."

Jake nodded his head and reached over his seat back and slapped Audy's knee. "I got you, Audy, we will didi mao first chance we get?"

Audy frowned at him. "I will not ask."

"Probably a good thing," Kyle called from the driver's seat as he flipped off the autopilot and looped around to head east. "Language lessons from Jake are just going to confuse you." Their camp was well south of here, but so far, he had made sure everyone, jets included, left the area headed east.

"You guys out of here this afternoon?" Jake asked ignoring his jibe.

"Yep," Kyle replied. "First to Fort Carolina, then we'll throw our Hail Mary tomorrow. You got this, here?"

Jake nodded. "Easy day. Besides, Colonel Pretty will be out here in a day or so to coordinate. He'll like your idea, I'm guessing. I suppose I'll have to listen to him."

"Ya think?" Kyle asked smiling.

"Don't worry about us," Jake shook his head. "You two idiots are stepping off into muj central. I think I'll suggest to Pretty he set up the kill zone, all I'll have to do is bait the bear."

"Sometimes you get the bear," Audy called out from the back, "and sometimes the bear gets you."

"He shoots and scores," Kyle smiled.

"Not even close Audy," Jake shook his head. "It's 'sometimes you get the bear, sometimes the bear gets the dog.'"

"Seriously?! You're filling his head with shit." Kyle was doing his best not to laugh.

"Clearly, you've never hunted bear with some of my cousins," Jake explained. "Problem is, I'm the dog."

"Just don't do anything stupid." Kyle said.

145

"Oh... Ok, Mr. I'm going to walk into the enemy camp."
Jake paused to spit. "Seriously though, if you buy it? Do you
have a problem with Elisabeth moving on with her life?"

Kyle laughed, "I suppose not, but she hasn't even spoke to
me since I told her I was going."

"She ever give in? Tell you who her step brother is?"

"Nope, it's starting to feel like a state secret."

"You could die not knowing? That would suck. Seriously
though, what's a proper mourning period with these things. I
don't want to piss off your ghost. I'm thinking she'll need a
shoulder to cry on, at least."

Kyle couldn't help but laugh. "I'd give her a day or so."

Jake gave flashed him a thumbs up and smiled. "Twenty-
four hours, not a problem."

"You people... think *me* strange." Audy threw in from the
back seat, shaking his head.

*

Chapter 11

"You are troubled?"

Audy's question filled the small cabin of the air car. It was an early model, it had been worked over to be airworthy, but its interior and most of the instrumentation were shot. And it was slow. They crept to the southeast towards Audy's clan at just under 100 miles an hour. The rattling defroster wasn't keeping up worth a damn and Kyle had a clear spot on the windshield the size of a dinner plate that he could see through. He kept the air car about 150 feet off the ground. Climbing any higher than that and the ice started building up on the edges of the engine nacelle intakes.

Audy sat in the passenger seat, wearing the uniform he'd been captured in and sat back with one foot resting on the dashboard. Audy looked just as relaxed as he always did. Seemingly at ease with the fact they would both be captured by the Jema and undergo some alien chemical interrogation by the end of the day, if ... IF everything went smoothly. They could just as easily wind up dead. Kyle was used to risking his life, but the idea of walking into an enemy camp, unarmed, put an entirely different spin on his emotions than what he usually went through before an op. Audy looked over at him in expectation of an answer.

"Elisabeth," he answered, sometimes one word, or one person was all the answer that was needed. "I've deployed countless times, I've never had somebody I worried about when I left." He didn't detail the fact that Elisabeth had refused to speak to him when he had delivered his decision to accompany Audy. She was angry, he got that. She had seen the post-strike videos from the attacks on the Strema Clan. In her professional opinion, as she had put it, and as he so clearly remembered; she didn't see how a world that produced such behavior, could produce another clan that they would be able to deal with.

Kyle had offered up Audy as a counter-example.

"I'm not disputing Audy's likeability, or even his character," she had thrown back in his face. "But the man was a prisoner

147

of ours. He's intelligent, he's adapted, done what he needs to. You're risking everything because you trust him."

That was part of it, a big part he knew. He also didn't see how they had much choice, but he hadn't said that to her. The air-strikes were devastating, but they were as Jake had put it, 'whittling on hickory with a butter knife.' They weren't going to build nukes, and he didn't see Eden being able to put thirty or forty thousand experienced troops in the field that it would take to meet the Strema in battle. At least not in the time they all feared they didn't have.

"She is well protected." Audy seemed almost surprised at his concern.

"If we aren't successful, it won't matter how well she's protected."

"It will be one thing in the end." Audy replied and then shook his head. "I do not butcher a saying of yours, it is one of our own."

"Well, we have that one too," Kyle answered. "It'll be, what it'll be."

"The same, yes." Audy replied. "Your worry, my desire for a future for my people, these things will weigh on us, but they will play no part in the future."

He had long ago picked up on Audy's *inshallah* attitude. It wasn't the lazier faire type that was so prevalent in the Muslim and maybe southern European cultures. Audy would work his ass off to get what he wanted, he just realized very clearly, there were some things one did not control.

"My people," Kyle replied, and "by that I mean my clan if you will, my countrymen of old, believe or used to believe that each person makes their own fate."

"You still believe that, or most of you do," Audy nodded in agreement. "I see this in your people. I believe this as well. You and I will give this mystical one hundred percent that you people are always talking about, but it will still be ..."

"... one thing in the end?" Kyle interrupted him.

"Yes," Audy agreed and then looked over at him. "You risk much coming with me. It shows courage and this will measure among the Jema. It will not seem so, but it will."

Kyle mulled that statement for a bit, and then looked back at his friend.

"Audy, I need you to promise me the mission comes first. You do whatever it takes, to convince your people we will help them. We'll give them a place among us, as long as they join us against the Strema. Do not worry about me."

"I still believe you can explain this better to them, than I," Audy replied. "If that changes, I will do what I can to protect you."

"I trust you Audy." Kyle said, knowing he didn't really have an option to trusting to Audy's plan. "The mission comes first, your people's freedom, a place to live and the survival of my people, you understand what I am saying?"

"Yes." Audy replied smiling. "Jake would say you are putting your ass out there, or on the line, which I think is the same thing – yes?"

"Yeah, same thing."

"There is *something* I don't understand." Audy replied after a moment of watching trees pass by beneath them.

"Jake said to me once," Audy had a questioning tone, 'Pretty chewed his ass.' I've heard you and I've heard Carlos say somebody 'had their head up their ass.' I hear 'get your ass in gear,' 'put your ass on the line.' Your father explained to you that Mr. Theo kicked Lupe's ass, and he said so in a manner suggesting approval, or maybe that Lupe had needed his ass kicked."

Kyle was trying not laugh.

"What is this importance that you people place on your ass?"

Kyle did laugh. It was a much-needed release. Anything that would get him out of his own head. "Honestly Audy, I've never thought of it until now."

"And lastly," Audy smiled in return. "What does it signify when Elisabeth says to you that sometimes, you can be such an ass?"

After managing to land the air car, they covered it with brush. The whole while Kyle doubted if it would ever fly again.

Audy trussed him up, with his wrists together and bound behind his back via a loop around his waist that doubled as a leash. Audy directed him to walk in front, as this was how a Chandrian would treat a prisoner in those few instances where they actually bothered to take one.

Kyle thought he caught a glimmer of a smile from his friend as he explained that.

"I will announce myself," Audy pronounced once they were walking. "They will be cautious."

"Shoot first cautious? Or curious cautious?" Kyle asked, turning his head to regard his captor.

"Yes." Audy answered with a grin and then gestured with his chin to move on. "You must not look at me Kyle, or at them when they come. If you look at me, I will strike you. You said I must sell it. This is what you meant?"

Kyle didn't look back. "You do what you need to do. I'll play prisoner all nice and docile like. Just like SEER school."

"You have a school to teach you how to be a prisoner?"

"Sort of," Kyle explained realizing how strange that sounded on the surface. "Mainly how to survive and escape."

"You people are strange, don't get taken prisoner should be the only lesson. Now quiet, they will be close."

They hiked along in silence for over an hour, much further than he'd thought they'd make it when Audy jerked him to a stop with a sharp pull on the leash and pushed him to his knees.

"They are here." Audy whispered. "Eyes down, silence."

Kyle had been looking hard and he hadn't seen or heard anything.

Audy shouted something unintelligible into the surrounding forest of mostly old growth hardwoods and the occasional pine. Kyle suddenly wished he'd made a harder study of the Chandrian language.

There was a two-word interrogative shouted back. It was basically 'who are you?' That much he could understand.

Audy shouted back again, and it seemed to Kyle that he sounded very authoritative.

"Not good, there is no officer with them." Audy whispered.

He saw two figures emerge out the brush not forty yards in front of him. They'd been so well hidden they seemed to just materialize there. They were both carrying those massive rifles held to their shoulders as they moved tactically. Having held one of those rifles he knew how hard that could be, the damn things were heavy.

Audy moved up from behind him, "I am sorry," he whispered.

Kyle wondered for a split second what he meant by that, but then he sensed Audy's rifle butt coming down. He heard Audy speaking again, as if far away or through the walls of the house he had grown up in. The sound of pounding surf and waves rose to a crescendo in his head and then there was nothing.

Audy was almost surprised that he'd been able to bluff these warriors who had been placed on outer picket duty. The task was generally given to those very hungry to redeem some past mistake. Given their aggressiveness, he was lucky not to have been shot. On the other hand, his story that he was returning from a secret scouting mission seemed to be working with these men. It may not have with a Bastelta or even a seasoned Teark. Then again, he could have talked to an officer and at least gotten a safe passage into camp. These men would be detained, officers would be brought to the gate and it would quickly turn in to what Kyle and Jake referred to as a 'dick measuring contest' between junior officers.

He'd been able to convince these warriors that the Shareki man needed to be brought to camp in no worse shape than he was at this moment. He showed them the assault rifle he carried and the compad from his 'captured' Shareki. They were suitably impressed, particularly with the electronic map on the compad that he "accidently" accessed as they were looking. The east coast of North America, complete with a blinking red dot that showed their location had impressed them. It was like nothing they had ever seen before. It was enough to convince them that whatever was happening, it was well above their current orders.

They had moved through the woods for just under an hour once they'd been joined by the rest of the Jema picket team. Four of them, all of the lowest Dadu rank, carried Kyle on a jury-rigged stretcher. Audy had read the secret signs on the trail as they neared the main Jema camp and stopped the group, pulling them off the trail into the woods. He grunted in approval as the four rankers carrying Kyle's litter dropped to a knee in a protective cordon after gently setting it down.

Audy signaled the leader of the group, a mere 'Dadus' away and walked a short distance from the group.

"What family name do you claim '*Dadus*'?

The man came to attention and looked him fiercely in the eye. "None, but the Jema. As is our shame, until the day."

"Good," Audy replied. "That day may be closer than you think, Dadus. I call upon your service today in the name of the Kaerin." He produced a tightly folded letter; the outside of the heavy paper had been printed with a computer by Dr. Jensen with his input. It had a large metallic symbol of the Kaerin, a simple golden sun and a smaller blue moon super imposed on it. The soldier had never seen a Kaerin message packet before, but the approximation of the official Kaerin seal had the desired effect.

The Dadus' eyes widened. "I'm yours to command, Bastelta."

Hearing his honorific after having been so long with Kyle's people almost took him by surprise.

"You will go into camp and deliver this to Bastelta Jomra'Sendai. You know of him."

The man nodded. "You have been long gone. He is Kaerdos, now. I will not be given leave to speak to him."

He smiled inwardly, Jomra' had moved up in rank with the Jema's coming to this world. Had he stayed, it may have been Kaerdos Audrin'ochal. It was of no consequence, he had always known his path would take him from the Kaerin, in one way or another.

He waved the small package under the man's nose and thumped the man's forehead with it. "You will be stopped, but you carry the seal the of the Kaerin. If you must explain, you are to say that you are instructed to deliver this only to Kaerdos Jomra' Sendai, and only him, on your honor."

"It will be so." The warrior nodded sagely. "Is he expecting this message?"

"I've been so long gone, he must think of me as dead. You are to say to him and only him; "This is from one, for whom words were not enough."

"A code?" The warrior nodded in understanding.

"Of sorts, he will recognize me in those words. Now, repeat to me the instructions I've given you."

When he was satisfied that the Dadus could and would deliver the message, he laid a hand on the man's shoulder.

"May your family be strong." It was the ritual saying, and it carried the shame of not having one, with the constant hope and yearning for a future with one.

He watched the man jog off toward his people's camp. Jomra would come to him, of that he held no doubt. Like him, Jomra' Sendai was among the oldest of the surviving Jema and he held to the old ways with conviction. He was a man of honor. He was also the friend that had shot him in the back as he jumped through the Kaerin's gate they had been guarding. He would either listen to him or look him in the eyes as he gutted him like a fish.

*

Chapter 12

The southeastern most Strema work camp was a much smaller version of the central camp they'd hit on the first day of the air strikes. There was a central wooden and earth perimeter wall surrounded by no less than eight observation or guard towers outside the walls. Regular roving patrols moved from tower to tower, overlapping with patrols from the other dispersed camps. The system of satellite defense in depth was effective in that it made getting ground troops close enough to mortar the central camp almost impossible.

That hadn't stopped what had become regular, two-a-day attacks from their four jets, harassing mortar attacks on the outer Strema patrols, and as of the last few days, artillery barrages and fly-by strikes by air cars equipped with either SAWs or unguided rockets. All of which just amounted to licking around the edges of the massive Chandrian presence in the middle of the continent.

That was all going to change today. If all went well, they'd be taking a bite out of them. Jake, with Colonel Pretty's input, had decided to target the southeastern most satellite camp at the edge of the Strema clan's massive footprint as their target. The course of the river and the gentle hills marching down to the river's edge made it the hardest camp to reinforce quickly from the enemy's perspective.

They had six mobile mortar teams, which for the day's operation, Jake and his fellow knuckle draggers had taken over command of. Jake would be leading one team, Arne, Jeff, Darius, Domenik and Hans would each have another. They were all the bait on the end of the hook, albeit bait with a bite. Jiro had an Osprey Mark II with a door and tail ramp gunner, each mounting .50 caliber machine guns that would play rover. Col. Pretty had a force of 740 hastily trained militia well dug into a prepared, defensive position three miles directly south of the enemy camp. They were the net, and as far as Jake was concerned, their biggest unknown. Would the militia stand?

Carlos and his new spotter Lupe Vasquez, were hidden up in the bluffs across the river and controlling two UAVs that watched the Strema, both the target camp and the narrow spit of land that the closest adjacent camp would have to traverse to reinforce the primary target group.

Jake checked his compad again. He'd been watching it for the last twenty minutes as the mortar teams slowly hiked north into their weapon's range of the target camp. Their aircars would have been heard had they tried to maneuver so close to a camp. The vehicles were parked back behind Col. Pretty's prepared position. Every unit on his electronic map showed green, even team three under Jeff Krouse. Jeff's team had had the farthest to hike with their soon to be disposable mortar.

"Mortar One – Actual," Pretty's voice sounded flat and unemotional, "all units green, you have the ball."

"Affirmative," Jake responded. He selected the artillery unit on his compad. It was located seven miles away on the west side of the river, south of where Carlos was set up. He pushed the button that started the show.

Seconds later the rolling rumble from the howitzer's shells broke through to them as their only deployed arty battery began firing at a diversionary target camp far to the north. The explosions from those rounds sounded muted and muffled, louder but not much different than distant shotgun blasts across the deep swamps of his youth as some other poacher had been killing something to eat. He knew though, that those 105 mm rounds were being directed by Carlos's drone and would be causing havoc wherever they landed. It would be a pinprick against the numbers the Strema had, but it was hoped they might start rolling reinforcements in *that* direction, away from him and the other mortar teams.

He was dressed in green and white winter camo, which for the hastily put together volunteer force was a hand tailored white bed sheet with a hole cut in it for his head, streaked with green paint. It had simple belt loops cut into it so they could still get to their pockets. Jake leaned back against the frozen hole he was in and stretched out his legs. He looked ridiculous, they all did, but that was the point. The Program had enough high-tech Special Ops gear for all the knuckle draggers and then some, but they couldn't outfit all the Militia in the same gear, at least not yet. He'd heard there was a settlement somewhere turning out real uniforms, but he'd heard the same thing about air to ground missile equipped aircars as well and they were still waiting for those.

"Dressing like the riff-raff," was how Jeff Krouse had put it. In retrospect, Jake had to admit it was a good idea. Their troops were green, very green. Having the knuckle draggers walking amongst them decked out in gear levels above what they'd been issued wouldn't have been good for their morale.

He listened to the distant arty mission that was putting out three round salvos and glanced back at 'his' militia mortar team. They looked scared, but they were ready, kneeling in position and primed to begin the hand to hand daisy chain of transferring the mortar rockets from the small hole they had dug to the single mortar tube they had packed in.

They all looked back at him expectantly. He smiled and thumbed his bed sheet camouflage. "Do I look as ridiculous as you guys?"

They all three nodded without a sound. One of them was Dean Freeburn, a childhood friend of Kyle's. He'd met Dean several times before and he was somebody who until this morning had called this mortar team – 'his'.

Freeburn, who Jake thought of as a good guy had the right temperament to be a soldier. But the man was thirty-five years old and had four weeks of intensive training and absolutely zero fucking experience. He might be as liable to break and run as the 50-year-old former community college track coach kneeling in the snow to next him. You just never knew who had the balls to stand behind their gun when the shit started falling.

Jake winked at Freeburn. "Flyboys come in after the shelling, then us," he whispered. "Be ready."

Jake remembered the moment he'd told Freeburn that he was taking over command of the mortar team for this engagement. He'd been worried about that. A regular Army nug would have been bitter. He'd almost laughed at the look of relief that had flashed across Freeburn's face.

It was a relief that would be short lived. The Colonel had other plans for the knuckle draggers. Pretty had been clear; his primary goal for this whole operation was to blood the militia, and prove to them that they could hit back and live. The recruits had all heard the stories, seen the recordings and had the living shit scared out of them for long enough that the Chandrians, particularly the Strema, had taken on a boogie man status. That had to change. The troops in training now and those waiting for a slot to open up would need people just like them, militia uprooted from their peaceful pursuits who were 'veterans'.

Jake knew that was true, but Pretty's whole plan relied on the militia manning his defensive position... today. To stand behind their guns in the face of a massed infantry attack, and he had doubts. He was self-aware enough to realize he was prejudiced as hell against the non-professionals. He'd felt the same way when he had to work with regular army in the past and most of them got to be pretty damned good. In fact, he knew from personal experience, looking at his three-man militia unit, that Rangers and Green Berets all started out as regular grunts.

War wasn't just the winnowing process it was often made out to be. He knew a lot of marginal troops, or worse, who lived to go home and make babies with their sweethearts. In his mind, war was an annealing process, dependent in large part to the quality of metal that was dumped into the forge in the beginning. Troops, any troops, were generally a lot harder coming out regardless of where they started, or where they were on the pecking order on the back end.

The three-minute artillery barrage passed quickly. The same could not be said, he knew from personal experience, by the ETs at the receiving end. There were truly shitty situations in life. Being on the receiving end of a targeted artillery strike was another, far deeper circle of hell.

With the last rumble of the final arty impact, he dug out his tin of chewing tobacco. It wasn't Copenhagen, but the can was. Some industrious colonist in California had started a nice little green house tobacco business a few months ago. The guy would be rich by the end of the war because the stuff was in such high demand.

Pretty had the ball on the Lightning strike, and he knew with the rumble of the last salvo fading, the jets had probably already begun their attack run. He put in a pinch of tobacco and laid his head back and closed his eyes running through contingencies in his head. He needed his team to relax. The adrenaline that would soon flood their systems, wouldn't be stopped. It would come in handy, maybe save their lives. If they let the rush carry them away though, it could just as easily produce some stupid heroic act that would get them or someone else killed.

He cracked one eye and smiled as his team was all looking at him like he was crazy.

"Relax guys, this is an easy day. Remember, steady and smooth."

They had only packed in six rounds as they had no idea how fast the ETs would react to localized fire, and the enemy would have no doubt the mortars were being launched from relatively close by. They were as loud as hell exploding out of their tubes and these had a rocket boost stage that could be seen. Not a design flaw, just something special added to the propellant for this particular op. They were bait. They needed the ETs to come out hunting them.

"And then run like hell," Jake pointed directly south. "Remember, the other teams will be on parallel tracks, converging at the kill box." He spat out a stream of dark tobacco juice that stained the packed snow at his feet.

He waggled a finger, windshield wiper fashion, "don't shoot the good guys, and don't stop." The rumble from the approaching two jets grew quickly. The nearest one almost overflew their position accompanied by a ground shaking roar. A second later, the forest on the far side of the low hills separating them from the target camp erupted with a series of explosions that they felt through the ground.

"Five hundred pounders," Jake grinned at his team. "They've got a particular snap to them." Not bothering to whisper anymore Jake was counting down in his head. The Strema would be diving into whatever hole they could find.

His guys looked like they were about to shit themselves.

"You know I usually have music going in headphones on this kind of op."

"Wha? What?" The former community college track coach asked. Jake couldn't remember his name, he'd ask later if the nug held it together.

He kept the count going in his head. Mr. ET would be huddled in his hole, looking to the sky for more planes.

"Mostly classical stuff, some Mozart or Beethoven, unless things are going to get really shitty, then I'd break out the Dire Straits from the eighties. Real warrior tunes if you listen to the words, Brothers in Arms, Iron Hand, Ride Across the River."

"Are you serious?" Freeburn asked coughing out a laugh with the other two breaking out into smiles.

"Do I look like somebody who'd tell you some bullshit just to lighten the mood?"

Freeburn jerked his head up and down. "Yes."

The Strema would be starting to come out of their holes, thinking happy thoughts, killing their wounded and calmly go back to work... "That hurts, it really does."

Something in his look made them all laugh.

He raised a hand to stop them. "Now, nice and steady, Fire."

The familiar *WHUUMP* from the mortar shell boosting out of its tube sounded deafening in the forest. The shell's ascent blew the snow off the overhanging branches around them. Jake ignored the cold sensation of snowy powder on his face and counted the other mortar tubes in the thick forest around them firing as well.

The first round hit just moments after they launched their second shell followed by the impacts from the other five teams. Jake glanced at his guys as they expertly handled the very touchy mortars with a calmness that impressed him. He nodded in appreciation of the training that Kyle's father had put them through. *Whuump........Whuump..........Whuump*

"Nice shooting," Carlos's voice came over the command circuit. "On target." The circuit included Pretty, the knuckle draggers and Jiro in his Osprey gunship. "ET force is marshalling outside of camp. We hurt em."

Whuump

"Numbers?" Pretty asked.

"The whole camp," Carlos intoned. The sniper was watching through two UAVs, one circling high over the enemy camp, the other farther north keeping tabs on the camps that could potentially reinforce them. "Wait estimate."

"Roger." Pretty sounded like he might have been responding to a pizza delivery.

"Whuump"

"Ok – I'll blow the tube," Jake yelled, "get moving and do not stop until you get to the trenches."

Freeburn waited expectantly standing, with his rifle held ready, "You aren't coming?"

"Be right behind you," he spit, "now git!"

Jake watched them go and noted that they were indeed running and in the right direction to boot.

Jake checked the three claymore mines he'd wired up in front of their firing position and gingerly pulled the pin on the trip wire. He waited for another minute or so and heard the Chandrians long before they crested the distant hill in front of him. They looked pissed and were moving fast. There was no order, just a mass of soldiers moving towards an enemy that had finally come out to play. They'd shown up too quickly to be from the camp, probably a patrol he realized.

No matter, they'd be the hunting dogs the others would follow. He lifted his head back from his scope and pulled a pin on a grenade. He dropped it down the mortar tube and started running.

The grenade was just to get their attention focused on him through the couple of hundred yards of brush pine and old hardwoods separating them, but it wasn't needed. More than a few heavy slugs whizzed by his head as he ran, closely followed by the massive reports of the rifles that fired them.

"I'm the Gingerbread man!" he yelled to no one, topping a small rise and sprinting down the other side. His team was out in front of him, but he'd run from game wardens the first time at the age of ten. Running through the woods was second nature to him. He closed the distance quickly until he was astride of Freeburn.

"Move it Fatty!" he yelled, smiling. He knew it wasn't fair, his guys were running the two and a half miles to relative safety, he'd been sprinting and was about out of lungs. He pulled off a decent pop-up slide, bringing himself to a quick standing stop with a thick tree between him and his pursuers. He waited just a moment, catching his breath, before peeking out around the trunk.

A rifle shot impacted the tree a few feet above him with a wet heavy slap.

"Fuck me." He yelled and started running again. A second later he heard his claymores trip accompanied by screams. That'll slow em down, he thought. He sprinted another fifty meters until he knew he'd have a vantage point to look back and circled back behind some thick brush. With nothing but the nose of his SCAR assault rifle pointing out he flipped the scope to full magnification and dropped two ETs that looked to be giving orders. The whole group was moving more slowly now. He didn't feel like pushing his luck. He slowly withdrew and when he was clear of the bush, started running again.

"Estimate enemy between three and four thousand, moving south on a wide front, claymores slowed the advance parties down." Carlos sounded a little worried.

Jake almost jumped on the command circuit to let everyone know he'd just personally serviced two, so they should revise the enemy count. He smiled to himself as he ran, knowing Colonel Pretty had a limit to the latitude he showed his knuckle draggers.

"Team three - Contact." Jeff's voice sounded pressed and the sound of automatic weapons fire could be heard over the command circuit. Jake could hear the gun fire in the clear as well, from the far side of a gentle ridge line off to his right.

He was still running and zipped his rifle's sling as tight to his body as he could and put on more speed. He caught up within sight of Freeburn and the track coach. He whistled them to a stop. He slid to a stop himself and pressed his team comms button on his collar. "Follow me, going right, and don't shoot until I do."

Jake half slid, half jumped into the next ravine and turned to the right running perpendicular to his previous southward direction. He heard Freeburn and the Track Coach laboring behind him, the third member of his team was just twenty years old and in shape. He was over the hill and running hard for home. Jake half nodded to himself, he was the only stupid bastard following the plan and the kid could flat out move.

Jiro's Osprey Mk II, the jet engines on the end of its wings pointed almost directly downward spun slowly in place above the tree tops about two hundred yards away. Heavy machine gun fire from the .50 calibers at its door and tail opened up, unleashing tracer fire into the woods directly ahead of them.

"Osprey - Team One, be advised blue force circling behind Team Three contact – keep their heads down."

The tracer fire was getting closer, dropping on a position directly between Jeff's team and the relative safety of the kill box still a long mile away. Jake sprinted and prayed that his two guys could keep up.

He spotted six of the Chandrians sheltering under a tangle dead trees deposited by the river's last flood. A dozen or more of the enemy lay unmoving already dropped by the heavy fire raining down from the Osprey.

Jake slowed and moved around to the bottom of the short hill and slowly started to climb giving his team time to catch up. "Osprey break fire, Break Fire!" The jet blasts from the Osprey had melted all the snow and frost in the trees above them, only the larger ones were still standing and it was practically raining on them as the Osprey dipped one wing and rolled away.

Jake looked at his two guys, and motioned with one hand, over the hill and shoot. Their eyes got big but they both nodded.

Jake surged to his feet even as the Chandrians on the other side started firing, at what he hoped was the heavily armed Osprey and not Jeff's mortar team.

Jake crested the hill and serviced four of the ETs before they realized he was there. He saw the other two Chandrians at either end of their position swing their guns away from the Osprey towards him. He waited to get shot, but he guessed wrong. The one he had a bead on just dropped his gun and started pulling at a short sword. Jake dropped him and waited for the impact he knew was coming from the last ET that was now almost behind him. Freeburn's rifle and that of the track coach barked almost as one, and by the time Jake spun back around, the last enemy was down.

Jake slid the rest of the way down into the former enemy position behind the fallen trees and quickly checked the bodies. One of the Strema was still moving with his guts blown out and he delivered a single shot to the back of the dead man's head.

"Team One - Team Three, Jeff get moving your twelve is clear."

"Team One – Osprey, concentrate on enemy force to north of team three."

"Affirmative Team One." Jiro's heavily accented and clipped English came across clear.

It was good to be working with professionals again. He looked back at his team, Freeburn and Coach. He no longer cared what Coach's name was, he was and would be "Coach" from now on. He'd earned a handle and a little respect. They both looked ill as they stood there looking at the carnage.

He walked up to them. "You did your job, you're alive." He looked both of them in the eye. "Focus on that, nothing else matters."

"Freeburn, you OK?"

"Yeah, geez, I think I'm going to puke." The man was still puffing heavily.

"It's the adrenaline, it's normal." He looked over at ...Timbull, that was his name. "How about you, Coach?"

"You ever get used to it?"

Jake glanced down at the sight around him and shook his head. "Used to what?"

"Just bury it," he said after a moment.

"Yeah," Coach nodded and Jake saw him looking at something behind him. He turned and saw Jeff helping a teenager up the hill. The kid had been shot in the thigh, but Jake could tell in an instant that Jeff had hit him with a nanostab. The wounded teenager was smiling as the half million nanites in his blood stream worked to stop the bleeding and cranked out enough artificial endorphins to float a fraternity for a weekend.

"Jake!" Freeburn yelled and started moving forward.

"What?" Jake asked, confused as Freeburn blew past him.

"It's his son, Jacob." Coach explained.

"Oh shit," Jake spit, and looped after Freeburn signaling Coach to follow him.

Jeff passed his burden over to the kid's dad and looked at Jake. "Thanks, I owe you."

"I wasn't doing anything else." Jake smiled and turned to Freeburn and Coach. "Run him back between you, and I mean run. He's feeling no pain – are you kid?"

"Feeeel fine, Sir."

"Sure you do, kid." He turned to the senior Freeburn, "I mean run, do not stop. We'll be behind you and flanking you, if we fire, you just keep running or I'll shoot you myself."

He watched them go, "Run, God dammit!"

Jeff smiled at him. "That wasn't strange."

"His own kid...shit, that's a first."

"Two of my guys were capped before I knew it, it was one of their patrols. I think I surprised each other." Jeff explained quickly.

Jake knew Jeff was a professional and wouldn't blame himself until later. "It happens, you know that."

"Yeah, how much time we got?" Jeff asked looking back the way he'd come.

"Not enough to stand here listening to your gang banger bullshit." Jake grinned, knowing they'd have to leave the bodies where they were, at least for now.

"Swamp rat" Jeff grinned back. "I'll go left."

The .50s on Jiro's Osprey opened up to the north of them maybe two hundred yards distant. Hundreds of the Strema rifles engaged the Osprey. They weren't going to waste the time Jiro was buying them. They separated and started moving south.

"You're lucky, kid," Jake tousled the wounded teenager's hair as they reached the rear lines on the back side of the trenched redoubt the militia had dug into the hill over the last 18 hours. The young man sat with his Dad, smiling a smile that could only come from the stupefying effects of the opiates in his blood stream. "Chicks dig scars."

"Maybe... might lose my leg." The kid, Jake, he remembered shared his name, smiled as he answered, as if the thought didn't bother him in the least.

Jake glanced at the senior Freeburn and shook his head. He saw the wound, it had missed the femoral artery and had gone clean through.

"No, but you're going to have a hell of limp for a bit. Right now, you're gonna go sit in one of those nice warm air buses."

Carlos's voice broke into the command channel. "Actual – Spotter, ETs forming up just inside the tree line." Carlos sounded irritated. He knew the man would rather have been out in the woods somewhere behind the Strema taking out officers from a kilometer away.

"Actual - Spotter, they're lining up in formation, old school, like Napoleon or something. They look like stacks of firewood from the air."

"Spotter – Actual, numbers?" Jake again heard Col. Pretty's voice and looked around and spotted him standing on the backside of the center of the low ridge they had dug into.

"All of them," Carlos answered. "The whole target camp, estimate between three and four thousand. Second UAV shows two adjacent camps falling in and moving fast. Repeat, two separate camps, each estimated at four to six thousand, repeat four to six thousand each group. Both groups reinforcing from the north on same track as target group. They will intersect initial target camp in estimate ten minutes, another plus fifteen before they make contact."

"Jake, where you hiding?" Pretty asked calmly.

"Behind you, Sir. Coming up."

Jake had helped lay out the trench works which had been dug into the side of the hill facing the clearing, and the edge of the forest that lined the far side of the open frozen ground. There were wide cuts with timber reinforced stairs on the back side and he fairly ran up the steps until he stood next to Pretty in the command bunker at the top edge of the ridge. Observation slits had been built into the facing earth and the sandbagged wall and he had a good view of the four lines of trenches that were roughly parallel with the low ridge top and stepped down to the level of the frozen, snow covered flood plain at the bottom.

In modern military terms the entire hill and its defense works were an anachronism. The men manning it could have been wiped out with a single air strike or ground down via artillery. A modern enemy wouldn't dare try a frontal assault against a prepared position. They'd isolate it, go around it or destroy it from afar. Everything they'd seen so far of the Chandrian tactics, as well as Audy's intel, said they'd attack. They had built an abattoir out of the clearing at the bottom of the hill. They desperately needed the Chandrians to assault them. Looking out at the killing field, the numbers Carlos reported aside, he almost hoped the Chandrians turned around. The whole thing looked to him like something out of a World War I battle manual. And that hadn't ever ended well for those who attacked, even when they managed to win.

"Done playing hero?" Pretty glared at him.

"Schucks, sir, I don't think I deserve a medal or anything."

Pretty just shook his head, eyes closed and ignored the statement. He pointed at the right most of the two compads he had arrayed on sandbags in front of him.

166

"You heard Carlos. I've got two fighters, standing by three minutes out. I'll send them in when the reinforcing groups reach the initial target camp, it'll give them a basket to drop in, maybe slow them down."

Jake nodded looking at the other compad which showed the transmitted feed from one of the UAVs overhead.

"Carlos wasn't kidding. Would ya look at that?" The Chandrians were forming up in what could only be described as firing ranks of three. Long lines, three men deep. The last time he'd seen something like that outside of a parade ground was a civil war re-enactment he'd seen as a kid.

"This is going to be ugly," he whispered.

Pretty frowned and nodded in agreement. "Doesn't make sense given they have accurate breech loaders. These dumb-ass tactics always relied on the will of the men in the ranks and their commanders. I haven't seen any evidence they are lacking in that department."

"No, Sir." Jake agreed.

"They may never make this mistake again, so we need to make it count and get our people out with a win."

"Where do you want me?"

"Get your band of trouble makers, you're going to be my flying squad if we need it and more important, my traffic cops which we will definitely need. Set up in the middle of trench three."

There were four total trench lines, all in contact with a zigzagging connector trench in the middle and at either end covering about a hundred meters of gentle downward sloping ridge line. They were on a small peninsula where the frozen river covered the line's ends. Trench one was just above ground level, four was directly beneath Pretty's position at the top of the hill.

"Anybody wavers, I'll try to direct you, but don't wait for me. You see a problem, fix it. Jiro is on line as well, but he lost his door gunners and is down to just his tail gun."

"Copy all, good luck, sir." He started forward but Pretty grabbed his collar and stopped him. The colonel jerked a thumb behind him. Six massive airbuses and dozens of aircars were parked, some of the latter out on the thick ice of the river.

"I'm not going to hesitate starting the withdrawal, forward most first. Don't let anybody rout and think it's a retreat"

Jake glanced down the hill at their very green troops. All he could see in most cases were their backs as they stood up on their firing steps facing the clearing and an enemy they were finally going to meet.

"Will do."

He worked his way down the zig-zagging central communication trench after learning the rest of the knuckle draggers were already waiting for him.

Jake slapped worried looking soldiers on the back as he went offering what little encouragement he could as he passed by. "Give em hell, stay up to reload - you'll lose your sight picture if you drop down. Remember, it's our mass of fire against theirs and you have this nice trench to hide behind and automatic weapons." He talked the whole way as he zigzagged down the trench pausing at each intersecting trench to have a quick word. He paused where the third trench branched off to the right when somebody up on the firing step excitedly proclaimed, "I can see em in the trees!"

"Let me see," Jake offered loudly and stepped up onto the firing step cut into the frozen earth and looked down across the flood plain into the tree line a little less than three hundred yards away. Jake stood there trying to strike a pose of 'casual yet concerned' when the truth was that against landmines, the militia's automatic assault rifles, three .50 caliber machine gun emplacements, three mortar tubes, and one 25 mm Bushmaster chain gun, the Strema were facing a wood chipper.

A part of him wished they'd realize that assaulting a prepared position was suicide. The hard job was over, this was going to be a slaughter. Another part of knew it needed to be. With just this first group forming up at the edge of the tree line the Chandrians outnumbered them somewhere between five and six to one.

168

"Yep, they're getting ready. Single shots if you can – make each one count. Short two or three round bursts if you have to. Anybody goes spray and pray and I'll cap you myself." He grinned at them, as he pointed at the group gathered.

"Anybody got a dip I can bum?"

Two or three guys nodded in the affirmative and started digging, but it was a hard-looking woman, late forties with a dirt smeared all over her face that proffered a can first.

He took the can. "Louisiana?"

"Hell no." She almost spit and then thought better of it. "Sir. I'm a Tar Heel."

He offered up a confusion. "That's Tennessee, right?"

The woman knew when she was being messed with and took back her can shaking her head.

"You were out there? How many we get?" The man asking had a soft, almost round face, and glasses. He would have looked at home in a dress shirt with a pocket protector.

"Air strike and mortars hit em hard. We got a few more while they were chasing us back here. The rest are out there right now," Jake said pausing to spit in the bottom of the trench. "We got enough fire power to toast these guys as long as you stand and pile em up. The Colonel has a few surprises ready for them. Don't break, don't hesitate to move when we tell you, and we'll be fine."

The Tar Heel woman glared at the people standing around her. "Ain't nobody here going to break, Sir."

"This your unit?" He asked

"Yep." Was all she offered back.

Jake smiled and nodded at her. "No, I don't think they will."

Jake hopped back down in to the trench and faced the woman. "Hold fire until they cut lose above you, good luck."

Two more zags in the central spine trench and Jake emerged at another wide intersection with its own firing steps and sand bags. Two trenches angled up and away from them, another two angled sharply down and away to either side toward the lower trenches. The rest of his crew was already there.

He saw Hans first. The man was seated on the firing step arranging ammo belts for his SAW that he manhandled like a personal assault rifle. One side of Han's face was red with smeared and dried blood.

"What the hell happened to you?"

"It is nothing." Han's slammed shut the upper receiver on his weapon clearly not wanting to talk about it.

"He ran into a tree." Darius said grinning from ear to ear.

"Do they give medals for that?" Domenik asked.

"You should see the tree, Hans won the fight." Arne said and then starting laughing, the big Norwegian sounded like a braying donkey.

Which was almost as funny as the look of embarrassment on Hans' face.

"White people..." Jeff interjected when the laughter died down. "Whole forest of muj out there and you take it out on the environment."

Jake relayed their orders once the laughter died down. "Basically, we stiffen up any unit that goes soft."

"That wasn't gay at all." Jeff smiled as he said it, and they all started laughing again.

Arne was up on the firing step glassing the forest edge and snapped his fingers repeatedly until he'd killed the laughter. "They come."

"Stupid bastards." Jake wanted to scream at them to turn around. All across the hill weapons came up atop the trench ridge or sand bags, safeties came off and cheeks went down against automatic assault rifles.

With a battle scream that set them all on edge, the forward most Strema firing line moved out in to the clearing about twenty yards from the tree line. There was no formal dress to the lines, no goose-stepping march, or swinging of arms. Just a tight formation that seemed to flow without pause towards them. It was three men deep and about eighty yards long, perhaps as many as 500 men. The enemy paused as if expecting to absorb some fire. The moment went on for too long where the enemies just stared at one another. With a scream from an officer that was picked up and echoed up and down the lines of the enemy, they broke formation and began sprinting across the open ground.

Jake just shook his head in wonder. He could appreciate the fearlessness in that charge. Even if they all had shitty Chandrian breechloaders, the charging force would expect to get hammered. Yet they came on, not in a cautious assault, but in a full out race towards the forward most of their trenches.

Their one big gun, a 25 mm Bushmaster chain gun adjacent to Pretty's outlook opened up and within a half second, the whole hillside launched a wall of metal at the charging enemy. Almost sporadically for a second or two, but the rate of fire quickly built.

Jake and none of the other knuckle draggers bothered to fire a shot, they just watched as the Strema were mowed down. The Bushmaster by itself took out the center of the enemy mass before soldiers in the trenches had even started firing. The chain gun's projectiles killed two or three of the tightly packed Chandrians with almost every shot. The charge melted away and was gone nearly as quickly as it had begun. A few panicked militia defenders fired their whole magazines on full auto in the excitement of their first engagement. Not as many as Jake would have expected, but a lot of rounds went down range long after there were no more moving targets.

Another Chandrian formation, three lines deep stepped out, with another just like it directly behind them at the edge of the forest. The forward most formation broke into a run across the clearing, while the second line walked forward a few paces, stopped and began firing. The impacts from the heavy Chandrian rifles smacked the wet earth all around the hill side. When they hit flesh, seeing as how most of the defenders only had their heads and maybe shoulders visible above the trenches, the destruction was horrific. Jake crouched down a little, suddenly appreciative of the enemy's marksmanship.

The .50 calibers and the Bushmaster opened up along the top of the ridge and scythed through the stationary rear of the Chandrian line that was visible. The militia fire focused on the immediate threat of those Strema that were running towards them, many with long knives or short swords rather than guns. Jake added his own fire to the rearward group that was actually firing on them, after checking the progress of the attacking line. The Bushmaster was doing the same. It's heavy slugs, at the rate of over 800 rounds a minute were fountaining up frozen mud and ice usually after blowing through one or two of the stacked-up attackers.

Jake watched through his scope as the larger group still in the woods, melted farther back into the trees in a steady flow. There was no harried retreat, it was a simple repositioning. The attack petered out. A dozen or so of the Strema had made it within ten yards of the first trench before they had been stopped by the defenders.

"Colonel," Jake pressed the command circuit on his collar, "recommend we pull out our forward trench now, let em see it. I don't want them waiting for the reinforcements."

"Concur." Pretty signaled back. "We'll make sure they see the airbus lift and leave."

Jake and the knuckle draggers broke apart and rushed into the lower trench and started moving people out. Some were more than ready to leave, others took it as a slight on their honor or some shit.

"Why the hell do we have to leave? We just..."

Jake didn't pause, didn't let the man finish whatever he was going to say. He just stepped up and cold cocked the one particular twenty-something that didn't seem to understand that he'd just been given an order. He pulled the punch and hadn't even really put his 'gumbo' into it as they used to say in the bayou. The kid scrambled up quickly enough and looked like he was stupid enough not to have gotten the message when those around him dragged him away down the trench.

The trench lines above them opened up in a furious fashion which stopped the whole withdraw process. Jake stepped up onto the firing pit and watched for just a moment as another Chandrian formation, three lines deep and sized the same as the first broke from the forest. This time they charged at a flat out run from the get go. Pretty held the Bushmaster in check this time, but the effect of the withering rifle fire from the individual militia members reduced the attack, just at a much slower rate. The enemy's charge would make it a lot closer this time.

"Keep moving!" he yelled as he dropped back into the trench. He could respect the militia's willingness to fight, but what was it about orders that they didn't seem to quite understand?

"Keep moving – get to your bus! We're gonna draw em in.... keep moving!" He felt more like a drill sergeant moving green recruits through the mess hall than he did a soldier but his section of the trench was finally empty with the notable exception of two bodies. The unit he'd just withdrawn would have noted their names. They'd had orders to do so. The two KIA in this trench, and he knew there were others, would soon get a burial worthy of any soldier.

The rifle fire fell off precipitously and he risked another quick look over the lip of the trench, stepping up on the firing step and dropping back down immediately. Two heavy rifle slugs slammed into the wall of earth on the outside of the trench wall, not that close, but he could appreciate how fast the enemy had acquired him. It was enough to remind him that there were Strema marksmen hunkered down in the forest fighting this engagement with more smarts than those compatriots of theirs who had just run headlong into a wall of lead.

Jake clambered back up the zig zag of the central trench to his squad's perch knowing the Chandrians would desperately want to close with them and he held no doubts as to the Strema's ability to win that kind of engagement.

He ducked instinctively as an F-35 roared directly over the battlefield at an altitude of maybe 300 feet. The departing rumble of its exhaust reminded him of other battles on another world. The fighter bomber ignored the Chandrians grouped to attack them and proceeded north to hit the reinforcing force.

By the time Jake collapsed into their fighting platform, the fighter had delivered its ordinance. He popped his head up long enough to see the angry roiling line of fire and the thick black smoke from the napalm or whatever similar weapon the

Program's nanobots had turned out. The line of fire was about three miles to the north. Knowing the number of Strema coming towards them in that reinforcing group force made it feel a lot closer.

Darius crashed into the earth next to him. "What now?"

"Hopefully they saw us pull back, maybe see the airbus lift."

"Two of them made it to my trench on that last charge," Darius shook his head. "Shot to shit, not that they seemed to notice. No rifles just these." Darius held up a massive knife, or short sword depending on one's perspective. Shorter than a Roman Gladius by several inches it was longer and heavier than a Bowie knife. "They don't go down easy."

Jake looked appreciatively at the knife. "I want."

"I know where they are selling them," Darius countered. "I'd go myself, but you should probably know that today is a famous Jewish holiday. I should not have even gotten out of bed."

"You slept in a bed?" Jake pulled out his plug of tobacco and tossed it over his head like a grenade into the manned trench below them.

"Bed, sleeping bag, I think God would not draw a line."

"Heads up," Pretty's voice killed Jake's comeback. "They look to be moving everyone forward."

The whine of airbus turbines grew and gradually turned into a heavy thrumming as the fans spun up and put out that funky resonance that seemed to put him asleep in about three minutes every time he rode in one. They couldn't see the bus, the hill was between them and its flight path, but as he edged his head up over to peek at the enemy he could see hundreds of Chandrian rifles tracking it in the distance across the river. A few actually fired at it, but most, given the distance, just watched the lumbering behemoth rise to an altitude of a couple of hundred feet and float out over the river. Not the most aerodynamic craft to begin with, it was loaded to its maximum payload and moving slow.

The rest of his crew filed into their firing position, one by one each giving him a thumb's up. Krouse was the last one and just nodded. "Lower trench is clear."

Jake reported into Pretty and climbed up the firing step between Hans who was laying out his belt of SAW ammo and Domenik who looked around at them and smiled.

"Roger that," Pretty responded, "Lower trench is clear, going hot on lower trench."

Another jet, the last one, Jake knew, came in along the river slightly to the west of the last jet. They all watched it for several seconds flying low and relatively slow until it released a series of long cylinders from under its wings. The horizon again lit up with the napalm.

Jake saw Domenik cross himself as he looked at the rising line of fire from the distant airstrike. No one liked to see that kind of strike, least of all ground pounders who could never really forget there were soldiers on the ground who had been the target. They could cheer the strike and immediately feel guilty about doing so.

"Heavy weapons hold until the Bushmaster opens up," Pretty intoned on the command circuit. Jake knew Pretty wanted to get as many of the ETs out into the open as possible before he really opened up the spigot.

"Is this a heavy weapon?" Hans asked, as he adjusted the lay of his SAW's barrel.

"Not for you," Jake answered.

"Osprey holding thirty seconds out," Jiro reported in over the command circuit.

Individual Chandrians rushed out of the forest, yelling what they guessed could only be obscenities involving their mothers. Sporadic rifle fire dropped them before most had taken half a dozen strides.

"Stupid bastards," Jake shook his head. "They're letting us play whack a mole just to gauge our fire, you'd think they'd have an idea by now."

Occasionally the Chandrians would fire as well and he could tell from the resultant scream or sound of the heavy slugs slapping a sand bag whether or not they found their mark. Whatever could be said about the stupidity of trench warfare, it definitely paid to be in one rather than attacking one. Defenses and superior firepower aside, Jake guessed they'd lost maybe two dozen casualties to enemy fire. That number was weighed against what was probably north of fifteen hundred Chandrians piled up below them, half of what this first group had arrived with. The other half looked to be getting ready to attack together. Something they should have tried in the beginning, but the enemy couldn't have known how green the defenders really were. They were totally unschooled in modern combat and had gained their experience in a different culture on a different world. Jake spit over the edge of the trench. Combat lessons were expensive. The enemy would learn though, they always did.

"Here they come!" Someone yelled from well down the trench above them.

"No shit," Jake said to himself. No one could have heard him, the entire hillside erupted in rifle fire as the Strema gave up any semblance of a tight formation and surged into the clearing like a wave hurdling the bodies of their fallen trying to close with an enemy that depended on keeping them at bay in order to survive.

The forward edge of the ET tide was about a third of the way across, many not even carrying rifles but running with their short swords pumping like relay batons when Pretty blasted across the PA circuit into every soldier's earbud.

"Trench two, immediate cease fire and withdraw."

Jake took a second out of servicing targets to observe the withdrawal which had a lot more impetus to it than the one they had managed. Some soldiers dropped their weapons and fairly ran, others stood their ground, emptying their magazines before being pulled down off the firing step by their trench mates. But once they started moving, they moved quickly.

The leading edge of the Chandrians was within thirty yards of the empty forward most trench and there were a lot more to that point than during any of the three previous waves. The enemy sensed the letup in fire due to those retreating and poured on the speed as they had far fewer bodies to dodge the closer they got.

"Trench two, withdraw to EVAC immediately." Pretty commanded when a lot of the stubborn holdouts from trench two stopped in the central trench or looked to find another firing slot in the upper trenches.

The colonel's command got them moving and soon the trailing bolus of retreating soldiers surged behind them, past their position and moved on upward to the crest of the hill in the wide connector trench.

Jake went back to servicing his weapon, selectively firing on rapid single shots. It was difficult to miss at this range. The enemy ran in straight lines, right at them, in areas still shoulder to shoulder and several men deep. Hans, manning the SAW on a bipod, was using short controlled bursts that would drop two or three ETs with every measured pull of his trigger.

The outgoing fire emanating out from the center of the line was doubly effective and opened up the center of the Strema line to the point the enemy was a lot stronger at either flank than it was in the middle. That was where the Strema would reach the now empty lower trenches first.

"Osprey start your run." Jake barely heard Pretty's command. The Colonel was playing this close, but now was not the time to doubt the operational plan. He swapped out magazines and swung his sights out to the end of the left line where the Chandrians with a blood curdling yell sounding of success, surged over the wall of dirt into the forward most trench. Seconds later the yell was heard again from the right.

Several small objects were thrown out of the trench as the Chandrians swarmed like warrior ants down the empty trench attacking a hill of a competing hive. The Strema grenades went off with loud crack dispensing a thick white cloud hiding sections of the trench from view.

"Fire in the hole! Fire in the hole!" Pretty yelled over the open circuit.

Their militia's defensive fire dropped off to almost nothing as every defender in the remaining in the two upper trenched jumped back down into their trenches and covered their ears and opened their mouths as they'd been instructed. Several

Strema grenades made it as far as trench three and the militia screams could be heard over the momentary relative quiet.

They had lined the lower two most trenches with claymores and explosives. Pretty watched from his protected perch as the Chandrians sensing victory swarmed up and over the first trench and into the second, some near the center, ran up the central trench into the second. The rest were still in the kill box, almost to the first trench.

"Fire in the hole." The Colonel's voice sounded reluctant.

The claymores in the walls of the abandoned trenches went first, followed a second later by a massive explosion that turned the bottom half of the hill into a wave form and shot tons of Strema bodies, frozen rock and dirt out onto the kill box. The hundreds of Strema in the trenches never knew what hit them. The enemy still in the meadow near the front edge of the trench complex had perhaps a fleeting glimpse of their death as the tidal wave of dirt, rock and shrapnel slammed into and buried them

The explosion stopped the charge of those still standing in the clearing, perhaps seven or eight hundred enemy. The Strema stood stunned for a half a moment, as if not understanding what had just happened and then resumed their charge just as the Osprey popped over the hill and bore down on them like its namesake. Instead of swooping down for a kill nose first, it slid sideways and moved out towards the river, its remaining .50 caliber on the back of its tail ramp chewing into the enemy.

The Bushmaster and the three .50 calibers at the top of ridge line opened up as well, as did the three mortars situated back at the evac area. The remaining defenders in the upper two trenches stepped back into firing position. Roughly three hundred assault rifles came up looking for targets of which there were very few remaining. The mortars continued to fall for far too long, the explosions throwing up fountains of frozen dirt and fallen enemy into unholy fountains.

Hank Pretty swallowed the bile rising in his throat and pushed his mic button. "Cease Fire. Cease Fire. General EVAC now. Wounded and trench three first. Let's move people."

He tapped Jake's channel. "Jake, move them out quick, then I want you and your team up here with me."

The last airbus lifted off behind them. The heavily loaded aircraft flew with a very slight nose down attitude and moved off south following the track of the frozen river, slowly increasing its altitude as well.

Pretty stood at the top of the hill with his motley band of international veterans and watched the edge of the forest from which the enemy had come. The volume of fire, particularly from the mortars and the Bushmaster and the .50 calibers had given the forest's edge a splintered visage like it had been gone over by the world's largest weed eater. There was none of the back-slapping bravado masking fear or manic relief at still being alive, that they had all just seen among the departing militia. There was only a quiet sickness at what they had just done.

The Eden Militia had just been given a victory by an enemy that had no answer to the firepower they had been able to focus. A critical, much needed morale boosting victory. One that sickened each and every man standing atop that hill.

"Movement," Hans was prone atop the layer of sand bags with binoculars trained on the forest.

"Scouts." Hans didn't look back and kept his face implanted within the powerful binoculars. "In cover, not approaching."

Between the combatants lay somewhere around four thousand dead or dying Chandrians, Strema sure, but men. A very few were still alive, dragging themselves forward towards their objective. It was a scene out of some old zombie movie. Somehow those still surviving, clawing their way forward were far worse to look upon than the enemy dead.

A minute later the far edge of the tree line shimmered across the field, as men emerged by the thousands and came to a stop looking out at their fallen clan mates.

Pretty pointedly walked out into the open and planted a pole in between the sandbags lining the top of the ridge. At the top flew a simple white flag with a round blue circle in the middle of it. When the Chandrians got close enough to see it, they'd recognize the blue ball as the planet, and hopefully get the intended message. For themselves, for the militia, below the blue ball of the plant were the words – Molon Labe - in ancient Greek. *Come and Take Them.* The militia referred to it as the 'Come and Take It' flag. This world had owners that would fight to keep it.

The two sides stared at one another in silence that was finally broken by a barked command from somewhere behind the front Chandrian ranks. A small group, half a platoon by his estimate began walking forward. He had no idea what to make of it, but a parley would have been beyond pointless with the language barrier and he had no intention of putting his veterans at risk.

"Enough theater." He said and turned to walk down the backside of the hill. "Let's go." He was tired of killing and glad to be leaving. That said, he'd already ordered the Lightnings to be turned around with fuel and ordnance as quickly as possible. The jets might be able to get back and hit this group hard before they dispersed under the canopy of forest. He couldn't afford to feel any mercy. This enemy had none.

*

Chapter 13

Audy stood up and moved away from Kyle who was still unconscious. His friend's breathing was normal and his pulse was steady. It is better this way, he thought. Awake, Kyle could offend their soon to be captors in any number of ways and end up dead.

He could hear men approaching through the woods. Jomra was not coming alone. Audy stood there passively and watched as the group emerged from the trail led by Jomra who had a junior officer in tow with half a dozen of his select men. The metal bands on their forearms marking them among Jomra's chosen elite.

His oldest friend stopped in the clearing and looked at him in what might have been surprise that lasted only for as long as it took Jomra to close the distance between them, sparing a dismissive glance at Kyle on the ground.

"Did my rifle miss?"

"You shot true, Jomra." He touched his chest beneath his collar bone where the bullet in the back had exited.

"Yet you live." Jomra's tone remained flat. Audy was keenly aware that his friend had yet to use his name, signifying he was Jema.

"I was found and healed by this man's people," he pointed at Kyle. "Whom you would make war on for the benefit and at the order of the Kaerin."

"The Shareki cattle took you in?" Jomra sneered. "You would have done better to stay among them."

"Perhaps." Audy motioned with his head toward Kyle. "You would be wise to listen to this one. He is a leader among his people and they have strength the Kaerin could not imagine. Jomra, they would have us join them and be free."

"You are mad." Jomra wasn't insulting him, he clearly believed it. "This is why you have returned?"

"I bring hope, Jomra... as does he," he pointed at Kyle. "He is a man of honor, a friend, and a great warrior. His people would offer us a home here. They offer us freedom from the Kaerin. A future with honor."

Jomra's face was an unreadable mask of stone. "Shareki always offer what we would take. They talk peace when they have no choice but to die under our blades."

Audy shook his head. "You think them weak because of the Kaerin's stories. Your masters came here before and slew farmers. There were no warriors among them. These Shareki fight with tools you or the Kaerin cannot imagine. They have never faced an enemy such as these. Jomra, listen to me if you have ever been my friend. The Jema have never had an opportunity such as this to break free from their control.

"You speak, as if you are still one of us." Jomra's words slammed into him. He had always held out hope that Jomra would have told the Jema that the Kaerin had killed him. Memory of him would have been that of a traitor to the Kaerin, but he would have "died" as a Jema.

"You ask that we break the writ again, now? When we are on the bleeding edge of regaining our honor?"

"The Kaerin sent the Jema to die here. You know this. You overheard the same words as I."

"Yet I did not choose to dishonor my people."

Audy took a step closer to his old friend. "I chose to leave the path the Kaerin laid for us. I chose to see the truth in what we both heard. I chose a path that would see our people free, not dead or serving the Kaerin for all time."

"Perhaps you chose unwisely." Jomra said after a moment.

He nodded towards Kyle's unconscious body. "I have always chosen my friends wisely."

"You can scourge me, I don't care. But you must listen to this man first. We will submit to the heart speak, both of us. You are a man of honor, Jomra, I ask you with the kinship we once shared. Listen for the Jema, not the Kaerin. Keep me alive long enough that he can speak to you."

"You have no standing among us to request this."

Audy smiled. "Why else would I have asked for you to come?"

Jomra raised a hand and signaled his men forward. "Gag him and take them to my tent under guard."

"The Shareki lives." A Dadus reported, kneeling over Kyle's body with the point of his double bladed *bouma* hovering inches away from his friend's neck.

"He may be useful," Jomra almost paused too long. "Make sure he is bound well."

Audy whipped his head back as a guard went to gag him, "What of Kemi?"

The reaction was lightning fast. The heel of Jomra's hand catching him square in the mouth. An inch higher, with a slightly upturned angle of punch and it would have driven his nose ridge into his brain. As it was, Audy landed on his back and was immediately dragged to his feet by Jomra's men and gagged. He ignored the pain and swallowed the blood welling in his mouth and stared back at his childhood friend.

"You have no standing to ask of her." Jomra looked angry enough to hit him again. He turned around, and with a wave to his men walked through the brush, back to the trail leading to their camp.

Audy spared one look back at Kyle, who was being dragged like a piece of fire wood between two Jema. Jomra was forty paces down the trail and almost out of sight by the time he reached it. He shouldn't have asked about Kemi. She was Jomra's twin sister and it had taken their discussion, such as it was, to a personal level. He had presumed too much on their past friendship but he wanted Kemi to know he was alive. He desperately wanted to explain to her why he had done what he had. Was she dead? Was that the source of Jomra's anger? Did he go to her now? Or was he intending to convene the council and see him scourged for treason?

The three of them, he, Jomra and Kemi, had been inseparable since the devastation suffered by their parents' generation. Kemi and he had intended to join hands and have children, should the Kaerin ever lift their judgment. Had Jomra told her that he had tried to kill him? If he had, he doubted they were on speaking terms. Then again, she probably would have tried to kill him as well. It was good to be home among his people.

"Well, they didn't kill us." Kyle managed to say with a very stiff jaw. It felt like he'd been in a dentist's chair for a week. He'd come to as they dropped him to the tent's canvas floor and tied his hands behind a tent pole. Audy was standing, tied to another pole ten feet away, looking at him.

"Not yet." Audy replied, looking more concerned than he had ever seen the man. He kept looking towards the tent flap like he expected the grim reaper to walk in at any moment.

"You hit me really hard." Kyle flexed his neck to the sound of popping gristle. His head was throbbing.

"It seemed like the thing to do. You would have offended them and been killed."

"What's going on, Audy?" The look on Audy's face was one of genuine worry and it seemed entirely out of character.

"I am uncertain. I have asked a man I once called friend, a high-ranking officer, to speak on our behalf to the Clan Leaders, of which he is one. This is his tent. I would have thought we would be brought before the council."

"Is he hiding us?"

Audy shook his head, his eyes never left the tent flap. "No, we were dragged through the camp. Our presence is known by all."

"This friend, you spoke to him?"

"Former friend, and yes."

"And?" Kyle prompted, pulling hard at what felt like leather straps around his wrists. He knew he sounded impatient. Melancholy wasn't an emotion he would have ever assigned to Audy and it was more than a little worrying.

"He may have believed me," Audy turned fully to face him and Kyle noticed the smashed lips. "He did not seem swayed."

"Great." Kyle swore under his breath looking around for something, anything that would give him some hope. It was clear he wasn't going to get anything positive out of Audy at the moment.

"What now?" Kyle asked a little more loudly than he had intended. Shadows moved at the bottom of the tarpaulin door, indicating a guard just on the other side of the flap, but he didn't think they were in any danger of being understood.

"We wait," Audy replied. "It will be one thing…

"Don't start with that shit, we make our own fate. Remember?"

Audy looked over at him with a face like a kid whose dog had just been run over.

"If it helps you to believe that – do so. Believe me when I say this, our lives are in the hands of others." Audy turned back to the tent flap waiting for the injured puppy to walk in.

"Hey." Kyle prompted. Audy ignored him.

"Audy!" He barked, finally getting the man to look over at him. "What are you not telling me?"

Audy nodded slowly. "There is a woman."

He didn't know if he groaned out loud or not. But his headache seemed to flare to the point of an aneurism. "The one you told me about? How screwed are we?"

Audy shook his head slowly. "You mistake my meaning. Kemi'sfrota is her name. She is the sister to the former friend I spoke to."

"Like the kid sister of a buddy close? Or close?"

"Close." Audy shook his head slowly back and forth. "We are not allowed families as you know. The binding of man and woman like your marriages is forbidden – but we still plan for the future, we choose mates or at least our women do, for the time when we regain our honor in the eyes of the Kaerin. Kemi had chosen me and I had accepted."

"So, she's your fiancé?"

"More informal than that," Audy replied, "but yes."

"How is that not a good thing? You're back."

"She is a leader among the Jema. She holds as much sway, if not more than her brother and I betrayed her. I did after all desert my people … and her."

"Great," Kyle flopped his head back against the pole and instantly regretted it. "Any good news here?"

"You can now be certain. I am not a spy."

"There is that," he acknowledged. But Audy's mien didn't waver. He doubted Audy would ever get this upset over the threat of death, but the potential of dying outside the embrace of his clan? He knew that was what was eating him.

"I ever tell you about the time I got taken prisoner by a village of Indonesian tribal types, for whom torture was an art form?"

Audy waited a long moment before responding. "You did not. I assume you escaped."

"Nah, turned out they were on our side all along. They just needed someone to convince them of that fact."

"And you did this?"

"Well, no. I got rescued by a squad of Australian Paras, who basically vouched for me."

"I miss the point of this story."

"It doesn't have one, Audy. I thought you needed to hear something with a happy ending."

Audy just stared at him for a moment and finally grinned a little, shaking his head. "You are a strange people."

A guard entered the tent an hour later and did a quick walking inspection of their bonds and then held the flap open with his head bowed in respect. In walked a woman. One look at Audy confirmed that this was his 'Kemi' that he'd spoken of. Kyle watched as Audy tried to stand a little a taller.

She was of average height, and solidly built like a gymnast. Her muscular physique did nothing to hide her curves. Her hair was braided in a thick flat rope that hung as far as her shoulders and her skin, like Audy's, had a Mediterranean cast to it. Her skin tone aside, holding a heavy spear that was taller than she was by a foot, Kyle immediately thought of an ancient Valkyrie. This woman was a weapon as much as the spear she carried. It was her eyes that Kyle focused on, one bright green and the other a cold gray-blue like a wolf. She glanced at him for just a moment and dismissed his presence just as quickly.

Ignoring him, she walked up to Audy and looked at him seeming to confirm that he was real. Audy had gone as rigid as the tent pole he was tied to, the moment she had entered. He didn't appear to have so much as taken a breath since.

The woman reached out slowly and touched his face. Like a blind person trying to recognize a long-lost love. Kyle suddenly felt less the prisoner and more intruder on something private.

Audy said something.

She nodded once and smiled at him. She brushed away a single tear that had stopped half way down her high cheek bones and then reached around Audy and hugged him tightly for a long moment her head buried in his chest.

Yep, definitely intruding, he thought. Not that there was a damned thing he could do about it. On the upside, it looked like Audy's concern over her reaction might have been overly pessimistic.

She broke the embrace and wiped away another tear as she stepped back. The smile disappeared in an instant. She struck out, driving a fist into Audy's face with a sudden violence that shocked him. He watched as Audy's head slammed back against the heavy tent pole with a hollow sounding thump.

She looked about to strike again but shook out the pain in the hand she had used. The blood, hers and his, she shook to canvas the floor with disdain. Kyle would be surprised if she hadn't broken her hand on Audy's face. She took another half a step back and whirled in place, the spear coming to the horizontal as she spun. The back end of the heavy spear was capped in an iron looking ball and it was driven with all her momentum into Audy's gut.

The tender moment had devolved into a beat down in seconds. *Ok, maybe Audy had it right in thinking she would be pissed.*

A look of satisfaction crossed the woman's face as Audy tried desperately to breath with a diaphragm that had suddenly decided to quit. The woman; the very angry, and skilled Valkyrie, adjusted the grip on her spear and turned towards him. Trussed to the pole as he was, under the gaze of those strange mismatched eyes he felt like a piece of meat.

She moved close to him and asked something with a calmness that surprised him. He had no idea what she was asking. He immediately recalled his SEER course. When you were going to get beat on, just go with it. 'Ride it like a rodeo bull' one of the instructors had said early and often, repeated with a sadistic smile. He'd never ridden a bull and had thought it was a stupid analogy then. It wasn't helping at the moment either.

Audy coughed out a single word and then after a struggled intake of breath let fly a string of Chandrian. Kyle just watched the woman's face for some indication that he wasn't about to catch the shaft of her spear with his face. Or worse, the very shiny, deadly looking double bladed spear point in his chest.

Something Audy had said seemed to register on her face. She pursed her lips in anger. Kyle, still expecting the spear, either end of it, just tried to hold her eyes with his own. She finally broke away and walked back to Audy and asked a question.

They spoke, alternating between shouts of anger and impassioned pleading on Audy's part for nearly thirty minutes. Kyle heard his name mentioned twice and the word Shareki half a dozen times by either of them. He knew from Audy, it meant 'outsider,' 'enemy,' or the 'soon to fall under our blades,' depending on the context. None of its varied meanings promised anything good.

The conversation, most of it having been carried by Audy wound down and Kemi seemed to relax somewhat. Though, at several points she'd shake her head in either anger or disbelief. When it was over, she said something to Audy that seemed to carry some formal weight to it. Turning to go, she stopped suddenly at the tent's doorway. She walked back to Audy. A short smile playing at her lips. She struck out again. This time a vicious back hand that split open Audy's bottom lip, again. She smiled at the sight of his blood and then walked up to him and gingerly kissed him on the cheek before walking out without so much as another glance towards him.

Alone in the tent again. Kyle just looked at Audy's bruised and bleeding face. "Well, I'm no linguist, but that seemed to go pretty well."

Audy turned to him, and offered up the best smile he could. Under the circumstances, it wasn't pretty. His teeth were red with blood from his cut lip. "Better than I expected."

"Is this an attempt to develop a sense of humor?"

"No." Audy shook his head and nodded towards the tent flap. "She thought me dead. Her brother Jomra, my friend, reported me dead."

"To protect you?" Kyle asked.

Audy shrugged. "I would like to know the answer to that myself. He's risen in command since I left them. It was he that shot me in the back before I fell through the portal."

"This just keeps getting better and better."

"He and I were on guard duty in the Kaerin compound. It was during a time of year when the portal gate was active. We overheard a conversation among some high ranking Kaerin speaking of us, the Jema. They thought we were of a different clan or perhaps it was a test of our loyalty as Jomra believed, but I decided to act. On my own, outside the Clan."

"Jomra tried to stop you?" Kyle asked.

"He nearly did." Audy nodded. "We fought and he shot me when I dashed for the gate. He told the Kaerin that my dead body had fallen into the gate. There was much blood I take it, as Kemi told me. There had been a gunshot and no body, I was gone. Jomra was questioned under the heart speak. He was believed."

"He never told his sister?"

"Until today, No. The story he had told the Kaerin was the truth as he saw it. He would not have dared to lie to them and put the entire clan at risk. The story he was ordered by the Kaerin to tell the Jema, was that I had been killed by them, trying to get to the portal."

"Where does that leave us?"

Audy shrugged again. "It will be discussed at Council. They will understand Jomra was merely following a Kaerin order, he had no choice. He has now put himself at great risk telling his sister the truth. It will be up to her whether or not the story is told to the council. At any rate, because of the Kaerin's explanation, I have lost all right to speak freely. I am no longer Jema." Audy spit out a mouth full of blood onto the floor of the tent.

"Kemi will decide whether to tell the council, and then they will decide whether to let us speak, using the heart speak, or they will kill us both."

About what he had figured. "So, third and long?"

Audy started to laugh, but it was clear his bruised and bleeding face hurt. "I would have said fourth and long, but there at the end... before she departed? Now I say third and long."

He figured Audy was referring to the kiss. "I did notice she has some very strong feelings where you are concerned." Kyle said.

"You are very perceptive, my friend."

*

"What kind of meat is this?" Kyle poked at chunks of dark meat floating within something like a watery stew. He didn't hate it, but it was a close-run thing. He was hungry enough that he managed to keep it down. They'd been there a full day and night and it was the first food that had been offered.

They were seated with their backs to their poles, under the angry gaze of a single Jema warrior that looked like he'd just as soon gut either one of them as take another breath in their presence.

"Mmmm...." Audy paused as if uncertain. "We call it Semat."

Kyle shook his head. "You do realize that we come from the same planet, as least in terms of animal life? What would I call it?"

Audy spooned in a large mouthful and chewed heartily. He swallowed and pointed at Kyle's bowl with his wooden spork.

"I think I know how you will feel, let us say only that this animal's hunting days are over."

"Dog? You eat dogs?"

"Given a choice, no." Audy replied. "They are pets to us as well."

Kyle stared down at the bowl, pushing a chunk of meat through the almost pungent gravy. He'd eaten worse, but he put the bowl down and focused on the coarse bread. "Loyal food?"

Audy tossed him his uneaten bread. "You must eat, you will need your strength if they allow us to speak."

"This heart speak? You've done it before?"

Audy nodded in the affirmative his mouth full. Kyle watched him swallow and almost felt sick at the thought of eating a dog.

"The Kaerin use it often on the leaders of the clans beneath them. Always, where the Jema are involved. The medicine or drug is not painful, but after .... after you will feel as if you have drunk far too much beer, only much, much worse."

"Wonderful..." Kyle chewed on the hearty bread and drank the water from their canteens that had magically reappeared with the meal. Audy shoveled the dog stew in like he was home from college and eating mother's cooking.

"The camp is not well supplied, it is strange." Audy said between mouthfuls. "They've been here less than one of your months, and already they are eating Semat. I don't understand this. The host is usually supplied for several decs, three or four of your months."

"Maybe they don't want to waste food on us."

Audy shook his head and looked directly at him. "Do not look at him, but our guard has been staring at your meal. He is hungry."

"Can I give it to him?" Cause I'm not *that* hungry, Kyle thought.

"I would not. Our culture views Shareki as less than the meat in this soup, it would offend him greatly."

"Of course, it would." Kyle wondered if it made any sense to try to ally themselves with the Jema, they were so different. "Different worlds."

"Yes," Audy said somewhat forcefully to drive the point home.

"If they let us speak, believe us, actually accept what we're offering, will they ever see us as anything better than dogs?"

Audy looked at him in confusion. "Am I not your friend?"

"Yeah, but..." Kyle waived his piece of bread around the tent, "forgive me, but I have a hard time believing you were ever... like this."

Audy stopped chewing, swallowed, and dropped his spork into the bowl in disgust.

"When I was new to your people. I could not understand why you trusted me as you did. It took some time for me to realize that I was not being tricked. Elisabeth explained to me, when I was still early in my learning your language, that you were a warrior but you did not wish to be. This is true?"

"Given an alternative, sure – I've had my fill."

"This I could not understand, I still don't in truth. Like a dog wishing he was a bird you understand. Like thinking of Jake without the laughing, it was something that could not be in my head. What else was there besides being a warrior? In my mind, I saw you as an equal, a warrior."

Audy looked at his own hands for a moment and then tapped the side of his head. "I could not imagine a warrior, a leader of men, and someone people followed not because they had to, but because of wanting to.

Audy pointed at him, accusingly. "This man was either lying or I did not understand...how his clan...worked.

"You were not lying, I learned. I had no concept of what else a man could do or be, except a slave to the Kaerin. Your people have a gift of freedom that you have almost forgotten is a gift. We..." Audy picked up his spork and twirled it around the tent, "... for us, it is a half forgotten, whispered legend from our long ago past. We have only our duty to the Kaerin. It's all we have had for generations. There is only our clan, and our enemies. There is nothing else."

"That's what I'm worried about." Kyle nodded slowly.

"I am not saying this correctly – I don't have the words." Audy pushed his empty bowl away. "You people have a saying, 'no badder enemy, but best friend,' yes?"

"Yea, sort of, no worse enemy, no better friend."

"This is what I am trying to say." Audy smiled. "If we are allowed to speak, and they believe us and accept your idea, we will not be allies, Kyle. You will become part of this clan. One of us." Audy paused and looked away for a moment... "or one of them. I promise you, you will see them different. No better friend."

"Or worse enemy?"

"True, they may still kill us," Audy agreed. "For now, we are the enemy, Shareki."

"I think they'll hear us out, they wouldn't have fed us otherwise." Kyle was trying to make the best of their predicament.

"The food means nothing," Audy rebuffed him. "The Jema would not kill a prisoner when he is hungry."

Kyle just regarded his friend, wondering what kind of people these Jema were when they weren't at war with you. "You need to stop talking now..."

Audy stared back at him for a moment and then broke out into a grin.

"I got you."

Chapter 14

He had no idea what came next, but the appearance of four very determined looking guards with those wicked looking short swords already drawn, left no doubt that they were going to find out very soon.

The guard who had been in the tent with them since they had eaten, untied them from their poles at a barked order and they were marched outside into the center of the camp which was a field of half frozen mud. Kyle was struck by how cold it was. The storm they'd been warned about was here. The light rain fell fast, almost ice, in small needle-like drops.

He was ready in his heart should the worst happen. He'd been in this place emotionally a couple of times before; no win missions where he'd honestly thought there was decent chance he wasn't going to make it. The resignation to accept what came next wasn't a new emotion, just one he didn't particularly enjoy. To make matters worse he'd volunteered for this trip, eyes wide open.

He had it right in his head and still believed he'd chosen correctly. If they didn't stop the Chandrian invasion and stop it hard, they'd soon be fighting the entire Chandrian home world and they'd all be dead anyway. He was going to go down swinging. Everything, Eden, Elisabeth and the future that they'd all found here .... he had more than enough to fight for or die for.

He had no idea how executions were carried out by the Jema, but there was no evidence of what his imagination had him looking for; no hastily constructed gallows, firing squad or a bonfire in site. Up ahead was a large tent with a crowd gathered in front of it, perhaps three or four hundred people were gathered in the rain outside. Maybe they'd just let the crowd beat him to death. He'd seen some of that on Earth; sectarian violence in India, or clan reprisals in Northern Iraq. Those weren't comforting memories. He looked over at Audy who walked like a wrongly accused man, clear eyed and head held high.

"Good or bad?" he asked.

The two guards leading the procession stopped and spun on him. He had a short sword held at his throat almost before he realized it was there. One of the guards barked something at him, and he got the message loud and clear. *Copy that – shut your pie hole.* He nodded gingerly in acceptance, he could feel where the sword had nicked his neck.

The gathered crowd, men and women started to part ways and allow them through. Kyle took his cue from Audy and didn't look away or down. He met every gaze that he could. It didn't feel like a lynch mob. The stares were more curious than anything else. It hit him suddenly. Every face out there was a man or woman of an age, somewhere between the late twenties and mid-thirties. As alien as the Jema were, the Kaerin took it to a whole different level. To have been able to order, and then carry out the execution of the entire adult portion of the Jema, only to keep the children alive and under their thumbs spoke to a level of evil that was difficult to conceptualize.

The entire Jema Clan, several million strong at some point to hear Audy speak of it, had been reduced to a single generation of children, now grown warriors. Cannon fodder for the Kaerin for the last ten years, they'd been reduced in numbers to the point there were a little more than thirty-four thousand of them still alive. It was a genocide that Kyle had a hard time imagining. Like the Nazis, only the Kaerin hadn't been stopped. He couldn't fault the Jema for being a little touchy regarding him and anyone else the Kaerin labeled Shareki. This entire Jema clan, its surviving members, had grown up and reached adulthood with a single acceptable path to redemption beaten into them - loyalty to the Kaerin. Their revolt, and the price they had paid, was still with them in the form of the elders and children that weren't there.

He could hear Elisabeth's arguments regarding cultural incompatibility playing in his head. At the moment, he had to admit she sounded very 'right.' Kyle knew their only chance, his only chance, needed to play on the fact the Jema had to be very pissed off as well.

And I'm going to ask these people to rebel again. Kyle couldn't guess how likely they would be to listen to a Shareki who was brought to them by a traitor. That is, if they were even going to allow he and Audy to speak and not do whatever the Jema did to Shareki prisoners they had no use for.

He'd expected a dark interior given the tent's size, but most of the ceiling seemed to be of a clear plastic that let in the gray soft light of the overcast sky. There were tables set up in a horse shoe pattern, down both sides and across the back end away from the entrance. Everyone sat with their backs to the walls of the tent, watching them as they were escorted in. No hooded executioner with an axe stood waiting, but there was a very solemn air and every eye of the fifty or sixty seated Jema regarded them both with a complete lack of emotion. The crowd was impossible to read and given the massive differences in their cultures, he'd probably just make a mistake in judgement if he tried.

Kyle immediately noticed the one familiar face he recognized, Kemi something, something. Audy's ex, who had made it very clear she had more than a few issues regarding her ex-boyfriend and his foundling Shareki, sat as impassively as the rest at the long table stretching across the back of the tent and forming the middle of the horseshoe. There were what looked like iron fire baskets hammered into the ground throwing off additional light. The scene was entirely too medieval for his taste. He was surprised to see one old man sitting at the center of the head table. The orbits of the man's eyes were walnuts of scar tissue and both of his arms resting on the table ended at the forearm and were capped by a bronze looking metal caps that reflected the torch light.

Another woman, sat between Kemi and the single Elder whispering into his ear. Kyle was reminded of the historical analog of the Emperors of Constantinople who regularly blinded and maimed the challengers to their rule. These Kaerin needed to be stopped.

The guards brought them into the center of the horseshoe, five paces removed from the center table and cut the straps that bound their hands behind their backs.

196

Kyle rubbed his wrists, willing the blood back into his hands and tried to look the men and women at the table in the eye, but they all turned as one of the Jema rose from a side table and approached them. He was slightly shorter than Audy, but heavily muscled. His eyes were a bright green, and he immediately recognized the resemblance this man shared with Kemi. There was no mistaking the fact that this particular Jema was a leader of soldiers. Everything about him screamed warrior and the crowd seemed to hang expectantly on his word.

This would be Jomra, he gathered. Twin brother to Kemi, and Audy's former friend. The same one that had tried to kill him and named him a traitor. He looked like real a hard case.

The man said something, a short sentence to Audy and then jerked his head in Kyle's direction. He then went on for a minute or two. Audy nodded a couple of times in understanding. When the man finished speaking, Audy dipped his head a little further in what might have been a grudging bow.

"I'm instructed by Jomra, to explain to you what will happen next. We will be judged." Audy's voice was clear. And Kyle could sense the shock amongst the crowd when Audy spoke in a foreign tongue. "You might think of this as a trial, though it will not be familiar as such to you, my friend."

"We will be given the heart speak drug I spoke to you about. I will be put to question first without any words from you. If they judge that my heart is true, you will then be asked questions through me. You will be aware of what you are saying, but you will say what your heart speaks. You will have memory of it, but no control of your words. I will speak your words to them, all of them, just as you say them."

"They could use what I say against my people?"

"Yes," Audy nodded, "and will do so if they choose to remain loyal to their masters. You, we, have no choice at this time. You could attack the guards, but all here know your potential value now that they see me speaking your tongue. They would take care not to kill us, it would only change the questions they ask."

"So, Hail Mary?"

Audy grinned. "This dog must hunt."

Jomra barked a harsh question at Audy. Kyle saw how Audy respectfully bowed his head as he nodded.

"Jomra wishes to know that you understand what I have told you."

"I understand, but I have a question."

"Speak it."

"The old man, who is he?"

"He was our first sword, our greatest warrior at the time of our clan's doom. An example to all of us from the Kaerin. He is a man of great wisdom."

"Can I be introduced?"

Audy looked at him like he was crazy. "We have no standing here."

Jomra fired another question at Audy. His tone left no doubt that he thought the private conversation between the Audy and the Shareki had gone on long enough.

"Are you prepared?"

Hell no, he thought. "Not like I have a choice."

Audy responded to Jomra with a short sentence terminated with a deep bow to his former friend and another towards those seated at the head table.

Another Jema, this one wore what he took to be a red leather trench coat that had the look of a formal uniform of some sort, approached carrying a wooden tray with two small ceramic shot sized cups. For all he knew, the guy was a waiter. The man held the tray out to Jomra, who ignored him, and just stared at Audy for a moment before indicating the cups with his chin.

Audy took the two cups off the tray and handed one to him.

"Drink it all now." Audy said. "Do not hesitate. Do not resist what you are asked. They respect truth and courage. Remember this."

Kyle watched Audy slam the contents of his cup back and swallow with a grimace like it was double shot of rot gut. He looked down at the thick brown sludge in his cup and figured whatever it was, he had tasted worse.

He was wrong, so very wrong. Battery acid was his first guess as his throat and stomach clenched in pain as the elixir slid past and landed painfully in his gut. He focused as hard as he could to keep it down and stay upright as his stomach muscles seized up in pain. The powerful wave of nausea was countermanded by the painful cramping of his stomach and the trail of lava the liquid had left in his throat. The pain radiated out from his stomach, up into his chest, down into his groin, easing as it went. A minute later, after nearly blowing his dog stew over Jomra and the scary looking Jema in the red leather coat, the pain had faded.

The silence in the tent began to take on a weight that he could feel on his skin. The flickering light from one of the iron sconces tasted like cinnamon, and when he looked up at the clear plastic of the tent's roof, the light bloomed in his head like a trumpet. He shook his head and tried to focus on the faces around the edge of the tent. The silent stares were unnerving enough without whatever crazy effect the drug was having. He looked over at Audy who stood stoically, his eyes locked with Jomra. He let his gaze wonder over those impassive stone faces seated at the head table. Most were watching Audy, particularly Kemi who may have looked concerned. But then again, he remembered that she'd been crying on Audy's shoulder in joy just before she started kicking his ass.

He caught himself stifling a laugh that came from nowhere as he thought back to Audy's reunion with his lady. It was much harder to do than it should have been. There were maybe half a dozen people seated at the end of the side tables on either side of him that he could see by turning just his head and he managed to catch a couple of them looking at him but they quickly turned their heads away when he stared back.

Fuck You, too, he thought.

Another minute passed and a tingling in his toes and feet of all places seemed to move rapidly up his legs. By the time the muscles in his upper legs started to itch, he was swaying on feet he couldn't feel. He was suddenly falling. He knew this only because the panorama of his vision was suddenly rotating

199

upwards rapidly at a crazy diagonal. He didn't feel himself hit the ground. His body, any feeling or awareness in his limbs, was simply.... gone.

He watched as his view changed again, he had been picked up and manhandled into a camp made chair. He knew this because he caught a glimpse of it as they dragged it towards him from the edge of tent and strangely because he could smell the pitch of the fresh hewn limbs of brush pine. He had no sensation of his body being thrust into it, or of the hands that seemed to adjust his head so he was roughly facing the front of the room. He could hear the chair flex as he was dropped into it, smell the pine sap, but there was absolutely nothing else. He was just a detached head propped up between two branches.

And we used to complain about the polygraph, he thought. This time the sound of his own laughter escaped, startling him.

"Not good," he heard someone say and then realized it had been him.

Intellectually, he knew he should be worried. He figured he'd be easy to flay alive in this condition. That prospect didn't worry him in the least. The fact that it didn't, did.

He couldn't turn his head, but in his peripheral vision he could see that back-shooting bastard Jomra standing off to his left looking down at what he assumed was Audy in his own bark-o-lounger, get it? Bark-o-lounger, it's a tree, a fucking tree!

He saw Jomra turn towards him with a look that even in his addled state left no doubt where he sat on Jomra's list of important things. Somewhere between a skin tag and a scab on a stray dog's dick. Gawd, I sound like Jake.

He heard Jomra bark something and the man in the red leather duster reappeared in front of him and shoved the edge of another tea cup between lips and clamped his nose shut. *Oh shit*, had he been speaking out loud? Had he said all that out loud? Surely, Audy wouldn't have translated that.

This new stuff was either tasteless or the first batch had melted his tongue. He wondered about that too, wasn't taste and smell related. He couldn't remember, but he dug through his memory for an answer with an intense focus that he couldn't comprehend.

Jomra started asking Audy questions. He knew they were questions only because the barking guttural shit these people called a language seemed to share the earthen human interrogative tone change at the end of a question.

The red leather coat wearing guy was still in front of him, watching him with what may have been an expression of concern but just as easily could have been the Chandrian facial expression for someone in the process of shitting themselves.

Audy and Jomra droned on and on. At one point, Audy talked longer than he had ever heard his friend speak. Kyle had the dimming light coming through the plastic roof to tell him the sun had slid behind the hills to the west. He realized that he must have blacked out at some point. It was dark outside, and noticeably dimmer in the tent. Newly lit lanterns lighting the interior looked like oil storm lamps.

"Backward ass aliens." This time he heard himself speak out loud.

"Oops" He licked his lips and smiled at or at least he thought he did at the red leather jacket pharmacist.

"Seriously, that jacket? Is that dog leather?"

The man stared at him for a moment without any expression and returned to his corner near the head table.

"Come back here! I'll bite your leg off!" He started laughing hysterically. Or thought he was, his diaphragm wasn't capable of doing anything but breathing in shallow tides. "I'm the Black Knight!"

He wasn't trying to be a smart ass, but the words just formed on his tongue and flew the nest as soon as he thought of them. There was no filter on his thoughts that seemed to run directly to his tongue and no thought of one

Audy was answering a question from someone at the head table.

"Don't know what he's going on about, but you should listen to him," he spoke out.

"You must be quiet, Kyle." Audy spoke to him from out of the space to his left. You will give affront."

"I can't stop, Audy... Audy? Not like they can understand me anyway. Shit!! What's in this stuff?"

"I've been translating all you say." Audy yelled at him.

It took a second for those words to register.

"Oh shit...everything?"

Somebody shouted something, yet another something he couldn't understand. Panic building in his mind and he knew that he was yelling every incoherent thought that seeped forth. Somewhere between embarrassment and knowing he was killing any chance they had, he was getting angry. He was getting pissed off, this wasn't fair, he had no filter, no inhibitions, but it wasn't his fault.

"It was the dog leather guy, blame him!"

There was a blizzard of activity around his head. Shit! He was talking out loud again. Something soft was put between his lips and suddenly wrenched tight. *That* he did feel.

Some part of his brain realized the gag had been doctored with something, just before his eyes slammed shut and his mind went thankfully quiet.

Audy's voice was a lifeline. I'm still alive. Audy's alive. If he could have reached with his hands and grabbed hold of Audy's voice he would have. It slowly grew clearer.

"You must wake, Kyle." The voice sounded closer now. "They are ready to begin your questioning."

"Do you have any idea how long it's been since I slept this well?"

"Matters not, my friend. The Jema are ready to begin."

"I don't give a shit, Audy. We'll kill them all, you tell them that. We'll take our chances with their home world, kill them all too. You tell em, I'm going back to sleep now." He could hear Audy translating. *Oh shit...*

Something slapped him, and his eyes flashed open with a surge of adrenalin. The man in the red leather coat was standing over him, with his hands on his knees. His strange alien face hovered inches above his own. He tried striking out with a quick jab of his right arm. An arm he couldn't feel, which didn't move.

He tried head butting the evil bastards face, only inches away, but the only reaction was a satisfied smirk on the face of the head pharmacist as if the man could read his thoughts. The witch doctor turned his head to address the solid presence of Jomra standing just behind and then slowly stood and walked back to his corner. Kyle half imagined the evil bastard had spun himself some sort of web there, that he would climb into and wait until he was needed again.

"What an asshole." Kyle muttered to himself and then he heard Audy translate something.

He saw what might have been a smile crack Jomra's face.

"You translated that?" He still couldn't turn his face and see Audy, but he could hear him just to his left.

"I have said all that you have spoken. I will say all that you will say." Audy explained. "Speak only to me, answer only me, think only of my voice."

Four men carrying Audy in his chair, swam in to his vision. They positioned Audy facing him, with his back to the head table. Kyle wondered if he looked as ridiculous as Audy. His friend looked like he'd been hit with a tranquilizer dart meant for an elephant. His head lolled from side to side until Jomra grabbed him by the hair and adjusted Audy's head so that they faced each other directly.

Kyle could still see the head table over and behind Audy's shoulders.

"Hello there." He would have waved if he'd had arms.

"Kyle, you must focus," Audy said.

"I can't stop saying whatever I think," he replied as calmly as he could. That fact bothered him a great deal, but there was a disconnect somewhere that prevented anything he said causing him any concern.

He listened for a moment as Audy faithfully translated everything he said or thought – not that there was a difference at the moment.

"Whose side you on here?"

Audy translated again.

203

"Hey did your girlfriend believe you? She want to jump your bones? Or grind you up and feed you to the dogs?"

"Look at me!" Audy raised his voice and Kyle didn't much like his tone.

"You look like shit, Audy," he said. "She cracked your lip pretty good."

Audy shouted out something in Chandrian and Jomra stepped up close to him and peeled back an eyelid with his thumb and then shouted something of his own. It didn't sound good.

The red jacketed witch doctor came back out of his shadowed corner and did the same thing to his eyes that Jomra had.

"This guy's breath smells like shit! Oh shit, why would I say that? Oh, hey they don't under.... Audy, stop it, don't translate that, I was just thinking out loud. I'm mean seriously! I just crapped myself or this guy has been eating dog shit."

"Kyle!" Audy yelled.

"Why are you yelling at me?!"

He was aware of the blow as it came in. He watched it in slow motion with a clinical detachment. The red jacket pharmacist rocked his head to the side with the open-faced slap. It barely registered and he managed to smile and cough out a laugh.

"Tell him he hits like a little girl."

Audy translated again.

"Seriously, whose side are you on?"

Dr. Evil faced the head table and was shaking his head as he said something. When he turned back around, he was holding another vial.

"I hope I puke all over that jacket."

The vial was shoved between his lips and he briefly thought about spitting it back at the man but he remembered why he was here, and swallowed through a force of pure will. The heavy hand over his mouth and another pinching his nose shut may have helped as well.

"You have too much of the drug in you." Audy explained to him. "That will help, but you must focus. Do not speak again, except to answer me."

"This is not a fourth and one, Audy. We don't even have the ball."

"Calm yourself Kyle, look at me."

He focused on Audy's face. Don't be a smart ass, don't be a smart ass, don't be a smart ass.

"I am not being a smart ass, Kyle."

"Shit! I meant me.... talking to myself."

"They will wait, close your eyes and wait for my voice. Do not speak."

"Course they'll wait, must be the best entertainment they've had in a while."

"Kyle..." The threatening tone of Audy's voice shocked him.

He actually managed to bite down on his reply.

A few minutes passed and he realized that he could breathe a little easier and it was slowly becoming easier to focus.

"Kyle? Are you ready to begin?"

"Like I have a choice."

Audy said something in Chandrian and something like a command was shouted back at him.

"Choose words carefully, Kyle. They have believed me, it is now up to you."

"Ok."

"Do you trust the man Audrin'ochal?" Audy asked.

"You think I'd sign up for this shit for fun?"

He listened to the translation and saw a glimmer of a smile crack Jomra's face from where he stood behind Audy's chair. It was Audy's voice he held on to, like a life line thrown from the back rail of a boat getting farther away with every passing moment, but it was the face of Jomra that he could see. The weathervane that was in control of his life.

Jomra spoke for a moment directly at Audy. He thought he could sense a friendlier attitude on Jomra's part towards his childhood friend but for all he knew of Jema social cues, the man may have been preparing to kill them both.

"The council has presented you with a choice," Audy said after a moment. "A simple decision. One, you will be allowed to leave and given safe passage by the Jema and I will be allowed to live again among them, as a Jema. They will remain true to the Kaerin's writ and wage war on your people."

"What's the other choice?"

"You will be killed for your knowledge of the Jema. I will be scourged and then killed. They will not wage war on your people, but the Jema would wish to disappear and start afresh on this world and be done with the Kaerin."

"If we don't stop the Strema and the Kaerin, the Jema will eventually be hunted down and enslaved or killed outright. Without us, the Jema are as good as dead, either at our hands or the Kaerin. You tell them that."

Audy translated and was stopped halfway through by a shout from the old man at the head table.

"I have explained this already to them. They say the question stands, you must choose one of the paths I have presented."

"The second choice." He answered without hesitation, taking the Jema out of the fight was the next best option to having them as allies.

"But when my people are done with the Strema and those dumb fucks in Canada, there is nowhere you'll be able to hide on this rock. We will find you."

Audy translated the response and there was a long pause before Jomra broke in with a question. Audy translated again.

"If your people are so powerful, why would you need us? Why not make your escape and fight us alongside your people?"

"Because fewer of my people will die fighting the Strema, and the Jema could survive, and be free, if we fight together. Besides," Kyle continued unable to stop himself. In a sense it was similar to being drunk, his emotions were jacked up, but there wasn't the accompanying slowness of thought, "after what the Kaerin did to you people, I like a good revenge story. We'd like to help."

"Is it not a warrior's duty to die for his people?" Audy asked after the back and forth.

"Yes, if he or she must. But we have a saying, it's better to make the other guy die for his people. We value our soldiers, our warriors. We fight …. very well. Sadly, it is the single thing my world had learned to do best." Audy was translating simultaneously, so he spoke slowly, managing as well as he could to find the right words.

"We came here to start a new life, one we are more than willing to fight for. But it is also a life we are willing to share. I thought a people like the Jema, who have been through what you have been through, would want another life other than as slaves. Who would perhaps be willing to fight for your freedom, as we are."

"It appears I was wrong. Audy told me that you were a people of honor, a people who had once chosen to not live as slaves. Do what you will with me. Let Audy remain with his people, I know how deeply he cares for you. You stupid bastards should listen to him. You can tuck tail and run, go ahead. If the Kaerin don't find you, do not doubt that my people will. To protect our freedom, if we have to, we will end you. It's why we are here."

He waited until Audy finished his translation and he watched his friend slowly nod at him. He'd made the right call, Audy accepted that.

Someone at the head table, directly behind Audy's head spoke, he couldn't see who.

Audy looked at him again and winked. There might have been a smile playing on his lips, but if Audy's face was half as numb as his, it was probably just the swollen lip.

"You freely accept your death, and that of your friend Audy to buy your people one less enemy to fight?" Audy nodded at him as he finished the question. Whatever he thought of the Jema, Audy had been good to his word.

"To fight at the same time," he corrected the questioner. "Yes, I do. Just don't go thinking you'll survive in the long run. If you were smart, which I'm seriously beginning to doubt, you'd stay slaves and team up with your masters and the

Strema. It would increase your odds. But putting you all in one place at the same time would make it easier for us as well."

The man in the red leather coat walked out of the shadows to take his place next to Jomra. He spoke a few words to Audy and then turned his head to look at Kyle.

"This is Bres'Trael, the leader of our Gemendi cadre, the ones most familiar with Kaerin technology, but make no mistake, he is Jema."

Oh shit. He managed not to say it out loud. "Not the witch doctor?"

"No, not the doctor." Audy said and then translated.

Bres'Trael smiled at him and begin laughing.

"What the hell?" Kyle could feel his world dropping out from under him.

Audy translated that too. And a few more people joined in the laughter, but it died the instant Jomra raised his hand. He turned to Audy and said a few words in Chandrian, finished and then added something at the end.

"Jomra apologizes for putting you through this trial. He has told me to explain to you, that I was able to convince them of our truth. You Kyle, you were merely tested... they needed to know what manner of man led your people's warriors."

Audy smiled. "He likes you, says that you have very large stones."

"They believed you? You could have told me."

Audy smiled at him. "I gave my word that I would not, and I am again and forever a Jema."

"I'm happy for you, now could I get out of here before I say something truly stupid?"

Audy translated loudly and this time almost everyone laughed.

Jomra walked up close to him and smiled with a nod. He said something and laid a hand on his shoulder.

The crowd stood and bellowed something in unison.

"That sounded good." He said to Audy

"Sri-Tel would speak," Audy said.

"Who?"

"Our leader, our sole remaining elder."

Kyle could see the movement behind Audy, and Jomra who moved to the side of his own chair. Kemi and another woman helped the elderly, maimed Jema stand.

The old man addressed the whole crowd in a booming voice...

"Kyle, you are now Jema if you wish it, and if it is allowed by your people."

He looked at Audy, who was translating, almost in shock. "You translated everything I said?"

"I did. Trust me, he understands. They all do."

Sri-Tel was walked around the table until he stood next to Jomra and began speaking in a deep sonorous voice that echoed through the large tent. Kyle desperately wished he could stand, or even move. His current helplessness, and the fact that he'd insulted all of them didn't seem to be a solid foundation to begin an alliance. Finishing, the blind warrior turned his head and seemed to look down at him with those pockets of scarred flesh in question.

"He has delivered the council's decision. I am Jema once more, and you as well, if you wish it." Audy said, his voice cracking with emotion.

Even through his swirl of emotion, Kyle could recognize the look of relief on Audy's face. His friend swallowed and glanced at Kemi before continuing.

"The Jema will earn their freedom at your side. He asks of you, although your answer will not alter the Council's decision. Do you believe that we can win?"

"Tell him, I would be honored to be counted among the Jema, and that yes, we will win. A few years from now young Jema will stand next to children of my own people, free. I swear it."

Audy barked an order an order and the four guards quickly approached and turned his chair around to face the crowd. Kyle was struck by how fast the soldiers had reacted to Audy's request. It appeared more than kinship had been restored to Audy.

Audy spoke loudly, and clearly. It was undecipherable to him but he watched as Audy paused for dramatic effect translating his last words. Those within the tent cheered with a frenzy bordering on a blood lust. He couldn't see the tent door from his handicapped vantage, but someone must have run outside and passed the message. Within a half a minute the entire camp exploded in cheers.

He looked up at their ancient leader who was staring down at him with sightless scar tissue, smiling at the cheers of his people. He watched as Sri-Tel took in his people's joy and then bowed deeply to him.

"Children ... I should have started with that." Kyle half mumbled to himself.

*

Chapter 15

The slate gray sky promised snow or freezing rain. Kyle could feel the dropping barometer add to the pounding in his head. Audy's gift for understatement was profound. Besides the excruciating headache, his entire body felt like he'd been put in a giant taffy twisting machine. The pain, nausea and fatigue aside, there was also the first sense of optimism he had felt since the Chandrians had arrived.

Yet another small group of Jema walked up to him in the camp's central parade ground. There were seven warriors, two of them women, the presence of which had long ceased surprising him – they were all warriors. He stopped, by now he knew the drill. They all smiled and bowed their heads slowly to him. It reminded him a lot of the way the Thai or Burmese people treated a stranger. Audy had explained that it was a sign of respect and simple greeting to one they did not yet know well, all rolled in to one. Audy had also warned him that his people were unused to meeting strangers. Since the Jema clan's sundering, most of their interaction with 'others' had been across a battlefield or perhaps an occasional ally in the Kaerin's unending orchestrated wars.

He and Audy had started this walk together. Their canteens of water, laced with something that was supposed to help with the hangover, but so far had done little. His friend had been busily introducing him to people that Audy had known all his life when Kemi had barreled into the group and dragged him off without a word. Audy had managed a sheepish grin over his shoulder as he had been led away like a pile of plunder.

He'd been left alone with a head that felt like it was inside the world's largest bell to greet his new clansmen. All of whom were very excited and shared not a single word in common with him.

He returned the bows of the latest group and then touched his chest.

"Kyle, Kyle Lassiter."

They in turn, with great formality touched their own chests saying their unpronounceable names that he couldn't even begin to try and remember. He nodded at each pronouncement and smiled just like he had done several dozen times in the last half hour. The small group bowed again and walked off talking excitedly amongst themselves.

Left standing there, was Jomra. He must have walked up during all the genuflecting. He said something as if he expected to be understood, signaling for him to follow. Kyle turned to follow and realized the man walked at a pace closer to a slow jog. It was all he could manage to walk at all. Every footfall sent blooms of white-hot pain trough his skull.

Jomra turned back to see him struggling, pulled up and looked at him with a lot more concern than he had the day before. He again said something in Chandrian shaking his head and holding out his hand for Kyle's canteen. He handed it over. Jomra shook the half full container and frowned. Removing the cap, he thrust it out at him, holding it under his chin.

Kyle accepted it back and took a long pull. He turned the canteen down and Jomra gently nudged it back up and said "Gra... Gra.."

He took another long pull and looked for approval. Jomra tapped his own chin and tilted his head back. "Gra sokee"

"Sure, Gra Sokee" Kyle muttered and watched a smile break out on Jomra's face as he managed to polish off the canteen by taking a few breaks and starting immediately again.

Jomra nodded with approval, smiled once and started speaking to him as if the fact they couldn't understand each other was irrelevant.

Jomra motioned for him to follow again and this time walked at his own plodding pace. His body felt like he had the flu, but he could already feel his headache lessening. No one had said to drink the whole thing at once. Or maybe they had, how would he have known.

By the time they had walked across the central yard of the camp which was surrounded by orderly rows of simple canvas tents, Jomra finished saying whatever he felt like he had to say and looked over at him with an air of expectation.

Kyle shrugged, "I'm sure you're right."

Jomra barked an order at a nearby group of guards and they moved back and away from whatever they had been gathered around. Kyle looked down at the pile of gear he and Audy had been relieved of. Their assault rifles, harness rigs and vests stuffed with full magazines were there. Their two compads, one of which they'd gone to great effort to bury, and assorted gear some of which had clearly been taken from the air-car that they'd tried to camouflage.

One of the soldiers was holding a chocolate candy bar wrapped in foil from the survival kit. He pointed at it and then to the soldier holding it. The man embarrassed, bowed quickly and tossed the candy bar, produced in Pennsylvania on a different planet, back onto the pile of gear.

Kyle walked over picked it back up and unwrapped it. He broke a piece off and handed it to the soldier who looked like he expected to be screamed at or worse by Jomra.

"Try it." He broke off another piece off and popped it into his own mouth.

The soldier looked to Jomra for help but got no reaction. The warrior put it in his mouth clearly expecting the worst. The transformation on the man's face was priceless. He exclaimed something loudly. Kyle broke off pieces of the chocolate and handed a couple out and then passed over the whole bar. He couldn't help but think of the GIs in WWII who had arrived in Europe with chocolate, or the countless desert villages he'd been to himself where the children quickly learned that most soldiers carried extra chocolate. Sure, the Swiss and Belgians did it better, no question. But, when it came to diplomacy, and goodwill, American chocolate was legend. Humans, he thought, same everywhere.

Jomra pointed at the weapons and then at him, motioning that it was OK to retrieve them. Kyle smiled in thanks and reached down and grabbed the weapon. He hit the magazine release button, pulled it free and then turned the weapon sideways as he cycled the bolt. He caught the spinning cartridge and handed it to Jomra.

The man rolled it around in his hand, shook it next to his ear, and held it up in the dim light looking at it closely, clearly understanding the principle of a cartridge shell. The Jema used thick waxed paper cartridges themselves. He shook his head in amazement.

Kyle held up the magazine. "Thirty rounds" and passed it over for inspection. He flashed his free hand six times counting in his head as he did so.

The magazine was a game changer. Audy had related that the Kaerin used belt feed machine guns, but that the Jema's only experience with them had been as targets. They didn't have the equivalent of a magazine-fed personal weapon. Jomra understood the significance immediately and excitedly passed the plastic magazine over to his underlings for inspection. Kyle suspected that among those gathered were some of the Gemendi that Audy had told him about, the techies, or what went for such among the Chandrian clans. They were the jacks of all trades; armorers, communications specialists, navigators, whatever needed specialized training at the hands of the Kaerin who tightly controlled all the limited technology on Chandra. The relief he felt in not seeing the red jacketed pharmacist from the day before was real.

"How about a demonstration?" he asked Jomra, "After all, we're going to give you all one of these."

He waited for a reaction and none was forthcoming, not that he expected an answer. Kyle pointed at them, his own eyes, and pantomimed shooting the weapon. He'd worked closely with locals in Afghanistan, Indonesia, Kenya and half a dozen other places teeming with people whose language he didn't speak. Translators were always busy and there was never one around when you needed one. This was no different. The Gemendi warriors caught on immediately and motioned for him to follow.

He looked over at Jomra in question, conceding that these weren't his troops to order about. Jomra was in command, he was the outsider. Jomra nodded in agreement and smiled at him. The man knew exactly what he had just done and smiled in appreciation.

They went through four complete magazines, alternating between single shot, three round bursts and full auto on the last mag. He showed them how to adjust the magnification on the electronic optics and how to load, unload, and safe the weapon. He'd given just this type of training a hundred times before in his past life. The first time had been with a group of Waziri tribesman who had been no strangers to firearms. The Jema took to the lesson with a discipline the Waziri would not have recognized and a humor that Kyle found comforting. These were not the mindless 'ant soldiers' they'd feared.

One of Jomra's men, hunched over the weapon's scope, and prepped to fire, accidentally thumbed the magazine release. The half full magazine dropped out on to the man's foot. The gathered crowd, which by then numbered well over a hundred warriors had laughed good naturedly. Jomra had made a great show of looking down range and shaking his head. The words he spoke were unintelligible but Kyle was pretty sure it equated with - "you missed." Which had really set the crowd to laughing.

More impressive to Kyle, was that the Jema warrior on the firing line realized he still had a round chambered even with people laughing at his expense. He reseated the stock and squeezed off the single round with a satisfying ping off the riddled metal bucket before picking up the magazine and wiping it off on his pant leg, reseating it and cycling the action.

The man glanced at Kyle for approval and he nodded back and flashed the man a thumbs up. "Good to go."

The Jema fired off three rounds, safe'd the weapon and passed it to Jomra who almost sheepishly looked over at him and asked something with a nod downrange.

"He wishes to fire," Audy stepped through the crowd behind him, "like the hummingbird – auto fire."

"I get it," Kyle answered Audy, who looked about like he felt. He nodded back in the affirmative to Jomra and gestured downrange. Jomra seated a new magazine and cycled the bolt. He fired a few rounds singly, one three round burst, then the rest of the magazine on full auto until the chamber locked back on the empty mag. The crowd hollered in excitement, many pounded their own rifles' stocks into the ground.

"Wow, they liked that."

"They see now, first hand," Audy shrugged, "what they have allied themselves with."

Kyle watched Audy listen to the excited murmurings of his people until his friend turned back to him with a smile.

"Many wonder if you and your people will use these weapons against the Strema."

"So will they," Kyle nodded, "rifles and ammo we have."

Jomra walked slowly through the crowd of warriors letting the gathered Jema touch the beat-up SCAR assault rifle as if it were some sort of talisman.

Kyle accepted the rifle back from Jomra and seated the last magazine he had brought with him from their returned supplies. Jomra stepped back and motioned down range inviting him to shoot.

"My head has had enough," he said to himself before taking a half step forward. With a half bow, he presented the assault rifle back to Jomra. The crowd noise dropped to nothing in an instant.

"Please tell Jomra that all his people will be gifted such a weapon, but his will be the first."

"Actually, I was the first," Audy countered with a grin, but he quickly translated what Kyle had said.

Jomra bowed deeply to him and then turned towards Audy, bowed again saying something in the process.

"You do him a great honor." Audy smiled. "I will not point out that I have carried such a weapon like this for months."

"Ya think?"

"I do what I can," Audy smiled at him as Jomra held the weapon over his head and shouted something to the gathered Jema who erupted again in cheers.

"Our grandchildren's children will tell the story of this moment." Audy smiled at him and nodded at his people.

Kyle looked at Audy. "We've got so much work to do integrating your people and training them up so they can fight with us, I don't want to think about it."

"I think you'll find the Jema willing participants, much more willing than you are used to. War is all we know."

Kyle nodded. He knew Audy was right, but the Jema were warriors. He needed them to become soldiers. That would be the hard part.

"I've got an important message to write and a diplomatic reception to coordinate," he said. "Can you keep them off my back for a while? I feel like an animal in the zoo. And linguists, Audy, find some volunteers, we are going to need a translator corps. You can't be everywhere and we'll need to pair them up with counterparts from our side and let them teach each other."

Audy nodded. "Of course, I will issue orders."

"As for the diplomacy thing... wait... can you do that?"

"Do what?"

"Issue orders, you can issue orders?"

Audy looked back at him feigning hurt. "I am now Kaerus Audrin'ochal."

"Kaerus? Like Jomra? They promoted you?"

"You speak as if you are surprised. Have I not hiked across this empty land with a hole in my shoulder? Lived among the enemy? Convinced them to help my people?"

"I have to admit," Kyle said, "said that way, it sounds a lot better than you were rescued by us before a lady farmer castrated you with a shotgun."

Audy grinned back at him. "I like my story better."

"I'll bet you do." Kyle held out a hand. "Welcome back to your people Audy, you did it."

Audy shook his hand. "If we fail, the Jema will die as a free people. The debt I owe you, will never be paid."

"We win this thing, we're even." Kyle nodded at the crowd. "They're good people, Audy. They deserve some peace. We all do."

*

St. Louis Center

Colonel Hank Pretty stood at attention as he said the appropriate words. He'd had a lot of practice recently. The

217

burials were the best object lesson that they could provide their green troops, most of whom had never been in uniform prior to joining the militia. A Chilean who had come from the same settlement in Northern California as the fallen, translated the words to the large contingent of Spanish speakers.

Jake stood respectfully, his hat in his hands, wondering what he could have done differently. Something, anything that wouldn't have resulted in the eleven body bags laid out in two neat rows adjacent to their graves. Pretty had blamed it on the language issue. Jake knew that hadn't been the cause. Half of them had spoken solid English, and the adjacent two squads had been Spanish speakers and had followed the order to withdraw without a hitch. Reasons didn't matter to him, it had been his op. It had been successful in every way, by any measure except that which lay on the ground in front of him.

The fact that they'd hurt the enemy to the tune of over 200 KIAs didn't matter right now. It had been a repeat of their rope-a-dope mission albeit on a much smaller, company sized scale. They'd nipped around the edges of a larger Strema foraging party until they'd led them into a trap. It had gone perfectly until it was time to withdraw and some had refused the order. Most of those were laid out on the ground now. Carlos had realized straight away what had happened.

"They're still green. They don't know machismo is the same thing as stupidity out there," Carlos had explained. Jake knew that had been the problem but it didn't help much at the moment. Pretty finished with a prayer and the crowd dispersed, walking slowly back to their sprawling camp alongside the Mississippi river that seemed to grow another row of tents representing another green platoon or company every day. As a group, he wouldn't call them veterans, but almost all of them by now had seen some action. There were some good troops here, some who would become very solid with more experience, but he would have said the same about the men they were about to bury as well.

"Wake up." Carlos' voice next to him snapped him out of his funk.

One of the men, Sergeant Suarez who had been on the op, was walking up to them, several of his platoon stood just behind him, hats still in their hands.

"Sir, we wish to tell you that our men have learned from this mistake. These men did not die in vain. My nephew and brother did not die in vain." The man turned to look at those standing behind him and then at the bodies laid out to the side.

"We wish you to know that you may trust us, that this will never happen again. We ask that you continue to use us. We would make amends for our fallen."

"I appreciate that, Sergeant, we all learned a lesson here today."

"Sir," the man finished solemnly and held out a hand.

Jake shook the Sergeant's hand and then watched the man start the walk back into camp surrounded by the other Sergeants in his company.

"What did you just learn, amigo?" Carlos was watching the camp in the distance.

Jake nodded at the departing backs of his men. Men who had lost far more than he had, men who wanted back in the fight. Soldiers, for the first time he thought of them as soldiers.

"Maybe we can pull this shit off."

Carlos nodded towards the camp. "Tough lesson, but very much needed. Come on, you can buy me a drink at the officer's club."

"We have an officer's Club?"

"Ok," Carlos relented. "You can share that bottle of rye I saw you trying to hide in your duffel."

"Sounds good."

They were halfway back to camp when both of their compads vibrated.

"Let me know if it's something I don't have to answer," Jake drawled. "If it's Seattle wanting another report, tell them to kiss my ass."

Carlos ignored him and read the message as they walked. He stopped in mid-stride.

"What is it?"

"Kyle..." Carlos laughed. "Damn if that hillbilly didn't pull it off, he's now a member of Audy's clan."

Jake pulled his own Compad out and started running thorough the message.

"So much for the drink, we're gonna be busy."

*

With Audy handling the crowd control directions and explanations, the Jema had ringed the central compound of their camp in a deep wall of flesh that pressed up against the log stockade walls. More still stood on the wall's ramparts, and several thousand were outside the camp lining the closest ridges. They may have been there for the view alone, but Kyle thought that the alliance was new enough that it made sense for the Jema to keep some force outside the walls. He'd pointed that out to Audy who had looked at him strangely.

"They are there because the camp is full. The heart speak does not fail, Kyle. You are trusted."

"So, you keep saying, I'm sorry." He gestured around the camp, every Jema stood with a rifle or spear, or both. He'd learned enough to know that the spear carriers were mostly of the Teark rank, akin to sergeants, and could and would wield the damned things to enforce commands.

"You sure no one will shoot? This is likely to scare them shitless."

Audy stared at him and ground his jaw for a moment. "As I've told you," Audy paused and grinned, "three times now. They have all been warned, no one will shoot. No one will think they are under attack. I've told them all to expect the sound of thunder announcing the arrival of your flying machines. Good enough?"

"Sorry, it's the first time I've brokered an alliance between people from two planets, what could go wrong."

Audy shrugged. "An interesting point, but you worry too much. You have done a passable job."

"Passable? Are you shitting me?" Kyle could tell he raised his voice a little too high.

"Perhaps I used the wrong word." Audy looked at him with a hangdog expression that slowly broke into a shit eating grin. "I got you again."

"You got me." Kyle felt like punching him but he also wanted to laugh. "Go do something useful." He stormed off. *I need somebody to yell at, that will understand me.*

He stood near the center of the cleared space that he thought of as a marshalling yard or parade ground, not that the Jema spent any time dressing formations. He glanced back at Audy who was standing with Kemi and Jomra, having a good laugh while pointing at him. He gave Audy a one finger salute and watched as his friend explained *that* to Kemi and Jomra, which they understood very well it seemed. Jomra was nearly bent over in laughter.

It was impossible for him not to like these people. They took war very seriously, especially where the opportunity to take on the Strema was concerned. In their downtime though, he'd found with Audy translating they were quick to laugh and seemed to appreciate nothing more than a practical joke.

He checked his compad again and smiled. He and Col. Pretty were showing off and he knew it. It wasn't vanity, it wasn't ego. They needed the Jema to work within their order of battle and Audy and Jomra had agreed the best way to do that would be a demonstration of what the Jema would have faced doing battle against their now allied Terrans or 'Terns' as the Jema pronounced it. Col. Pretty had agreed that a demonstration of sorts was warranted.

Kyle had made a few suggestions and Hank had added his own. There would be no telltale rumble from the approaching jets. They would be coming in at supersonic speeds, at what Pretty had called 'airshow altitude' on full afterburn. The shockwave would arrive after the jets blew over the camp.

He glanced at his compad again, amazed at how fast the two yellow carats indicating the strike jets were moving across the map.

"Audy - heads up!" He pointed to the west where the southern chain of the Appalachians began to roll.

He watched every head in the fort follow Audy's pointing and then they all stuck fingers in their ears as Audy had instructed them. Knowing what to look for, Kyle saw the two small dots high above the distant hills, descending and growing rapidly in size. The murmurs grew until it seemed they were all shouting or cheering at the approaching planes as they dropped below the background of the mountains and were lost to view. He wondered if the crowd thought the pilots could hear them, the Jema could be amazingly naïve regarding technology but no one could fault them for that.

Mere seconds later the jets tore over the top of the fort at an altitude of no more than 300 feet. He didn't have it in him to watch the crowd's reaction as he was nearly blown off his own feet. He was just starting to look around when the sound wave trailing the supersonic jets exploded over the fort. *Holy shit*, maybe airshow altitude was a little much, he thought. He couldn't tell if the Jema were shocked, afraid or angry but slowly the deathly shocked silence built into a roaring cheer that chilled his blood. There was excitement in those screams but something else as well. The Jema wanted payback on the Strema, and they'd just had a taste of what it may look like.

He glanced back at Audy who was grinning at him and flashing a thumbs up. Ok, so far so good, he thought. Two tilt wing Ospreys II's appeared along the same ingress route. They were much bigger, more easily seen, and were moving a hell of a lot slower than the F-35s had. The Jema were almost shuddering in excitement. He knew Jiro was flying one of them and even he who had spent half a lifetime riding in the damn things was impressed at how they flared out over the camp's central field, killing their momentum. The two craft slid into position and circled each other slowly, nose to nose at one point until they came to rest accompanied by the ear-splitting roar of their jet turbines at the wing tips.

The back ramps came down quickly as the engines were spooled down and wound to a stop. He was looking at Jake and Carlos, rifles slung on their backs standing on either side of Col. Pretty. He waved at them and started walking forward, with Audy, Jomra, Kemi, the single Jema grey beard Sri-Tel and a handful of other Jema officers whose names he couldn't remember or pronounce. The rest of the knuckle draggers were close behind the first trio and a second later Jiro appeared with his flight helmet in his hand.

Kyle turned to Sri-Tel who stood next to Jomra. "You will have to forgive us, we do not know your ways and we may offend, but I'd like to introduce you to my friends and colleagues. He waited for Audy to translate, at which point Sri-Tel shook his head.

"It is we, who must be concerned of value," Audy hesitated in his translations, "of worthiness in your eyes. That you have such tools and power that have been described to me and that I have just heard and felt... It is we that we who are honored."

The old man continued for a moment, seemingly awed at what had been described to him. "Sri-Tel, in his mind's eye can see the eagles of his youth, he wishes to know if he may be permitted to ride in the flying machine?" Audy was going to have a busy day translating.

"He may, at some point you all will." Pretty answered for him.

Audy translated both ways and the introductions, especially for Hank were onerous. Kyle had had three days to at least get used to alien sounding names that the Jema took so seriously. Pretty had a look on his face somewhere between confusion and terror.

"Relax, Sir," Kyle threw out over the top of the conversation being carried by Audy, "they don't expect you to remember their names."

"Duty calls," Jake nudged his arm and then nodded to the second Osprey. He spotted Elisabeth immediately and figured Audy had things well in hand and made a beeline for her.

Coming down the ramp behind her were his parents, Zarena Gonzales, and her two daughters, Lily and Sophia. The girls were wearing their best dresses and carrying flowers. Behind the first group was his high school buddy Dean

Freeburn, and his two teenage boys, the eldest one Jake, on crutches.

He reached Elisabeth and swept her up in a big swinging bear hug.

"I'm so sorry," she whispered against his neck.

"No worries, you were almost right."

Their kiss lasted longer than it probably should have.

"Is this a breach of protocol?" She asked pulling back with a smile.

Kyle grinned back at her, "It's what I do best."

The crowd which had been at a rolling din went silent as he was hugging his mom.

He turned to see five-year-old Lily Gonzales walking right into the middle of the group of officials as if she belonged. She stopped in front of Kemi and presented her bouquet of flowers. The crowd watched in stunned silence.

Supersonic aircraft, VTOL Ospreys, automatic assault weapons were great, but if you really wanted to cut to the quick with the Jema, bring out the children.

Kyle glanced over at Elisabeth. "Your idea?"

She nodded once watching the scene herself. "Good or bad?"

"Look at Audy's face, she did that."

Kemi looked stunned, not at the flowers, she clearly didn't know what to do with them. But she knelt down and gently touched the young girl's face seeing something that had not been allowed among the Jema for a quarter of a century. When she stood, there were tears in her eyes and in many others eyes throughout the gathered Jema host.

"Good idea." Kyle squeezed Elisabeth's hand. "Duty calls." He hugged his mom again and shook his dad's hand and escorted them over to the main group.

"Sri-Tel," Kyle stood in front of the sole Jema 'graybeard' as he thought of him, and pointedly looked to Audy as he spoke. "I'd like to introduce my mother and father, Christine and Roger Lassiter.

Sri-Tel, the scarred orbs of his eyes looking at him as if they could see, bobbed his head with a bow when Audy finished translating and then went on for some time speaking to the air between where Kyle stood and his parents.

"Lassiters," Audy began, "Sri-Tel wishes to apologize that their son has joined with the Jema. On our world, in days past, this was done only with the consent of the mother and it was cause for a great celebration. He apologizes that he was not able to speak with you before this."

His Mom, never a diplomat, looked at him for a moment with a 'what have you been up to' look and then turned to Audy.

"Please tell him that our son has long since stopped asking our permission, but we are pleased by his choices and his new friends."

Way to go, mom! he almost pumped a fist in celebration but limited his reaction to sharing a look of relief with his father. One never knew what one would get when Christine Lassiter was asked to speak.

Hearing the translation, Sri-Tel threw back his head and laughed.

Audy listened with a smirk on his face. "Sri-Tel says, this is the way of children. By the time they are old enough to heed your wisdom, they believe it to be their idea. You no doubt are the ones to be credited."

Audy continued with the introductions. Kyle backed off a step and looked for Elisabeth in the crowd. She was already working, and he spotted her marshalling a group of hand-picked linguists from their side ranging in age from teenagers to a couple of people that looked to have retired years ago. No doubt some more college professors, of which Eden seemed to have recruited in large numbers.

He bumped into somebody standing behind him.

"Where you think you're sneaking off to?" Jake sidled up next to him.

"Ahh, ugly, but friendly," he clapped his friend on the back.

Jake smirked at him and saw where they were headed. "Translators the first order of the day?"

"You volunteering?"

"That's funny." Jake shook his head slowly. "You know I never volunteer for anything." Jake slapped him hard on the back. "It's good to see you too, buddy. Don't think poorly of me, if I had a few moments of worry."

"I was worried myself for a bit there. These are a hard people."

Jake pointed back towards Audy and the group they had just left. "Speaking of ugly faces, what gives? They play toss the Audy?"

Kyle laughed. "He got worked over pretty good by his girlfriend, the one that accepted the flowers."

"Seriously?"

"As a heart attack," Kyle nodded. "I'd say she was less than pleased with him leaving. She'd thought him dead all this time, besides being a traitor to boot. She came very close to running him through with that pig sticker she's carrying."

"Such a tiny thing." Jake tilted his head sideways a little, like a confused dog. "Kinda hot though, in a Sheena the warrior, meets east European stripper."

Kyle nodded to himself in agreement. "With a little Bruce Lee thrown in, so tread carefully. At any rate, they've made up. Surprised either one of them can walk right now."

"Good for Audy." Jake nodded as if all was right in the world.

"What'd I miss with the Strema?"

"Hit and runs." Jake shook his head and grimaced. "More run, than hit. The day before you messaged us, we had a group go macho and failed to break contact, they hurt us. But Carlos seems to think his people are learning."

"His people?"

"The Latinos, the South American crowd. They've been fighting down there amongst each other for so long, they don't really have to have military experience to be worth a shit in a fight. Among the militia, they're the best we have right now, sometimes they just don't listen very well when it comes time to break off."

Kyle pointed around them. "Liable to be an issue here too. I'll bet they don't have a word for withdraw. That'll be a different problem down the road, but they've got a serious hard on for the Strema, especially with our rifles."

Jake shook his head. "We could use some of that right now."

Kyle watched Elisabeth through the crowd hoping they'd be able to get some downtime. She was going to be as busy as he was for the foreseeable future. The compads she was handing out to the Jema had a language instruction program in them, as well as dictionaries, children's pictionaries, and anything else that might speed up the learning process. It was the best they could come up with in the few days since he'd set this reception in process. Elisabeth was justifiably proud of what she and her team had managed to put together. Given time, he knew he was going to have to learn Chandrian. He was counted as one of them, he'd need to speak the language.

"Speaking of which," Jake pointed at the horizon. Eight air buses were slowly growing closer in the distance. "First load of food, weapons, and ammo, in that order. Pretty thought some sort of feast would be appropriate."

"Oh, it will be."

Jake was silent for a moment looking at him, and then slapped him on the back again. "Thirty-four thousand trained soldiers, you sure you never did a recruitment rotation?"

"Warriors, not soldiers," Kyle clarified and then pointed back towards Audy.

"Audy did it, I just confirmed what he said under some sort of truth serum. He convinced them to back his play, and they'd let him back in the fold before I was even allowed to speak. I think the fact that we were already taking it to the Strema is what sold them. Like I said, serious case of the ass. You see the old guy, no eyes, or hands?"

"Yeah, he kind of stood out."

"Courtesy of the Strema, acting on Kaerin orders. The Strema were also the tool used by the Kaerin to execute all the Jema."

"So, by hard on for the Strema, you mean full-on, ball peen hammer..."

227

"And then some," Kyle agreed, doubting he or any Edenite could fathom the score that the Jema had to settle. "I think their chance at freedom was just gravy. What they really want is a shot at the Strema. Clan honor, nothing we haven't seen before."

"We going to be able to control them?" Jake was looking at a trio of Jema warriors standing twenty feet away looking at them with open faced, unabashed curiosity. There was almost a challenge in their look.

"Not sure," he shrugged. "Direct them at least. Audy and I have had a couple of long discussions with their tactical commander," Kyle pointed at Jomra who stood behind Kemi watching the air buses come in and land at the far end of the erstwhile landing field. "His name's Jomra, that isn't all of it, but he answers to that."

"Jomra," Jake rolled it off his tongue. "Sounds almost Javanese or something. He the real deal?"

"In spades, they don't have ring knockers or an OCS, everything with them is merit-based. Audy and I are thinking that it may be a good idea to get our team of miscreants together, with Audy, Jomra, and a few of their leaders and show them what we can do. Show them what soldiers, backed by air power can do, versus a group of warriors hacking at each other."

"The guys will like that. Will this Jomra cat listen? Or is he stuck in his ways?"

"I think he'll be open to anything that kills Strema. He's also Audy's childhood friend, the same one who shot him in the back before he jumped through the Kaerin's gate to translate here. Jomra reported him dead at the order of the Kaerin. He's also Kemi's, Audy's fiancé's brother."

"Freaking alien soap opera." Jake mused.

Kyle shook his head. "No drama though, just very angry and a little bit hungry. The Kaerin basically dumped them here, thinking that they'd be in a fight with Fort Carolina from the get go. Didn't bother with much in the way of logistics or supplies."

Jake nodded, and pointed at the approaching line of air buses. "We can do angry, we can fix hungry."

"Half their women will be pregnant in a month," Kyle pointed at Audy. "His fiancé has literally dragged his ass back to her tent every couple of hours. This is a whole clan that has been forced to punish pregnancy with death since this generation hit puberty. Which is to say all of them, excepting the old man. No kids, no families. The whole camp has been moaning for the last three nights, not wasting anytime in guaranteeing their survival as a people."

Jake shook his head in disbelief. Kyle watched as a whimsical smile slowly broke out across his friend's face.

"You don't think they'd be interested in expanding the ol' gene pool? I mean some serious swamp dwelling alpha hunter type."

Kyle tried not to laugh and failed.

"I'm serious," Jake looked offended. "Among some cultures, outside genes are highly valued."

"You ever seen one of these cultures?"

"I read about it."

"Like in a book?" Kyle was almost crying with laughter.

"I'll have you know I'm a heavy reader in my downtime."

Kyle knew that was true. You just really had to get to know Jake before that ever became evident.

"Easy killer, I think non-frat is the way to go, at least for now. Unless you get knocked over the head and dragged into a tent. No families or kids for a generation, there are some serious biological clocks kicking in right now and I don't have a clue how we'd fit in to that, if at all.

Just then a group of four Jema women approached them and barked out some unintelligible gibberish, but they were all smiles, even holding their long rifles, with the bouma blades strapped to their waist.

"Well, hello there." Jake smiled and did a little bow.

"Did you hear anything I just said?"

The women stepped in close and felt up their arms and one of the women smiled at Jake and thumped him on the chest with the back of her hand.

"I heard blah blah blah," Jake said ignoring him, and holding out his hand. He gently placed the woman's hand in his own and shook it slowly, up and down. "It's a pleasure, Ma'am."

One of the women yelled at the warrior who was eyeing him and getting ready to thump him in the chest. She explained something and pointed at Kyle and then over to the crowd where Elisabeth was working with Audy and the translators.

"I think you just got shot down buddy," Jake drawled, smiling at the girls and shaking another hand to a storm of laughter. "...and I feel like I've just been hit over the head."

"I admit, maybe I was wrong." Kyle didn't think these women were about to abduct Jake, but the invitation was clear as day. "Just be careful, they likely take parenthood seriously."

"Yes, sir." Jake smiled and clapped him on the back as he followed the two warriors who were signaling him to follow. "I'm going in for some high-level diplomacy, I'll find you at the barbeque."

*

Chapter 16

Audy approached the back ramp of the Osprey with Jomra, and two other Jema Bastelta who would be accompanying them on the patrol. Kyle was getting better at recognizing the rune looking symbols on the Jema warrior's arm bands and he could tell the two Bastelta, one man, one woman, were "senior" Bastelta. Warriors who had been at that rank long enough to have the experience needed to move up.

"Kyle, this is Juni," Audy, introduced the woman standing next to Jomra. "She is the leader of our scouts."

Kyle returned a bow and then awkwardly shook hands with the woman, hoping she wasn't going to ask about three of her warriors that had disappeared during the first couple of days after the Jema's arrival. He knew the Jema well enough by now, to know it wouldn't be held against him or the other *Terns*. That said, it was a worry. The last thing they needed was this patrol or demonstration as he thought of it, to turn into a dick measuring contest. Their goal was to demonstrate how they fought, and more important, how the Jema could be trained to incorporate the new weapons they'd been provided. It was the classic game of showing warriors that soldiers usually won.

Jake, Carlos, and the rest of the knuckle draggers were already in the field tracking a large foraging group, in the heavy frozen forests, west of where the Twin Cities had been back on Earth. That was where they were headed. Juni's hair was blonde, cut in a high and tight, except for a long pony tail that hung down far enough that she had pulled around her neck and tucked it beneath the shoulder strap of the small bag she carried. The woman looked past him into the interior of the Osprey and asked Audy something.

The other Bastelta, who Kyle thought he recognized, seemed very interested in Audy's answer, which he was certain included an assurance that they would indeed fly there in less than a day. Jomra caught his eye and pointed at the Bastelta on the other side of him, "Esta Parkin'jela."

231

"Park," the man said, with a knowing smile, and held his hand out. Kyle shook it, and remembered where he'd seen this man before. He'd been the guy that had almost cut his throat the day he and Audy had been marched to the central tent. He didn't let on that he remembered, but he noticed Audy looking at him strangely for a moment before he spoke.

"Park is the Captain of our strongest hand, a force of about four and a half thousand warriors."

"OK, then." Kyle indicated the ramp and pointed to the overhead shelf fronted with cargo nets for their bags and benches along either side. He handed out the thickly insulated ear muffed headsets and didn't have to explain further. He could see Audy pointing at his ears, no doubt explaining to them why they called the Osprey II the *Harpy.*

A half hour into the flight, Jomra, the two Bastelta and Audy had completed their visit to the cockpit where Jiro had done his best to explain *how* he flew the plane and they seemed convinced enough they weren't about to die that they'd stopped staring out the small shoe box sized windows.

He watched as Jomra, lifted the headset off of one ear for a moment, before letting it snap back into place. He nudged Audy with a foot and asked something in Chandrian over the open circuit. The only word Kyle recognized in the question was Strema.

"Jomra says the Strema are without honor, but they have ears. How will we sneak up on them in this beast?"

"We are going to land at Ft. Carolina and transfer to a Blackhawk, and then an aircar from St. Louis Center, much quieter. We'll still land a good way away from them, and hike in to meet Jake and Carlos."

He watched as Audy tried to explain what a Blackhawk helicopter was, with his hands before he remembered his compad and showed them a video of one in flight. He had to smile at the new look of fear on Jomra's face. He couldn't find fault in that. He hated helicopters with a passion. In his opinion, the only thing worse than a helicopter was the underpowered, barely air-worthy, original eggbeater style Osprey.

The rest of the trip passed quickly, it had basically just been a short jump over the hump of the southern Appalachians to the location that the Jema were supposed to have been inserted to; on the doorstep of Fort Carolina. At the bottom of the ramp, Jomra stopped and looked around at the parked aircraft to include two F-35s that they'd been buzzed by a nearly two weeks ago. Another F-35 could be heard receding into the distance somewhere above the clouds.

"On its way to attack the Strema," he explained. "We hit them two or three times a day from the air."

Jomra and his two Bastelta seemed appreciative of Audy's explanation, but Jomra was already pointing at the assembled aircraft; Ospreys, Blackhawks and aircars as well as the redoubts and defensive lines built into the hillsides surrounding the landing field. He said something to Audy and shook his head.

Audy answered him, and then translated. "Jomra is thankful that the Kaerin could not aim well, and were not able to send them against this encampment. He still thinks they would have won though."

Kyle nodded, "Tell him that we'll ask that question again, after our little demonstration up north."

They transferred to an air car that he flew himself. As opposed to the Osprey, the occupants could see outside very well, and speak, and hear. Kyle took great delight in listening to them chatter back and forth in excitement as he flew northwest to St. Louis center where they'd switch to a Blackhawk before heading northwest to rendezvous with Jake and Carlos and the rest of their team.

"I've explained to them that this is a civilian vehicle, designed for a family and not for military purposes," Audy said after a while. "Listening to them, seeing this through their eyes, I am remembering how difficult it was for me to come to believe what I saw in your tools." Audy shook his head grimacing, "and I had the benefit of learning in a hospital bed, watching war movies on your television."

"Well, if you think that kind of exposure would be helpful, we can talk to Elisabeth. I'm sure she can put a familiarity program together, videos and what not, might save some time."

"Yes, I am thinking this would be useful. Perhaps, I could provide the sound in Chandrian?"

It took Kyle a second to realize what Audy was talking about it. "That's a great idea. Call it 'Audy's *New Ally 101* course,' explain some of our technology, and the comp boards especially. That's going to be key to integrating you guys."

"What will be key," Audy tapped the dashboard of the air car, "is your acceptance that we are a different culture, a very different culture. We will need to be accepted as we are, before we will be as you say... integrated."

Kyle was about to agree but something in Audy's tone stopped him. "You do realize I was talking about just the military side of things, right? Just to give your fellow Chandrians a leg up in utilizing our gear and tech, we're going to need to be able to communicate, support, and reinforce each other."

"You are correct, of course," Audy nodded in agreement.

"Audy?" Kyle could tell the conversation between Jomra and his subordinates didn't seem to be involving Audy at the moment, "What were you talking about?"

Audy shook his head. "I am not looking to give offense, nor is our Council who asked me to bring this up should an opportunity present itself."

"Audy, what's going on? I'm a Jema too, remember?" he tried smiling.

"Your assistance, the medical help, the food for our encampment, the assistance with our indisposed warriors...

"The pregnant ones? Audy? Is that what this is about?" He knew there were close to four thousand Jema women that had discovered they were pregnant in the last five or so days, and the number would only go up. The Jema clan had a biological clock that hadn't been allowed to progress and the dam had broken with a vengeance. They were taking no chances with the future of their clan, and most of the pregnant women had removed themselves from the 'active' list of Jema warriors.

"Yes, in part,"

234

Kyle had rarely seen Audy so circumspect regarding what he clearly wanted to say.

"Just tell me for God's sake!"

"Your people that have come to assist, have been a great help, we have no experience of our previous generations to help us with this, but they are requesting information that we will not give."

"You've completely lost me,"

"Your people from the Program, they are registering us, in a census, I believe they call it, a counting?"

Kyle could feel his blood pressure climbing with the simple mention of the Program.

"We do not have a problem with being counted Kyle. We understand the support you are providing requires an accurate count, not to mention the military side of the logistics. It's important, we understand that. But they want information that we are not yet prepared to give."

"Like what?" Kyle scratched his head, wondering if they had some sort of taboo over shoe size, because he knew there was what he thought a very popular effort to get them all modern boots underway.

"Our last names, Kyle. The names we took from our parents." Audy said it loud enough that it stopped the conversation in the back seat.

Jomra leaned forward and asked Audy something.

Kyle saw Audy nod in response, and then turned to look back at him. "Kyle, it may seem strange, but we will not speak the names of our parents, our family names, until we have earned that right in our own eyes. That won't happen until we earn it on the battle field against the Strema. Your people from Seattle, have a requirement to register us, and I gather that their database requires a last name. It's becoming an issue, delaying our receiving the compads in some cases. A few women were told they could not receive medical care until they had completed the form. We don't understand how this can be so important to your people.

Kyle's fingers ached before he realized how hard he was squeezing the steering yoke of the aircar.

"Tell Jomra, that I will fix it. It's not important at all, just bureaucrats doing what they do. I know a lot of the helpers we sent out are young people, they are probably being asked by their superiors back in Seattle to collect the data. I'll fix it."

"Thank you, it will help avoid misunderstandings."

Audy turned to Jomra in the back and explained it in Chandrian. Kyle heard Jomra grunt in satisfaction. A moment later the Chandrian war leader was leaning forward and over the back of the front seat and started counting off statements on his fingers to Audy.

He watched as Audy nodded in agreement. "There is also the issue of asking us about our religion, we have none, other than rumors of what was believed long ago. Our education levels? We are warriors, we have learned to fight. Our professions? Again, we are..."

"Warriors," Kyle finished for him. "I get it, Audy, I do. Tell Jomra we'll put an end to this shit the moment I have time to get in contact with Seattle."

"Thank you," Audy said. "I do know how speaking to Seattle upsets you, but it will be for the best if we are allowed to be Jema until we are truly free to choose the parts of your culture that make sense to us. Schools for instance, when we have time to learn skills beyond the battlefield, we will wish to learn all we can. For this moment, the Strema remain and that is the only future we concern ourselves with."

"I wish my people could see things so clearly."

He fumed as he listened to Audy translate to Jomra who replied calmly.

"What did he say?'

"He says, he believes the fact that your people in Seattle can worry about such unimportant things in a time of war speaks to the power of your people. He now sees the truth in what I have been telling him about how it is only a select few of your people who are trained as warriors."

"Soldiers, Audy, soldiers. And yes, he's right. Far too few of our people know what it means to fight."

"This is a better thing," Audy agreed. "Far better than your entire people having no choice but to fight. The Jema will adapt, but we must be allowed to first earn that future."

Audy translated again and Jomra gave his customary grunt of acknowledgement that he had come to learn was acceptance or agreement. But Jomra, still leaning forward, spoke directly to him.

"We will earn our right," Audy translated, "to stand next to you, with you or apart from you, as we see fit. This is what freedom means? Yes? The Jema will not trade one master for another.

Kyle nodded in agreement. "That's exactly what it means, and tell Jomra to never forget it."

They switched to a Blackhawk on the outskirts of the St. Louis Center, the burgeoning base, located on the edge of the Mississippi river, some seventy miles or so southwest of where the city had been on Earth. Kyle ignored the looks from a lot of the gathered militia as they walked across the landing field. He knew that for most of them, the only Chandrians they had seen had been from a distance, over rifle sights. Even then, not enough of them had that much experience. For most of them, it was their first exposure to the Jema and the curiosity they showed towards their new ally was understandable if bordering on rude.

For their part, Jomra and his two Jema officers ignored the attention and just stared at the helicopter. It did look scary, when he stopped to think about it. A big metal beast with a twirly thing on top and another at the rear. Its blades were just starting to rotate as they approached. He nodded in appreciation as Audy demonstrated to them how to approach hunched over. Audy may have overdone the demonstration of the danger, as he pointed at the spinning rotor blades and made a chopping motion at his own neck.

Kyle laughed a little to himself. It was better to have them safe than sorry. It was difficult not to laugh at the open fear on their faces as the blades spun up into a hurricane of wind and sound. By the time the Blackhawk lifted off and dropped its

237

nose to fly to the northwest, Audy was the only other occupant in the back with his eyes open. He picked up the locator beacon on Jake's compad just under an hour later and directed the pilot to insert them well to the west of the blinking icon that the pilots had been tracking to. He'd introduced himself to both the pilots as they boarded. He hadn't recognized either one of them, which he took as a good sign. The call up plan was working.

They sat down with a gentle bump in a natural meadow amidst a dense, dark forest. They were at the western edge of the mixed pine and deciduous forest that stretched from the shores of the Atlantic to the Great Plains. The Strema had been sending a steady series of foraging parties west in pursuit of buffalo on the edge of plains, taking deer and elk from the forest they traversed. The foraging parties were two legged locusts, spread out in a wide line, a thousand men strong, beating through the woods and driving the game before it into large nets or into the range of the hunters at the far end.

Jake and Carlos had been trailing this group that had progressed to where the forest had just begun giving way to the plains. Utilizing the thick foliage along the banks of a tributary of the Clark river they had remained hidden and observed as the Strema party had come back together to make camp and preparations for their return east, back to the Strema main encampment. It was a trip that promised to be a painful one for the Strema.

Right now, Kyle had to get his group of Chandrians in position without being spotted by the Strema scouts, as well as making sure one of them didn't go Rambo on the first Strema they came across. He was also aware that he was being judged. The militia was being watched, just as they were trying to observe the Jema. He had to admit that getting this party to where they needed to be, without embarrassing himself in way that could set back the new alliance was in all likelihood just as important. He had no idea as to how the Jema thought of them as individual warriors, but he was certain that if they could be successful on this operation, the Jema would come away with a new appreciation and understanding of what soldiers could do.

Once he was certain they had all their gear on and slung correctly, he stood back and took in the four Jema. Standing there in their MOLLE gear, with slung assault rifles, digicam BDUs and green/black face paint, they looked just like any other squad until one noticed the bouma blades scabbarded at their thighs. He checked his watch.

"It's 1430, we can move fast for the first two or three miles and then we'll have to go stealthy and stay hidden from any scouts we come across. We will not engage," he emphasized. "Not until tomorrow, when all the pieces are in place. If we have to engage, we do so quietly." He pointed his HK at a tree and triggered a suppressed round. "Even that, only if we have to. Our plan is for tomorrow, and it relies on surprise."

Kyle waited as Audy translated. He could tell the Chandrians were looking at their assault rifles in surprise and it took another five minutes for Audy to explain how the suppressor worked.

Juni, the warrior goddess, fired a question at Audy. She didn't sound happy.

Audy abashedly looked over at him and answered her directly. Audy's response didn't improve the look of disgust on her face. Kyle noted how Jomra stepped in, raising his own voice. She acquiesced with a frown and a frustrated kick at the dirt under her boots.

Kyle didn't need a translation, she didn't like the idea of sneaking around and letting Strema live, none of them did. Between Audy and Jomra, it looked as though they'd be able to keep the aggressiveness of Juni and Park under control.

"Ok, I'll lead off. This," he held up a fist, "means we stop and drop to cover, whoever is next in line, will repeat the signal until we all stop." They'd gone over tactical hand signals the day before but given the looks on Juni's and Park's face he thought it a good idea to emphasize that one.

He started off slow, allowing his legs to stretch after the flight. If the Jema suffered from the stiffness he felt, they didn't show it in the slightest. After a quarter of a mile or so,

239

he dropped onto a game trail and picked up his pace into the thickening forest to something a little more face saving. He ran for thirty minutes before calling a halt. It was stupid to be pushing himself this hard just to save face, when they were getting closer to where they might expect Strema scouts at the edge of their hunting camp. Kyle took a knee and checked the map on his compad, struggling to control his breathing. Jomra, who he was glad to see was sweating hard in the chilled air, looked over his shoulder at the screen. Kyle pointed at the five green carats on the map indicating all of them. "This is us."

He scrolled the map to the north seven kilometers and two green carats showed up. "This is my team." He scrolled back to the area between them and the Strema camp and indicated a couple of rough red circles. "This is where my teammates have spotted Strema patrols."

"Strema?" Jomra asked. Kyle scrolled the map further east following the dotted blue line of the stream they'd been following. The shallow stream, maybe ten yards across, broke between two short, forested hills ahead. Beyond that, another five klicks eastward, the area opened up a bit in a large natural meadow where the Strema hunting party had made camp. The area was indicated by another red circle, this one notated with *"bad guys"* written within. Kyle rolled his eyes, Jake was being his usual smartassed self.

"We'll cut north from here, slowly," he explained as he scrolled back to their position on the electronic map. He input their projected route to Jake and Carlos' position on the flat screen with a series of green dots. "My team will see our line of approach on their screens, they'll know where and when to be looking for us." He waited for Audy to explain and Kyle was rewarded with a few words and a grunt of acceptance from Jomra.

"Very useful," Audy translated.

"It is, at that," he pointed at Jomra's own compad, and gestured for it. Jomra powered it up and comfortably went to the map application, and with a hint provided by Audy, brought up their current position. His eyes went wide as it displayed an identical screen to what Kyle had just powered down.

"Everyone will carry one of these," Kyle explained. "From you to the lowliest of your warriors, you will be able to control what level of information they see, but everyone can keep a picture of the battlefield in their mind as they move or prepare to engage."

Juni said something and nodded excitedly.

"My scouts can communicate without returning? I can know where they are at all times? Miraculous." Audy translated.

"It's not without issues, which we'll discuss later," Kyle nodded. "But yes, we call it tactical command and control, and it's a game changer."

He could tell they wanted to talk some more, but he waved them off. "Later."

They moved off again heading north, at a right angle away from the creek their game trail had been roughly paralleling. It was slow going, as he picked his way through the brush, paying more attention to his own sound discipline than he had in years. For the most part, he tried to stay to the rocks as they gradually climbed uphill, mindful to stay below the line of sight of any Strema below who might happen to look up at the wrong time.

They crossed over a shallow exposed ridge on their bellies, dropped down to another game trail on the back side of the ridge, and continued to move slow, until the trail crested back across the summit again. There, Kyle halted them, and pulled out his binoculars and scanned the stream's narrow valley below them. It took him a moment to spot a Strema scout team, and he pointed out the pair of enemies to the others holding the binoculars out to Jomra.

Jomra accepted the binoculars, but just held them against his chest as he pointed out two more pairs of scouts that he hadn't seen. He didn't think Jomra meant anything by handing the binoculars back to him unused, but he couldn't help but be impressed. He could see the other scouts, now that

Jomra had pointed them out. He nodded in appreciation of the man's skills.

Not to be outdone, Juni's arm reached over Jomra's shoulders and pointed out another pair that Kyle couldn't spot until he brought up the binoculars to confirm the sighting. He shook his head and smiled. True, they had a better idea of what to look for than he did, but they all seemed to have the eyesight of hawks. He pulled out his compad and updated the positions of the enemy scouts, adding the two new locations with a note disparaging Jake and Carlos' ability to either see or count. Audy who had learned how to read English before he could speak it very well, suppressed a laugh and explained the notation to the others. He was more than happy to see the Jema take some pride in their native ability. It would make the mental leap they had in front of them that much easier.

An hour later they crossed the ridge again, until they were high above the main Strema foraging camp that faded in and out of sight as they moved slowly through the heavy foliage. He halted them when they reached a flat knoll, shielded from the meadow below by the pines growing up from the hillside below them. The area was thick with ground cover and he dropped his pack and took a knee in the middle of it, motioning them all down around him.

He looked over at Audy, "Let them know we're here." He indicated the others. "We'll wait here till dark, as long as they," he nodded down into the meadow below, "don't pull a night march on us."

He watched as the others nodded in understanding and shed their packs. It took more control than he had imagined not to smile. Even Audy was looking at him strangely.

Jomra looked around the clearing, and asked Audy something.

"Were we not to meet Jake and Carlos here? Audy translated.

He looked at all of them, Park had shed his pack and was playing with the map on his own compad. Juni watched the enemy below them with unconcealed anger locked into her face, her mouth set in a hard line, brow furrowed. Jomra just looked at him in expectation of an answer.

"They are here," he smiled and waited for Audy's translation.

"Jake? Carlos? Come on out."

The bushes moved behind Jomra, and another lump of plants rolled on to its side directly in front of Juni.

"What took you guys so long?" Jake sat up and started digging in his pockets for his can of snuff.

"Ola..." Carlos waived from where he was laying atop his sniper rifle, and then slowly, rolled back, becoming nearly invisible again, even though he was practically laying at Juni's feet.

He pointed at the amorphous blob that was Carlos. "We call that a Ghillie suit, we use them to blend in to the environment," he explained, happy to see the looks of surprise on all of their faces. "Somebody like Carlos," he pointed at the non-descript bank of bushes and ferns next to Juni, "is an artist. He can sneak into just about any area with ground foliage, get into the range of the enemy's leadership and take them out."

"Hey, what am I? PFC Smedlap?" Jake came to one knee; his Ghillie suit a mass of brown and green strips of cloth. Grass, ferns and sticks had been inserted at every angle imaginable. Even right in front of them, there was very little edge to outline his frame.

"Anybody can be taught to wear a suit like this," Kyle explained ignoring Jake's middle finger scratching his forehead. "It takes a lot of training to do it right. Jake's very good at it, Carlos is an artist."

He listened to Audy's translation, his eyes meeting Jomra's, who grinned at him and nodded in acknowledgement.

'Tied up, one – one,' he thought, before hastily reminding himself that this wasn't a matter of showing off. 'The hell it isn't.'

Park pointed around Juni, at Carlos, asking something with a gesture toward the enemy below them.

Audy answered immediately, nodding his head up and down for emphasis.

"They think Carlos is too far away to hit anything."

"Tell them, the far edge of the Strema camp is well within range."

They all openly scoffed at Audy's translation of Carlos' statement.

"Show them this." Kyle looked over at the lump of undergrowth that was Carlos, a blackened hand appeared beneath the Ghillie blanket covering him, holding a shiny .50 caliber round.

The shell was passed around with looks of amazement. It was Park who slid a 5.56 round from one of his spare magazines and held the two shells next to each other. He fired a question off to Audy.

"He wonders how a man can survive firing a shell this large."

Kyle laughed. "The sniper rifle is designed to absorb a lot of the recoil, there's still a good bit of sensory feedback."

"Sensory feedback?" Audy asked.

"Pain, Audy," Carlos intoned from under his camouflage.

Jake crawled on his knees into their circle and introductions went around. When they were finished, he pointed down the hill.

"They've pulled in their hunting parties, and packed up a good bit of their camp. Early this morning, about two hundred departed straight east, same way they came in. There's just over five hundred remaining, not including their scouts. Dom, Jeff, Hans, and Darius, are at the far end of this ridge. They reported this morning's group went past them about midday. They'll definitely be out of the picture for tomorrow's fight."

"Where will we meet them? As they march?" Jomra asked through Audy. "How many warriors do you have hidden in these hills?"

"Forty-three," Kyle said, and indicated all of them, "including us."

Jomra laughed quietly, shaking his head at Audy, before saying something that Kyle was sure was something along the lines of 'these guys are nuts.'"

"Jomra thinks your balls may be bigger than your brains, he means no offense."

Kyle smiled and scratched his head, smiling. "None taken. We think we have plenty of firepower, we want to show you how we fight." He smoothed out a place in the cold dirt of the hillside, grabbed a stick and started to draw, exchanging a knowing glance with Audy. Their first conversation had literally been stick figures drawn in the sand.

"This is what we'll do..."

*

Chapter 17

Before night fall, they moved as a group three miles to the east. They stayed in the hills above the shallow valley on constant lookout for Strema scouts. Arriving shortly after sundown, Kyle and Jake had departed downhill towards the meadow, towards the expected path of the Strema's travel. Carlos could tell the Jema contingent was not happy about being left behind amidst the short line of trench and breast works that they'd been preparing for the last three days. By his way of thinking, the Jema were Audy's problem to deal with. It wasn't like he could say anything to them that they'd understand. They could meet up with Kyle and Jake, tomorrow, after the show.

Carlos figured their Jema allies would get their fill of action in the morning. The whole Strema hunting party was going to be led by their balls into the killing ground they'd prepared beneath their dug in positions. They'd be covered by the mortar team that the Jema crowd was inspecting behind the breast works, three M-60 machine guns, his rifle, and thirty-seven other Eden militia. They weren't basic recruits out of St. Louis base, they were veterans of their country's militaries on earth and of the unending wars there and basically the best of what the militia could scrap together.

Audy approached with his clansmen, and clanswoman, he corrected himself. Juni looked to be interested in nothing more than kicking ass and taking names. He knew how Audy felt about the Strema, but in Juni's case she had seethed in anger each time they'd spotted a Strema scout during their march.

"Ahh, my spotters," he stood and gave the *'Thai bow'* to them. "Has Audy explained how we'll do this?"

"I have," Audy answered. "We'll locate the officers, and direct your fire."

"Right," Carlos scratched his head, he knew he probably had all manner of bugs crawling on him at the moment and he did his best not think about it. Laying in concealment for a couple of days with Jake to keep him fed and watered was easy duty. After all his time laying hidden at the edges of battlefields, one could be forgiven for thinking he'd be used to things crawling on him. They'd be wrong. The hardest part of his job was spiders. Ants, even snakes didn't bother him. Spiders were a different story.

"OK," he began, pointing downhill from their trench. "We are going to prioritize a bunch of targets before the shooting even starts. When they are in the draw below us and coming up, that will be more fluid. But when they are still down on the road passing by, or preparing their assault, you'll point out each target, wait for me to acquire it, and then we'll move to the next."

Audy faithfully translated all of that and then provided the follow on.

"How will you keep the targets in your mind when they are all moving through the brush below?"

"I'll service them when they are still in the meadow, as you point them out. As many as I can. That's why we have to prioritize. Will you be able to identify whoever is in command?"

"We will," Audy answered him directly before passing on his words to the other Jema.

"No one can shoot that far and hit something." Audy pointed at Park as he translated, and then gestured down the hill to the narrow track the Strema would be marching through. Audy clearly didn't want the comment attributed to him.

Carlos wasn't offended, he was used to that sentiment among his own people who understood, at least in principle, what a sniper rig could do. Among the Jema, the only frame of reference they had was their own technology.

He smiled and pointed down at his rifle. "It's not magic, it's the weapon. Anyone can learn to do it, with enough practice."

Audy turned to his wards, "Carlos credits the weapon for his skill, though it is said amongst the Terrans, no one can shoot like him. It is truly magic what he can do."

"You tell them what I said?" Carlos asked.

"I did," Audy replied, "I think they'll need to see it to believe."

*

Jomra hadn't slept well for the few hours where he had even tried. There was something he wasn't seeing here. His allies weren't stupid, their tools alone gave proof to that, and yet ... He stood on the firing step of the camouflaged defensive trench cut across the top of the draw between two shallow hills looking downwards through the six hundred yards of scrubby short trees below them. Besides the fact the Strema would outnumber them better than ten to one, it was the shallowness of the hills to either side that bothered him. There were draws on either side of those flanking hills, much narrower, but did their allies think the Strema would not see them? Not utilize the other draws to flank them?

Many Strema would no doubt die in the draw beneath their prepared position in the face of the massive fire the Terran rifles could produce, but the approach to their flanks along the backside of the hills to either side of the draw couldn't even be seen from where he now stood. The Strema were without honor, but they were not stupid. There was no way they would not see and exploit the covered approach up the hill side. Approaches, he corrected himself, one on either side. He would not have thought his new allies could be this foolish. There was courage, but it could easily walk into the territory of pride. Warriors were wasted in that land.

Audrin though, knew what the Strema could do, and having lived among them, he also knew what the Terrans and their weapons were capable of. His friend, at his feet, looked to be sleeping without a worry. Audrin had been no different the night before when Juni and Park had pointed out that they did not have the numbers to defend this position. Audrin had only nodded in agreement. It was as if Audrin as well, expected the Strema to run straight into the teeth of their weapons.

Jomra knew, many Strema would do just that. They would sacrifice themselves, fixing the attention of the Terrans while the flanks were exploited. No one knew what Audrin was

248

thinking, ever. Least of all him. The fact he'd come alone to this world, and how he'd come here proved that, but his friend wasn't stupid or blind. No, it was he that was missing something.

"You look worried, Jomra."

Audrin was awake, rubbing at his face, sitting up in his sleeping bag. Yet another wondrous device they'd all been provided with. Looking down at his oldest friend he could not imagine what he'd gone through during his first contact with the Terrans, or the desperation that had driven him to do what he had done. The man had risked everything. Jomra was thankful that he had. No matter what happened here on this empty world, they would die free. He and the rest of the Jema owed Audrin a debt that could never be paid. And yet, as he glanced around at their defensive position and the killing ground in front of their trench, he couldn't help but shake his head. He had not expected the death to come so soon.

"Jomra?"

"I know they wish to show us something of their power here," he indicted the draw beneath them, "but this is too...

"You think their pride has taken a bite that they cannot chew?"

He felt himself nod, the saying was strange, but it fit very well with what he was thinking.

"I need coffee," Audrin grunted as he climbed out of sleeping bag, "and one thing you can always count on with our new friends, they'll have coffee in the morning."

He watched Audrin make his way through the trench to the dug-out area where a small space for supplies had been designated. He came back holding two paper cups of the black tar juice that he had tried once before at Kyle's insistence. To him, it smelled wonderful but tasted like something dirty leggings had been washed in. He looked doubtful as he accepted the cup.

"I had smelled it brewing, I did not know if it was for everyone."

"It is," Audrin sipped at his cup with his eyes closed. "It's addictive like Haaka leaf, but good for you, or so they say."

249

The bitterness wasn't quite as strong as he remembered. "Like warm mud, strained through sweaty socks."

"I'll ask what you think, in another moon or so," Audrin grinned at him, and then joined him on the firing step, pointing over the berm.

"They wish to shock you, Jomra. Surprise you with their power. They call it making a point." Audrin took another sip and regarded him with a smile, "and I agreed."

"You haven't forgotten how to read the ground before a battle?"

Audrin just glared at him for a moment not bothering to answer. But he did spread his arms wide in response. "You worry the Strema will see that our flanks are unprotected?"

"You are clearly not worried about this, nor it seems, are our new friends. *That* is what worries me."

Audrin nodded, "I would be worried had I not studied their wars and tactics. This is what Jake calls a rope-a-dope. Leading the enemy to where we want them, make them think they are doing something on their own initiative, before you make them pay dearly for their mistake."

"Jake is the one that makes people laugh? Chews the Haaka leaf?"

"Yes, that's him."

"Does he have some sort of magic to defend our flanks?"

"He chose this battlefield," Audrin pointed around him. "They have been preparing it for a several days. You can trust their ability as soldiers."

"That word again," Jomra had heard it used much by Kyle. "Soldiers? Kyle says this is how we will win, if the Jema can learn to fight as soldiers, not warriors?"

"Watch with an open heart. It's all they ask."

"They are so powerful?"

Audrin shook his head. "No, Kyle would admit that most of their soldiers, take away their tools and technology, are no match for our own warriors." Audrin pointed to middle of their defensive line where Carlos was making ready with his personal cannon that he called a rifle.

250

"Carlos, and," he pointed at the dark-skinned warrior standing behind him, "Jeff, as well as all those with Kyle concealed in the forest beneath us, on the other side of the Strema's march, they are warriors our equal, with or without weapons. But they are very few. Most of their soldiers," Audy indicated the others coming awake within the trenches, "have joined to fight only for the duration of the war. They were something other than soldiers before, and will go back to that after."

"That one," Audrin pointed again, "I know him well, he was a physical therapist before."

"What is a physical therapist?"

Audrin shrugged. "He helps people heal more quickly by helping them exercise."

"You are being serious?"

"I am," Audrin confirmed. "They are soldiers, some have been soldiers before, but they all, with the exception of Kyle and those he calls knuckle draggers are something else."

Jomra glanced at the soldier Audrin had said helped people exercise. "But he is no warrior?"

"No, he is a soldier, and a pretty good one. The difference between the tactics of soldiers and warriors is what Kyle wishes to show you. To make his point."

"I'm convinced they will all be prey to Strema blades if they do not realize our flanks are unguarded."

"They know Jomra," Audrin nodded, "they know. Their plan relies on the Strema seeing that too."

Jeff, the dark-skinned warrior, walked up to them and asked Audrin something. The warrior, soldier, he corrected himself, put his palms together under his chin and seemed to be pleading with Audrin. He really must learn this English, he thought. Whatever Jeff was asking Audrin, it was clearly important.

Jeff turned to him and pointed down the hill. At the bottom of the draw, was a small meadow. Bisecting the clearing, still visible, was the cart path the Strema had cut through it on their way here. The path had been used the day before by the smaller group of Strema that had gone on ahead of the main group they would be seeing soon. It wasn't by any measure a road, but it was clearly a wide path that been cleared to allow the passage of the Strema's supply wagons. Fresh meat was the reason the Strema were out this far from their main encampment.

The Terran's words came across to him as a question and Jomra glanced at Audrin for help.

"He asks only if we are ready."

Jomra flashed a single upturned thumb from a closed fist, Audrin had explained that it meant he was prepared or all is well.

Jeff smiled at him and bumped his fist against his own and said something else before moving further down the line to where Carlos was adjusting something on the massive rifle. He had seen the shell that the fifty-caliber fired. He did not believe a single man could fire such a rifle, but Carlos had assured them that his rifle was designed to do just that.

"What did Jeff ask you?" He turned back to Audy.

"He begged that I prevent you and our other Jema friends from going Leroy Jenkins on the Strema, and to stay behind cover and observe. I think he fears Kyle, should anything happen to you."

"Are we children to them?"

"No, Jomra. No, but you will need to see how they fight, then we can talk of it with Kyle."

"And who or what is Leroy Jenkins?"

"I don't know," Audrin confessed. "I'm still learning their tongue, but I believe he was a great warrior, with perhaps too much courage, not enough," he tapped his head, "brains."

"Battle mad?"

"Perhaps," Audrin shrugged. "But not in a good way."

"Their ways are so strange, we have much to learn of these Terrans."

"And they of us, it's natural we both have questions."

He indicated the flanks to either side of the draw directly in front of their prepared defensive works. Hills which gently rolled above them. Not only would the enemy be able to utilize the flanks to advance without being fired on, they would be in a superior position when they crested over the two hills flanking either end of their line.

"Right now, I just question these tactics."

"Patience Jomra, with luck the Strema will question it as well."

He shook his head. "Fine, I will observe and learn. Though I will probably have to sit on Juni."

"I'm not sure she would complain," Audrin replied. Audrin had long predicted that Juni would at some point ask to him to clasp hands.

"If she did," he said, "I'm not sure I would survive."

Jeff was waving them over, and he recognized the hurried preparations and whispered orders that progressed through the trench work, which was nothing more than a camouflaged hill, with a firing step cut into it and a trench behind that. Everyone seemed to be grabbing their rifles, tightening belts and straps, and stuffing handfuls of food into their mouths. The men behind the large hummingbird guns, the ones their allies called *emsixties*, handled long belts of ammunition that he did not quite understand. Would they not have to put those shells into the magazines for the guns to function?

Some things were the same on any planet, and he noticed warriors preparing for a battle, was one of them. They followed suit, and Jomra watched closely as Juni and Park cycled their newly gifted rifles and readied them to fire. He dreaded a friendly fire incident that Audrin had warned them about.

A pulse of excitement ran through him at the thought of the firepower he had in his own hands. He would take more enemies with one magazine than he did in in most battles. The fact that they were outnumbered more than ten to one was forgotten. They would soon be in battle. "We are Jema," he said to Park, to Juni. "If our allies fall here today, we will fall with them."

Jeff and Carlos turned their compads towards him as they approached, so that he and his people could see what they were looking at. Jeff explained something to Audrin who translated.

"Those are images of the Strema camp, at this moment."

"How?" he could see the tiny figures on the monitors. The Strema beginning to fall into a long line of march, blocks of warriors, Audrin had called them company sized units, and there were five of them. Well over five hundred Strema, separated by the heavy wagons being pulled by the same warriors. There were thirty-seven people in their defensive line, and Kyle had six more within the tree line at the far side of the clearing below. He waited for Jeff or Carlos to call a halt to this madness. They didn't. They only looked at him expectantly.

"How is this possible? You have an aircar above them? One with large weapons I am hoping?"

Audrin translated, and then responded directly to him. "No, it is called a drone." He held his hands out stretched. "A mechanical bird, a machine that flies by itself, or can be directed by a person far away. At this moment, one of the men with Kyle below is directing it. It has a camera, the images are transmitted here, like a radio."

Jomra felt himself smile, finally a piece of the technology that Audrin had said would change the way the Jema fought forever. He could see the possibilities in his mind. "And it carries a large weapon perhaps?"

"No, just a camera to take the pictures."

Maybe not so miraculous after all, but it was still amazing to watch the enemy prepare for their march that would take them through the meadow below. He mentally shook his head. If their position here was weak, the one held below by Kyle and the others was foolish in the extreme. No matter their firepower, they would be swarmed under by the massive assault that would surely come the moment they opened fire.

He kept his mouth shut and watched the images of the Strema camp that he knew was three kava away, the Chandrian unit of march was slightly longer than the mile the Terrans used.

"They will be underway within moments," he said to Audrin. Juni and Park at either side of him nodded in agreement. He listened to Audrin rephrase it in English. New allies, new technology and they were going to lose here today, because the Terrans wanted to 'prove a point.'

*

Kyle heard Audy's voice in his earbud from Carlos' mic pick up imbedded in his compad.

"Enemies moving," he passed down the line on his own tactical channel. He had Dom, Darius, Jake, Hans and Arne with him. His whole original 'test bed' contingent minus Carlos and Jeff above, with Audy. Jiro, who was probably asleep in his cockpit five miles to the north of them, and John Wainwright who had been among the first casualties of the invasion fully rounded out their original group.

They'd carried enough ammo down here to fight all day if they had to, so much, most of it was stashed at their fallback position, a hundred yards further back into the woods. He knew if they needed it, the ammo, or the fallback position, things would have already gone tango uniform and neither would make a difference in the end. That said, he couldn't imagine very many Strema surviving the blender that Jeff and Jake had prepared.

"Carlos, you and your spotters have the ball, I'll give a one click warning when we have them in view. Shouldn't be more than a minute after that, you'll have line of sight on their leading edge."

"Copy that, one click warning order," Carlos replied. "You guys don't let the Cajun do anything stupid."

"Shoot straight, jarhead," Jake jumped in on the circuit.

Carlos just responded with a single click.

"Must have his game face on," Jake responded with a mumble that Kyle barely heard. Jake was ten yards away behind another log.

He laid his head down on his forearm and closed his eyes. In his mind's eye he pictured everyone's position, the zones of fire, his own lines of sight that were so critical to the plan that Jake, Carlos and Jeff had worked so hard on. He knew a forest fire sometime in the last couple of years was the culprit behind the cleared meadow and the near barren hills rising from the far side. It was the lack of thick forest growth at this location that made their plan feasible. He could see directly across the clearing and up the slopes of the broad grass and boulder covered hillside that led to his friends, old and new alike. The leader of their new allies was up there as well. No doubt anxious to go toe to toe with an enemy force that outnumbered them better than ten to one. What could go wrong?

He wasn't sure how much time had passed when Darius' voice whispered into his earbud. Darius held the far western end of their position with Hans and Arne.

"Two scouts, jogging fast."

Less than a minute later, two Strema jogged through the meadow, their heads on a swivel, focused on the dense foliage that hid his team at their edge of the meadow. They glanced up at the hillside on their left but saw nothing that alerted them and were soon out of sight continuing down the rough path to the east. Kyle almost wished them luck, maybe they'd get far enough away that they wouldn't try to come back and help. From everything that Audy and Jomra had related regarding the Strema, he wasn't hopeful on that score.

It was nearly ten minutes later when Darius reported the lead elements of the Strema column was in sight. Kyle sent his one click warning to Carlos who responded in kind.

*

Jeff Krouse, who, as Audrin had explained was a former SEAL, perhaps the most elite of the Terran's fighting forces on their home world. The SEAL had just finished explaining to them in whispered tones what a Jarhead was. It made no sense to Jomra. So little about the Terrans did. For that matter, Seals were hardly a paragon of martial example within the animal kingdom. They were hunted widely on Chandra by several clans and it seemed odd that the Terrans would claim such an easily hunted beast as a symbol for an elite fighting force.

And this man Jeff, seemed entirely too at ease for the desperate battle they were about to face. Again, he was missing something here, and he wished Audrin would just say what it was. The warning click on Carlos' radio was heard by

256

all of them in their small group. Jeff's relaxed smile disappeared and he flashed a series of hand signals to those around him, and Jomra watched in appreciation as the men readied themselves quietly.

"Ok," Carlos whispered to Audy; this was a word that Jomra was coming to recognize as having many meanings. He tried to follow Carlos's words, but was lost immediately, and growing frustrated until Audrin turned to them all.

"I've told him to look for the armbands of the Tearks, possibly a junior Bastelta. Use your binoculars, and tell me where you see them in reference to the grid I showed you." Audy turned to the meadow below and with a hand counted off four zones in Chandrian, "I will relay the sighting to Carlos who will kill them to begin the battle."

"From here?" Park, who was counted among the best Jema marksman, peeked over the lip of the berm and shook his head. "It would take two hands of our best long shooters to make that killing shot, and then only if one of them was very lucky."

"He could make that shot if the distance was doubled." Audrin replied shaking his head. "I warn you, plug your ear closest to his gun."

"A war party this large," Juni jerked her chin at the meadow, "if commanded by a Bastelta, he'll have two or three ass lickers with him."

"Anything important?" Carlos asked. His head remained down against his rifle's scope.

"Just that if they have a Bastelta, a junior officer, he'll probably have several Tearks, all with the arm bands by his side."

"Copy that, group of muj with arm bands," Carlos replied.

"There, the tardan bastards are here," Park pointed over their berm, whispering. A group of Strema, loosely ordered came into view, they moved quickly, appearing out from behind the hills on the right flank that hid their approach into the meadow. The lead group, a finger of warriors, numbering a little over a hundred warriors, carried their weapons ready in two hands. Jomra knew this was the enemy column's best finger, company, he corrected himself, happy that he had remembered the Terran name for the unit that Audrin had taught them. They were unencumbered, looking for signs of trouble and moving across the meadow below them from right to left.

That group was half way across the meadow before the next company came into view, weapons slung on their backs. This group were all pulling on a network of ropes leading to the first couple of wagons heavily packed with the meat they'd taken, most still wrapped in the hides of whatever animal had been harvested.

Jomra could feel the hate roiling in his gut, and he gently put two hands out onto the shoulders of Juni and Park and gave them a squeeze. They could well die here, unless the Terrans were truly magicians, but they would take many Strema with them. When they looked back at him, pleading, he gently shook his head.

"We'll do as our friends ask, we'll stay behind these walls. The enemy will be here soon enough."

The first two wagons, were almost across the meadow when another finger of troops, likewise pulling wagons appeared. Jomra glanced at Audrin who lay prone with binoculars next to Carlos, the long shooter. He was proud of what his friend had done to try to find the Jema another path. It was a pity that it would probably end here today. Just because their new allies had, in their own tongue, bitten off more than they could chew. He didn't know if it was pride, or tactical stupidity. It mattered not. The Jema would stand.

They all saw the Bastelta appear, near the middle of the column, and as they had guessed, he had two Tearks with him. He could hear Audrin whispering something to Carlos and saw his friend stick a finger in his ear. He followed suit. The concussion from Carlos' rifle struck him like a slap across his entire body. Even expecting it, he barely managed to keep his binoculars focused on the Strema commanders.

One of the Tearks, was hit, and blown back ten feet out of the route of march. Carlos had missed the Bastelta and hit a lowly Teark. An impressive shot, no doubt, but the enemy

258

commander wasted no time. With a surprised glance at his dead subordinate, he looked up the hill towards them and shouted an order. Carlos fired again, and the second Teark, standing next to the Bastelta, had his head removed by the shot. Carlos hadn't missed, Jomra realized in shock. The long shooter was letting the Bastelta issue his orders.

The Strema in the meadow, two fingers worth, almost 250 warriors swarmed up the hillside like an avalanche in reverse, coming directly to where they waited, all 37 of them. Jomra's eyes caught the Teark directing that first wave of assault, and then watched as the man was folded in half and blown back into his advancing warriors by Carlos' third shot.

"Truly magical," Park sat against the inside wall of their berm, looking across at Carlos, his mouth hanging open in surprise. Carlos fired again, and Jomra didn't get turned around in time to see who he had targeted that time, but he had no doubt another Strema Teark was dead. He located the Bastelta quickly, and could see he was young for the rank, he'd be aggressive. He wasn't stupid though. The Strema leader wasted no time in stopping additional fingers coming up behind him from entering the meadow. He was clearly directing them up the hidden draw on their right flank.

Carlos fired again, and a Teark running towards the Bastelta, no doubt to collect orders was hit and blown off his feet to slam against one of the wagons. The man had been running! Carlos, if anything was better than what Audrin had described. That had been an impossible shot. Jomra shook his head, as the Strema, two fingers worth that had already transited the meadow, reappeared for just a moment but were shouted back, and no doubt directed up the draw on their left flank.

"Audrin," he yelled, "they are coming up both flanks now! Do they see?

"They see!" Audrin yelled back. "Now the Bastelta!"

Jomra managed to see the impact from Carlos's shot explode the Bastelta's upper body and take down another Teark who been unlucky enough to be standing directly behind him.

He heard Jeff shout something, from farther down the line, and the Terran troops stood up in the trench and laid their weapons over the berm. They all fired in their single shot mode, he knew from personal experience how hard to control the weapons were on automatic. He still thought of it as the hummingbird mode. He was doing his best to think of things in their terms. Even firing singly, the thirty or so rifles reaped a glorious bounty on the Strema who were in their headlong run towards them up the hill. Strema fell across the front of their assault, but the human wave did not stop. Just as he knew it would not. There were too few of them to stop this tide, let alone the hundreds that were now climbing the hillside, unseen on either flank.

The Strema below them reached within three hundred strides, *yards* he corrected himself, of their camouflaged line when Jeff shouted another order. The three large guns, *em-sixties*, Audrin had called them, opened up. Each had two men serving the weapon, one firing, and another feeding the weapon with belts of cartridges from a can that he had mistakenly thought were convenient way to carry ammo. Now he could see that the linked belt had a deadly purpose.

He noted Park and Juni firing as well, doing their part. He did not join in. He had much to learn from his allies. A lesson he was just beginning to appreciate as he watched the Strema assault below them run into an invisible wall of lead and die by the dozens. The charge faltered under the incredible volume of fire being put out.

Another shouted order from Jeff, and a strange *thump... thump ... thump* sounded behind him like small explosions. Some soldiers had dropped their assault rifles and were dropping what looked like grenades into tubes they called mortars. The explosions below him in the draw brought him back around. Fountains of dirt, rock and Strema body parts blew skyward in the narrow draw, as the Strema halted their climb and scrambled for cover. He knew it was only temporary, they would wait for an order and then charge again as a group, however many were left. He was not worried about them. The unseen Strema that he knew were climbing the hills on either side of them, would soon have them bracketed and be firing down on them from two sides.

Surely, the Terrans, with the tools they had, could see this. Perhaps the grenade tubes could be targeted there, and lobbed over the hill, but it would have to be soon. Any second now, they would be here.

Jomra ducked involuntarily, as the horizon to either side of him erupted. It felt like an earthquake amidst a long, continuous series of sharp explosions that echoed through the hills. Had the Terrans hidden troops guarding the flanks? He hoped not, as no one could have lived through the roiling and angry cloud of fire just now coming over the lips of the hills framing the draw.

*

Kyle sat the switch board aside. He'd just used it to cook off the more than forty claymore mines lining the natural defiles that had just a moment earlier been packed with well-ordered Strema striving to reach the height of their target before swarming down on them. The half dozen buried 105 rounds mixed in with a few canisters of napalm had immediately followed. He felt sick to his stomach, but he had a point he had needed to make with his allies. Their existence on Eden, for the Jema as well, depended on winning - period. Against the Strema, that meant killing all of them. That had to happen before they could call on reinforcements from Chandra. It was a binary solution set, either/or, survive/or die. They couldn't afford to fight fair and have a chance of surviving. He hoped their new allies could understand that. He hoped he'd made his point.

There were a few dozen Strema hunkered down in the middle draw, under cover from the militia's fire above them, probably wondering what the hell had just happened. They were two hundred yards away, uphill and directly in front of them, exposed.

"Finish it," he spoke into his mic, to his own team. They opened up, and it was over within a minute. Coming under accurate fire from their rear, the Strema who didn't break cover, died. Those that did, were targeted from above, and died.

*

It had taken an hour to police the battlefield and dispatch any surviving Strema. The idea of taking prisoners would have been as ludicrous to the Jema as it was logistically impossible for the militia. There had been precious few of the enemy that could have been saved from their wounds in any case. The Strema had simply continued their attack, despite wounds. It was an ugly reminder of what they were up against.

Kyle had the drones up looking for any Strema reaction force, and Jeff had positioned his militia team along what had been the planned path of Strema march a half mile east of the meadow just in case. He and Jake were meeting with Audy, the Jema, and Carlos down in the meadow itself. From there, looking up, the undulating hills and three body choked draws were clearly visible. The two on either end were charred and blackened, half buried Strema bodies were already drawing great herds of turkey buzzards and clouds of other scavenger birds.

Jomra, turned to him and asked something, Audy translated.

"You could see their approach the whole time."

He realized it wasn't really a question.

"We try to pick our battlefields," he said. "Strategically, we think offensively and are aggressive. Tactically, it's usually better to get the enemy to attack a prepared position. Especially against an enemy this aggressive."

Jomra seemed to accept the answer once Audy had translated, and responded with something that of course he had to wait for Audy to translate...

"When you were under the heart speak, you said that if we fought you, you would hunt us down and destroy us... It was heart speak, so you believed the truth of what you said. At the time, I admit to thinking you underestimated us, the Jema, and perhaps even the Strema. Now I see, it was I who was wrong. You are far more powerful than I could have imagined.

262

You did not even have your airboats here today and accomplished something I would not have credited had I not seen with my own eyes."

"It's just technology, Jomra," Kyle shook his head. "We've had generations of war using our technology. Our tactics have grown up around it. Man to man," he looked at Juni, "or woman, I'd put a Jema well ahead of most of our people in an honest fight. But we don't fight fair, we fight to win. So, every trick I, or we, can think of, we'll use and keep using until the Strema are gone, the Koryna as well."

He hadn't had an update on the northwest group, the Koryna clan, in a few days, but he knew they'd abandoned the west coast as a target and were on a route of march to the southeast. They were being tracked by Colonel Pretty's SF guys. Barring another storm, they'd reach what had been the Canadian border with eastern Montana in another week or so. It was an enemy that could wait for the moment.

"Of course," Audy replied for Jomra. "You should use the Jema as bait for the Strema war party, and then attack them as you did here."

"No," he said it louder than he intended. "We don't have the numbers to do that, not yet," he replied. "We need to get your people integrated with our own, get them trained up on tactics that would see your people not just fight for honor, but survive. We had one casualty today, wounded, he'll be able to fight again in six weeks. Even with the help of our weapons, how would you have fought this battle?"

Kyle paused and waited for Audy's translation to catch up, and before Jomra could reply,

"You would have won, I'm sure. But, how many people would you have lost? How many times can you fight that kind of battle against the Strema before there are too few of you left to survive as a people?"

Kyle listened to Audy translate and watched as Jomra regarded him. Was it surprise he saw there or anger?

"Your concern for Jema lives does you honor, but warriors will die in this fight."

Kyle nodded in agreement. "Yes, but soldiers win, and hopefully go home to raise families, and live. You forget, I'm Jema as well now. I would see the Jema come to understand our ways, not just our tools. With an eye to the future, the Jema need to be on equal footing with my people. After we finish the Strema and Koryna, the Kaerin will still be out there, so will the governments of earth. We need allies in the Jema, not bait."

Audy nodded his head at him in approval before translating what he'd said to the others.

Audy, listened to comments from all three of his fellow Jema before turning back to him and bowing his head again.

"You will have your allies, Kyle." Audy faced Carlos and Jake as well, and bowed his head again, "and friends who can the see the honor and wisdom in what you say."

*

Raleigh-Durham, North Carolina, Earth 1.0

"It's official, Gannon's been relieved. RUMINT has it he was arrested as well."

The rest of TF Chrome stared back at the just arrived Jenn Bowden, aka Captain Jennifer Bowden formerly of the Army's Aviation Test Group. Her husband Rick, another Army Captain stood next to her nodding. "House arrest, but arrested."

Captain Derek and Lt. Denise Mills, sat on one couch. His babysitters, the Souzas, Brittany and Tom, both Captains, rounded out the three married couples of the strangest Special Forces team he'd ever heard of, sat on another. No doubt the Souza's terrible twins were around the corner at the top of the stairs listening in.

He'd been here, a 'guest' of the Souzas for nearly eight months and there'd been no contact from Gannon. No contact from anyone. Sir Geoffrey Carlisle was truly dead as far as the world was concerned.

"He failed to put down the riots in Boston," Jennifer Bowden shrugged, her long dark hair was tied into a single thick pony tail. "One story has it the ROE plan he put forward was too lenient from the administration's perspective, the other has it that he refused to order the deployment given the ROE that had come down from above."

The ROE - the rules of engagement - something US military officers had been having a great deal of trouble with regarding what exactly the rules were with respect to US citizens who were rioting or in some cases openly revolting. He knew it wouldn't be much different in Europe either. The situation got very confusing when the other guy started shooting, regardless of shared citizenship.

"I always thought Gannon was an asshole," Derek Mills shook his head. "Maybe he's not all bad."

Sir Geoff had by now worked out the division of labor of the Task Force charged by Gannon 'to sit on him.' He'd gotten to know them well enough that he had a degree of comfort with them. Derek and his wife were African Americans recruited by the Army from some Silicon Valley start-up; they were the hackers. The Mills were both former Army SF pilots; Jennifer now flew for rich corporate VIPs and Rick for some energy company. Those were cover jobs he knew, but they were real, as far as any job was real these days. The American economy was grinding to a halt and the riots, like the massive one in Boston, were now regular occurrences.

President Donaldson's economic reset wasn't going as smoothly as he thought it would. Any pretense of it being a bottom up exercise in people power was an open joke. It was being enforced by a military that was plainly caught in the middle but still following orders from the top.

"So, what now?" Tom Souza was rubbing the bridge of his nose, and he looked over at his wife Brittany. Captain Brittany Souza could have been a model. She pretended to sell real estate and was active in raising the two smartest kids he'd ever come across. She was also the senior officer in command of their Task Force. If it was still indeed a Task Force. It had been defunded almost a year earlier, kept on covert life support by General Gannon. Now, that was gone as well.

"We're exposed," she said simply. "They'll question Gannon. Anybody think he'll keep his mouth shut?"

"Me either," she shook her head in response to the silent stares back at her.

There were more than a few glances in his direction. "We need to move," Tom Soares spoke up. "The sooner the better. We can be at Hilltop in three hours."

"We have lives here," Denise Mills spoke up, holding a hand over her belly. He'd been in the room a week ago, when the young woman had announced she was 3 months pregnant.

He husband reached over and put his hand over hers. "Our lives... all the more reason to move."

"But," she glanced around at the others in the room, "our orders were official."

"Orders in direct opposition to the President's," Tom Souza spoke up again. He pretended to sell insurance to the same clients his wife pretended to sell real estate to. "Denise, these people running things won't even debate the need to disappear us."

"I'm truly sorry," he said, "for all of this."

"You don't have anything to be sorry for," Rich Bowden spoke up as he moved around and pulled up a bar stool to sit. "You're as much a victim here as we are."

"Technically," he sighed, "I'm already a victim. Already dead. I'm the evidence that needs to disappear."

"That isn't going to happen." Tom Souza said with a shake of his head.

Sir Geoff met the stare of Tom's wife and commanding officer. Brittany was gauging him with a look that put her husband's declaration in doubt. He understood her calculation, could even agree with it. He knew them all well enough by now to know why she was the one in command. She wouldn't hesitate to give the order to bury him in the backyard. She'd probably do it herself, as he surmised it wouldn't be a popular decision. He understood the angles at least as well as she did. He'd made similar calls in the service to his own country. At this point in his life he wasn't about to pretend otherwise.

"Under some circumstances, it may have to." He said simply, nodding back in acquiescence to the unreadable stare of Brittany Souza.

"You're supposed to give me reasons to keep you alive." Brittany wasn't there in the calm demeanor, the set of her jaw and the cold eyes – it was all Captain Souza.

"I'm sorry." He barked a short laugh, "I was thinking of your children, present" he nodded to the staircase, and turned with a smile to Denise Mills, "and future."

He leaned forward, elbows to his knees. "I've lived my life, you simply have to do what's best for the children."

"Not going to happen," Tom spoke up again, this time directly at his wife. "Hell, the boys think of him as Grandpa."

"Uncle, surely," he protested.

"Get real old man, you're Gramps." Tom smiled over at him.

Brittany shook her head, "I wouldn't have taken Gannon's order to hide him if I didn't think it was the right thing to do. It's still the right thing, you'll come with."

Brittany looked between the two other couples. "This goes beyond anything in our brief. TF Chrome is over as of this moment. Make your decisions to come with, or not, but we all need to be on the road. And Hilltop is out, have to be somewhere else for the long term. It was purchased by one of my alias accounts. They'll find it in the records once Gannon talks. We should get there and to our bug out packages, but we'll need to move on. There's nothing to say we have to stick together, nothing holding us."

Her head swiveled back to him. "You up for a road trip Gramps?"

He almost shuddered at the thought of being shut up in vehicle with the Souza twins and their questions. "I'll manage."

"We're in," Rich Bowden spoke up glancing at his wife for confirmation, "right?"

"Yeah, we're in," Jenn nodded.

"I can't have a baby on the run," Denise Mills' eyes were watering. She looked up at her husband in near panic.

"Babe, the road is safer than if we get caught." Derek looked at his wife and grasped at her hand.

She nodded her head, a couple of times struggling to hold back tears.

Sir Geoff watched it all with a practiced eye. They could be playing him, he knew. He didn't think they were. Denise wasn't an actress, she was a world class hacker. And the cold calculating gaze of Brittany had been very real. Burying him in the backyard had most definitely been on the table for a moment or two there.

"Ok, we go." Brittany came to her feet with her hands planted on her hips. "We get to Hilltop, we'll figure out the next stop from there."

"Which direction is Hilltop?" he asked.

"Why would that be important?" Brittany's wariness peaked, as did the corner of her mouth in what may have been a smile.

She's even sharper than I thought. "I may have an idea for a longer-term solution." That would be enough for now. It would have to be.

"West, up in the mountains, near the Tennessee border."

Brittany didn't turn away. She was looking at him again with a smile that seemed to say, '*You aren't fooling me.*' "You been holding out on us?"

"No, nothing like that," he lied just like she clearly expected him to.

"Let's get moving then." Brittany pointed at her husband, "I'll see to the boys, get the car loaded." Turning to the others, "we'll meet at Hilltop, it's a three-hour trip, that puts us there around midnight. We shouldn't stay there more than a day or two, tops. If you're delayed, we'll leave bread crumbs at the dead drop at the bottom of hill."

The Bowdens and Mills stood up to leave. Denise Mills gave him a look that he couldn't quite label. She no doubt blamed him for her predicament. He couldn't imagine being responsible for a child right now, or an unborn one, with the world melting down around them.

She whispered something to her husband and waited for the others to leave the room.

She stared at him for a moment.

"Mrs. Mills, I'm truly sorry it's come to this."

"You think we have a better future on the run, than turning you over?"

"I believe I'm justifiably prejudiced in thinking that yes, running is your best option." He tried to make light of the situation and failed miserably. She looked about to cry again.

He walked up to her, "I've never been a parent, Mrs. Mills. My wife was killed in an embassy bombing nearly fifty years ago. She was pregnant at the time and I don't suppose I ever got over that. I do understand the decision you're weighing. Turn me in to a government that is arresting its own generals for not attacking its own citizens, or hope for the best and trust that we can find a solution."

She didn't answer him. She didn't have to.

"Please trust that I have a solution." It was as far as he was willing to go at the moment.

Her hands moved over her flat stomach protectively. One wouldn't know she was pregnant looking at her.

Her head jerked once in a nod., "For the moment," she said clearly. "You put my child at risk, I'll put you in a hole faster than a dog's bone."

He had to smile at the comment but he didn't doubt the young woman in the slightest. These were truly his kind of people.

"I would dig the hole myself."

"Ok then," she sniffed, and turned to the open door. "Just so you understand," she threw back over her shoulder.

He was alone in the foyer of the house. His suburban prison these last months. He could hear the excited voices of the twins upstairs, packing, echoing 'Yes mam' to their oh so capable and dangerous mother. His time of lying to these people was at an end. He wanted to protect them and with each passing day it looked more and more like he was going to have to. The Program had a backup site hidden in an abandoned silver mine in Idaho. *That*, he had lied about. But if they didn't understand his reason for keeping the second site a secret, they weren't the sort of people he thought they were.

It wouldn't be easy, crossing the country in the midst of a civil war, while being hunted by the US government. I'm too old for this, he thought. But he'd been saying that to himself for a long time. At some point it was going to be true.

*

Chapter 18

Lupe Flores was having second thoughts over having begged Kyle to let him join the militia proper rather than stay back in Chief Joe and help with training. Looking across the short expanse of concrete at his platoon mates, a mixture of militia and Jema warriors, he had no doubt it would have been a lot safer to stay home as a Sheriff's Deputy. Their mortar squad had been stood down until they received the newer, heavier air car that could safely carry the weight of a mortar team and enough ammo to make it worthwhile.

The MMS team had lost an air car to the enemy a month earlier. A single, heavy .48 caliber bullet from a Strema rifle had gotten lucky and shredded Paolo's turbine blades. He'd watched his squad mate and friend, along with three other members of the Chief Joseph MMS, go down into the forest trailing smoke followed by an explosion that no one could have survived. They'd been promised new air cars, but he wasn't holding his breath. Scuttlebutt around the massive camp at new St. Louis said the *royal they* needed infantry more than anything. Militia members who had gained any experience and were considered veterans at this point, were all being assigned to joint militia-Jema platoons.

Nothing was as frightening to him as the fact that somebody out there considered him a veteran. A year ago, less he realized when he stopped to think about it, he'd been a part-time hunting guide in the high desert of the Owyhee range in southeastern Oregon. He'd work three months a year guiding wealthy, tourist hunters from the Portland area who were lucky enough to draw a tag for a bighorn sheep or antelope or who'd just driven across the state for the chukar and pheasant. If he was going to be honest with himself, he'd also have to add slacker, poacher, and part-time drunk to his resume.

He'd been dragged to Eden by his sister and brother-in-law and given a second chance that he'd initially done his best to waste. Everyone here had a dream, someone or some job. It was why they'd come. He'd been someone else's baggage. It had taken him less than two days to fall back into what he knew. He could now see the promise of this place. Not just the new planet, but the fresh start it offered. Everybody else talked about what they could do here in a general sense. They were concerned about building a civilization and society that was truly free. That sounded great to him as far as it went, but it paled in comparison to what he wanted. A chance to be someone that didn't make him cringe in the mirror every morning.

The Deputy Sheriff back in Chief Joe, Theo Giabretti had given him a chance in a way that hadn't hurt too much, beyond a bruised jaw and ego, and he'd jumped at it. He'd talked to Theo last night and told him that he was part of a new joint platoon of Eden militia and Jema warriors that would soon be going out on its first patrol. The first fully trained unit of its kind. He'd been proud saying it. He knew Theo would let his sister know. Theo, a former Marine, must have heard the fear in his voice, the doubt that he'd never admit to, but couldn't deny. The old geezer had asked if he'd wanted some advice. He owed Theo a lot, everything, truth be known. "Sure," he'd said.

"You're already dead, no need to be afraid." Theo had somehow made it sound logical. "The guys that buy it, are always the ones counting down the days until they go home. You fight like an animal, for the guy next to you, knowing that your last actions are what's going into the letter that your sister will get. Don't be thinking of home, getting back to base, the last time you got laid, or anything other than what's in front of you. If you can do that, you'll be alright."

He could do that, or at least try, he told himself looking at a pair of Jema, sitting on the tarmac a few feet away from him. They sat, their backs leaning into each other, playing with their compads. He wondered when the novelty of the things would wear off. For the moment, the Jema all seemed to be addicted to the new technology like a bunch of teenagers. The Jema always seemed at ease, not a worry in the world to look at them. They'd been like that since day one of their joint training. Thinking back on Theo's advice, he couldn't help but think the Jema would understand and agree.

It would be one thing in the end... they'd all adopted the Jema saying. They'd trained together for six weeks, in his case, his first actual, military style training. In the case of the Jema, they were lifetime warriors who were learning how to be soldiers.

He knew he had it easier than some of the other militia. He'd been somewhat accepted by the Jema in his unit, and in particular by their platoon leader, Jadis a'Tera, or something like that. They called her Jadi, or Lieutenant Jadi, and if the Jema warrior cared what her people called her, it didn't show. The only thing she seemed to care about was that her orders were carried out. He supposed the fact that he could out shoot any of his fellow militia, as well as any Jema in the platoon with his .308 rifle, went a long way in explaining his special status. He'd tried to explain to her once that he wasn't a soldier, that he could shoot because he was a hunter.

He was getting pretty good with the pidgin Chandrian they all seemed to be using, and Lt. Jadi's English wasn't half bad as long as she stayed to the bare basics. The instantaneous translation provided by the compad helped a great deal, but he couldn't help but think the program had missed something when he'd tried to explain the kind of hunter he had been.

Lt. Jadi had just smiled and nodded, and pointed at the Jema half of her platoon. "We are hunters as well," she'd said.

Not the same, he'd wanted to explain. Jema hunted game that went on two legs and shot back. The closest he'd been to combat were three shoot and scoot missions with his mortar team. He wanted to get her to understand, but in typical Jema fashion, she'd smiled, punched him in the arm and walked off before he could think of a way to re-word what he wanted to say.

Now, he was watching Captains Bullock and Delgado, he knew them as Jake and Carlos. He supposed that familiarity, due to him having come from *Kyle's clan*, had bought him something special as well. For his own part, Kyle was somebody he knew, barely. A hometown guy, that had moved away to the Army a long time ago. But Carlos? That was different. Carlos was dating his cousin Zarena and could end up family. Probably would, given the way Zarena's little girls had taken to him.

Both of the officers stood near the nose of a Blackhawk helicopter, heads bowed in conversation with Lt. Jadi, an ever present compad carrying the majority of the translation load. He noticed that Jake and Carlos were geared up as well. They'd been told the *knuckle draggers* were going to act as their Quick Reaction Force or QRF. He'd come to trust his militia platoon mates, but they weren't professional soldiers any more than he was. The platoon's Jema contingent was blood thirsty enough that he figured they'd tangle with the first group of Strema they saw. Having professionals around sounded pretty good to him right now. He just hoped there was more to this QRF than Jake and Carlos.

"Lupe," the Jema seated at his right on the tarmac, Nodri, nudged him and jerked a chin toward the gathered officers.

"You know," he pointed at the group, "the long shooter?"

He nodded. "He's dating my cousin, we've met." He'd had this conversation with Lt. Jadi a couple of days earlier.

Nodri listened to the audio translation that his compad provided.

"You are of the same clan?"

"Not really. Captain Kyle," he knew last names were a taboo subject among the Jema, they didn't use them, "grew up in my home town. Captain Carlos is his friend, that is how I met him."

"You look same," Nodri patted at his own face and hands.

"You mean my skin color?"

Nodri nodded.

"We're both Hispanic. Our people came from the same place, long ago. Now though, we are from the same country."

Nodri pointed at Enrique and Juan Edelman, the brothers were from Chile and sons of a doctor who'd brought his family to Eden. "But a different clan than them? You speak that other tongue with them."

He agreed with a nod, "Spanish." He knew he was out of his depth trying to explain the concept of countries, and ethnic groups to the Jema, let alone the fact that the Edelmans were Jewish and originated in Germany. "They speak the same language as Carlos and me, but they are from a different country, or were, when we were on earth. We don't have clans, like you do."

Nodri listened to the translation and smiled, and punched him on the arm. "Now, we are soldier clan."

"I guess so," he couldn't argue with that.

"Lupe! Come here a sec." Carlos was waving him over.

He jogged over and saluted like they'd been taught.

"Stop that shit," Jake shook his head. "You're in the field, last thing we need is for the Strema to figure out who our officers are."

"Right."

"Lupe," Jake nodded at Lt. Jadi, "Carlos and I are going to be coordinating two other platoons besides yours in the same general area. You're going to be our radio man slash translator for the Lieutenant here, she singled you out. You stay attached to her hip. Understood?"

"Ok," he said with a lot less enthusiasm than he felt.

"Keep your commlink in your ear, keep us updated, OK? Don't wait to be asked what you're up to. We can see your team's movement on our boards, but we don't know why you're moving, and we need to know, got it?"

"Yes, sir." He sure hoped Lt. Jadi had asked for him; he didn't want special treatment.

"That's it, then. You'll be fine."

He knew when he was being dismissed and turned to go, as Carlos slapped him on the shoulder and walked away with him a few steps.

"What gives?" the sniper asked him.

"Sir, you know the only reason she asked for me is that she thinks I'm somehow part of your clan. Because I know you from Chief Joseph, because of Zarena."

"Zarena? What does she have to do with this?"

"Lt. Jadi asked the other day how I knew you," he shrugged. "You know how hard it is to explain shit to them. I said that you were dating my cousin."

"Zarena's your cousin?"

He managed a smile. "Second cousin I think. You know how it is. We're all cousins, I didn't know what else to say. Easier than trying to explain how you knew Kyle and all that."

"Don't worry about it. Jadi asked for you, because she thinks you speak the best Chandrian among her militia people. That's it."

"Ok, I got this."

"I know you do," Carlos slapped him on the back. "Be safe, Primo."

Lupe couldn't help but laugh, as he walked back to his platoon. They were all cousins.

*

It had been going so well, Jake thought. He sat in the open door of the grounded Blackhawk, his feet dangling, enjoying the spring sunshine. Carlos was racked out in a nap across the row of web seats, and the rest of his QRF were sunning themselves on the far side of the helicopter, stretched out in a haphazard, plopped down pattern atop their packs. He didn't begrudge any of them their sleep. They all needed more than they'd been getting. Carlos would spell him in another hour or so, or would have, he thought. He concentrated on the moving icon representing one of the squads of 1st platoon, that was set up on a beautiful ambush location. An icon that shouldn't have been moving. He gave the blue force tracker one more 15 second update. It showed a squad of Lt. Jani's 1st platoon still in motion.

"Well, shit..."

"Problem?"

So, Carlos was awake, he could have sworn the guy had been snoring a few seconds ago.

"We got an ambush squad moving out in what looks like pursuit of the muj."

"Shit," Carlos echoed and sat up reaching for his own compad.

It had been going perfectly. The Strema security patrol, perhaps 250 enemy, had picked up the trail of the patrolling 2nd platoon. The patrol was leading the enemy directly past the ambush site set up by 1st and 3rd platoons. Their track of march had entered the kill box too far north of 1st platoon for it to act as the anvil, but 3rd platoon was perfectly positioned and waiting. Once the ambush was sprung, 1st platoon would have moved in force, and caught the Strema in a perfectly executed L shaped ambush. The 2nd platoon acting as bait would have been the hinge that anchored 1st and 3rd platoons coming in from two separate directions. At least that had been the plan.

But somehow, one of the squads of 1st platoon hadn't been able to maintain their position when the Strema marched past, and were now in pursuit. It put the whole plan at risk, not to mention, the eight soldiers of the wayward squad were in danger of being rolled up in an area where they had no direct support. He'd thought Lt. Jani had better control of her platoon.

"Get your boy on the line," Jake told Carlos. "I'll get us up."

"My boy?"

"Lupe. You're cousins, ain't ya?"

Jake hopped to the ground, and left Carlos mumbling behind his back. He went around the front of the helicopter, pounding on the lower glass port of the cockpit that he could reach. Might as well make sure the pilots were awake as well.

He took one look at his QRF, the fellow knuckle draggers, they'd all picked up on the conversation and movement on the helicopter. He wondered if it was still possible for any of them to actually sleep soundly. Consummate professionals, he appreciated the fact that they were all sitting up, tying off boot laces and in Hans' case, shrugging back in to his shirt. He tried to block his eyes looking at the massive Dutchman, who was several shades whiter than he thought a human could be.

"Hans, you part Yeti or something? You're glowing."

"Has been a long winter," Hans shrugged.

"What gives?" Domenik asked, as he stepped off a few paces to relieve himself.

"We got a wayward squad from 1st platoon, going on the offensive all by themselves."

"What does a squad hope to do?" Hans had a gift for stating the obvious.

"Die gloriously," Darius threw in, coming to his feet.

"Or just die," he countered.

Carlos stuck his head out the open door of the helo, "Jani is requesting to move in support of her idiot squad, they aren't responding."

Fuck...

Jake could see everyone looking at him, waiting for the answer they knew was the right one. You tied off a shot off limb with a tourniquet. You survived to go home, teach your kids to fish with one arm. Lt. Jani's platoon had good ground. A solid defensive position they were going to need desperately when the Strema patrol reversed course. Lose a squad, or a platoon? He put in a fresh dip and worried at it with his tongue before spitting. He looked back at Carlos and shook his head.

"Denied." He waved at the pilot and circled his hand over his head, and the Blackhawk's turbines begin to whine through their start up.

*

Lupe's panic fueled brain was doing strange things as another Strema grenade went off close enough in the dense forest that he felt the concussion. He was confused at what he was trying to do; hug the rock he was behind even tighter, or somehow crawl underneath it. He caught himself trying to do both at the same time as the rational part of his brain screamed at him to do one or the other. The rational part that Jake had told them they all needed to ignore. *'Follow your training.'*

Jake's training talk was a long way away right now. Lt. Jani's bullet-riddled body was a lot closer. She had been sheltering behind this same rock.

The Strema seemed to have given up on the massed rushes that had killed Jani. At least for the moment. They were content to dart forward in small groups, or skulk around in groups of two or three trying to reach their defensive line. Teark Banja, or 'Banjo' as they'd all called him, and his entire squad had gone off after the Strema like a chihuahua chasing a train. And then they'd caught it. The Strema patrol had reversed course over their corpses and started backtracking toward where the surviving three squads of their platoon waited. They'd watched them come in, moving slower than he expected. They'd been told to expect a frenzied charge.

Lt. Jani had waited until there were almost forty or fifty enemy in sight before she triggered a claymore, and the rest of them opened up at ranges that were far too close for comfort. An enemy massed salvo, from an unseen position farther back in the woods had slammed into the rock that provided cover for Lt. Jani, Nodri, Vance Littlefield, and him. Lt. Jani had strangely come to her feet when a round slammed into her shoulder. A second later, successive wet sounding slaps tore her body apart. Littlefield's body lay just behind hers, the top of his head missing. Then the Strema had charged. They'd stopped the initial assault, barely.

Nodri shook his head and said something that his translator didn't catch, and moved to fire around the far end of the large rock ledge whose top broke the dirt surface of the hill like a half buried stone cigar. Lupe wiped away the sweat from his eyes and realized it was blood from a cut on his forehead. The top edge of the rock was discolored where chips of stone continued to be chiseled out by Strema lead. He was lucky he hadn't lost an eye.

What the hell were they supposed to do now? Lt. Jani was dead. Second and Third Platoon had been moving up to support them, but there was a lot of gunfire coming from the distance to the south. Something had stopped them. He and his platoon were now on their own, without an officer. They were going to die here. He almost panicked again. But the massed fire of his platoon's assault rifles behind him snapped him out of it. Training kicked in, and he came up over the ledge of rock and added his own fire to help stop the current assault.

His rifle's action slammed back on an empty magazine and his hands felt like he was wearing mittens as he struggled to get a fresh one inserted. *'You're already dead.'* Theo's voice spoke to him clearly as he ran through half of the fresh magazine with series of aimed three round bursts, the last of which he saw stitch up the torso of a Strema in the process of throwing a grenade.

The whoomph! of the explosion wasn't so far away that it hid the screams of the other Strema it took with it.

"Good shoot!" Nodri yelled.

"Shot," he yelled back, "Good shot!"

Nodri moved to a different position behind the rock, popped up, fired again before dropping down to reload.

The Jema smiled at him. "Is good fight!"

Crazy bastards. "Nodri? Who's in charge now?"

"Jani say hold, we hold."

He almost nodded in agreement, but there was a lot more Chandrian fire coming from the south, on the far side of the next hill over, than there was being thrown at them. He was starting to think maybe the whole Chandrian patrol hadn't come at them. Maybe that was why they weren't charging anymore.

He tapped the command channel on his compad, knowing he was screwing up. Carlos had more important shit to do right now than give him some advice, but somebody had to know what they were supposed to do.

"Actual here, go 1st platoon."

"Uh, this is Lupe, we are still holding. Lt. Jani is dead."

"Who's in command?"

"That's why I'm ... I don't know, Sir."

"That means it's you, Primo. Hold one, we'll have a drone overhead in thirty seconds."

Lupe looked over at Nodri while he waited, the Jema was actually grinning in excitement. "We hold, yes?"

Jake took one look at the take from the drone they had over 1st Platoon's position, and nodded at Carlos. He drew a line right through the Strema that held them pinned down. They had to consolidate and quickly or they were going to lose all of them. It was on 1st platoon to move, 2nd and 3rd platoons were slowly moving back, under fire, further south back to 3rd platoon's original position. A location they might have a chance of defending against what was coming from the north.

Carlos shook his head. He liked Lupe. The dude was scared shitless, but so far, the former poacher was doing the right thing. He glanced at the large force of Strema reinforcements moving south fast, directly toward the remnants of Lupe's platoon, which according to the blue force tracker was down to twenty-two soldiers.

"Primo, Actual, I got bad news, and really bad news..."

Lupe listened as best he could over the sound of gunfire from Nodri's assault rifle. Twice he had to ask Carlos to repeat the orders, because he couldn't have heard right. He had.

He stowed his compad in his thigh pocket after switching to his platoon circuit. He grabbed up Lt. Jani's ammo and pointed at Littlefield's body. Nodri understood immediately and did the same.

"Platoon, we have new orders," he tried to remember to speak as plainly as he could, "We are being held here by these Strema. They do not attack because they have two patrols, maybe three, coming up fast behind us. We are to charge forward, through this enemy." *Don't use the words retreat, or withdraw,* Carlos had said. "We move to the sound of the gunfire on the other side of the hill. Straight through, up the hill, down the far side into the backs of the enemy attacking 2nd and 3rd platoon. *Pump em up, give em a reason to fight, glory to be had, all that shit,* Carlos had said.

"We will move out in one minute, we will rescue 2nd and 3rd platoon. Edelmans? You on?"

"I am here, Juan is ...dead."

That meant it was Enrique. He wondered how many of what was now his platoon were alive in the positions behind him. He thought of checking the blue force tracker, but realized he didn't want to know.

"Enrique, you grab the grenade launcher, we'll all move after you fire three rounds on my command. Do you understand?"

"I have only two left."

"Two then, two rounds and we go. Make sure everyone understands, we leapfrog, like we practiced, pair up, one fires, one moves. We leapfrog all the way to 3rd platoon. Nodri, do you understand?"

The man nodded at him and flashed a thumbs up as he could hear the machine translation repeating everything in Chandrian. He didn't trust the compad.

"Repeat it all in Chandrian," he ordered Nodri.

You're already dead, make it count, do it right.

He listened to the Chandrian over the platoon's circuit and didn't hear anything that he clearly knew was wrong with Nodri's translation. Then again, he picked up maybe three words in ten, and one of those was 'leapfrog.'

"Grab up the ammo from our fallen, we'll need it."

He waited another twenty seconds and was about to order Enrique to fire when a group of three or four Strema in front of them charged forward. They were quickly put down.

"Now Enrique!"

The first round from the grenade launcher hit a tree limb and deflected uselessly into the killing ground right in front of them. He'd been watching when Nodri pulled him down behind the rock. He felt the explosion through the ground and could hear the shrapnel spalling off of the far side of his rock. The second grenade sailed further into the trees and exploded. He didn't wait to see if it had been effective.

"Go, now!"

He was up and running for a fallen log twenty yards ahead when he heard a round zip past his head like a pissed off hornet. He realized Nodri was next to him matching him step for step. In his excitement, he'd forgot to designate who'd move and who'd provide cover fire between the two of them.

Stupid! Fix it, if you live to the tree.

Nodri collapsed next to him and looked at him embarrassed. "I run, you shoot," Nodri said.

"Right."

He looked back in time to see one and then a second of his people go down. The first he couldn't tell who it had been, the second was female which made her a Jema. He hoped it wasn't Mella...

You're already dead, asshole! Concentrate.

"Ok, go," he yelled at Nodri, and came up firing, trying to sight in on a muzzle flash in the wood's deep shadows below them. He waited until Nodri found cover and started firing again before popping up and running forward towards a shallow depression ten yards to the Jema's right.

He ate dirt as several rounds zipped by. He ignored the tug he felt on his pants leg. He moved to his back and lay there for a moment. He was less than twenty yards from where he knew there were a bunch of the enemy using a thick pile of deadfall as cover. He unclipped a grenade, and pulled the pin, holding the spoon in place like they'd been taught. He raised his head enough to see several of his platoon fall into cover roughly in line with him.

"Grenade assault," he ordered, "on my throw." He yelled the order as loud as he could. They'd practiced this, with real grenades. It was one of the few things they had a lot of.

Dead, you're already dead.

He waited another ten seconds, the more people that had time to prepare a grenade, the better. He glanced over at Nodri, the man had slung his rifle and was holding his fucking short sword. His friend was still grinning at him and trembling in anticipation. He felt himself grinning back.

What the hell was wrong with him?

"Now!" he screamed and spun to his side, whipping the heavy grenade out as far as he could.

There were too many explosions to count, but he was up and running towards the enemy position before he realized what he was doing. He saw nothing but a Strema directly in front of him coming up with his sword. He was there before he knew it, before the Strema warrior could react. The full auto salvo from his rifle caught the man's shirt on fire. That had to be his imagination, he thought, as he blew through him and fell on the next group, most wounded, bleeding and dazed from the grenades. There were too many of them, and those holding rifles were starting to realize he was among them. In slow motion, most of them were swinging his way.

Already dead...

There was tug on his scalp as one of the Strema guns went off, a split second later his world exploded in pain and noise as every gun in the world fired at once.

He came to his knees, shaking his head at the buzzing in his ears. He became aware of being surrounded, awareness coming with pieces clicking together slowly in his head. What were the bastards waiting for? He was finished, were they gloating? Then he realized it was Nodri in front of him looking at him in concern. His Jema friend held his short sword dripping Strema blood in one hand, an assault rifle in the other.

"Can you go?" Nodri asked.

He pulled himself to his feet using a branch of the deadfall and looked around. Strema dead, at least half a dozen lay around him. There was blood dripping in his eye, and he wiped it away, the pain making him instantly aware of the furrow of skin missing from his scalp. He looked around for his helmet, and another Jema handed it to him shaking his head and saying something with a smile. The Kevlar helmet was creased on the side, a flap of it still held together by the sewn fabric on the outside.

"Holy shit..." *I got shot in the head.*

"You alright?" Campos, the corporal from third squad asked, stepping forward to look at his head, "besides being one lucky son of a bitch?"

Lucky? "I'm OK, I think," he said looking around as the men around him started scrambling for cover. Nodri moved quick and pretty much tackled him, they landed on the bodies of the dead Strema.

"More come," Nodri whispered, as he angled his gun down the hill, his barrel resting across the top of a dead Strema's back.

"Second platoon here! Identify!" He could hear the shouts coming from below them.

"Friends," he whispered to Nodri, "hold fire, tell them, hold fire." The buzzing in his ears was back with a vengeance.

*

Jake smiled at the feed from the drone that had followed 1st platoon's assault. Some Jema had carried Lupe up the hill above 2nd and 3rd platoon's position. There, the little guy had managed to regain his feet. The first Strema patrol had been dealt with. The recombined company, its survivors at any rate were now filtering back to 3rd platoon's original prepared defensive position.

The relief Strema force had stopped for some reason in the location of where 1st platoon had started. It wasn't like them not to charge, and that worried him. Were they learning? Why had they stopped? They were coming in for a landing now, maybe the helicopter scared them off, but for the moment the Strema were a ridge line away, maybe two klicks, just watching. It was weird, not at all what he expected of them.

He glanced back down at the image of Lupe on the compad that Carlos was leaning over. "Looks like we might have our first battlefield commission."

"He did all right, didn't he?" Carlos acknowledged in rare praise.

"Tough little bastard."

"Might be my cousin, someday," Carlos shrugged.

Jake rolled his eyes and bit back his reply. "What the hell? The Strema reinforcements look to be falling back the way they came. That's a first."

He watched the Strema move back via the drone, many of them did not look happy and were being corralled by their Tearks. "They could put a hurt on us. Why pull back?"

"They already did," Carlos spit out the door of the helicopter as it touched down, "1st platoon had fifty percent KIA, 2nd's looking at ten dead, sixty percent casualties."

Jake shook his head, "I thought they were ready."

"Use it," Carlos looked at him. "We chew their ass, have Jomra or Audy rip a few heads off. They *were* ready, Jake. That idiot squad of Jema didn't go Leroy Jenkins, this would have worked."

Jake just looked down at the compad, confirming the Strema were still moving away. He knew Carlos was right, but it didn't help.

"No sense waiting for them to change their mind," he tapped at the side of his helmet, and looked over at Darius. "Get 1st and 2nd platoons moving to the exfil. Third platoon will hold here with us until everyone else is away."

*

Not very many things could stop a Strema war party, not once it had its Shareki prey in sight. The discovery of Jema warriors, fellow Chandrians, fallen in battle next to what could only be their Shareki allies was unthinkable. Pamish'd Hotta, the Bastelta in command of the three fingers of Strema warriors in pursuit of the Shareki, knew this had to be reported to Bres'Auch Tun without delay. He looked down at one of the bodies his men had stripped. There was no mistaking the Jema tattoo, or the Jema bouma blades. It was the Shareki uniforms they wore, the boots on their feet and the Shareki weapons they carried that stopped him. How in the name of the Kaerin was this possible?

That their own kind was allied with the Shareki had thrown his men into a wild rage. He'd had to dispatch two of them with his own blade before he could restore order. This discovery took precedence over pursuit of a Shareki war party. He would withdraw and make haste to the main encampment. One thing they'd all learned in the last moons, there would be other Shareki to hunt. They were like the clouds of flying blood suckers that seemed to follow them like a noisome cloud. They were everywhere and nowhere, constantly dashing in to bite and then disappearing.

Unless of course they retreated to a prepared position which they seemed to have done once again. His scouts reported that they had stopped their flight and turned to meet them. The enemy seemed to be daring them to attack. Denied within, and certainly remaining unspoken, he had no wish to assault another Shareki prepared position. Ever.

The finger that he commanded now, had been among those who moons ago, had arrived late to the first battlefield, along the frozen river. He had seen with his own eyes what the Shareki had done with their weapons from a prepared position. Yes, he would return to camp and report the betrayal of the Jema. The relief he felt in leaving this deadly ground would not be part of his report.

*

Chapter 19

New Seattle

"Who are these people, again?" Kyle was stopped outside the conference room door with Hank and Elisabeth. He'd caught a glimpse of Paul Stephens, Doc Jensen, and a couple of other program folks at the table, but there were a group of people sitting on the far side of the table that he didn't recognize.

"The New Colonist Leadership Council," Elisabeth answered, "led by Richard Kiley. He's convinced a good number of settlement chiefs to sign on to his petition for the meeting."

"I know that guy," Kyle remembered the politician 'wanna-be' from the bar, months ago, "he's a leech." Pretty had ordered him back to Seattle for this meeting. He didn't want to be here, and he had more important things to do than listen to somebody bitch. A million other things.

"Leech or not, he's got enough SCs and colonists to sign his petition of redress to convince Paul to sit down."

"Redress of what, exactly?" Hank shared a look of pain with a glance at Kyle, before turning to Elisabeth.

"They want more say into the decisions regarding the Jema policy and the war in general," Elisabeth shook her head. "The petition was very general, high level, but Paul thought it best to meet with them. They aren't that numerous, but they make a lot of noise."

"The Jema policy?" Kyle closed his eyes and shook his head. "Trust me, if the Jema ever found out there was such a thing as a policy regarding them, they'd laugh their asses off. Right before they gave us the finger and walked out on this fight. They don't plan on giving the Program, let alone the New ..."

"Colonist Leadership Council," Elisabeth finished for him.

"Whatever, they aren't going under the thumb of anyone, ever again. Can't say I blame them."

"This just gives them an air of legitimacy," Hank shook his head, jerking a thumb at the door.

"You know Paul," Elisabeth replied. "He's all about buy-in, and inclusiveness. Let them state their case, then you can shred it. Paul's already let a lot of air out of their balloon."

"I don't have time for this shit," Kyle almost bolted.

"Yes," Pretty laid a hand on his shoulder, "you do. These settlements are feeding the war effort. Trust me, according to Paul, a few of these SCs share your opinion of Kiley, but they still have concerns. Come on, welcome to my world."

Paul came to his feet at the head of the table the moment they walked in.

"Ladies, Gentlemen, allow me to present Colonel Hank Pretty and Captain Kyle Lassiter, the two people most responsible for our common defense."

Doc Jensen started it. He shot to his feet and started clapping. He was followed immediately by Jason Morales and a couple of the visiting Settlement Chiefs. It was pure theater, but he managed to absorb the mock enthusiasm without rolling his eyes. Kyle noted his memory of the name Richard Kiley was spot on. It was the same guy that had confronted Jason in the bar months ago. It looked like he'd gone from playing up to stressed out colonists, to cultivating a new constituency. For now, he was all smiles and clapping enthusiastically along with the rest of the room.

Kiley noted his glance of recognition and smiled back at him with a slight head bob, as if to say; "Yes, that was me."

The single exception to the round of applause was one of the SCs, a middle-aged guy, that looked like a lumberjack from a beer commercial. He'd managed to come to his feet, but held his hands together at his belt, red faced. The man either very much didn't want to be there or had a serious case of the ass against him or Hank, the program, or some combination of all the above. Whatever it was, it wasn't feigned. Anger radiated off him as he glowered at all of them.

Hank waved away the applause and begged everyone to sit down. Once they had, only he and Paul were still standing.

"I know I speak for Kyle as well, when I say, thank you, but the men and women we all owe, are those out there right now, under arms, taking the fight to the enemy, and to those we have lost, and to those we will lose before this is over."

"Well said, Hank," Paul nodded gravely, and motioned his friend to his seat.

"I'd be remiss if I didn't introduce Dr. Elisabeth Abraham. I assume most of you already know her. She approved your selection as a Settlement Chief. She has two PhDs, and a solid background in organizational psychology and history, to go along with the diplomas in Psychiatry and Anthropology. She walked away from a tenured position at Stanford to join us here, so it goes without saying her council is heavily relied upon."

"Next, we have Dr. David Jensen, our Chief Scientist and head of the technical aspects of the program, those few that haven't been turned over to the individual settlements. Jason Morales," Paul indicated Jason, who leaned forward and waved down to him.

Kyle returned the wave with a grin that screamed, I'm here against my will too.

"Jason is our Chief Economist, and I believe you've all, with exception of Mr. Kiley, worked extensively with him and his team."

Kyle appreciated what Paul was doing. Just simple introductions, and a few innocuous statements that were already drawing lines in the sand. Technology already turned over to the settlements. A subtle hint that the Program itself was winding down. Jason's team was already working with these people, all of them, except Kiley. Kyle figured that was the real issue here - Kiley's role.

"We have," the oldest of the SCs spoke up from down the table next to Paul. "His assistance has been most welcome, but it does play on some of the issues we'd like to discuss."

"Granted," Paul allowed, "thank you, Ernesto." Paul seated himself. "Perhaps we can work our way up your side of the table, with intros."

"Fine," the man smiled and waved at them all, "Ernesto Jimenez, I'm the SC in Rio Plata, but I'm here with the blessing and authority of my fellow SCs in Havana Nova, Caracas City, and New Lima."

"Susan Park," the middle-aged Korean woman raised her hand, "SC in New St. Louis, representing my colleague in Orleans as well."

Kyle had traded a hundred e-mails with her but they'd yet to meet. Their largest base and center of operations was outside New St. Louis, much of their logistical support flowed through her organization. She'd been nothing but the consummate professional and helpful at every turn, he couldn't imagine what complaint she had.

"Peter Tashvili," a young man, same middle thirties as himself waved his hand, "SC in Houston."

"Martin Kostens," the angry lumberjack spit out, "Astoria."

Shit. He recognized the name Kostens from one of the many letters he'd had to write.

There was a slight delay of stunned silence at his anger, but Kiley sitting next to Kostens, recovered quickly and laid a comforting hand on the man's forearm with a practiced nod of solidarity.

"I'm Richard Kiley, and I'd like to personally thank you all for agreeing to this sit down. While I'm not an SC, and I hold no official post with the Program or any settlement, I've been asked by many of our citizens and the SCs present, and those represented by proxy to present our petition. We've, as you've seen, collected over a hundred thousand signatures from all across our population."

Kyle imagined he was keeping a straight face, bordering on dismissive disgust, as he sat looking at Kiley. The very picture of a passive, impartial statue. He did not feel he was doing anything to deserve the soft kick to the shin delivered by Elisabeth under the table. He did his best to relax and get over the desire to reach across the table and throat punch the leech.

"Andrea Gordon, Central Valley California," a young, stout woman waived her hand, "or Farmville, as our people are starting to refer to our settlement. It seems agriculture is all we're deemed useful for."

"Andrea," Kiley tried to reassert control, "we'll discuss it."

"We will indeed," Paul took charge. "Thank you for that. Now that we all know who we have across from us... a statement of scope from me. I've gone through your brief in fine detail, as has Dr. Abraham and where relevant, Dr. Morales has been brought in. In many cases we are already working the problems. Let's begin with what I believe is the most pressing issue, and that brings us back to you, Ernesto, and the SCs you are representing."

"A point of order, if I may?" Kiley interrupted. "Are we to accept that you have decided which of our grievances we'll discuss? We were all under the distinct impression that our entire list of issues would be discussed."

"That's a fair point, Mr. Kiley," Paul pointed at the paper in front of him, and let his finger drop until it rested on the list.

"You just provided the answer to your own question. We have a long established, approved and functioning process to air and adjudicate grievances. They exist in every settlement, and they exist here at the program level believe me. Open, transparent and entirely citizen run, with zero input from any Program official. Each and every one of your grievances will be handled by that process. That said, your petition raised several *issues* of broader import, some ancillary to the aforementioned grievances, but significant enough in scope that they made my list of discussion points. So here we are...." Paul looked at each of the SCs and again at Kiley, and finally back to Ernesto.

"Mr. Jimenez, you're up."

Ernesto opened his hands in front of him, atop the notes he'd brought, "As you all know, many of our colonists of Hispanic background have chosen to settle in what was Latin America on Earth. Whether out of familiarity, or I suspect as was the case with myself, a desire to do it right this time. No latifundista social class, without the corruption, the racism, what have you. I'd like to think it is working. It's early days, but we are on solid ground.

"I'm not here to complain that the vast majority of new industry related to the war effort has been, to date, stood up in North America. I'm a former businessman, I understand the necessities of logistics. Proximity is important, it may even save lives. I am not here to complain that this trend, if it continues unabated, runs the real risk of recreating some of the disparity in economic development between North and South America that so characterized our old world.

"What I have been authorized to impart is our concern. We place no motive behind the trend, but nonetheless it is happening." Jimenez paused and pushed his briefing paper away. "This occurs, as our region supplies numbers of militia volunteers far in excess of many communities in the north. I'm the last person in the world to accuse anyone of any racial bias, my own children and one grandchild are serving. They do so as volunteers, with a genuine wish to play their part. We, myself and those SCs I represent, ask only that this trend not be allowed to continue. Something needs to be done before we recreate a pattern we all left behind."

"If I may add," Kiley spoke up again. "I agree, it's not intentional, but I don't think we should be so quick to dismiss the potential racial aspects at play."

Kyle *felt* a physical switch inside him flip as his blood pressure seemed to double in an instant. Hank must have seen it on his face, maybe he was vibrating in his seat. But he laid a heavy hand across his forearm. Kyle shrugged it off.

"I'm sure you don't," Kyle agreed with a genuine smile. "After all, if this were truly just an issue of economic fallout from real world issues of transport and logistics that we can try to address, there's no political angle for you to play is there?"

"That kind of insinuation is not helpful, I for one..."

"Mr. Jimenez?" Kyle cut in loudly leaning across the table towards Kiley, his eyes locked on the man. "Are you, as the representative of these affected communities claiming any sort of racial motive or malice?"

"No, of course not," Jimenez countered. "As I said, we know why it's happening, we seek to ameliorate the affect."

"And you Mr. Kiley? Are you in any way associated with any of these affected communities?"

"That's hardly the issue here, it's a..."

"So, the answer to that is NO, I take it."

He looked back to the end of the table and nodded at Mr. Jimenez politely. "I can't begin to say enough good things about our militia volunteers, especially the Latino contingent who as you have correctly noted, have volunteered in such large numbers. Please take our thanks back to your communities."

"And a promise," Jason spoke up. "We are already working to get some of the higher tech production moved south." Jason leaned forward and looked back down the table towards he and Hank. "We've got production schedules for your new heavy aircar in place, if we move it south, it'll add a two-day transit with teamed pilots flying non-stop, if you can live with that."

Hank nodded with a look of chagrin. "We've been waiting months; a couple of days won't be an issue. In fact, the AGM, the modified maverick missile that it'll carry, is useless to us without the platform. You can move that production and assembly south as well."

"I thought so, too," Jason nodded towards Jimenez. "It's already on the list, as well as a few other items. This is my fault entirely. We went with logistical expediency in most cases, little thought was given to areas not getting production lines. It won't happen again."

"Next item," Paul cut in with a huge grin.

"Not so quick," Andrea Gordon of California's Central valley added. "Different area, same problem. I realize we were set up as a breadbasket site. Hell, farming is all my family has done for four generations, but I've got a lot of people interested in doing something other than farming. We need some diversification, plain and simple, beyond another plant turning out MREs."

"Noted," Jason answered, "The list I referred to has the all the breadbasket communities in mind, as well those communities in Texas and Oklahoma that focus on hydrocarbon extraction."

"I don't expect you, Andrea," Paul turned back to Ernesto, "or you, to take any of this as an empty promise. We'll meet again, and monthly on this issue, it's a wide spread problem, but we are already working it. You think you have issues, you should read my e-mails from the settlements in Europe. They are almost wishing the fighting was in in their backyard. I'm sure that's in jest, but it's been said more than once."

"Fair enough." Ernesto said.

"Can we get to the primary issue?" Kiley looked like a man surprised and more than a little frustrated that the meeting wasn't going his way.

Kyle had his issues with Paul, but the way he'd limited the scope of the meeting from the outset was sheer brilliance.

"You're referring to the issue of the Jema?" Paul asked.

"I see you recognize it as the primary issue as well?"

"Actually," Paul clearly tried, but failed to hide his grin. "I was just going by the four asterisks you had typed next to the underlined, bold font on your list. I'm reading now; "The issue of the integration of the Jema, Why, in a military sense? and how? socially, post conflict."

Paul placed the paper back on the table. "That would entail quite a lot, and I'll set us all straight right now. Military matters," Stephens paused and looked at all of them, "tactical or strategic, are not the purview of this group, or that of the Program. The Program's singular role in that regard is limited to organizing the supplies and support that Colonel Pretty and Captain Lassiter have requested."

"Even when those decisions are getting good people unnecessarily killed?"

Kyle had to hand it to Kiley, the asshole could pull off sad and smug at the same time.

"I'm not about to allow Monday morning quarterbacking of military decisions," Hank sounded polite, but there was a warning tone. Kyle could tell Pretty's switch was about to be flipped as well.

"My son is dead," the lumberjack next to Kiley said softly. "Three weeks now. Dead because we insisted on integrating the Jema with our militia. Dead, because some Jema went off on a rampage, that got a lot of people killed."

"Your son was in the 1st Combined Regiment, A Company?" Kyle asked.

The man just nodded in response. "He was asked to volunteer, some sort of combined elite unit. A lot of good it did him. We've heard the stories, these Jema have a blood feud, a thousand years old, and it got my son killed."

"It did," Pretty admitted. "You're right, and there is nothing that will change that. The surviving Jema of that same unit, offered themselves up for sanction. They weren't even the ones at fault. In their culture, sanction is a slow painful death, saved for the worst of transgressions. We talked them out of it, thankfully. That unit, the poor judgement shown by individual Jema, all killed in the same action, is now an example that the Jema leadership uses to instill and enforce our tactics. The lives that will be saved in the future, not to mention the capability in battle that have been gained, are too numerous to count."

Kyle glanced between the lumberjack, probably a fisherman, from Astoria and compared him to Kiley seated next to him. One had given everything, the other absolutely nothing.

"None of which will bring back your son," Pretty added. "I can't sit here, and pretend to know what you are feeling. My children aren't of an age to be fighting. But I can say, that I've buried a dozen close friends over the years. One of them closer to me than my own brother. It doesn't get easier, but you do come to understand they died for the man next to them. I'm very familiar with your son's case. He died for the Jema in his squad, because he and three other militia members wouldn't be left behind when their Jema brothers in arms acted without orders.

"I'd only ask that you take into consideration and remember what your son did for his brothers in arms, militia, and Jema alike."

Kyle felt himself nodding. "If we have a hope for what the future will bring with our Jema allies, it starts and ends with us fighting together."

"You honestly believe that?" Kiley almost snarled at him.

Kyle had never wanted to cave someone's throat in so badly in his life. He bit down on his anger, reminded himself that Elisabeth was sitting next to him.

"I do, so do the militia members fighting alongside them," he answered softly, struggling to control his breathing. "And before you continue to insult the Jema, I'll advise you to be very careful. I'm a part of their clan, took the oath so to speak, and when I give my word I keep it.

I'll not allow you to use the death of this man's son, or those who will fall in the future to score political points. This enemy will not stop until they are killed. The Jema are prepared to die, as a clan... all of them, to stop our common enemy. Do you have any concept of that kind of sacrifice? Right now, they are willing to die, are dying, for you Mr. Kiley. For all of us. The least we can do is respect those that step up and do their part."

"There is no disrespect intended," Kiley seemed to have checked his own emotions. "But if you think I'm the only one who thinks these Jema can't be integrated, you're sorely mistaken. I'll say it now, and I'll keep on saying it, they'll be the death of us."

"Stop." The lumberjack waved a hand in front of him. "Just stop."

Kyle gave the grieving father a firm nod, and stood up, purposely ignoring Kiley. It was time for him to go before he did something stupid, something he'd very much enjoy but regret later.

Elisabeth was glad Kyle had left. She knew there was a limit to his patience once frustration started to build. To her, Richard Kiley wasn't just frustrating, he was dangerous. She'd been correct in assuming that Kiley was someone looking to exploit the social and security unease amongst the colonist population to his own benefit. But his use of a public petition circulated through the same population was worrisome.

She watched him closely as the meeting continued. The SCs had additional issues, and they were addressed each in turn as they went around the table.

At each issue, Kiley took notes. It only took her a moment to figure out why. She mentally shook her head. They were giving him the ammunition he needed. Kiley wasn't here to air grievances, he was here collecting evidence of how the Program made decisions, wielded authority. She could almost write his next petition for him –

'They say the Program is dead, that all authority has been pushed down to the settlements, and that it no longer plays a role outside that necessary to coordinate our common defense. And yet, when we take our petition of grievances to them, who meets with us? Who tells us what can and will be done? Who makes the decisions that will in the long run affect each and every one of you? Who has already decided that we will integrate the Jema among us, on their terms? The Program, the same Program that would have you believe they don't play a role in your lives. We need a say in our own future! None of us signed up to live under an oligarchy or under the thumbs of the founder class. Speak up now, before it's too late, blah blah blah...

There would be enough who would at least listen to what he was saying, and that made him dangerous. He was playing the long game, and she doubted if Paul realized what was happening. She was right about Kiley, but very much mistaken regarding her half-brother. She shouldn't have been surprised.

The issues ran their course, the SCs were for the most part mollified or at least content to take a wait and see approach.

"Mr. Kiley," Paul held up a hand. "Your attention and concern regarding these issues is laudable, and I do appreciate you helping to bring them to our attention. I think we could use you here at the Program. Perhaps we need an Ombudsman, whatever title you think is appropriate. Would you be interested in ensuring that the people who have felt free to bring their issues to you, are heard? For my part, I believe it would be a good idea."

Elisabeth enjoyed the look of surprise that crossed Kiley's face, but he was too savvy to be ensnared and recovered just as quickly.

"I appreciate the offer, I do." Kiley smiled, "I think my role, such as it is, would best be served remaining independent of the Program."

I'll just bet you do, Elisabeth thought... *For now.*

*

Chapter 20

"Our Teark, she give her order for the company to march out, to her most senior sergeant." Kyle listened to Jomra, whose English seemed to improve every time Kyle saw him. It wasn't fair. "Again, the militia sergeant asks her a question. He not refuse order, I do not wish to say the man was ...sekarmani?"

"Insubordinate," Jake offered up the word.

To hell with fairness, Kyle thought, this was just wrong. Even Jake had better Chandrian than he did at this point. It was like there was a huge hole in his brain that didn't allow for the Chandrian language. The Jema were all picking up English. They spent what little free time they had conversing in it with their militia counterparts or watching the endless library of video entertainment the compads offered. He used to worry about putting that particular cultural foot forward, but the videos, everything from new production music videos coming out of New Seattle, to old video files from Earth that they'd brought with them; it was all available on the compads. Everything from old war movies, documentaries and sitcoms, for better or worse, it was all there.

He didn't understand their taste in entertainment. Coming to grips with the fact that recordings of the 'Golden Girls' were among the most popular shows among the decidedly warlike clan proved difficult for him. Elisabeth said it had something to do with the fact that the Jema didn't have elders of their own. Whatever the reason, he just couldn't get around the fact the Betty White was probably the most recognizable Terran face among the Jema.

"Yes," Jomra pointed at Jake, "that is the word, your militia sergeant was not.... direct with his insub..ord-ination, he was crafty."

"Had to have been a sergeant with some old world, big army experience," Kyle added. "A lot of them, were as you say, crafty."

"Yes, he was very polite. Yet he did not the carry the order to march to the soldiers," Jomra continued. "Our Teark, by this time is puffing up. Her face is red, she is becoming angry. I watch this all from a distance. She repeats her movement order to the sergeant, for a third time."

"Three times?" Sri-Tel was incredulous, his scarred face looking somehow more dignified inside the glow cast from the fire they all sat around at the end of a long day. It was far too hot for a fire, but the smoke kept the mosquitos and no-see-ums down to nuisance level. "This sergeant lives?"

"He lives. He is a large man," Jomra added. "Sergeant Riley, very strong, his men fear him I think, but he is ...."

"A stubborn asshole," Carlos nodded. "I've had the pleasure of dealing with him. He's more than competent, just thinks no one's qualified to give him orders."

"Yes, stubborn," Jomra nodded in agreement. "A good word, some would say this about the Jema? Yes?"

"We're more prideful, when we are stubborn," Audy explained. "This sounds like he is stubborn, because he is ... an asshole."

"Yep, that's him," Carlos agreed smiling, to laughs all around.

"So how does this asshole still breathe?" Sri-Tel asked.

"I don't know what happened," Jomra shrugged. "I see our Teark, the top of her head to here on the Sergeant," Jomra held a bladed hand at the middle of his chest. "She leaned in close to him, spoke something to his ear. The Sergeant turned white. I swear it. Next, he is screaming at the platoon Tearks, like he is on fire, and the company begins to march."

"Problem solved," Audy shrugged. "She probably just threatened to castrate him with her bouma and whispered it to save him embarrassment."

"The story is not done," Jomra was smiling. "I do not see this company for five days, and then, it was back at the base, they were on rest. I see our same Teark walking, holding hands with your Sergeant Riley. At first, I am very confused. They were ... together. The Sergeant, he is moving quite slowly, has trouble walking, and as they get closer, I see his face. His eyes black, going to blue. You say, beaten like a drum, yes? The Sergeant, struggling to walk, is wearing a huge prideful smile, hand in hand with his Jema officer."

They all laughed, Sri-Tel slapping at his knees said something in Chandrian.

"It seems Jema discipline can take many forms," Audy translated for him.

The laughter was needed as much as the downtime around a fire. The ops tempo had picked up appreciably in the last month. The combined units, mostly under command of Jema Bastelta or senior Tearks, and the Jema proper, operating independently under militia officers, were hitting around the edges of the Strema host daily. The air mobility gave them tactical opportunities that the Jema couldn't have imagined, let alone planned a few months ago.

He and Colonel Pretty were pleased. The Jema had an esprit de corps that was bleeding over and mutating inside the mixed units. They were still losing people, it was impossible not to when the enemy was willing to sacrifice huge numbers of their own warriors to get within knife range. But morale was high, and the constant attacks, in addition to the airstrikes, were starting to whittle the enemy down.

The majority of the militia was directly under Colonel Pretty now, in a separate theater to the northwest. The Colonel and the militia were doing the same thing to the much smaller Koryna force in the northern plains, near what had formerly been the border between North Dakota and Montana. There, the Koryna didn't have the cover of the deciduous forests the Strema moved within, but they were beelining it south by southeast, moving as fast as they could, to try and link up with the Strema. For their part, the Strema were undeterred in their march south along the Mississippi River. They'd been whittled down to roughly sixty thousand warriors, or twelve hands as the Jema counted them.

The laughter petered out until Jomra grunted to himself with a pointed glance towards Audy.

"Just say it, before you explode trying not to." Audy shook his head.

"Sergeant Riley looked worse than you, after my sister got done with you."

The laughter exploded again. Audy chagrined, accepted the comparison with equanimity. "May the Sergeant be as cured as I was."

When the laughter died down, Kyle turned towards the Jema elder. The only one.

"Sri-Tel, can you tell us about the Chandrian gate to the south? We've talked to your Gemendi cadre, they just know it's there, somewhere. They said you might know something of it from the old stories or myths."

The old man's face turned to the fire as he spoke. Audy was listening as raptly as he was and after a moment began translating. "Only foggy memories of tales told to me when I was young. Stories of strange peoples, machines from another world coming to Chandra through great storms. Perhaps they came from your world. I know the gate lies on the water, or near it. Somewhere in the Gray Bite to the south, or along its shore."

"The Gulf," Audy added. "Maps are kept very secret by the Kaerin, but most clans have kept hidden, old maps of where they came from. About six hundred years ago, the Kaerin moved us all, great migrations. We know now, after looking at your maps, the Kaerin moved us to Iberia, a place you call Portugal. Originally, we came from Karelia, what you call the Baltics. The Gray Bite, Sri-Tel refers to, is of course your Gulf of Mexico."

He'd always wondered where the Jema came from, in an ethnic sense, but he sat that aside.

"Sri-Tel, is the gate the Strema seek always open?"

Sri-Tel shook his head after Audy translated. "I cannot say. The gates seem to follow a schedule, with the seasons. I know the Kaerin plan around this, but it is just one more thing they do not share."

"Well," Jake said, "it explains why they seem locked on to N'Orleans, they're headed for the swamp gas."

"What?" Kyle rubbed his eyes, it had to have been the smoke.

303

"Going way back," Jake shifted his feet, stretching out his long legs, settling in to tell a story. Kyle had already decided to cut Jake off, the second he mentioned hunting dogs, his inbred uncles, or his illiterate cousin-brothers living in the bayou.

"Way, way back, to the Choctaw, and Chitimacha tribes, there's always been stories of people and ships just being swallowed up by the fog, off coast in the gulf or from the bayou itself. A French Galleon disappeared in the early 18th century, a whole flight of P-40s just before WWII, and a whole host of rednecks and Cajun navy have turned up missing over the centuries. Used to call it the swamp gas monster when we were kids."

Jake stopped and realized everyone was looking at him.

"I'm just saying..."

"This swamp gas?" Audy asked. "Is it year-round?"

"Nah, mainly in the spring and fall."

"That's just nuts," Kyle started.

"I'm serious," Jake said a little defensively. "I'm not saying it's the gate we're talking about. I'm not saying I think it's anything other than the bayou swallowing things, cause, well because it's a freaking swamp. I'm just saying, a lot of people and shit has gone missing over the centuries and the stories go way back. Hell, even Doc Jensen thinks the Bermuda Triangle is somehow related to the natural gates that link the universes or realities, whatever we are calling them today."

Kyle just looked at his friend. He was almost certain Jake was being serious, he hadn't tried shocking them with bullshit stories of toothless, shoeless relatives once. "Well, that's one theory," he allowed.

"I do not know what I think," Audy allowed. "There is a gate there. More importantly the Strema know there is a gate."

"They are trying to return," Jomra added, "to report. That is the only part of their writ left to them. Conquering you, preparing this planet for the Kaerin to populate is not going to happen. At least not with the forces they brought with them. This time."

This time. That was the nut of the issue, they couldn't let the Strema escape, or Kyle knew the next time would come far too soon.

"They will still try to destroy us, the Jema," Jomra continued. "If they make a return, with word of how few you... and we are, with word that the Jema fight at your side, the Kaerin will bring all their strength to bear before we attack them."

"We have no intention of attacking them," Kyle added.

"That may be, but they would not even consider that you have any other thought." Jomra shook his head as he spoke.

"This is truth." Sri-Tel said in English. "Power is all to them, they judge only power, in themselves, in others." Sri Tel went on in Chandrian.

"You are either under their leash, or you are a threat to be destroyed," Audy translated the balance of the old man's statement.

Kyle knew Doc Jensen was working on something that might play into this, something related to having identified the gravimetric harmonics between Eden and Chandra. It might be able to provide them with some defense against further incursions or allow them to take the fight to Chandra. A large part of him wanted the physicist to fail, at least in the latter. He was tired of fighting.

Sri-Tel broke in and went on in Chandrian for a moment before Audy began his translation.

"You have to understand that Chandra had no knowledge of the gates before the Kaerin arrived, the gates brought them and they have kept the knowledge to themselves, as they have kept their tools from us."

Kyle felt as if he'd just been slapped. "Wait, you mean the Kaerin don't come from Chandra?"

"I thought you knew this." Jomra said. "They came in numbers the size of a small clan, long ago, with fantastic weapons that even they no longer have. They conquered us, all of us. It has taken centuries, but Chandra is theirs and has been for a long time."

"No, we didn't know." Kyle shook his head, the ramifications of that didn't play at all in their current fight, but it could weigh heavily down the road. Had the Kaerin been marooned on Chandra? Or was it an invasion from another world that for some reason hadn't been followed up?

"Hell, maybe the Kaerin are just trying to get home." Jake's thinking clearly was following along the same lines.

"Does it matter?" Jomra asked. "They are there, they want to come here."

"Point," Carlos agreed.

"Let's table the Kaerin for the moment," he said, swatting at a mosquito that had landed on his arm. "The issue at hand is the Strema. Colonel Pretty is going to stop the Koryna soon, but we'll be splitting off a large part of the militia to do that, as well as some of our air support."

They were going to miss that, he knew. But they'd been receiving more mortars, heavy weapons, artillery and finally the long promised heavy air cars. More importantly, the troops, militia and Jema alike were gelling and gaining experience with the new equipment.

"I think we're almost strong enough to stand toe to toe with the Strema."

"Yes!" Jomra's fist slammed into his leg out of enthusiasm. That was going to leave a mark, he thought.

He held up a hand, trying, in what he knew was a wasted effort to stem Jomra's enthusiasm.

"*IF* ..," he glanced at Audy and Sri-Tel, and back to Jomra.

"*IF* we can find the ground we want, if we can lure them there, and if we can dictate the fight on our terms. We fight Kaerin style, we'll lose. Or just as bad, we'll win a battle that destroys the Jema in the process. Neither of which, we are going to allow to happen. We are going to win, and after," he looked around at the other faces around the fire, "the Jema can be free, decide where they want to live and how, and I can go fishing."

"Amen to that," Jake drawled.

"We must win first," Audy added. "I too, am anxious to live ...a different life."

"You will be free Audrin'ochal," Sri-Tel grinned. "You will need to learn to defend yourself from your wife."

They all laughed at that, none more so than Jomra. "That is easier said than done with my sister."

"She's already decided that we will live in the north," Audy said, almost apologizing. "She has seen pictures of settlements in Vermont and Montana. She wants to live in the snow."

Carlos just shook his head. "She'll get it there. I spent a very cold month at Ft. Drum once, teaching army guys how to shoot. It's well south of Vermont. I don't think I ever got warm."

"I do not like the cold," Sri-Tel shook his head. "With hope, your people's reservation for us will be somewhere warm."

Kyle laughed along with the rest of them, and then stopped himself as what Sri-Tel had said registered. *What the hell?* He glanced at Jake for a second who was looking at him, eyebrows popped halfway up his forehead in question. He'd heard it too.

"Sri-Tel, where did you hear ... about a reservation?"

"From your people, the ones who work in the camps. This is a problem?"

Kyle didn't know what to say. If the confused stares from Jomra and Audy weren't bad enough, Sri-Tel the Jema elder seemed to be looking at him in accusation with those scarred pits that had once been his eyes. Carlos was looking at him in what may have been sympathy at the old man's question. Jake for once, was silent. Kyle watched him take out his knife and begin picking at his nails.

"From your face, I'm thinking this reservation place is not what I had thought in my mind's eye," Audy followed up.

"Audy," he leaned forward until he came out of his camp chair and knelt in front of the small fire and added a few sticks. They were going to be a while.

"Before, I answer, I need to know more about who has been telling Sri-Tel this, and what exactly they've been saying. I wouldn't ask, if it wasn't important. Because the Jema will be able to live anywhere they want, they won't be limited to a reservation."

"Is not a good thing?" Sri-Tel asked, but it was more of a resigned acceptance.

Kyle closed his eyes a moment, feeling his jaw clench. "No, it's not a good thing. I think some people who do not have authority to make these decisions have been trying to sell you on the idea. In the hope that when they propose it amongst my people, you'll have already said yes."

"We will begin to say no, now." Jomra declared. "I'll make certain all of our people who speak with these officials do the same."

"What is a reservation?" Audy asked. "I thought it to be a place set aside for our own use, that would be ours."

"Oh, it is," Jake shot back. "The same could be said about a prison."

"Jake?" Kyle turned his head, "you're always talking shit about how your Dad's family is part Cherokee, that true?"

"It's true, no shit."

"Tell them."

"Audy, you like to read," Jake said. "Read up on the term Trail of Tears for some details, but I can give you a you a condensed version right now."

Kyle stood as Jake begin to tell a story, as only he could. "I need to call Elisabeth, and find out who's behind this, but I think I already know."

*

"Hammer them, fire all tubes." Jeff kept his voice calm, denying his own excitement. The role of Forward Area Observer was not something he'd done in a long time, and not ever from the position of being in command of a regiment's worth of troops. Troops that came from two different worlds and were fighting for the right to call a third, *home*.

Then again, most of what he'd done in the last two years was outside the norm of what former SEALS found themselves doing. But it was worth it. His parents, his sister, brother-in-law and three nephews were here on Eden looking at a fresh start. They had all been evacuated to New Baltimore within a couple of days of the initial Chandrian invasion, and had already decided to make it their permanent home. He approved. Their original settlement along the Great Lakes had never really been threatened, but he was done with Michigan winters. Growing up in Detroit had cured him of that.

He watched the fountains of mortar and artillery fire explode through the thick forest along the Mississippi River, or Mud River as the Jema had accurately named it. In the last several weeks the Strema had learned the hard way that they had two options when they met a large contingent of combined militia-Jema forces. They could charge and try to overwhelm it with sheer weight of numbers.

Something they hadn't been able to do yet because the whole offensive game plan against the Strema was focused on attacking the edges, going after patrols or foraging parties of a size the joint force could handle. If a prospective Strema target was large enough to make standing off a full counterattack problematic, they simply avoided it and waited for a target they could handle.

Their tactics didn't stop the Strema from attempting to just roll over whatever force attacked them, but their massed charges died abruptly and repeatedly in the face of automatic rifles and crew served machine gun emplacements. Just as this latest one had fifteen minutes ago. They'd ambushed a Strema 'finger' patrol, roughly a thousand warriors. A third, maybe more of the Strema, had been taken out quickly in the initial attack or in the stopping of the initial counterattack.

But the enemy was adapting. Of late, the Strema, when lacking the numbers they needed for a successful local charge, would usually withdraw a short distance away to await reinforcements before launching an attack that the Strema thought would overwhelm them. Until recently, the combined Eden forces had been using that time to move or withdraw, to plan for the next attack or ambush the next day. The key tactic to fighting the Strema was not to wait around to be outnumbered. If he were a Strema, he'd be pissed off. He'd have an enemy that continually denied him a battle he could win, while chewing off smaller pieces of his host on a daily basis.

Now though, he felt himself smiling as the artillery rounds fired from six miles away fell upon the Strema awaiting their reinforcements. They now had the airlift capacity to sling in enough 105 mm field artillery pieces to emplace semi-mobile artillery in support of their ambushes. It was WWII era artillery, but it was simple to make, relatively light weight, reliable and oh so effective against unarmored infantry.

At the moment, from the Strema perspective, the four-tube battery was raining death on them from a position they weren't even aware of, let alone could see or counter while they awaited reinforcements. The Strema commander, if he still lived, had a simple choice. He could watch his men die from an enemy he couldn't even see, or he could attack the enemy he could, now, with what he had. He knew enough of how the Strema worked from their Jema allies, to know that to retreat or withdraw was just another way to commit suicide for a Strema officer. In the end, the Strema Bastelta, or whoever was giving orders in the woods down below him, gave up on waiting for reinforcements.

He pulled the binoculars away and shook his head in disgust. The Strema, somewhere between four and five hundred remaining from the original ambush and the subsequent shelling, came out from under whatever insufficient cover they'd found and started up the long but shallow incline, into the teeth of their prepared position.

"Stupid bastards," he whispered to himself, having nothing but disgust for whatever system produced such mindless servitude. Maybe it was their culture, maybe it was fear of what would happen to them if they didn't. He couldn't have cared less. He didn't have any sympathy, these ass clowns wanted New Baltimore too. He pressed his throat mic. "Here they come, hold fire until they hit the second marker, give em some hope and then take it all."

He'd been fighting true believers of one sort or another for almost fifteen years straight. He no longer held any illusions regarding what it took to win. Destroying their so-called 'ability to wage war' that they'd been taught at the Naval Academy wasn't enough. It wasn't even the right battlefield.

You couldn't destroy their 'will to fight' either, not when their entire existence was tied up in whatever they believed, whether it was religion, communism, or loyalty to some tribal code as was the case with the Strema. No, the Jeff Krouse method of war was the shortest line between two points. You just destroyed them.

The charging Strema went down in massive numbers as his dug in troops, backed by half a dozen M-60s, and two mortar squads opened up. He followed the man he suspected was the Strema Bastelta, through his binoculars until he disappeared in a dirt and flesh fountain of an exploding mortar round. He knew the Strema by now, they'd follow the last order that had been given. Hell, his Jema were wired the same way, but they were quickly learning to think on their feet as well.

Victory and the survival of his troops assured he watched and listened with a practiced ear to the fire his units were pouring down the hill. He nodded in approval. They weren't any over the top one-man charges by any of his Jema. The first time he had seen that happen, even though Kyle and Jake had warned him, it had come as a shock. After the battle, he had made every one of his Jema walk out to where their fellow warrior had needlessly died.

"This man will never kill another Strema," he'd screamed pointing at the body. "He'll never again stand shoulder to shoulder with his brothers and sisters in arms. He is dead and the Strema still live. This," he had screamed, "is a waste."

His Jema translator had translated the words accurately, and the message had seemed to get through. His words had carried some weight, and finally, the whole concept of live to fight another day was filtering down into their thick, proud Jema skulls. He had gained a reputation among the Jema as the 'black soul.' It was a moniker used with reverence and had nothing to do with the color of his skin. He was known among the Jema as the one who hated the Strema as much as they did. He'd never admit it to them, or let it show, but he didn't hate the Strema. He just wanted them gone. If that meant killing them, he'd kill them.

The fire was beginning to wind down. He was already thinking of the after-action report he'd send to Kyle. The second mixed regiment, in his opinion, was ready. They'd stand their ground. Their tactics were about to change. The Strema would need to be careful what they wished for. They were very soon going to get the battle they sought.

*

Chapter 21

The background din of the gathered Jema and militia officer and NCO cadre was a welcome difference from the first gathering of this same group five months earlier. Back then, at the original Jema encampment, this combined group had numbered a little over a hundred, almost all of them Jema. The discussion, such as it had been, consisted of Audy translating for Colonel Pretty and Kyle describing the overall strategic situation and their intentions. For the Jema, that first gathering had been little more than an opportunity to get to know their new allies. What little trust there had been, was solely due to Audy. The Jema had taken what Audy had told them at face value, but there had been a healthy 'wait and see' element to the gathering as well. The new assault rifles they'd been issued at the end of the meeting had helped a lot.

Since then, they'd made huge strides in integrating the two disparate forces. This group was now over two hundred men and women, who had been working together in fits and starts for the last five-plus months. To listen in and watch, the conversations were a strange polyglot mash-up of Chandrian, English, and Spanish due to the fact that so many of the militia were from Latin America. The conversations Kyle could hear were mostly English, though there was a heavy dose of Chandrian curses, used by all, and a lot of pantomimed 'hand talk' as well.

At least they were talking now, Kyle thought. As painful as the integration had been at times, it continued on its organic path based on the hard realities and necessities of their operations. He had to laugh at the hardcopy pocket dictionary that some program official had issued the joint force. No doubt, it was someone in Seattle's bright idea and pet project. It was meant to create an official canon of language that the Chandrians could use when communicating with their new allies. Thousands of the things had been printed up and distributed to both sides of the alliance. Seattle had been touting the dictionary program as huge success, as extras were

313

constantly being requested. Kyle and Col. Pretty had let the requests and deliveries continue until Seattle had started using the dictionary program as an example of how they were able to assist and guide the Jema integration effort. Then, Seattle began making noises that they were going to create a *cultural* integration program.

That was when Col. Pretty had let them know that the dictionaries were being carried into the field by Jema and the militia as very conveniently packaged toilet paper. Seattle had not been amused that the word 'dictionary' had come to mean 'ass-wipe' in the literal, field expedient Chandrian. What was happening with the Jema and the militia was entirely organic and problems aside, it was working. It certainly didn't need any input from Seattle. They'd decided early on to go with mixed units. It had been painful at times, and still caused issues on an almost daily basis, but it was paying dividends.

At times the nearly unintelligible patois that developed naturally in any given mixed unit made inter-unit operations more difficult. They'd learned though, generally when units communicated with higher echelons or another unit by radio, they'd put like to like on the horn to avoid confusion and then let the individual units parse out the orders. It was a problem, but a manageable one. It was also the first step of an integration process for two interplanetary cultures that was going as well as any of them had a right to expect.

Kyle listened in and couldn't help but think on how far they had come and for about the millionth time thanked God for the natural linguists on both sides of the cultural fence that had helped the techs program and update the audio translation program into everyone's compads. He'd often wished he'd been born with the linguist gene and had always been envious of the few brothers in arms who seemed able to pick up a new language within a few months of hitting the ground somewhere. That particular skill had never been his, and his experience with trying to learn Chandrian wasn't proving to be any different. He was getting better, slowly. Thankfully, so was the audio translator program on his compad. It was almost enough reason to not want to accidently misplace the damned thing.

At this point, every Jema and militia officer as well as NCO, Teark, and sergeant alike, were now equally cursed with the electronic anchor. The translation software was one of the few good things coming out of Seattle these days. When he had time to think and dwell on it, which admittedly wasn't very often, he knew that Paul was losing control of the Program. The growing bureaucracy that was feeding the war machine had its hands in just about every aspect of the Program at this point. That same bureaucracy was tying itself in knots with worry over their new allies.

The concerns were legion; from the effect the Jema were having on the militia - all to the good as far he was concerned, to how they were going manage the integration of the Jema if they could manage to bring the war to an end. The latter concern was laughable to Kyle. The Jema were done being managed, by anyone. Least of all a faceless bureaucracy that hadn't stood shoulder to shoulder with them in a fight. If he had to write one more screamer back to Seattle to keep their noses out of militia – Jema relations, he'd need some allies for whatever fight came after the one they were already in. It was a fight that Elisabeth was convinced, was coming. She had to deal with the bureaucrats every day, and she was sounding more and more worried.

The heart of the argument was driven by what was happening in the mixed units. In short, they were working, and at this point he was just one of many 'Terns' that had been adopted by the Jema. Every unit represented in the room had militia personnel that had, in the words of the Program bureaucrats, *gone native*. There were two competing vectors coming into being. One was happening organically. A warrior caste, for lack of a better term was growing up through the mixed units. On the other hand, the Program was worried enough about the formation of a mixed warrior class made up of militia veterans and Jema, that they were reactively pushing for a semi-formal, two-class system made up of Terrans and Jema.

315

They said the right things and hid their intentions under blankets of bullshit labeled with palatable language like, 'the protection of indigenous Jema culture.' He had to laugh at that. Jema 'culture,' among the Jema was an almost forgotten myth. They'd lived in an armed camp, commanded by the Kaerin for nearly five centuries. Their dominant cultural trait, up until five months ago, had been slavery enforced with ritualized warfare. At any rate, it was a fight that could wait, at least for him. Elisabeth had to deal with it every day.

"A moment?" Audy walked up to where and he and Col. Pretty stood waiting for Jomra to arrive.

"Sure thing," he replied. "The Colonel is just trying to keep me awake."

Audy looked tired too. They were all exhausted. Nonstop operations, training, and managing the war left little time for sleep.

Audy pointed at the screen behind the podium. "Your visuals will be useful," Audy explained. "But they need to hear you speak from your hearts."

"We get that." Pretty looked out across the gathered crowd. "We realize our management school leadership tactics don't play well, we're learning too."

"You have their respect, as do your soldiers." Audy bowed his head slightly with the statement.

"Jomra and I agree with your attempts to get the Jema to accept a new way of battle." Audy shook his head slowly, "making soldiers from warriors, is a ... process. But it is working as you know. Jomra spoke to them, again, this morning in our own tongue regarding this. I think you'll find them attentive."

"He rip them a new asshole?" Jake had walked up and caught the last of the conversation.

Audy smiled. "We have improved much. Yet many of our war ... soldiers have yet to grasp the idea of a war, based on your concept of attrition, movement, and logistics. For generations we have engaged in set battles, more or less scheduled by the Kaerin. This has been very different."

316

"Still too much warrior, not enough soldier," Kyle said. The problem boiled down to that, the rest was semantics. To make matters worse, a lot of the militia could at times, in the confusion and kinetic clash of a fight, get seduced by the warrior mentality of those Jema fighting next to them. He thought back to his meeting in Seattle with the SC from Astoria. The man who had lost his son for that very reason. Like Audy had said, it was a process, and the cultural integration naturally flowed both ways.

"Yet you, and many of your militia have growing reputations as warriors." Audy said.

"No, Audy," Pretty answered. "We may hold to the warrior ethos, but in the end, soldiers will beat warriors nearly every time."

"I've seen enough to know the truth of this," Audy answered with a nod. "Jomra agrees, as do all Jema by now. I only ask that when you show them what can be done as soldiers, you speak to them as warriors. That is where their hearts are."

"Show them the rope-a-dope fight," Jake said. "We stacked em up like cord wood."

"You had a drone up recording?"

"Of course," Jake answered. The light bulb went off in Kyle's head.

"Wholesale slaughter on the big screen?" Kyle scratched his cheek with a smile. "Pictures are worth a thousand words."

Pretty already had his compad out. "I'll feed it to the tech running the show."

"Just need some popcorn." Jake walked off shaking his head.

He turned to Audy and glanced at Col. Pretty. "This plan of yours is the best one we have, Audy. But if it's not done right, you're all dead. As much as you are able, you and Jomra need to emphasize the point that much more is possible acting in concert, with precision, with timing, than as individuals making a name for themselves or counting coup."

"I'm not familiar with that term." Audy replied.

"Jake would call it measuring dicks." Pretty smiled.

"Aaah, I understand."

317

"I see Jomra, I'm going chat him up too." Kyle bowed out of the conversation and made his way across the floor of the massive flight maintenance hangar. It was, he realized, the single largest building on the planet east of the Rocky Mountains. Jomra was doing the same, Kyle's old assault rifle slung on his shoulder like a trophy. An ever-present sign to his people that things were very different from whence they'd come.

The Strema were as unused to fighting on the move as the Jema were. Chandrian military strategy was built around set battles that had been scheduled by the Kaerin and were a struggle of sheer willpower and ferocity more than the tactics, strategy, and logistics that every 1st lieutenant since William of Orange had learned. They were learning quickly though, both sides, which was a sword that most definitely cut both ways. The Strema host was no longer bunched up. The enemy marched along a dispersed front, twenty miles wide, and ten miles deep along the west bank of the Mississippi. A fact which significantly dulled the impact of their regular airstrikes.

The dispersed nature of the enemy made hit and run, squad and platoon level tactics possible, but mixed squads of militia and Jema working together left it up to the strength of leadership of each team to pull back when it was time to pull back. Problem was, pulling back, breaking contact, or God forbid a tactical retreat, were all alien concepts to the Jema.

The Jema were getting better. For every Jema *Teark* or Sergeant that kept his rankers under control, there seemed to be one who'd go 'berserker' and take his squad or platoon willingly down the same path. Militia casualties were way up since joining forces with the Jema. It couldn't be helped, they needed their Jema allies desperately. More importantly, they needed the respect of the Jema. If that meant taking part in an ancient blood feud then so be it. But they had to do it on their terms. There simply weren't enough of them to fight the war by Chandrian methods.

Jomra approached him trailing his mixed translation team through a group of subdued Jema officers that had accompanied him. He had spent enough time around their allies at this point that he immediately picked up on their mood. They'd just had their asses chewed. It was something any soldier could recognize at a hundred paces.

He held out his hand. "Jomra, it's good to see you."

Jomra shook his hand somewhat softly. The Jema hadn't quite figured out that custom yet. They were worried about squeezing too hard and turning a greeting into yet another dick measuring contest which was what a great many things in the Chandrian culture boiled down to.

"Captain Kyle."

"What's with your people?" Kyle indicated the somber group of officers taking their seats and nodded at Audy who had just joined his fellow Jema.

Jomra, whom Kyle knew understood him, looked to his Jema translator who had a confused look on his face. The Jema war leader shook his head in disappointment and turned to the elderly militia translator, Carlton by his name tag, who was paired with his Jema counterpart.

"Sir, could you rephrase that question?"

"Sorry," he was used to dealing directly with Audy and had gotten spoiled. "His people seemed subdued, quiet. Is everything all right?"

The translation chain skipped Carlton as the Jema translator, half of Carlton's age had seemed to understand him and quickly asked Jomra a question.

Jomra grinned a moment, nodded at him, "Eshani troo, dalla."

"Sir," Carlton spoke up, "Jomra Sendai asks that we inform you that he and Sri-Tel have told the entire Jema host that all postings or rank, maybe social position, I'm sorry sir, it's a difficult concept for us. It will all be based on something other than man's individual kills in battle – once this war is over, they must learn to live again as men. That they have only known war on behalf of the Kaerin and only in the manner that the Kaerin allowed. The way they fight was developed by the Kaerin, for the benefit of the Kaerin to keep their numbers down. They will from this point forward fight only as men, not as slaves or there will be no men left to raise their young."

319

Kyle smiled, "Somehow I doubt he said all that Mr. Carlton."

"Sir, I was allowed to attend the Jema gathering this morning and have discussed little else with my translation partner since."

"I see. Thank you both." He nodded his thanks to both the translators.

"You welcome, War Leader," the Jema translator said.

He looked back at Jomra and smiled and flashed him a raised thumb, they all understood that.

The Jema leader nodded once at him and grinned making the hard lines of his face appear skeletal. Jomra spoke far better English than most of his Jema translators, but he never seemed to tire of making them work.

"Is this to be another ... power point?"

"No, I think we have something much better to get our point across."

*

Chapter 22

"You know," Kyle fished out his dip and threw it into the Mississippi. "I'm beyond tired with this socialization bullshit coming out of Seattle." He held his compad in one hand and resisted the hourly urge to frisbee the damn thing and forget it forever.

"I'm just tired," Jake drawled in reply.

They were all exhausted. Constant operations and the training schedule had not let up a bit, but it was paying off and an end was in sight. A risky, balls to the wall end game that was Jomra and Audy's idea. It was so crazy it might work. If it didn't, Seattle wouldn't have to worry about socializing and integrating Jema warriors. There simply wouldn't be any left to work their bullshit on.

The program's army of bureaucrats had been on rapid fire of late, as if they had just realized, six months after the fact, that they had allies who were from a different planet fighting side by side with them and who were expecting their own freedom after the fighting. It was more than some of the *wanna be* politicians sitting safely a half continent away could stomach. Richard Kiley was actively directing the worst of it. Somehow the politician had gained a not inconsequential following within the program itself. The more he thought about it the angrier he became.

Audy had warned him and Pretty, at first politely and becoming more strident of late, that having escaped the control of the Kaerin, the Jema would never again accept any control outside of strict military needs.

"Fucking bureaucracies," Kyle's jaw was clenched and it came out just above a whisper.

Jake jerked a thumb over his shoulder towards the camp. "Pretty jumped on an Osprey, said he was gonna rip somebody a new asshole over this latest ... guidance."

Kyle nodded, he knew that. Pretty would make certain no one would be dumb enough to think they were going to tell Audy or God forbid, Jomra, that their entire Clan needed to attend mandatory 'cultural sensitivity' training. He smiled at

321

the thought. It would actually be some decent entertainment to watch Jomra's response.

Jake, who was down on one knee at the edge of the floating dock, shifted legs and let loose a stream of spit into the river. "Personally, I love the effect the heathens are having on our troops, kicked up the testosterone level a notch or two."

They both smiled. The Jema simply said what they thought. They of course had their own societal filters on their conversations, and actions. For the most part though, they were a world apart, literally, from anything that made sense to anyone born and raised on Earth. What understanding did exist, was in the field, in a fight. Back at base was a different story all together.

Initially the complaints against Jema Tearks from militia under their command had worried him. The typical Jema Teark, was roughly equivalent to a senior Sergeant in mentality and attitude with the command authority of a 1st Lieutenant. As a group, they had exactly zero patience or understanding for someone questioning orders. The friction between the two forces was easing up, in large respect due to the Jema's willingness to listen to advice and counsel. There was also the painfully discovered understanding on the militia's part that an order by a Jema Teark, was not in any way to be confused with a suggested course of action.

The discipline had often been enforced back at the base, after the patrol or fight. More than a handful of militia had come out with broken noses and black eyes. Some of the Jema, when they'd failed to listen to the advice of their militia counterparts, received the same from their own betters. Complaints were filed of course, Seattle would spin up, but by the time they tried to involve themselves the parties were usually 'over it' and working well together. He and Hank had to talk to more than one militia officer and explain to them that the newly formed alliance was in the simplest of terms, more important than their loss of face, or the use of their jaw for a couple of months.

At times, the militia gave as good as they got, some of them were tough as nails and didn't have it in them to back down any more than the Jema. People that had given up everything to come to Eden were for the most part a hell of a lot harder than the average American, Chilean, or Englishman that they had all left behind.

The fights, those amongst themselves, as well as those against the Strema, had led to a genuine respect between the groups. Friendships and romances were rampant across the two groups. Conflict still occurred, but it was now far more likely to be between one mixed unit and another, which was a time-honored military tradition among both societies and one in which the leadership of both camps encouraged and leveraged.

"So, do I," Kyle replied to Jake's testosterone comment. "I think they have a lot to teach us, or remind us of, actually."

"Well some of us aren't technically Jema certified like you, don't be going native on me. I'd have to report you."

"No worries, but you know what I mean."

Jake nodded, "I do. Hell, guys like us have a lot more in common with Jema warriors than we do with most of our own people, especially some of the noobs. We've been fighting one war or another our entire adult lives. We had leaders who didn't have the balls to want to win, and their fuckin Kaerin made sure nobody won. Brothers in arms and all that."

"Maybe, but I think it's deeper than that." Kyle said. For him it was far more than having a shared background of having been soldiers. The Jema had something that Earth's people had lost at some point, certainly the civilized West at any rate. Not totally forgotten, he'd always thought of it as the 'caveman gene,' the embers of it were still there. That ancient piece of humanity's wiring that had allowed mankind to beat larger predators, ice ages and other humans intent on killing them on a constant basis. Humanity owed its very survival to the ability to commit violence in the name of a greater good or for individual survival. That particular human trait in one form or another, had long since been driven into remission by advances in civilization and technology. He could feel it making a comeback on Eden and the Jema were helping fan the flames.

The basic concepts of right and wrong, personal honor, a person's word; all were suddenly in vogue among the combined force. It was one more dynamic that worried some in Seattle. Elisabeth kept him very well informed. The royal 'they' were already talking about the 'mistake of allowing the formation of a military class.' The same 'class' that was fighting and dying to protect those at home worrying, wanted nothing more than to end the fighting and return to whatever life they'd come from. And the Jema, damn! If ever a people were anxious to be doing something other than warfare as a way of life, it was the Jema. He thought they could be forgiven for striving to kill as many of the enemy as quickly as possible. They had more than enough history and cause.

The notion of a joint military class rising up was laughable. The Jema wanted nothing more than to end the fighting and raise the first children their clan had seen in twenty-five years. Most Jema female warriors were worth two militia in combat, it was an accepted fact. That didn't stop the pragmatic Jema from reasoning that those who were already pregnant were very much protected from the fighting and back at their camp in the Carolina hills.

"Caveman gene, lizard brain," Kyle smiled at Jake, "it kept us alive as a species through our darkest days. Civilization almost killed it, and here we are, needing it again and the Jema haven't lost it. I think we all feel that ancient call."

Jake rolled his eyes and just looked at him for a moment squinting. "You're making my head hurt."

"Think about it, you can't tell me, you or any of us, don't slip into that place where rage and violence keep us alive. Where do you think that comes from?"

Jake looked out across the river and shook his head. "Mommy issues? Wild Turkey? unrequited love? Seriously, the how? the why? I'm too tired to give a shit. It'll be one thing in the end."

"Shit, not you too?"

Jake nodded, "Me too. Maybe I've been fighting too long," he smiled. "You have to admit it has a ring to it. Course, I've never been accused of being a worrier."

"Or a thinker."

Jake grunted in agreement. "Look where that's gotten you."

"You might have a point there."

"You bet your ass I have a point. I have enough to worry about keeping my guys alive." He came to his feet and slapped a meaty palm on his shoulder. "That said, when this is over, and you want to move on Seattle... say the word." Jake winked at him and smiled. "This ends? Really ends? I'm going full monkey tilt swamp rat – no one's going to find me unless I want them to. So before then, you need a pipe hittin redneck to knock the holier than thou out of some of these would be politicians, you know who to ask."

Kyle glanced down at the compad on his thigh and up again at Jake.

"God, I hope Seattle hasn't bugged our compads."

A look of panic flashed across Jake's face for just a moment. But he laughed and tilted his head downward towards his own compad holstered to his leg. "Joking.... PTSD, lack of sleep."

He spent the next half hour slapping at mosquitoes that dared to test the DEET fog around them, listening to Jake tell hunting and fishing lies.

They both heard the hum of the boat's engines a few seconds before the Kevlar molded twenty-six foot riverine appeared around the north end of a heavily forested island in the middle of the river. Kevlar was one of those great materials that the nano production could spit out in huge quantities relatively quickly and molding the hull of a boat was different from body armor only in its size and shape.

The boat's twin jets had the craft launching a rooster tail of muddy water churned white as the craft turned and barreled towards them.

"Not sure I want to be standin on this dock." Jake joked.

As the boat rapidly approached, they could see Audy standing at the central console, a huge bug eating grin on his face. They needn't have worried. Audy had been inserting assault teams up river against the Strema for over a month.

325

Their friend lifted one hand off the wheel and waved before throttling down and swinging around sharply as the v-hull dropped deeper into the water.

Audy reached down and brought up a brace of ducks as he passed by the dock and came about in a tight circle. Pointed up river, the current slowed the boat further until it drifted into a nice docking position.

Kyle glanced over at Jake who was looking at the ducks. "Son of a bitch, knew I should have gone with."

Kyle pretended he didn't hear Jake. "Good hunting?"

"Good hunting," Jomra answered from the back of the craft, as he high stepped over the side to the dock. Two Jema rankers and their *Dadus*, or corporal, jumped out fore and aft and quickly secured the boat. Jomra turned back to the boat and pointed at Carlos, who was just starting to come awake, his sniper rifle in its case and cradled in his lap. "Good hunter."

"Why do I think you mean something other than ducks?" Kyle shook the man's hand.

"Ducks?" Jomra looked confused.

Just when he was amazed at how fast Jomra and the other Chandrians were picking up English something would happen that would remind him of how far they still had to go.

Audy gave some orders to the warriors quickly followed by a barked admonition from the Dadus when he thought the two men under him weren't moving fast enough in retrieving the ducks. The three warriors were at the end of the dock at the head of the trail leading back to the camp, a quarter of a mile away when Jomra asked something of Audy with a smile.

Audy laughed and jumped down to the dock leaving Carlos in the boat looking like he was in no hurry to move anywhere.

"Jomra thinks the news must be bad to be met like this."

"Jomra's plan is approved," Kyle said. He looked towards Jomra and then Audy with an apology ready. "But..."

"I hate this word," Audy growled. "You people always have a 'but'." Audy flashed Jomra a thumbs up and then delivered a sarcastic "But!..." to his friend and rolled his eyes.

"No – but," Jomra shook his head. "Is a good plan, will work."

Kyle nodded in agreement. It was a good plan and one that they would never have thought of, or even imagined. It was a Chandrian show and almost guaranteed casualties in the realm of an engagement from the US Civil War or the trenches of World War I.

"Please convey to Jomra," he turned to Audy, "I agree with him. It's our best plan. Colonel Pretty agrees as well and is on his way to Seattle to report that we are going forward with it. Regardless of what they think. General Majeski, and others are uncomfortable at the level of risk to the Jema and the number of casualties you seem willing to absorb."

Audy shook his head at him, as if to say Jomra already knows your concerns and doesn't give a shit, but he translated as asked.

Jomra's face exploded in frustration. "Is why !!...is reason!" Jomra gave up and looked pleadingly at Audy.

"This plan will only work if the Strema catch the Jema without your support. We understand the risk, we do. We welcome it. There is a not a man or woman among us that does not believe we must make a stand. We feel the need of it, it is not a poor choice, is not a choice at all. It is necessary. We have a debt to repay that does not involve you. What involves you," Audy pointed at him and Jake, "is what comes after. We will not be a refugee people. No reservations and we will earn our right to live here."

"Three days!" Jomra interrupted Audy holding up as many fingers.

Audy nodded up river. "We spotted their forward scouts, they can be here in three days if we give them a reason to come."

"OK," he nodded at Jomra, and then at Audy. "I'll get our people moving out, we have some serious work to do."

Jomra stepped up to him and Jake and went on for a moment in Chandrian before looking over at Audy and gave a nod to translate.

"Jomra says that having you as allies is the greatest boon the Jema have received in the history of our people. He reminds you that some prices must be paid by those who hold the debt, willingly paid, to secure a future. He gives you his oath, that not a single Strema heart will beat on this planet when we are done."

Kyle nodded in response. He didn't doubt Jomra's oath, that wasn't what he was worried about. He held out his hand and Jomra with a huge smile gripped his forearm, in Roman fashion. He did the same, it felt right.

They were joined by Carlos on the dock.

Kyle looked around at his friends and brothers in arms.

"No more half measures, no more containment, no more attrition. We've all sold our souls killing other men for no real reason." A lifetime wasted, he thought. "You to the Kaerin, we to a bunch of politicians that believed in nothing but their own power. We'll fight for an end to this, to the end."

They shook hands again, all around.

"My inner redneck is smiling." Jake said to no one in particular as the five of them walked the length of the dock on to the shore.

"Inner?" Kyle and Carlos asked together with perfect timing.

*

Chapter 23

Bres'Auch Tun looked skyward at the shouts of his men. More Shareki airboats in the distance. Four of the large boats, the ones he knew the enemy used to ferry large numbers of troops in for attack and back out of danger before his host could retaliate. The strange aircraft were miles away and moving in the now familiar diamond formation to the northwest, just as they had the whole day before. He knew the Shareki base was somewhere south of the host's position along the river. His scouts had gotten that much to him before contact had been lost.

What he would give to know what the Shareki were up to. Were they shifting their troops to the northwest to meet the Koryna? Perhaps his allies threatened a city in their march to meet up with him. Perhaps it was a trick. It would be just one more in a long list of feints and strange tactics that seemed to always result in defeat for his war host. He only knew they had not been attacked for two days. That was new.

He was more certain than ever that these Shareki, while powerful, and well trained in their own art of war, were few in number. Very few. He desperately needed to reach the great gulf and return to the Kaerin to report. This world could be theirs, but only with far greater numbers than he had to command. They may be few in number, but these Shareki had very sharp teeth. This was the source of his divided mind. A much heavier invasion force, one including the Kaerin themselves could win here. But that would require returning to Chandra with news of these Shareki, their powerful weapons, the Jema treachery, and his failure to subdue them. Not only would the rewards for his people not be forthcoming, he'd be lucky to survive the delivery such news.

In the back of his mind, what had started as doubt moons ago had grown to fear. Not for the Strema, but for all of Chandra. If these Shareki could reach Chandra in numbers, with the Jema to guide them, all could be lost.

He dared to hope that the Shareki were moving to engage the Koryna. It was far past time for the Koryna to finally join this fight, make their presence known. The Strema had waged this war alone against the Shareki who were supposed to have been just a nuisance to be swatted aside. Yet, the enemy had managed to kill half his host without ever offering a true battle. Once the Jema treachery had been proven beyond doubt, he'd ordered the Koryna to swing southeast at their best possible speed, to meet up with his host at the confluence of the two great rivers.

They would march south to the great bay together, to the gate emergence that naturally linked this world to Chandra in the days of late autumn. He'd planned to throw the Koryna against the Shareki, and create some tactical space in which his host could win their way south, survive and get a warning to Chandra.

That had been the plan, but now this. The Shareki, yet again, did not react as expected. Perhaps, he was correct in his assumption that the Koryna path of march put some Shareki holding or large dwelling at risk. He had no way of knowing and the enemy's ability to appear and disappear from the field had sapped the morale of his host far more than their heavy losses. Losses were expected. There could be no glory, no value in what was won without sacrifice. It was the inability to hit back that hurt. It was not a position that a Strema War Leader had ever faced.

Those cursed flying boats; the big ones carrying the enemy in such large numbers, that could fly in minutes what would take his host a day to march. They were what haunted his dreams. Given an opportunity, they were what he would kill first. The small boats, the ones that dropped their bombs, were amazing in their speed and the effectiveness of their ordnance, but they did not hurt near so much as the enemy's ability to appear and disappear across miles.

Whatever the Shareki air boats were doing now, and had been doing since the previous day, he could not afford to ignore it. His enemy would know this as well. If he'd learned one thing since their arrival, Chandra's military tactics, his own leadership included, was less than wind against the

Shareki weapons, the mobility of their warriors and worst of all, the thrice cursed flying boats.

The enemy, which now included the treacherous Jema, had managed to nip at his edges, like a pack of elytee, darting out of reach, content with killing those who turned to fight or fell behind. How the Jema could have found common cause with this planet's Shareki he did not know. The act of breaking bond with the Kaerin and mother Chandra itself was unthinkable.

The Kaerin mistake, and with them a world away, he would call it that - all those years ago, had been letting any of the Jema survive. He swore, given the opportunity, he would tell them as much. The surviving Jema now represented a threat to Chandra itself. They could bring the Shareki to Chandra and guide them once there. All thoughts of winning honor here had been forgotten long ago. His host had but one mission now and that was to get back to Chandra, deliver word and prepare.

"Bsrat."

"Yes, War Leader."

"Prepare the host to night march, we will not be stopping. The fists are to remain separated, I don't want to them bunched up in the morning's light." In case the Shareki renewed their attacks, he thought to himself.

"It will be so, War Leader."

"Perhaps we'll steal a march on them." Bsrat commented, watching the massive airboats drift past the horizon.

"Perhaps," he allowed. Hope was hard to come by on this cursed world.

"If it is not a feint to lure us," Bsrat turned back to face him. "Perhaps the Shareki go without the Jema. We have seen no evidence of the airboats where our scouts have reported the Jema along the river."

He nodded in response and recognized the flicker of hope in his heart. "If they have done so, we will empty the veins of the Jema host if it costs us everything."

331

Bsrat had been his second for many years, he didn't need the danger spelled out to him. The man nodded his agreement.

"The Kaerin were very much mistaken, War Leader." Bsrat shook his head as he spoke a simple truth that would have seen them both gutted a few months ago. If they disputed the truth now, between them, then all was truly lost.

"These Shareki?" the younger version of himself continued as if the lack of rebuke gave him license. "This must be a colony world, we know they are but few. The land is empty. If a mere colony has such power, we cannot allow them to have an ally of our home world. You are correct, destroying the Jema is all that matters. It will be one thing in the end."

*

Six miles south of the Jema lines.

It was as nice as an evening got in late August along the banks of the Mississippi River. Earlier in the evening, as the blue sky was going to purple, Kyle had imagined a baseball game at Busch stadium some forty miles north and a planet away. Hot and humid, a moonless dark sky, with thousands of moths and other bugs dancing in the stadium lights as the Cubs and Cardinals battled for a Division crown like they seemed to every year. He had to wonder if they were even playing baseball back home, this season. Things had been coming apart last summer, he doubted if they were very much improved at the moment.

There were no stadium lights here. No baseball. Just several large fires to keep the bugs at bay. Five hundred soldiers, four companies consisting of their best mixed units. The mood in camp was strange. They'd received word several hours before of Colonel Pretty's attack on the Koryna near what would have been called the Nebraska/Iowa border, near a small town called Plattsmouth, neither of which, the border or the town, existed on Eden. All their maps, as accurate as they were, were filled with meaningless lines and dots

332

representing roads and towns that didn't exist here. And never would if they didn't win.

Pretty's force had hit the Koryna hard, caught them in the open and destroyed more than half of the forty thousand soldiers marching to reinforce the Strema. The Colonel though, had paid a huge price losing nearly five hundred militia and twice that many wounded. Casualties, deaths, wounds meant nothing to the Jema and they were having a hard time understanding the somber mood of their militia comrades. By the Jema's way of thinking, they'd just won an unimaginable lopsided victory.

Five hundred men and women who had given up a life on Earth for the uncertainty and hope of a better future on Eden were gone within the space of a few hours. Closer to home, Hank had sent Jake and him a personal message relaying that Darius Singer and Arne Jonsen had been killed in the action. They had led a platoon in relief of several companies in danger of being surrounded and routed. They had kept a channel of escape open, saving the lives of hundreds. In the end, only eight men and three women survived from their platoon. Darius and Arne had stayed behind manning the heavy guns until they had run dry of ammunition and been overrun.

Kyle had already said his silent prayers for the five hundred he didn't know and his two friends. He recognized one of the overrun companies as being commanded by his father's friend, Glenn Ada. Since the invasion, nearly 2500 militia had been killed. Their population on this planet was small enough that nearly everyone knew someone who had died, or knew someone who had lost a loved one. He said another wordless prayer knowing those numbers were nothing.

Not a drop in the bucket, to what the Jema would lose tomorrow and that was if, freakin IF, Jomra's plan worked. If the plan failed, the only Jema left would be those pregnant women warriors tucked away safely in the Smoky Mountains. What scared him the most, was the simple fact that Audy and his clanmates would probably think that a fair trade as long as they killed all the Strema in the process. Their hatred, their need for revenge ran that deep.

Even with a very heavily prepared battlefield, somewhere between 45 and 50 thousand Strema were going to roll into less than 15,000 Jema. The Jema had weapons superiority, plans for tactical surprise and complete dominance in Command, Control, and Intelligence, as well as Kyle's own plan for the five hundred handpicked shock troops camped with him on the river's edge. None of which would prevent a lot of Jema dying tomorrow, in fact, Jomra's plan depended on it.

Kyle couldn't bring himself to hate the Strema. In the dark, with only the sound of popping green wood in the fire to distract him, he realized that what they represented was almost too alien to hate. He would fight to kill them. They were anathema to everything he believed in. He would seek to end them, but it was just another battle. One in a too long line of battles against people raised to hate.

His own enmity, he saved for those humans born of his own world who created their own reality in their minds and then went about with some self-justified authority, making sure everybody saw the world as they did. Some of these people had come to Eden, others here had since given in to that particular strain of insanity evidenced by an inability or unwillingness to fight for their own survival. Others had suddenly discovered their 'courage' in a milieu that held no risk to them, politics. Many of the nascent bureaucrats cum politicians in Seattle seemed to have no compunction against attacking or undermining those who *were* willing to fight.

"The old man was right," he whispered.

"Pretty?" Jake asked. His friend was as silent as him staring into the flames across from him sitting on an upright log. "He usually is."

Kyle nodded in agreement even though that wasn't who he'd been thinking of.

"I meant Sir Geoff."

"About what?"

"You remember that last night in the HAT?"

334

"Kind of hard to forget." Jake spit into the fire. "Wasn't the first time the Air Force tried to kill me. But it was the first time it hadn't been a mistake."

"The old goat pulled me aside and warned me if Eden was invaded, he had no doubt that we'd win out. But winning would take the building of a central authority. A government that would be at ass end with every reason we had for coming here. He said I'd be amazed how fast the Program would be used, be manipulated and altered to start pressing its own agenda."

"The old goat was psychic."

"I think he just understood people."

"Fucked up, you mean."

"Yeah," Kyle whispered in agreement. "In the end, maybe that's all it is."

"Nah," Jake shook his head after a moment. "There's always going to be the one percent out there. Evil dickheads, at both ends of the political spectrum, just wanting the power. They're nothing, one percent, if that. Easily ignored if it weren't for the nasty, efficient, ambitious, back stabbing fifteen or twenty percent that don't believe in anything one way or another. They just feed off of the power and authority, and in turn, grow it, protect it. I don't care if it's the New Caliphate, South American Junta Republic, the Central Asian Bloc, Nazi Germany, Mao's China, the Soviet Union, or hell, Russia at any time in the last 600 years. It comes down to the bureaucrats that owe their allegiance to the system or entity that employs them and everything they'll do to grow and protect the power they see as theirs."

Kyle turned away from the fire to look over at his friend.

"Who are you? And what have you done with Jake?"

Jake grinned and tilted his head to the side in what might have been a shrug. "I gots me some schoolin."

"You don't fool me, Jake."

Jake looked at him for a long moment. "Sir Geoff give you any final orders or anything?"

"Something like that." Kyle answered.

"Well," Jake stood and stretched with a long-winded yawn. "When this is over, I'm with you, you know that. Bureaucrats need reminding what consent of the governed really means."

Kyle looked up at his friend and nodded, "Get some sleep, I'm right behind you."

*

Audy and Jomra stood in the main Jema trench line behind a heavy bulwark of tramped down dirt thrown up between them and the advancing mass of Strema less than two miles off, and unknowingly tracked by a trio of drones that circled lazily above them. The earthworks were still growing as a thousand shovels had dirt flying, adding to the sought-after image of a Jema force that had been caught unaware and was now trapped between the river and a Strema force that outnumbered them more than three to one.

Audy shook his head at that thought. It may be part of their plan, but that didn't change the fact, they *were* trapped. Their Tern weapons would alter that balance quickly, but the plan called on an initial sacrifice to lure the Strema into an all-out attack. They simply couldn't use the modern weapons until the Strema believed they could overwhelm the Jema. Many would fall, every warrior accepted this. No one doubted the sacrifice would be worth it.

Sri-Tel himself, was to play an integral part of the plan and he looked somehow taller to Audy, more substantial than he had in recent memory. The old man was guided to a place in the trench between him and Jomra. Sri-Tel dismissed his bodyguard, with the ritualistic parting of the Jema. The one they had privately used since the culling of the Clan at the hands of the Strema a generation past.

"Traver, today you will remember your father's name," Sri-Tel spoke solemnly.

The guard looked at Sri-Tel and nodded. Then looked at Audy and Jomra. "It is on my lips. After today, all will hear it."

Audy nodded. He had his own father's name in his thoughts, something he could not claim while the Jema were

336

shorn of their honor. If he survived, he would scream it to the heavens. His mother and father would hear him.

When the bodyguard was gone. Sri-Tel's sightless gaze was focused on the space between them. "Describe the field to me."

Audy moved forward and squared Sri-Tel's shoulders with the expanse of meadow in front of their lines.

"In front of our lines," he began. "A large flood plain gone to grass. Firm ground until the middle where there are some large puddles, no more than ankle deep. Beyond the middle ground, the low point and then more flat meadow stretching to the edge of the forest land from which the Strema think they hide their approach. Their scouts are at the edge of the meadow, watching us even now."

"How far?"

"Seven hundred long strides all the way across, perhaps eight hundred for you." Jomra answered.

"The Mud River runs straight past on our right. We are facing upriver." Audy glanced at the river as he was speaking, "Behind us the river bends sharply to the west."

Sri-Tel's head came up smiling. "They will think they have trapped us with our backs to the water."

"They do," Jomra said. Sri-Tel couldn't see Jomra's nod of resigned acceptance. "We've no escape from this ground."

"This plan relies on their pride." Sri-Tel said. The old man was silent for a moment as if remembering something, and then nodded to himself. "A good bet, as our new friends would say."

"At any rate, our timing was good. We spotted their scouts in the woods while we were at march. They have watched us entrench, we do not believe they realize that we have prepared this this ground for three days."

"And the hills?" Sri-Tel asked, pointing accurately to the west where bluffs climbed out of the forest and stretched out above the left end of their line, following the bend of the river. "They are prepared?"

"Yes, the militia artillery troops assure us that they are ready, they have given Jomra control of the device."

"You can work the device?" Sri Tel turned his head towards Jomra.

"It is a switch, simple, like most of our friend's tools. It is easy to use, more difficult to time correctly."

"That, I trust you can do," Sri Tel nodded with a smile. "What of our friends?"

"They will come by river," Jomra answered. "A mixed force, led by Kyle and Jake. Once the battle is joined, they will land on the Strema's riverside flank with some five hundred warriors and heavy weapons."

"Soldiers, Jomra, they are soldiers as we must become. Today will prove that. We... you must learn this new way."

Their entire plan relied on the Jema acting as soldiers, not as warriors. It was a difficult thing to go against what one felt in the blood.

Sri-Tel turned towards the river that he could not see.

"The long-shooter? He is out there in the river?"

"On a wooded island in the river, yes. Some twelve hundred long strides from your destination, perhaps farther."

Sri-Tel shook his head in disbelief. "He is confident he can make that shot?"

"We all are." Jomra answered. "It is not natural what that man can do with his rifle."

"Good," Sri-Tel smiled and seemed to grow taller still. "I will walk out alone to meet Bres Auch-Tun. His pride will guarantee that he'll want me under his own blade. I want to be the last Jema warrior to fall. Today, those that fall after me, will fall as free men, soldiers. You two, you must make certain that we never give our freedom up again, that we learn these new ways. Learn to live as a free people."

"We will," Jomra and Audy answered almost in unison.

"When I fall, the long-shooter on the island will avenge me." Sri-Tel held up a hand to stifle the argument Audy saw building across Jomra's face.

"I have spoken to Kyle of this. It is proper that we allow our new allies to avenge me. It must be done, and as you have said, the long-shooter on the island is like nothing we have. It will fire the blood of the Strema host." Sri-Tel smiled to himself.

"We will lead them by their balls on to the killing field. Not unlike what the Kaerin and the Strema did to us in the battle that took both your fathers. The Kaerin used our pride, faith in the old ways, used our honor to lure us into an unwinnable position. We will do the same to them, here."

Audy watched as Jomra slowly nodded an assent that Sri-Tel couldn't see.

"You have been our light Sri-Tel, our father and our mother when we had no other. Our children will know your name and your story." Audy was not surprised to see Jomra's eyes watering.

"And their children's children," Audy added.

Sri-Tel nodded slowly. "That is a fine thing, but I'd rather be remembered as an example of what happens when people bend knee to another. Remember that part as well."

Sri-Tel turned toward him, "Audrin'ochal ...Bess'triata, for that was your father's name, I remember him well. As a warrior and as a man. I use his name today, as you will use it for the rest of your days. You have long understood the evil of the Kaerin. Long before we were ready to listen. I task you with finding our people a place in this new world, alongside our new friends. They have their own ways as you know and as we have spoken, you must preserve what it means to be Jema. I would not have us win this day only to lose ourselves."

"It will be done." Audy ignored the tears streaming down his face. He knew his father's name. He had not heard anyone use it since he'd been a child of seven years old.

"Jomra, you will lead our people. You have the respect of all, and you are smart enough to learn from my mistakes and to listen to Audrin'ochal's wisdom. I leave the Jema in your hands."

"I'm honored, Sri-Tel."

The old man nodded once and then grinned. "Now somebody find my sword and bind it to my stump. I've long dreamed of this day and I find myself at peace."

*

Kyle awoke slowly enough that he was unsure of having slept at all. He checked his watch. He'd had his head down for a total of four hours, that had to count for something. He swung his feet off the makeshift cot and pulled the tent flap back a few inches. The false dawn, across the river and far to the east was just a hint of a glow beneath the horizon.

He sat up and pulled on his boots lacing them tight. They were the same boots the program had secreted him into, a year and a half ago, while they were dressing his unconscious body and dumping him on Eden. Back then, he'd initially thought Eden was part of some sort of virtual reality. He'd come a long way since then, they all had. Somehow the bloodshed of his past was still with him.

He clicked on his electric lantern and with his elbows in his lap he paused and looked down at his hands.

How many more people were going to die at his hands today? At his orders? There had to be an end in sight. This had to mean something. Sitting in a tent, the morning before a patrol, a fast assault, or a covert insertion – he'd been here a hundred times, more, over the last fourteen years in other tents, on another planet getting ready for a battle that in the end, had meant nothing. He'd killed for nothing, ordered men to kill for nothing in the grand scheme of things. Just a pawn in a geo-political religious struggle, that his side had the wherewithal to win but had steadfastly refused to do so. This morning was different.

He'd become so cynical with his past life that this feeling of …justness before a battle was more than strange. It was wholly unknown to him, but familiar in its comfort like sharing a beer in adulthood with a childhood friend and picking up a conversation that had lain fallow for decades without missing a beat. He was at peace with what he would do, with what he would order others to do. They had no choice but to win.

The Jema were willing to risk everything. They understood the necessity in a way he and the other Terrans never would. Kyle said a short prayer, on bended knee. "Lord, give me the strength to do what must be done, that the sacrifice of so many will not be in vain."

Jake was already awake, sitting on the same log he had been the night before.

"You crashed before me, you didn't sleep?"

Jake waved the stick he was poking the fire with. "Couple of hours."

Kyle stretched his aching body. He'd come close to pulling something in his hamstring a week past and it was still tender. His back popped liked a string of firecrackers, his left leg quivered under the strain and his neck a fraction of an inch out of alignment, momentarily locked before releasing with a loud pop followed by the sound of gristle rubbing against scar tissue that shouldn't be there. He couldn't even remember where it came from.

"You sound like I feel." Jake shook his head without looking up.

"I hate this part," Kyle answered. "The before."

"May there be another," Jake toasted with his canteen.

"Amen to that."

"I'm going to ask a favor," Jake suddenly looked serious. "If you say no, I'm likely going to draw down on you, or threaten you with some bluegrass music till you give in."

"Name it," he laughed. He liked just about every kind of music there was, but bluegrass was a particular kind of hell to him.

"I can tell you haven't read your messages yet. I'm going to insist you wait till after the fight, we need you clear headed."

"Seattle?"

"Yep," Jake just nodded and he looked pissed.

"I'm in a good place right now," Kyle responded. He nodded more to himself than to Jake, surprised he believed it. "Just tell me. I promise, I'll do nothing till after, if there is an after. If we don't win, Seattle's not going to matter?"

"Good enough," Jake nodded after a moment.

"Apparently, the Council," Jake held up a pair of finger quotes and then lifted his palms skyward in his best gospel music hallelujah, "hallowed be their fat asses, think Colonel Pretty fucked up. Cited his losses, he's been relieved."

Kyle was dumbstruck. The Koryna had been stopped cold and were half the size they had been a day earlier. Over twenty thousand fewer enemy to deal with.

"They want you to leave the Jema to deal with the Strema and assume command of all our forces, but first you need to report to Seattle asap, to be blessed or some shit."

"Un... fucking... believable..." he started reaching for his compad.

"Kyle!" Jake warned. "It'll wait."

His hand doubled up into a fist, but he left the compad in its holster.

"This was from Stephens?" Kyle couldn't believe what he'd just heard.

"Negative," Jake shook his head slowly. "He wasn't even cc'd, which is strange."

"I will burn that place down if I have to."

Jake stared at him. "I'll bring the matches."

*

Two hours later their mixed force of militia and Jema handpicked soldiers, five hundred strong were fed, caffeinated, and geared up milling along a quarter mile of muddy river bank. A small armada of boats were pulled up to the shore, held in place with staked ropes. Several larger boats were anchored in the river just offshore. There were bass boats, ski boats, pleasure boats, a couple small river tugs, and their entire force of seven Kevlar molded riverine assault boats. Most of those were tied to the large barges they'd be pulling. Forty-seven craft all told, and the four company leaders stood in front of Kyle, waiting for him to say something. Three of the company commanders were Jema, two men and one woman, who was a Jema equivalent of a second cousin or something to Jomra.

Is'mra hadn't made this cut by nepotism. Standing next to Jake, she was as solid an officer as they came. Her reinforced company was a unit they had come to rely on. Her troops, militia and Jema alike, would follow her into hell. That trait probably had something to do with the fact that she was the women's champion among the Jema at Tar' Sega, their

342

indigenous unarmed martial art that Audy had gone to great lengths to instruct Kyle in. To him, it felt like a mix of the Israeli derived krav maga and karate with a little ultimate fighting thrown in the mix, without the wrestling.

Jomra had told him that were less than three dozen Jema men who could beat Is'mra, and that they would all have to work for it. She'd not been shy dealing with early militia discipline problems in her unit through her own personal one on one counseling sessions, aka beat downs that moved bruised egos back into line quickly as fiercely loyal soldiers. A great trait in a commander, even better, her troops would do what they were told to do.

"Is'mra, how are we doing today?"

"Good to go," she grinned and flashed the now ubiquitous thumbs-up that the Jema seemed to use instead of nodding.

Next to her, were Dik'strala and Jai'nee, two brothers, twins who would forever be Dick and Jane. The genesis of "Dick and Jane" had been explained to them and no one thought it funnier than the twins. Standing next to the positively Amazonian Is'mra, they looked like a pair of short overly muscled Portuguese fishermen. But they both seemed to have a knack for languages so of course they'd been in command of some of the first mixed units. That they were natural leaders and always seemed to know what the other would do, led to a situation where their two companies often worked in concert.

"You two ready?"

"I not like boats," Dick, at least Kyle thought it was Dick, said looking out at the river in anger.

"Fastest way to the Strema. We are ready." Jane answered for him.

"We all know the plan," he said. They'd rehearsed and practiced unloading from the boats for hours yesterday.

"Tell your people to not shoot at anything moving on the big island. I doubt very much they will see anything, but our sniper team is there. We stay in the main channel behind the island until we get the signal from Jomra. Waiting is going to be hard, when your people..." he stopped himself. These

343

people weren't Terrans and hadn't grown up watching sitcoms or soap operas. "When there are so many Strema to kill, waiting for your blades. But we will wait until we get the signal from Jomra."

He looked at each of them in turn and got a thumbs up from all of them. He glanced at Jake who had a knowing grin on his face. "Nice speech, Boss. I hear ya."

He flashed a thumbs-up of his own. "Ok then, let's go."

*

Chapter 24

Seattle

"Have you heard from Kyle?" It was a strain for Paul to speak, the slurring of words impossible to miss. The medical nanobots in his bloodstream could repair a lot. Fixing all the damage from the stroke he'd suffered the day before in the council meeting was at the limit of its capability, and he knew it, just as she did.

Elisabeth looked down at her much older half-brother, after a quick scan of the monitoring equipment that he was plugged into. She did her best to smile. "I imagine he's a little busy right now."

"...should have listened to Geoffrey." Paul's eyes begin to tear up. "He said this would happen."

"Nothing has happened Paul, other than some bureaucrats overreaching. Hank, Kyle, Jake," she paused wondering what the Jema would do if they survived, "all of them. They'll put things right. You have to know that."

"Fight our own people?"

If we have to, yes. "It won't come to that, Paul."

"No such thing as good government," her brother was smiling as he said it. She thought he may have started to laugh to himself when he was gripped with pain that was evident on a face that had gone white with strain.

"We'll make it right, Paul. For now, just get some rest, you've bought us our freedom, let somebody else make sure we keep it."

"Kyle... and Hank, they can't listen to them." It was a struggle for him to say anything more. A graduate of medical school, she had a better notion than most of what was happening inside the network of arteries and veins of his brain.

"Shsssh, Paul, you need to rest." Her thumb triggered the muscle relaxant which was all Paul needed to finally sleep.

She watched his monitors for a moment and then almost stifled a giggle at the thought of Kyle listening to the arguments of Kiley and the council that he seemed to have recruited. When did her spear thrower ever listen to anyone?

She remembered her initial evaluation of Kyle's psych profile and his military jacket. The final report had been written by a Johns Hopkins Doctor of Psychiatry on loan to Walter Reed where Kyle had been sent upon discharge for evaluation.

'Subject is burned out after fourteen years of high intensity conflict across half the planet. He has lost faith in his command structure and has become psychologically numb to his environment. He's borderline anti-social at this point, particularly towards the upper echelons of his command structure. Very strong loyalty complex to his men, his unit, family, and friends – no one else matters to him right now.

Subject is very self-aware. He knows it's time to leave the military. The only social danger this analysis foresees, is that when subject begins to care about something again, it's liable to be intense. If he should adopt anti-social or anti-authority attitudes, be they towards civil or government authority, subject has the potential, given his experience and training to be very dangerous. He bears watching and gradual assimilation back into society through the auspices of the NCWA. Recommendation, approve honorable discharge, furtherance of file to NCWA induction program.'

She had read the recommendation several times and finally taken it to Sir Geoffrey for a final decision. She'd been in charge of recruiting and vetting all of Sir Geoffrey's *'specials.'*

Sir Geoffrey, had read the file in advance, and acted as if he couldn't understand her concerns, or maybe he could. His way of getting people to face the kernel of truth at the heart of most things was to deny the existence of all else, the fluff he called it.

"He's burned out, angry, and maybe a little depressed... he's been at war his entire adult life Elisabeth, why wouldn't he be?" She could remember the look of confusion on Sir Geoff's face.

"But is he stable? You had me looking at him as one of your specials, basically your insurance policy should things go bad."

"Oh, they'll go bad my dear, I guarantee it. The stress of what we are doing guarantees it will go to a knife's edge at some point. People like this young man won't notice. He'll take it in stride and in the end do what he thinks best. He's taken orders for too long, true. But I'll turn that out of him quickly enough. I'll make sure he has the authority to do what is needed."

"You're sure?"

"Heavens, no," the old Scot had sworn. "He could be an absolute nutter. In which case, we'll move him out to the NCWA and he can make a run for the nearest Italian or Australian recruiting center. I'm never sure, Elisabeth." He grinned and patted her on the head as only someone born in the middle of 20th century could get away with. "But, I'm not wrong, bring him on."

She looked down at her brother, and honestly felt he had nothing to worry about. Kyle would put things right, she only hoped he was alive to do it and that Paul would recover well enough to see it.

She stepped out into the hall of the hospital and was instantly confronted by Richard Kiley, the ex-political spin doctor turned new Council Chairman. He was bookended by two security officers she didn't recognize.

"Dr. Abraham, I hope Mr. Stephens is doing well."

"You'd better pray he lives, Mr. Kiley. After what you've done, his calming influence may be the only thing able to keep you alive."

"I can see you're upset." He looked concerned but the sentiment didn't reach his eyes.

"You would be correct."

"Doctor," he looked apologetic for just a moment, "I'm afraid I'm going to have to confiscate your compad. It was recently brought to my attention that you're involved with Mr. Lassiter who has refused to respond to our messages this morning. We'd like to speak to him on a level playing field so to speak, not one that has been prepared by, well," he paused, "by someone upset concerning this recent family tragedy."

She did giggle then, she couldn't help it. "You actually think you're back on Earth. That the same bullshit applies?" She handed over the compad with a slight bow. "Take it, Kyle's never been much of a writer."

She couldn't have been more wrong.

*

The slow boat ride upriver was just over an hour in length. Plenty of time for Kyle to read the message from Seattle that he'd promised Jake he would ignore. He sat for ten minutes, fuming, lost in his own rage against the steady thrum of the big Evinrude outboard driving the overloaded twenty-four-foot converted fishing boat up river against the relentless weight of the Mississippi at a sedate five knots.

Then he started typing out a response to Kiley's summons. He cc'd everyone in his address book, smiling ferally as he imagined the 'Oh shit' moment when the Council, who had ordered him to Seattle, read his reply. He read it through, satisfied it conveyed his intended message and hit send.

He felt much better and could concentrate on the coming battle. He managed to close his eyes and try to relax for a few minutes until he realized another boat was pulling up alongside his.

He opened an eye and saw Jake had taken the wheel of a large bass boat, its swivel chairs removed and sporting a blast shield in the front of the boat with a .30 caliber M-60 machine gun resting on a spindle mount where the front chair had been.

"You evil bastard! You promised," Jake yelled.

He smiled back, "I'll owe you one."

Jake smiled back at him and then did something Kyle never expected. Something he had never seen Jake do before. His friend came to attention and saluted him. There was no middle finger, no peace sign, no lazy flopping of a wounded duck elbow. It was a proper salute.

Returning it, was the only thing that came to mind. He was speechless.

Jake grinned and gave a whooping howl and veered his boat away to fall back into its original position in the line of gunboats.

*

Richard Kiley was still flanked by his bodyguards walking across the large central arrival plaza toward the admin building. It was very early in the morning, but he had much to do to consolidate his new authority and had already been up most of the night communicating with those who supported him, building a list of those who didn't. His compad buzzed at him, and he noted that Dr. Abraham's had chimed at the same time. He looked down at the screen, Kyle Lassiter seemed to have responded after all. He couldn't help but smile at the thought of Lassiter's reaction to the news he was now sitting at the head of the Program's council. He opened the message, noted immediately the page and a half of addressees and began reading.

"Sir, is everything all right?"

"Sir?"

His voices of his bodyguard reached him as if through a thick wall, until his eyes focused on them. It brought him back to the present and their shouting suddenly seemed very loud.

"Are you all right? Sir?"

"I'm fine, I'm fine." He heard himself saying the words, his mind far away from the moment focused on the very descriptive e-mail he had just read.

"He can't do that! It's not... right."

"Sir?"

"We... I can't ... this can't happen."

"Sir?!"

"What? Damn it! I'm trying to think." He didn't notice the spittle that flew from his mouth as he turned on his guard.

"Sir, may I suggest we get you inside, you've ...uh had an accident, Sir."

349

"What?" He followed his guard's eyes down until he realized he'd pissed himself.

*

The Jema skirmishers and scouts amidst the narrow band of trees at the water's edge and atop the opposing bluffs high above the prepared battlefield had been exchanging sporadic fire with their opposite numbers for the past two hours. The Jema were using only Chandrian weapons and they steadily gave ground toward the battlefield as the Strema main body continued to move up through the woods reinforcing their numbers.

Audy watched the scouting battle take place along a familiar pattern. The battle, was unfolding utilizing the same tactics clans of Chandra had employed for nearly a thousand years. Now though, he watched the forces unfold and the enemy lines form on his compad through the feeds from the high-flying drones above them. It amazed him that the small Seagull sized machines could stay aloft using just the tiny propeller in their tail. That they could broadcast images back to him he took for granted, it worked in the same manner a radio did. Leave it to the Terrans to take a toy, and turn it into something they could use for war.

He had no idea if the Strema had any concept of the recon and communication technology the militia had gifted the Jema with. If they did, they clearly didn't assume that the Jema possessed the same capability in the absence of those militia forces. Watching the Strema, it was clear that their behavior so far was based on their belief that the Jema were without support of their Terran allies.

He watched as the enemy commanders continually scanned the sky expecting at any moment the aircraft that had killed so many of them. Yet they continued to move forward massing at the edge of the opposing forest, gaining confidence as time passed without the familiar rumble of jets or the high-pitched scream of the slower air boats that the Terrans called Ospreys.

Their plan was working. So far.

"Not how we imagined this moment of glory as children, is it?" He motioned his compad towards Jomra who was intently studying his own.

"No." Jomra smiled. "I like this better. Dying sword in hand, wrapped in honor is a good thing. Winning is better."

The battle was not yet joined and that outcome was far from assured, Audy thought to himself. "There they are, look with number three."

Jomra had picked up their allies' technology as quickly as he had. It was so much better that the bits and pieces of Kaerin technology they were allowed to have back on Chandra. All of it, from the weapons to the communications to the drones themselves, it was all designed to be used by anyone. One didn't have to have a Kaerin blessed Gemendi priest to operate any of it. For the thousandth time, he wondered at how his world had developed or failed to develop compared to Kyle's home world. He knew the Kaerin were to blame for that as well.

"They look ready to fight," Jomra replied once he had switched drone feeds. "Tired as well; they look to have marched through the night."

"How soon before their main body reaches the clearing?" Sri-Tel asked, sitting calmly in the trench just behind them. He was dressed in his formal jacket, the embroidered eagle of the Jema at its breast, the sleeves pinned up to accommodate his handless arms. His old sword, the Jema's ceremonial *First Sword*, was strapped to a stumped forearm with a web of leather strips. The jacket and the sword he had managed to keep hidden for almost thirty years. Once Sri-Tel was standing in front of the Strema, both would only further enrage the enemy, as would the forbidden flag waiting to be raised above the Jema trench line. Enjoyable as the symbolism was, Audy knew it was like spitting on an angry tiger. There was little need to inflame the hatred between Jema and Strema.

It was Sri-Tel's idea. The uniform, the sword, the flag; beyond the mere possession of the items, using them here today was a message for their fellow Jema as much as it was bait to the Strema. A complete repudiation of everything of

351

their past lives. They would no longer allow anyone else to be an arbiter or judge of their honor. They would make their own.

"They are here," Jomra answered, "still forming up in battle lines just within the far tree line."

"Signal our skirmishers to halt fire and withdraw as they are able." Sri-Tel stood as he was speaking. Audy watched him pause and turn to the mid-morning sun, warming his face in the light he could not see. A moment that would be among his last. When he turned back to them his face was set.

"Raise the Black."

"Yes, sir." Jomra signaled men waiting in the middle of their line at the small rise they had used to anchor their trench stretching from the river on their right flank to the base of the bluffs on their left. A large black flag with a white eagle on either side went up almost immediately.

"It is done."

"Someone point me in the right direction, a blind man's journey needs to begin true."

Jomra jumped down into the trench and grabbed Sri-Tel's elbow. "I'll escort you myself."

"You'll get me out of this foul-smelling ditch, on flat ground pointed true and you'll leave me there. My last command to you, Jomra."

Jomra flashed a look of annoyance at him.

Audy just nodded back as if to say, let him go.

"As you say, Sri-Tel."

*

Chapter 25

Bsrat approached him at a run and pulled up with a face vacillating between surprise and anger.

"What is it?" Bres Auch-Tun challenged him, expecting to hear that the Shareki had tricked him yet again and were waiting for them.

"They are flying the black; they should not even have one, yet the Jema are standing under it now."

"Their dishonor knows no bounds."

"Sri-Tel himself, the old man, stands in front of their host, sword in hand."

Not in hand, surely. Bres Auch-Tun smiled to himself. "No bounds at all." The Jema had no call on Strema honor, and Sri-Tel had no standing to challenge him. Yet the Jema battle flag flew, and Sri-Tel stood in defiance. So, the faithless traitors wanted to die with honor. He was beyond caring with rage. Let them go to the earth thinking whatever they wanted, as long as they went.

"I will take the old man's head, like our fathers did his hands and eyes. Then Bsrat, then we will destroy these shadows of men." He looked around through the thick growth of spindly river pine they hid within at the edge of the battlefield.

"Order the host to form up for an assault. They can eat what they have on them. I'm not going to delay battle while the Jema await their Shareki friends to return."

*

Carlos watched the blind, handless Sri-Tel walk slowly across the battlefield through his rifle's scope. At times, it seemed as if the old man could somehow see where he was going, then he would stumble, go to a knee, and slowly regain his feet and continue on. Through the scope, he could see the deadly Jema bouma blade strapped to his forearm. The old warrior walked with a proud, slow gait, his head held high. He was in no hurry and Carlos could see the smile on the old man's scarred face very clearly.

Carlos swung his rifle, his personal .50 caliber, modeled after the Barret M82, but built molecule by molecule to his own specifications by the Program's nano-production. He'd used it exclusively for the last three months and at this point it was an extension of his will. The Strema leader had been marching out as well and had reached the halfway point between the two forces. There he stood, enjoying Sri-Tel's struggling blind walk.

"The bastard's just going to wait for the old blind guy to find him." Carlos said, not lifting his eyes from the scope. He had a comfortable "sit" with the rifle laid out before him across a dead fall log that he'd chopped a firing port into so that it was at the perfect height to index with his prone body stretched out behind the log. He wouldn't dare pull away and ruin the sight picture he had. His scope's aimpoint traced an outline around the face of the Strema leader who stood there with his own sword arrogantly balanced on one shoulder.

Lupe Vasquez sat next to him watching through a spotting scope with a built-in laser range finder on a tripod. So far, the "civilian" had done very well, and he was a natural stalker.

"Nine hundred and sixty-two yards," Lupe whispered. "You can do this?"

The Strema and Jema leaders were coming together about halfway from the river's edge to the base of the bluffs running along the far side of the flood plain. From their position on the island, Carlos would have to shoot across the narrow river channel created by his island and half the battlefield.

"Everybody's good at something," Carlos replied as he watched the Jema leader slip and go down ten yards short of where the Strema leader had been calling him in, taunting him. He watched as the Strema leader laughed and said something in that crazy talk that he couldn't begin to understand no matter how much time he spent with the Jema.

"You're already dead, asshole. You just don't know it." Carlos whispered to himself, willing Sri-Tel to get up out of the mud and close the distance.

"You could at least keep to your feet, old man. Your host, such as it is, is watching."

Sri-Tel privately cursed his blindness but managed to keep his composure as he regained his footing and tracked to the mocking voice.

"Your predecessor took my eyes and hands, while I was bound by ropes and surrounded by your Kaerin masters. He didn't have the honor to fight me. I doubt you'd be here now, in front of your own host if I had both."

"You mean if you and your people still carried their honor? If you had the right to fly a black flag in challenge? If you hadn't allied yourself with the cursed Shareki of this world? I'd still meet you here, as I have done, you know that."

"Perhaps you would have." Sri-Tel answered, closing the distance slowly to the source of his enemy's voice. "The outcome though, would have been very different."

"Stop your mewling Sri-Tel." Bres said his voice rising. "The Jema will die today, as you and they should have died all those years ago."

Sri-Tel smiled. "The Jema that fall here today, myself included, will fall as free men. While you will still be a slave."

Sri-Tel lashed out with his shortened sword arm with a vicious upward swing aimed at where he thought his enemy to be. He put three decades of shame and anger behind the strike.

Bres Auch-Tun parried the strike easily, his counter swing taking off what was left of Sri-Tel's sword arm just past the elbow. He looked down at the pitiful heap of a man. A creature without honor, in the mud before him, and grunted in laughter.

"You are destined to die in pieces it would seem." He reached down and grabbed the old man by the hair and dragged him to his feet. How he wished then that Sri-Tel's eyes had been spared all those years ago, so he could see what was coming.

Sri-Tel's head snapped forward slamming in to the grinning face of his enemy.

355

Carlos watched the Strema leader's head snap back in a spray of blood from a shattered nose. In what seemed like slow motion, the Strema bastard held out Sri-Tel at arm's length and ran his sword through the man's chest and then let him drop to his knees pulling his sword out as he did.

His target stood there with a smile, and it took every ounce of control Carlos could muster to resist applying that final ounce of pressure on his trigger. Sri-Tel, with Audy translating had made Carlos swear he would wait until it was over.

The Strema leader took a half step to the side and spun in place, his sword following in a deadly arc.

The Strema leader paused just a moment before reaching down and lifting Sri-Tel's head up by the hair and presented it towards the Jema's lines.

Carlos thought of, and just as quickly dismissed the familiar 'God forgive me' that he always intoned before squeezing the trigger. As usual, the rifle's recoil surprised him. He could see the trail of marbled air created by the passage of the heavy bullet through his scope, humid air at this distance guaranteed it. It struck the Strema leader in the left arm-pit as he held his trophy out in front of him at arm's length.

The 660-grain bullet was still moving at just under three thousand feet per second when it penetrated into the upper torso of the Strema leader, mushrooming as it struck bone. It transferred its kinetic energy into a shockwave of pneumatic pressure inside the man's chest, far higher than the body's capacity to contain it. The top third of the Strema leader's torso simply exploded into a cloud of bloody mist. His head popped straight up a foot or so and landed next to that of Sri-Tel's in the mud.

Both sides had watched the lopsided struggle, the outcome never in doubt. As the report of that single rifle shot echoed across the river plain, rebounded off the bluffs and back across the gathered armies, silence reigned for a short moment. Carlos swiveled his rifle into the forest on the right side of the plain. He couldn't know the reaction of the Jema was one of silent respect, of bowed heads and tears. They'd just lost the man who had raised them all.

356

Among the Strema, the reaction could not have been more different. Shocked outrage as they surged forward, their leaders were barely able to hold them back. Carlos scanned the scene looking for that one individual that he knew would now be trying to keep his army in order.

Bsrat reacted as quickly as he could when the Strema host that was suddenly his to command surged forward seeking vengeance for the warrior had that carried their honor for more than a decade. The Fist commanders were looking at him, half threatening, half pleading to be released. It took him less than a second to realize there would be no topping this tide.

He jumped up on a fallen log. "Hear me!" he shouted. "First, Second, and Fourth Fists up the hills to our right! Flank them! Move fast, we will attack directly."

He nodded as the gathered Kaerus and Bastelta officers began screaming his orders and his host under the cover of trees writhed like a nest of vipers in preparation.

"There will be one attack and one only. The Jema have sided with the Shareki, they now threaten our home itself. It is upon us to stop them and finish what should have been done thirty years ago. Today is the Jema's last."

He stepped down as the shouts from his host rose in fury. He grabbed the Gemendi Priest by the shoulder. "You will unleash the Kaerin gifts." It wasn't a request and the Priest did not take it as one.

"They are being prepared." The Priest might have bowed his head slightly. Bsrat knew he was not Bres Auch-Tun, not in status nor name. None of that mattered to him, as long as the Gemendi brought forth their weapons.

"We will need them."

*

Audy watched his compad. There were enough breaks in the foliage to see a large portion of the enemy moving to his left as he faced them across the plains. While the Jema fought, organized by Fists as did all Chandrians, they did not recognize individual units other than as an organizing

357

principle. The Strema however, as vainglorious as ever, created much competition in between the individual Fists. Each followed their own banner, whereas for the Jema there was only the Eagle.

All this made it easy to see the flags and banners of three Fists, some fifteen thousand warriors, as they broke from the foliage and started up the hill to the top of the bluffs that towered nearly two hundred feet above the left side of the battlefield.

"Only three Fists to the hill," Jomra said looking at the same image.

They had hoped for more, it would mean nearly thirty thousand Jema would remain to attack them across the wide meadow.

"More for us," Audy answered. Just the same, he checked the river and the unmoving icons that represented Kyle's boats sheltering behind the island. Most were packed to the point of sinking with soldiers, some were large enough to have mounted heavy weapons.

"If I were them, I'd wait to attack until those on the hill were in a position to fire on us from above." Audy nodded up at the hills and glanced into the trenches at the looks of grim determination among his own people.

"But you are Jema," Jomra answered, "and Strema think with their balls."

Jomra stood up in the large marshalling trench behind the hill they'd created preparing the battlefield. "First Fist! Make your line on the field and advance."

*

Bsrat turned to watch a Fist's worth of Jema surge over their breastworks, form up in front of their lines, and advance fifty meters. Someone over there was holding to the old ways.

He looked closely at them through his field glasses, they were carrying nothing but Chandran rifles. The Jema were renowned as marksman but they were too few, far too few to carry this day. Some honorless bastard in the center of their line waved the black flag mockingly. The day was without a breeze, but with every wave of that black flag the Jema

358

insulted the Strema's very existence. It infuriated him as much as the bloody remains of Bres Auch-Tun in the middle of that field.

"Form up for attack," he shouted.

He grabbed the nearest Bastelta. "Inform the Gemendi that they will join the attack, all weapons authorized."

He stared out at the enemy's firing line as the Strema host ordered itself for an assault across the flood plain. A small part of him thought of the honor that would fall to him should they end the Jema here today, and manage to get word back to the Kaerin of the threat that this world posed. He pushed the thought back down. All that mattered was preventing the Jema from leading the Shareki back to Chandra.

"Bastelta Toruda?"

"War Leader?" It took a second before he realized that Toruda was addressing him with that title. Toruda and his team of scouts, twenty of the ablest warriors the Strema possessed, stood nearby. They were all chosen men, and Toruda himself stood within arm's reach, no doubt anxious to be given the honor of leading the charge.

He handed over a sealed leather satchel containing the records of their invasion, detailed maps, and fantastic drawings and accounts of the Shareki weaponry.

Toruda's face fell.

"You know what this is?" Bsrat asked. "Bres Auch-Tun spoke to you of it, yes?"

Toruda glanced down at the oiled leather satchel in his hands. "He did, War Leader."

"Take your chosen and leave this battlefield now. Strike northwest for two days, before swinging back to the south. Take yourself to the sea and find the gate. No matter what occurs here today, this message must get back to the Kaerin. Our honor lives with this packet. I ask you to do this, others I would order."

Toruda glanced out at the battlefield. "I am honored that you ask. I will see this done. I will also tell them that the Jema died here today."

"Go." Bsrat slapped the man on the shoulder. He would not dishonor him, by thanking him. "Avoid the Shareki at all costs, get home."

Toruda nodded sharply once and barked an order at his men, who fell immediately on the dropped packs of nearby Strema warriors.

Bsrat took a moment to observe what was now his host to lead. They outnumbered the Jema, but he knew a great many of his host would fall here today no matter the outcome. The Kaerin had scourged the Jema for a reason, they refused to bend knee and had almost won those many years ago before he had been born. For a short moment he wondered what his life would have been like had the Jema's revolt succeeded.

*

Audy stood at the top of the earthworks looking down at the meadow and at the backs of the heads of the Jema First Fist. From his vantage he could see the narrow field trench they had dug the previous day about a third of the way across the meadow. Its fill had been carefully carried back to the main breastworks, the enemy couldn't see it. The Jema's First Fist marched in line across the meadow toward the enemy, stepping across the unseen trench until they came to a stop just beyond it.

He turned to look back at Jomra whose attention was focused entirely on his compad, monitoring the Strema who were climbing through the sparse pine on the hillside to reach the bluffs. Audy saw Jomra nod to himself. His lifelong friend looked up to see him watching and flashed him a thumbs up.

Audy turned back towards the meadow where the front ranks of Strema were moving out towards them in neatly ordered blocks of men, each a thousand men strong. The dreaded Strema block; a hundred warriors wide standing shoulder to shoulder, ten lines deep. He saw no reason to wait for more blocks to form up.

"First Fist," he screamed. "Fire!"

The front rank of Jema kneeled, the back two rows formed a solid line behind them. The heavy long rifles fired in a ripping burst, their targets almost five hundred meters away, mostly still within the forest. Nevertheless, the leading edges of the Strema formations were staggered as hundreds fell. Six seconds later, the Jema second rank fired. Audy recognized the deadly rhythm of Jema battle fire; fire, break the breach, eject the smoking cartridge, insert a fresh round, close the breech, fire again. The Jema firing line was renowned across Chandra for its deadly calm. The three ranks of the Jema First Fist, stretching across the width of the battlefield poured a steady stream of fire into an approaching enemy that they could not stop.

The Kaerin's hand in the development of Chandrian technology, the strict enforcement of battle tactics that guaranteed mass casualties. It was all by design, Kaerin design. On Chandra, no single clan, or even alliance of clans could bring enough firepower to bear to overcome the numbers the Kaerin could muster with nothing more than a promise of a power over a neighbor, or a year without taxes, or simply a promise of continued Kaerin favor and goodwill. This was the last time the Jema would use such tactics. They'd learned well at the hands of their Terran allies, and it cut to his very soul that they were ignoring those lessons now.

By the eighth salvo, the Strema were pouring out of the woods, falling into staggered blocks that took up the width of the meadow, with more still forming within the woods. The Strema had replaced the front two formations that had almost ceased to exist. The Jema line against the Strema block, one last time. Today, Jema and Strema alike, recognized the Jema line, for all its courage, was too thin. The Strema began marching, firing as they came. The front rank would step out in front of the enemy's block formation, kneel and fire, before being passed and swallowed up by the advancing formation. The new front line would repeat the process. In terms of frontage, it didn't bring as many rifles to bear at once, as the Jema lines, but there were a lot of the Strema columns and they had a depth to them that could absorb and ultimately overwhelm the Jema firepower. By the time the third Strema salvo was fired, large gaps were showing in the Jema First's front line.

Audy's heart vacillated between pride and anger at what was being sacrificed. All the while, wishing he was standing among those Jema in the First Fist. The names of those in the field standing before the Strema, giving everything, their futures, would live forever.

Bsrat watched in satisfaction. The Jema fire was as deadly as ever, but they were far too few. Soon, very soon, the enemy would be taking Strema fire from the bluffs as well. He glanced up to his right, only the trailing end of the three Fists worth of men he had ordered up the bluffs were still visible. The rest had gained the top and were already approaching the edges overlooking the battlefield.

Strange that the Jema had not invested the bluffs, but it explained in his mind what had indeed happened. They had caught the Jema unready, without their Shareki allies. They flew the black, they expected to die here.

There were now less than three hundred strides separating the two lines in the middle of the field. The Jema front rank had been savaged, perhaps half of them remained standing. He wondered how many more they had hidden behind their breastworks. The forward most Fists of the Strema had been nearly destroyed, but there were fresh Fists taking up their place as they stepped over their fallen. There was no sense in waiting for the Shareki to reappear.

"To swords, signal the charge, all Fists!" Bsrat looked to his left and to his right. Three Fists not yet committed would cross the battlefield with him. "Gemendi are to open fire!"

Audy saw the large puffs of smoke from the forest's edge. "Trenches!! Now!" he yelled. Most Jema officers and Tearks had the commo pieces in their ears. But orders could only be repeated so fast.

The Strema artillery rounds were much faster. In the back of Audy's mind, he knew the Terrans would have classified them as heavy battlefield mortars. He could almost see their arc onto the battlefield. They fell near the midpoint between the two lines, their massive explosions spraying shrapnel in a circular pattern, hitting both sides with a vicious impunity. Three gaps appeared in the Jema lines where no one was left standing and the Strema blocks opposite those gaps looked as if large bites had been taken out of the mass of warriors.

The remaining Jema of their First Fist, perhaps less than half of the original five thousand that had stood out there in the beginning, having finally gotten his order, retreated a few steps and dropped into their field trench where their Shareki assault rifles awaited them.

The counter-arty, manned by the Terrans left behind by Colonel Pretty, came from three miles behind the Jema lines. The rounds split the air with a heavy tearing sound. The entire front edge of the opposing forest erupted as twelve, *One O Fives* dropped rounds on their pre-targeted grid. Audy knew the 105mm was not a big gun as far as Terran militaries counted them, but the effect of the precision fire was like nothing he had ever seen. A second salvo of friendly artillery savaged the Strema blocks of men at the far edge of the battlefield, most still picking themselves up after the edge of the forest behind them had been reduced to naked spars of scarred wood.

Bsrat slowly came to his feet covered in mud and blood spray from the nearest explosion. The Shareki are here, he thought. It would be one thing in the end. He could not have called back his host had he wanted. The Strema host was committed. Something moving on the bluff, caught his eye. For a moment his mind didn't register what he was seeing as the hillside itself changed shape. Along its front edge massive geysers of dirt and rock shot skyward. A moment later the sound and shockwave hit him as the bluff seemed to double in height along its entire length.

His fury was paired with his pride. "Unfurl the black, blow the horns." He screamed, and screamed again until the order was acknowledged.

His signalmen reacted quickly. A large black flag, a white snake on either side went up on a standard pole near him. Half a minute later someone found the battle horn and its deep resonance worked its way across the battlefield as all the firing ceased. It was but a moment later the Jema's own horn sounded its reply, followed by more gunfire than he imagined was possible. The Jema had Shareki weapons, yet they had them. They had stood there and died, to lure him in.

There were no more orders to give. He drew his blade and started forward amidst the twenty some odd thousand remaining Strema.

Shouts from his left flank caused him to look towards the river. He noted, with a detached fatalism, that his left flank was swinging toward the river to meet the Shareki who were arriving by their powered boats. The amount of fire chewing into his men from the river was surpassed by that issuing from the breastworks where the enemy had at least three of those horrible big guns that fired almost as fast as the Shareki personal rifles. The big ones would often pierce four or five bodies at a time when they hit a tight formation. The horrendous fire poured directly into his host that died by the hundreds with every step it took.

Screaming defiance, his gun forgotten, he began running towards the enemy lines. Their only chance was to overwhelm the Jema and their Shareki weapons before he ran out of men.

Audy dropped back into the trench as their heavy weapons opened up. He dropped his breechloader and picked up his heretofore hidden assault rifle. The massed fire from their emplaced 25 mm chain guns, and from the single half-buried APC that carried the same deadly gun on its turret, merged with the automatic rifle fire from every Jema. The top of the entire earthworks fired over the heads of the remaining Jema in the field trench directly into the advancing wall of Strema.

The front line of the Strema seemed to shimmer red before it wavered and started to disintegrate. But the Strema had almost reached the hidden field trench full of wounded and dying Jema who all had their weapons up firing directly into a growing wall of bodies less than thirty paces away.

The entire Jema clan reacted as one, without orders. He knew Jomra would not try and stop them. He couldn't have if he had tried. The Jema poured over the lip of the breastworks, firing as they surged forward. Their targets would crest over the growing pile of Strema bodies in waves, only to be blown back, adding to the wall of dead.

Audy slammed another magazine into his rifle, un-clipped the holster lock on his gifted "forty-five" and joined the swarm of men rushing to meet one another in the killing ground. They'd be at swords soon. He welcomed the thought, even as he heard the heavy fire still pouring into the Strema flank from the river.

Mortars firing from the boats loitering off shore landed amidst the tightly packed Strema towards the rear of their formations even as the water borne M-60s on the Riverines continued to flay those that turned to meet the threat coming from the water's edge.

Kyle wanted to scream at what he was seeing. The Jema were giving up their superior position to close with the dying Strema host. Audy had warned him this would happen; Jomra had tried in his own way to explain to him why it *had* to happen. Different worlds, different values. He knew he would never understand the Jema's need to pay such a heavy price for a victory that had been assured the moment the Strema began their charge.

He did understand that it was price he would need to pay as well.

"Land all boats!"

He cursed Jema honor, most of the Jema piloted craft were already shorebound by the time his order had been passed. His own skipper, a Jema warrior, threw her throttle to the stops, tied off the wheel, and started firing inland over the plexiglass windbreak. Seconds later the unmistakable sound of props screaming out of the water met his ears as the smaller boats were simply driven aground.

His own boat hit something at the water's edge, Kyle registered it for a split second as probably a sunken log or large rock, but it was completely forgotten when they ran up the bank almost on edge. They were all thrown forward in a pile against whatever happened to be in front of them. In his case it was an unlucky ribcage of someone and he heard the snap of a bone against the side of his head. Adrenaline accomplished the impossible and the pile of limbs fairly exploded apart as the soldiers pushed off and flung themselves over the side of the boat accompanied by some very imaginative cursing in several languages. Kyle found himself, how he wasn't certain, lying in muddy grass, pointed in the general direction of the Strema.

He was servicing targets that were sprinting towards them, most with swords in hand before he realized what he was doing. Thankfully one of the machine guns started working again on one of the grounded boats, or they might have been overrun. They were still too few to coordinate any fire as most were still unloading themselves from the boats.

"Get down!" he screamed at those around him. They needed to let the gunships still loitering out in the water to create a beachhead amidst their already landed boats. One of the small craft, somebody's donated bass boat, exploded in a fireball off to his right.

To his left he caught sight of Jake tackling a Jema warrior. He looked up as best he could, aware of the mass of lead passing by mere feet above their heads. He watched, sickened as a squad of seven or eight Jema on the far-right end of his line, those closest to the Strema rear, stood and charged into the Strema. They cast aside their assault rifles and drew blades. Kyle wanted to scream at them to stop, but could see in an instant what they were doing. A large group of Strema, ready to overwhelm them, changed direction and flowed toward that small vulnerable pocket of Jema steel that dared to challenge them.

It all happened within a handful of seconds, but it wasn't wasted. The machine guns and auto cannons from the river ceased firing. His command stood and charged forward as one, firing as they went. They made it thirty yards inland where a small flood channel gave them an opportunity for cover. This channel, boot sucking mud at their feet, had been their objective. They went prone in the mud, somewhat protected and started firing again into the flanks of the enemy. His mortar teams started dropping shells well past their position into the packed mass of Strema. Out of their line of fire the gun boats opened up again with horrific effectiveness.

He felt bile rising in his throat, the slaughter was something he had told himself he could get past. He focused on what a victory here meant for the Jema, and on the genocide that had been carried out against them at the hands of the Strema. They fired until they stopped the last wave coming toward them.

The Strema, those remaining, were focused at the middle of the battlefield under the two black flags in a furball of steel on steel and the occasional rifle shot.

"Advance, stay in your groups! Gunboats cease fire, I say again, gunboats cease fire."

The last was a meaningless order. The Strema may have been perfectly willing to fire into their own troops. His gunners on the boats were not. Besides, the blood bath occurring under the two flags had no lines. Just two peoples with a hatred so deep it defied words.

Kyle and Jake lost complete control of the Jema under their command, as they ran forward into the rearmost of the surviving Strema. The ancient foes would pair off one on one, the victor would turn to fight another. The Jema knew they had already won, and they fought like it. The Strema, were defeated, knew it and wanted nothing more than to take a Jema with them.

Kyle limped over to Jake and realized for the first time the pain in his knee. Probably the graceful boat landing, he thought.

They watched in shock as the Strema were pinched off into smaller and smaller groups, surrounded by Jema blades. Kyle and Jake skirted the fight in unspoken agreement. Their help at this point would not have been appreciated, they'd be interlopers in something ancient. There were no runners, no deserters. Wounded Jema and Strema alike were out there on the battlefield right now, crawling towards the rapidly shrinking bloodbath.

"War should always be like this." He heard himself say it before he realized he had spoken.

He looked over at Jake to explain himself. But Jake was nodding in agreement.

"This will end it. It'll be over."

The maelstrom of violence continued only a few more minutes until an ear shattering yell went up from the all the Jema. The swords were all held skyward ready to strike. There were no more Strema.

Except one. The solitary Strema, wounded, stood as upright as he could. The pole carrying the Strema banner was holding most of his weight.

Jomra emerged from the front ranks of where the melee had occurred. He was covered in blood and gore and clearly had been wounded himself. He limped out to where the single Strema warrior stood and waited expectantly without a word.

The Strema bowed once, as best he could and then struggled to drop his flag pole and use it as a spear directed at Jomra.

Jomra caught the pole, yanked it from the Strema's grasp and let it fall behind him in the churned mud at his feet. Without warning, the Jema's leader, their new ally and their friend, took one step forward and thrust his sword up under the rib cage of the Strema and screamed in defiance as the blade broke through and punched out the man's back. He didn't gloat, he didn't pose. Jomra threw the body aside, pulled his blade and thrust it skyward.

Another shout went up from the Jema, this one lasted as long as long as their breath held. Kyle and Jake, Jema and Terran alike screamed in release. Screamed at the horror of what they had done, at the vengeance gained, at the freedom won.

Kyle noted the bodies. Tens of thousands of them, and he realized the horrible price the Jema had just paid. Blood to cleanse the past, purchase a future.

*

Chapter 26

Late September, New Seattle

"There's been no contact, Sir." Franklin Dawkins' response to his question held a tone of inevitability, resignation even. Richard Kiley didn't care for either.

"None? How about Colonel Pretty, Dr. Jensen, or that so-called whiz kid they had running the economy into the shitter?"

"Nothing on the Colonel since we received word two weeks ago that he had linked up with Lassiter and beaten what was left of the Koryna."

"Killed, you mean," Richard Kiley turned on Dawkins. He'd leave no room for doubt with anyone, where exactly Kyle Lassiter stood on his shit list. Kiley had thought of himself as a leader, and he had advised politicians his entire adult life. He knew he'd lost an opportunity to sway Lassiter to his side in that bar more than a year earlier. He'd realized it for the mistake it had been, once he'd learned of how far up the food chain the former soldier was. In his defense, he'd been playing to a different audience at the time and he'd said things he wished he could have taken back.

Any opportunity to recruit someone as capable as Lassiter shouldn't have been thrown away to sway a few scared colonists. It had been a different time. He couldn't take it back, nor could he reverse the course he'd been committed to for the last year. To do either would be seen as weakness. His goal had been the destruction of the Program or as it turned out, the subjugation of the same Program to his will. The latter he'd brought about, the former forgotten. But he'd made enemies along the way, including Kyle Lassiter and the men he commanded. The militia was now an opposing base of power he'd either have to destroy or bring under his civilian control. It was time people knew the degree of danger the militia represented. That had to start with his own people.

"I don't think what they did could be construed as beaten. It was murder on a grand scale. Carried out with no input from the civilian authorities."

Dawkins didn't seem swayed. "I'm not sure that opinion has much support Sir, if you'll excuse me saying so."

"We'll change that," he waved away the comment. "Dawkins, you can always speak your mind around me. We are going to be completely transparent to everyone and that policy starts with me."

Dawkins was a recent arrival as well. A former college professor of Antiquities who had always considered himself a strict constitutionalist. His wife had run off to make a life with someone else in the wilderness somewhere down in the Sierra Nevadas. Kiley figured that had a lot to do with Dawkins' fervent desire to put the Program's significant technical and industrial sector to work building a facility to send them back home.

Kiley wasn't about to let that happen. He had a real shot at building something here, and he needed an organizer of Dawkins' capability. The man had been easy to sway. He heard what he wanted to hear.

"What about Jensen? The rest of the Program staff?"

"It's what I've been trying to get across to you since last night. I almost put it in an e-mail, but I know you think the Program still has admin privileges, so I've been waiting." Dawkins was frustrated, they all were. He was enough of a realist to know this wasn't going to be easy.

"Your EA wouldn't let me in the building," Dawkins whined. His chief advisor almost stomped a foot in protest. *Might need someone with a little more backbone.* He could wait, soon everyone would want to work for him. He'd could have his pick of talent then.

Kiley stopped him walking and slowly turned to face him. "We've got security concerns as I'm sure you can understand. Ms. Serrano was just doing her job. We seal this place up tight every evening. It's probably the safest building on the planet."

"I realize that, Sir, I do, but..."

"Speak man, I need your counsel."

"Sir, no one outside your council has seen you in two weeks. It doesn't look good to those on the outside looking in."

"It doesn't, does it? Well they weren't the one threatened!... By that, ... psychopathic goon."

Dawkins looked at him like he wanted to say more, but he didn't. He'd always been able to make people see his way, back down when he had to.

"So, what was so important?"

"Dr. Jensen, Dr. Morales, and his wife are gone. Jensen sent an email to some friends yesterday from a fishing boat out of Yachats Bay. We've managed to get his e-mail account mirrored."

"So, the man went fishing, and Morales? Not like we weren't going to put him and his wife out to pasture anyway. They've screwed the economy enough as it is. But I'll use that, Dawkins. I'll let the people know the mess they've left me to clean up."

"Sir, my people went out to check on the nano-plant. It's empty, no one is there. Jensen's entire staff is just gone and, ... and the production center has gone cold."

"Good riddance, I say. Turn the shit back on."

"Sir, the master computers are shut down, and we don't have the passwords to re-initialize the system."

He glared at Dawkins for a moment. Could Dawkins not tell he wanted solutions, not problems? And make no mistake, lack of access to the computers that controlled the nano-production was a problem. He knew his team had to see him as a man of action. "Is everyone meeting us here? I'd say that news just got bumped up to item one on today's docket."

He pushed through the double doors. *Who are all these people?*

He was confused for just a moment until he recognized Col. Pretty, standing behind Paul Stephens' wheelchair. Both Doctor Abrahams, mother and daughter flanked Stephens. He took that in, in the split second before he realized Lassiter was standing next to Elisabeth Abraham. He'd spent enough time worrying about the man that he recognized him instantly. His spine suddenly felt like it wanted to be anywhere but in his body. He wouldn't let it show. He noted his own council was still here as well.

"A little late, but welcome nonetheless." He managed to say.

It was quiet in the room, quiet enough that Paul Stephens' labored speech could be heard.

"When you build something costing upwards of a trillion dollars over two decades ... and you have a Chief of Security like Sir Geoffrey," Stephens applied his oxygen mask and took a deep breath as the room waited. "You put in a few back doors that no one knows about."

"Apparently," he managed in response. "What would you like me to say?! My grievances and those of my supporters aren't legitimate? That my duly elected position as the Program Chair doesn't hold weight now that you are here? ... and that I'm likely..." He paused and looked directly at Kyle Lassiter whose blue–gray eyes reminded him of a wolf. "To be handed over to the Jema."

Lassiter threw back his head and laughed. "Oh, there's a large part of me, and the ten thousand veterans surrounding the city as we speak, that think that would be a grand idea." Lassiter was pointing out the window but turned back to look at him. "But, I was outvoted."

"I see," he managed. "Did you conduct this vote yourselves? or did you allow my council to vote?"

Lassiter shook his head slowly at him. "No, in the end, it was the only kind of vote that really matters. The consent of the governed. No one here has the slightest problem with you walking these halls pretending you're in charge of something that doesn't exist. The rest of us are simply leaving, to places that grow their own food, produce their own goods, to live without the weight of a government that no one needs or wants. You Sir, are in charge."

"I see." He knew where this was headed. "And the production facility?"

"Mothballed, until needed." Col. Pretty answered him, but he couldn't help but look at the evil grin on Lassiter's face.

"Incidentally," Pretty continued, "several hundred Jema count themselves as fishermen, or at least they'd like to be as I understand it. They were quite taken with Whidbey and the surrounding islands. Good neighbors I'd say. I wouldn't think you'll be able to buy them off."

"But you should try," Jake Bullock grinned. "It might work, never know unless you try."

"You would starve us?" he managed.

"Not at all," Lassiter piped in. "You've never had more than five or six thousand hard core supporters. Assuming you can convince them all to stick it out with you, you probably have an entire year's worth of supplies already laid in."

"Closer to two." Jason Morales spoke up.

"Two years' then," Lassiter smiled. "Sounds like plenty of time to get done what you need to get done."

"You're all mad."

Lassiter took two steps towards him, and he was immediately ashamed at how he recoiled.

"No, we believe in liberty. Call yourself President, Shah, High Grand Moose, I don't give a shit. But something you should think about," Lassiter grinned and paused, "well, two things actually. The first was pointed out to me by Doctor Morales. Say your people actually get their shit together and start working, learn a skill. Something they are going to have to do, if they are going to survive. If they do that, there's two hundred plus other settlements out there that will welcome them with open arms no strings attached. Why would they stay here under some government that just lives off their fat? Something to think about as you do whatever the hell it is that you think needs doing."

"Tell him the other thing," Jake blurted out, "he should know."

Lassiter smiled again.

"I wasn't bullshitting that we put this to a vote among the soldiers that have just protected this planet, knowing full well they'll likely have to do it again. The Jema voted as well. All twelve thousand plus of their survivors that we had with us. After losing nearly five thousand dead in a single day, we all felt they had earned the right. They weren't too happy when we asked them what we should do with you and your so-called Emergency Council. To a person, they thought you should be dealt with."

"I think scourged, is how they referred to it." Jake offered helpfully.

"Our own troops outnumbered the Jema almost two to one," Lassiter continued after letting Jake's comment sink in. "The motion to leave you in charge of nothing, won the day."

"By forty-one votes," Jake added with a snort of laughter.

Lassiter stepped closer to him.

"Don't think for a moment that we wouldn't have carried out the other motion had it passed. That is what consent of the governed means Mr. Kiley. With our level of technology, no one needs a government, at least in the traditional sense that creates a class of politicians who in the end just live off of others. We used to have a nation, and we let power hungry assholes like you steal it. Now we have a planet. This time we'll keep it."

*

Smoky Mountains, Tennessee - Earth 1.0

"Alright, what gives?" Brittany disappeared from her face in an instant and Captain Souza reappeared before him in visage, intensity, and mannerism the moment her children were out of ear shot. One second, she was a doting mother kissing the tops of her children's heads and shooing them off the wood deck, back into the mountain cabin. The next, Sir Geoff had a flash of concern that this was the moment the Special Forces Captain would use the silenced .22 she carried, the one she affectionately referred to as her "*Hush Puppy,*" to put a round in his ear.

This is a remarkable woman, he thought. She was cold, calculating and most of all professionally detached from emotion to a degree that only another operator could appreciate. Now though, there was a fringe of anger or frustration in her mien. He imagined that having the safety and lives of her children thrust into her professional decision-making loop had a lot to do with that.

"I'm sorry?" he managed. He was stalling for time, hoping to get a few more cognitive cycles in. He could see the flash of annoyance in her eyes, she saw right through him. Perhaps she had done so from the beginning.

"Sir Geoff," her head canted to one shoulder peering at him, "give me some credit here. I know my team. You said something to convince Denise not to turn your ass in. Which I appreciate, because I'm pretty certain it would have been the end of us. What was it? You spin a fairy tale? Or did you come clean?"

He could see that lying to this woman, right now, would not end well.

"I asked her to trust me."

She just held his eyes for a moment, looking for some indication of falsehood. In her stare, he could almost feel the phantom muzzle of the *hush-puppy* pressed against his forehead. She broke her gaze and turned to look back through the sliding glass door off the deck of the mountain hideaway, their interim stop on wherever TF Chrome and their voluntary prisoner would go next.

Her husband and both the Mills were hunched over a pile of maps on the kitchen table. Denise Mills had her laptop up, hacking into DOD systems trying to ascertain whether anyone was on their trail. The Bowdens were both out trying to procure them transportation.

Captain Souza turned back to him, her voice dropping an octave, sounding a little more like Brittany.

"We've trusted you, we've protected you, are protecting you now. I'm asking you to trust us, fully. This isn't some put-up crisis to get you to come clean. Which I'm sure has crossed your Byzantine mind. Geoff, my children don't know where they are going to sleep tomorrow night. They think this is some cool adventure. I'm less amused."

"I can sense that."

"I'm dropping the 'Sir' bullshit, Geoff. My kids look at you like the grandparent that they've never had. Like it or not, and sometimes, I don't – you are part of this family. So please, with sugar on top, if you have some place for us to go where my kids don't have to live out of duffel bags, tell me now. And before you answer, as much as we all like you, you screw with me here, you will become *another* grandparent my kids never knew. Their young, they'll get over it."

"Idaho." He'd decided earlier that he would be coming clean, but he so enjoyed his professional conversations with this woman, and as she said, he had to be certain he wasn't being played.

"Idaho? Your program has a facility there? Off the grid? Because if it's at all associated with any of your missing flock, it will be watched."

"Not a facility, so to speak." He scratched his head, he was the last person in the world to try and explain the quantum linkage that the portal technology was based on.

"The first time we sent a manned exploration to Eden, we had to have a portal there to get them back. Think of a round trip flight. Your originating flight has to have an airport at the destination, a place to land, refuel, and take off from again."

"Ok, I get that. How could you have had that? If it was the first trip?"

"That was the nut of the problem. What we sent, with a team inside it, was another portal with a self-contained nuclear reactor to power it. The same type as used to power a nuclear submarine. It became the first portal site on Eden until we could build a permanent station. Once we were up and running, that self-contained unit, about the size of two large shipping containers, was sent back here and mothballed for contingency purposes."

"In Idaho?"

"In Idaho."

"Can you run the thing?"

"Heavens no. I wouldn't step into the thing if I had anything to do with it."

"So, how does that help us?"

"I think if we can power it up, and by we, I mean Denise. I think it should establish a link or a carrier signal, whatever it's called, my colleagues on Eden might see it. They can come and assist. If, and it's a big if, they don't think it's the government that found the unit."

She shook her head at him. "So, it's a long shot. Belize is another option."

"They'll find you here, anywhere here, eventually. You know that. An alternate universe, is a long shot by definition. But your children would be safe on Eden."

"If we can make it across the country, while it melts down into civil war."

"There is that," he agreed.

She glanced back inside for a moment before turning back to him. She sighed heavily with her hands on her hips. "Ok... it's a shot. You've almost made me happy we didn't bury grandpa in the backyard.

He smiled and bowed his head. This woman could have been his daughter. Granddaughter he corrected himself, she thought just like he did.

"Rest assured, Grandpa shares the sentiment."
*

North East Oregon - Eden

"OK, let it down slowly..." Kyle half shouted from his end of the log. Chains, tackle hanging from jury-rigged tripods clicked and groaned as Audy and Jake played out their rope and the log dropped into place. They were up to the fifth log level and Kyle no longer had to bend over to inspect the cut outs he was making with the chainsaw. His cabin was coming along nicely. With some luck, they'd be able to start on the roof by tomorrow. He had a pile of metal sheeting waiting back in town for that.

He and Jake shared a look of disdain as they all heard Jake's compad beeping. Kyle had 'accidently' left his in the air car parked uphill fifty yards. For just a moment, he felt his heart kick into high gear and his blood pressure rise. He forced himself to remember the war, the fighting was over, for

378

now. It was getting easier for him, but not enough time had passed to push it into long-term memory. He was still feeling it, like an extra layer of clothing in warm weather that he couldn't shed.

After the 'Battle of the River', transport had come and the Jema had linked up with Pretty's force to prosecute the end of the war on the surviving Koryna. That host's end hadn't come in a single fight. The enemy had splintered into three different groups and each one had to be hunted down and destroyed in turn.

After helping their Terran allies finish off the Koryna, the Jema had split up themselves. Forced to live together as a host their entire lives, Audy explained that they were all a little tired of living in a communal camp. In the old days, he had explained, Clan identity was really only important during warfare with other groups. In times of peace, a time of distant memory before the Kaerin, they lived apart in several settlements, even a city or two. With their freedom won and assured, they selected more than a dozen different sites to live in. Some alongside Terrans, others in new settlements they established. One group was waiting for a ship to take them to what had been Northern Germany or the Baltic coast on a different planet. They'd now seen maps of the world for the first times in their lives and the legends described and passed down by Sri-Tel seemed to indicate that was where the Jema had originated.

Audy and Kemi were living with about 300 other Jema twenty miles away at the end of what Kyle thought of as *his* valley. At night he could see their camp fires. Chief Joseph was booming and was just over the mountains behind him. Elisabeth, now two months pregnant, was living with his parents until the cabin was finished.

He watched as Jake scrolled through the message a smile breaking out on his face. "Well, it's official," he said. "Richard Kiley was forced to step down in Seattle. His people are asking to be let back in to our "joint human community." Jake held one hand up giving air quotes.

"I guess this means you and the Program people can go back to work in Seattle," Jake continued. "You're no longer a fugitive from the long arm of the law."

"Gee," Kyle smiled. "I was really starting to worry about that."

"Yeah, I could tell, you've been bleeding concern this last month.

"He has not been concerned," Audy added, failing as usual to pick up on the irony.

Jake rolled his eyes. "Thasss what I'm sayin."

Jake looked around the interior of the half-finished walls and dropped his compad with a decided lack concern onto a pile of tarps.

"If you two are done yapping, our next log is waiting," Kyle threw his handful of rope at Jake. "I know you'd rather talk than work."

Jake let the coil of rope hit him in the chest without making any effort to catch it. He held up a hand and walked to the middle of the cabin. A single wall separated the structure into two halves with a wide doorway cut into it.

"Speaking of which, I know this isn't the final, built out floor plan so to speak, but where's my room going to be?"

"About six miles that way." Kyle couldn't help but laugh, as he pointed over the mountains towards Chief Joseph.

"That's not gonna work for me," Jake shook his head. "It's no way to treat family."

Audy burst out laughing, slapping his leg, braying like a donkey. Jake just winked at him. Kyle looked back and forth between them. Audy looked like he was about to pop a seal. It hadn't been that funny.

Kyle had a sinking feeling as Jake joined in and started to laugh. He felt the blood rise in his face. All the pieces started filling in.

"Nooo..." It was all he could think of to say.

Jake pointed at him and he started laughing so hard he was almost crying. "I'll bet you feel like you've just been kicked in the stones."

"You're the brother?... Elisabeth's brother?"

"Just a stepbrother," Jake was grinning from ear to ear. "My dad, the original bayou swamp fox, and Doc Abraham senior were married for about ten years after Ellie's dad died. She was teaching at LSU, he collected gators and swamp samples for the science department – who knew? It didn't last, but your bride-to-be and I pretty much grew up together."

"I don't believe it."

Jake smiled and pointed at him, "Yes, you do. Relax, we don't share any DNA."

"I guess that's something." Kyle managed to suck in a deep breath when he noticed Audy grinning.

"You knew?"

"Was obvious," Audy clapped his hands together once. "It came to me, so I asked Jake. I was sworn to secrecy. We Jema like a good joke," Audy laughed, "and this one was very good."

"Holy shit." He blew out a breath, "Doc Abraham and *your* Dad?"

Jake just winked at him. "The Ol' dog had it going on."

"I can't get my head around ..."

"I'll just bet you can't," Jake answered walking over to the next log and affixing the choker cable. "One of these days over a beer, I'll tell you a story about two good looking kids, living under the same roof, hitting puberty at the same time and not being related. I mean, not really."

"Oh, Dear God, no..."

"Oh, yeah." Jake nodded, "Sis was a bonified hotty."

"Stop talking, Jake."

"Ok, Ok, I get it. Too soon and all," Jake stood and walked to the end of the log, "But seriously, where's my room?"

*

Planet Chandra
Private Estate of the Kaerin Prelate

Noka S'kaeda leaned forward with his knuckles on the marble table of his personal study and stared down at the hand sketches of the miraculous machines and weaponry the Strema had encountered in the hands of the planet's Shareki.

Six Strema scouts were all that had survived from the failed invasion. The Strema survivors had managed to bring back their War Leader's reports, along with these sketches of devices that sent a cold chill down his back.

He'd read the reports earlier. Read them before, after, and during, especially during the questioning of the returned scouts. That, he had seen to personally. The news they returned with, as well as the details and thoughts they had given up to him under the influence of the heart speak and his own blades, held danger for the Kaerin. It was a strange sensation; fear. These Shareki were advanced, perhaps as advanced as the world that had abandoned his people here centuries past.

The aircraft and weapons were of a type he was not familiar with, but he was very much aware of what they were in terms of function and capacity. The Kaerin had possessed much the same when they'd first been marooned on Chandra a millennium ago. His ancestors had been soldiers, all of them, sadly. Not a scientist or engineer among them, and it had taken less than a generation for most of their equipment to wear out.

For all he knew, these advanced Shareki could be the descendants of the people of Kaerus, cousins of a sort. His people had always been conquerors, perhaps they had conquered the worlds in a line, and were now almost here. But that, he knew, was wishful hubris. The Strema scouts had reported that the small numbers of Shareki that had been captured before falling under their blades had spoken a language entirely alien to the Gemendi priests.

"No, these are Shareki." He said, thinking out loud.

"You're certain, Prelate?" Gasto Bre'jana, his trusted colleague, perhaps the only one on the council he would name such, had wondered if the Shareki could be from Kaerus as well.

"No," he admitted. There wasn't enough information to be certain. "Yet, there is no evidence to suggest that they are of our blood, no matter the separation of years."

He looked up at his friend. "Am I missing something?"

"I've known you to be wrong from time to time, Noka. I've never known you to miss details, or evidence."

"Your confidence in me notwithstanding, I'm basing my theory solely on the reports of their tongue."

"Unrecognizable, without commonalities." Gasto nodded in agreement, quoting the report. Strema were slaves, but they were well-trained and obedient. Their war leader, Bres Auch-Tun had kept immaculate records. His friend took a sip of the wine grown a few miles away on this estate.

"It was known," Gasto continued, "all of Kaerus spoke one tongue, and had for many centuries by the time of our ancestor's ill-fated travel here. I too, doubt the language of our people could have altered so much as to be unrecognizable."

"I'm of the same mind, and assuming we're not both wrong," he took a sip himself, "it would signify these are indeed Shareki, and if the Strema slaves are to be believed, they are not indigenous, but a colony from the next world beyond. An advanced world to be sure, certainly their arts of war are beyond ours at the moment."

"There is the reserve." Gasto, said after a moment. "We've always kept it safe."

He nodded in agreement. "Yes, but we've always preserved it to insure our survival here. Sooner or later, we'll need it here, against the clans."

Gasto nodded in what was probably acceptance of the argument, not agreement. "I was thinking of the Jema. These Shareki now have allies of this world. Why would they wait for us to come again, to fight them on their own ground?"

Noka tapped his own chest and then pointed at his friend. "You, me would think that. Any Kaerin would think that. The Jema, their hate for us notwithstanding, would think that of us. They'd so advise these Shareki. They'd expect us to attack."

"Should we not?"

He gifted his friend with a nod of respect. But he was pleased to have taken something else from the analysis of the reports. Something that had escaped his friend. Then again, he had recognized the pattern during his interrogation of the

Strema scouts, and Gasto had not been present for that, by design.

"The reports, Gasto... these Shareki are aggressive only on the defensive, and quite ably at that. But they do not attempt to strike head on. They led the Strema time and time again to a location they controlled, and only then did they unleash their might."

"What of their numbers?" Gasto threw back at him. "The Strema weren't idiots... well, Bres Auch-Tun was not, at any rate. He believed them to be very few and if true, such a strategy on their part makes sense."

"It does, but perhaps they are marooned as our forefathers were. I wonder, why did the might of their home world not come into play? Eh?"

Gasto looked at him as if he had just realized why he led the council. "You're right, I did not think of their home world. You suggest we use their strategy against them? We don't attack, and walk into the killing land the Strema described. We do the same to them here?"

"Yes, Gasto." He nodded solemnly. "We prepare a similar welcome for them here. They'll be vigilant waiting for us. We'll let them grow impatient. Remember, they'll have the Jema pushing them. Let them come, we'll return the favor. I will need your support to release the reserve weapons when the time arrives.

"You'll have it, you know that, but why wait? There are some among the Gemendi who have long called for releasing the ancient weapons for study. They believe we have progressed in knowledge enough to warrant the risk to the equipment. If we could produce a fraction of what our ancestors held in their arms upon the battlefield...?"

"You speak of Tima?" Gasto's eldest son was high up in the Gemendi priesthood. A veritable wizard with gadgetry. Gasto was doubling down on his support of the plan to risk his own son in such a way.

"Among others," Gasto affirmed. "But yes, he's long believed we are ready to crack the mysteries of our elders. I've

384

never agreed myself, as you know. The need for such a drastic measure was not... what it may be presently."

"I'll see what I can do." He said after a moment of thought. He'd have to get Tima promoted. He could do that, or rather someone else who owed him a favor could. Let the young man see what could be discerned from the weapons of their forefathers. There was no need to tie himself to this plan until it worked. The Kaerin did not suffer failure.

***

I hope you've enjoyed this story. There is much more to come...

Your review on Amazon and Goodreads, or even sky writing would be very much appreciated if you are so inclined. Sky writing would be cool. If you enjoyed the story, please tell your friends, family, colleagues, and the strange guy that restocks the vending machine at your favorite gun-range... I've learned from a lot of readers, that word of mouth is still alive and well in our age of electronic media. We should all be thankful for that.

As always, you can sign up for my newsletter on my website, www.smanderson-author.com or follow me on Goodreads. I believe, I've remained true to my promise of answering all the e-mail. I very much enjoy corresponding with my readers. Don't hesitate to reach out if you are so inclined. I haven't sent out any messages beyond a single update and a notice this volume was available – that practice won't change.

Its December 20, 2018 as I write this, so I'll close out by wishing you all a grievous and enlightening Festivus as well as a Merry Christmas, Hanukah, and Happy Holidays!

Made in the USA
Las Vegas, NV
28 December 2022